Review

MW01230129

Another winner in this series!

Reviewed in the United States on January 17, 2023

In Departures, book 4 of the "The Navarre Link Chronicles: Change of Leads" series, Napoleon (Leon) fights depression in a harsh prison environment. However, he has loyal friends who are using their influence to restore his freedom, freedom the previous governor had promised. Author A. K. Brauneis does an impressive job of describing the various personalities in the story, from the loyal ranch family who have befriended Napoleon and his partner/nephew Jack, to a particularly vindictive guard at the prison, and to Napoleon as he struggles to cope with his dire situation.

Mary Trimble *Maureen*

Loved this Wild Ride!

Reviewed in the United States on January 23, 2023

In "Departures" the fourth book in this Western series set in the late 1800s, the dashing Napoleon (Leon) Nash suffers through his twenty-year prison sentence. His nephew and one-time partner Jack Kiefer, freed for the same violations in a separate trial, suffers terrible guilt as he enjoys his life on the idyllic Marsham ranch.

Leon's life in prison becomes increasingly brutal at the hands of both jealous inmates and a vindictive warden and his guards. At the same time, Jack's affection for a young Marsham daughter turns to love as she grows older and he settles into a life spent breeding horses, rounding up cattle, and experiencing a loving family like the one he was torn from as a boy.

But Jack's guilt threatens his perfect life. As a result, he visits his uncle frequently, bringing some light into the older ex-outlaw's grim existence. Jack also leads the fight for Leon's release through the only means possible, a pardon from the governor.

Brauneis' extraordinary ability to put us in scene and pay it out with vivid descriptions of action held me spellbound. Both Leon and Jack are appealing characters with compelling backstories. Strongly recommended with a caution: some graphic violence.

Carol Pierson Holding

Lovable Outlaws!

Reviewed in the United States on January 21, 2023

The Navarre Link Chronicles: Change of Leads: Departures, is the fourth book in this heart capturing old west series. Our favorite outlaws have decided to turn over a new leaf as one lives free under the pardon of the government, while the other does time in prison under dire conditions. The struggle to survive the hatred and heavy hand of a brutal guard bring Leon to the brink of desperation as Jack fights on the outside for the justice denied his partner: the pardon promised by a governor no longer in power.

A.K. Brauneis draws the reader into the story hook, line, and sinker. And once again, we can't get enough of our beloved bad boys!

Mary Ann Hayes *The Carnelian Games*

CHANGE OF LEADS

BOOK FOUR

DEPARTURES

THE NAVARRE LINK CHRONICLES

CHANGE OF LEADS

BOOK FOUR
DEPARTURES

A. K. BRAUNEIS

First Printing: 2023
Printed and bound in the USA
ISBN:

Two Blazes Artworks
710 Terry Lane
Selah, Washington
USA

www.twoblazesartworks.com

Cover art, interior illustrations, and design by A. K. Brauneis.

Dedication

To my husband, Paul. Though often shaking his head at my chaotic creativity, he has always there with his love and support throughout this whole process. Love you, Babe. You're the best thing to come into my life.

To Peter Deuel. Though gone from this Earth for many years, he was, back then and still is now, my creative inspiration.

Acknowledgments

Where would I be without the westerns! Movies, TV, books, they were all my sanctuary, my private world where I could go anytime and disappear into a world filled with fun and adventure.

Jimmy Stewart, Audie Murphy, and Ben Johnston, to name only a few who kept my eyes glued to the screen. Wagon Train, Wanted Dead or Alive, High Chaparral, Lancer, and my all-time forever favorite, Alias Smith and Jones. Westerns were abundant when I was growing up, and I'm sure I watched every single movie and most of the TV series that were out there.

Charlie Russell! Oh my, what an influence he had, and still has, on my creative endeavors. Attending the Out West Art Show in Great Falls, Montana, has become one of the highlights of my year.

Max Brand was my favorite western author, and though I read books by others, his were the ones that kept me coming back.

Today, I watch most of the new western movies that hit the silver screen, giving my support to a genre that has lost its way but is struggling to make a comeback. At the very least, these more recent westerns have been entertaining, but there are a few that stand out as gems: Butch Cassidy and the Sundance Kid, Tombstone, Silverado, Dances With Wolves, Appaloosa, and yes, I did enjoy Cowboys and Aliens!

I thank all these creations, and the many people that helped in their production for giving me a love that has lasted a lifetime. Now, here I am, writing my own western series, and enjoying every minute of it.

For those people in my life now who have helped me along the way I would like to thank:

Lisa Baird for the many hours she dedicated to proofreading this manuscript, and for her knowledge of legal proceedings and terminology.

Bob Schrader for his invaluable assistance in accurately depicting the courtroom scenes and other legal proceedings, with some leeway for creative license, of course. Any and all errors are completely my own doing.

Renee Slider, curator at the Wyoming Territorial Prison National Park, for all of her assistance in tracking down the details.

S. Whyment for her support and contributions toward character development.

Eric Hotz for his technical support. For someone, like myself, who is computer illiterate, his advice and assistance has been invaluable.

Also, to the various online writing sites that offered me a safe place to get my literary feet wet and for helping me realize when it was time to move on.

And, of course, my writing critique group. This group has shown me so much support and encouragement, both in fine-tuning my manuscripts, and in weathering the stormy waters of self-publication. You're a great group of ladies!

Thank you!

Also available on Amazon

ICE: Prelude to the Navarre Link Chronicles
ISBN 987-1-7335920-3-1

CHANGE OF LEADS: THE LOST SHOE
ISBN 13:978-1-7335920-0-0

CHANGE OF LEADS: AFTERSHOCK
ISBN 978-1-7335920-1-7

CHANGE OF LEADS: DANGEROUS GAMES
ISBN 978-1-7335920-4-8

Prelude

Leon's situation becomes even more precarious. He finds himself in a dangerous situation with Warden Mitchell blackmailing him into becoming a snitch, and the inmates who already suspect his alliances.

He decides to play a dangerous game in order to keep both sides at bay and also hold onto his special privileges that are the main things keeping him alive in this hostile environment.

Jack and Steven make plans to approach the new governor, the Wyoming Board of Penitentiary Commissioners, and the Wyoming Supreme Court, to question the validity of the Auburn Prison System and to appeal Leon's harsh sentence.

Penny, with the help of Dr. Mariam Soames, infiltrates the prison to find out for herself how brutal life is behind those walls. What she witnesses makes her even more determined to assist Jack in his quest for justice.

All Leon has to do is hold on and stay out of trouble. Not an easy feat when the warden suspects his duplicity, and the alpha wolves in the warehouse are circling.

Table of Contents

CHAPTER ONE
THE AMBUSH

Wyoming
Spring 1887

Jack Kiefer sat in the passenger car, his body moving slightly with the swaying motion as the train clattered along the tracks. He rested quietly with his arms folded, and his head leaning back against the headrest, looking out at the passing landscape. It was a cold and gray day, with some white patches of snow still scattered here and there along the terrain. But for the most part, the bare, wet ground dominated the territory, and the hope of warm spring days to come was in everyone's mind.

The train had already chugged its way past Laramie, but Jack had stayed on this time, going all the way to Medicine Bow. Taggard had sent a telegram, requesting that Jack come for a visit with him first, before seeing Leon, as there were things they needed to discuss.

Jack didn't think anything of it, assuming it had something to do concerning the interview with the governor. He'd caught the mid-week northbound instead of the weekend special and was going the extra distance. If he timed it right, he could visit with Taggard for a day, then backtrack and still visit with Leon at their usual time.

There weren't many other people on board, as it was still chilly for unnecessary travel and most families waited until a trip would be more pleasant. Besides, mid-week was usually more for business travel anyway, and Jack wasn't surprised that his fellow passengers were men. The atmosphere, though filled with cigar or pipe smoke, was quiet and relaxed, with very little conversation amongst the occupants. Most of them read newspapers or, like Jack, simply stared out the window at the passing terrain.

Departures

Jack wasn't really seeing the landscape go by him; he had been long this route so many times now, it really didn't hold any interest for him. His mind was on other things; things miles away and into the future. He wondered how Kenny was going to respond to the letter he had written to Leon at Christmas. The one that had included the little aside to the guard concerning their plans. Would Kenny be willing to help? Would Dr. Palin? It was asking a lot, and Jack knew that; it could be putting their very livelihoods at risk, and good government jobs were not that easy to come by.

Penny had wanted to come with her friend on this visit, but Jack didn't think this trip was a good one for that type of get together. This was more of a business trip: a gathering of information and a testing of the waters. Aside from that, Jean had been right in the surmise that Jack wanted his first visit with Leon after the winter hiatus to be private. Just the two friends reconnecting. Of course, a guard would be there, but they were used to that by now and generally ignored his presence. Not much they could do about it, anyway.

Penny could come next time, Jack promised her, after they had a better idea of how things stood. Who knows? Maybe after their meeting with Governor Moonlight, Leon would have his pardon and there would be no need for Penny to come out to the prison again. Somehow Jack felt skeptical about that, like it would be too easy, and it wasn't Leon's fate to have things come easy.

Jack frowned as he became aware of a disturbance in the atmosphere of the passenger car, and he dragged himself back from his inner thoughts to re-assess his surroundings. It was unlike him to be caught daydreaming, and he admonished himself for allowing his attention to slip. His first awareness of something different was the nervous countenance of the other male passengers; the second indication was the presence of a very large man making his way down the aisle in Jack's direction.

Geesh, that guy's big!

Jack found himself mimicking the reactions of the other passengers in his attempt to avoid eye contact with the man, thereby, hopefully, avoiding notice. Then Jack groaned as the mountain stopped beside him and then—oh no— slid in between his seat and the next, and sat down, facing Kiefer, and expecting some kind of response.

18

Jack saw nothing else for it; to avoid being rude and possibly angering his new companion, he put on a smile and acknowledged him. Then his jaw dropped as he realized that he recognized him. Suddenly the mountain wasn't such a threat after all.

"Deputy Schumacher," Jack greeted him. "What are you doing here?"

"I was about to ask you the same thing, Mr. Kiefer," came back the quiet, unassuming response. "Didn't really expect to see you back in Wyoming."

"I'm on my way to see Sheriff Murphy in Medicine Bow, then Leon in Laramie," Jack informed him. "I ain't seen Leon all winter, so this is the first chance I've had. Sheriff Murphy is expectin' me, so . . . is there a problem?"

"Nope," Mike answered. "Just so long as that's the only reason you're on this train."

"Ah, yup," Jack assured him, thinking this was an odd conversation. He smiled to lighten the mood. "How is Rick Layton doin'? I ain't heard nothin' about him for over a year now."

"He's fine,' Mike informed him. "He doesn't do work for Morrison anymore. Not since, well . . . you two. He used his share of the reward money to upgrade his ranch and then he went and took himself another wife. A young widow who came with a whole parcel of ready-made young'uns. He's got his hands full now."

Jack smiled. "Yeah, I guess he does. Glad ta hear things are workin' out for 'im."

"Yup," Mike agreed. "All right," he said as he used his bear-paw hands to push himself to his feet. "My advice to you, Mr. Kiefer, is to keep your head down and stay outta trouble."

"Yeah," Jack agreed. He frowned, wondering where this was coming from. "I'll certainly try ta do that, Deputy."

"Oh," Mike massaged the side of his jaw that still tended to ache on occasion. "When ya see Nash, tell 'im no hard feelin's."

"Sure. Yeah, I'll do that."

The big deputy turned and walked back the way he came, leaving several relieved gentlemen in his wake who had, thank goodness, avoided his attention.

Jack sat back and folded his arms.

What in the world was that all about?

But before he could spend time pondering this question, he felt the train slow down, then heard the engineer lean on the whistle for all he was worth. Jack sat up and, looking out the window, a dreadful feeling of déjà vu swept over him.

For sure and wouldn't ya know it. They were in familiar territory, and as the brakes on the locomotive shrieked painfully in their efforts to stop the train, Jack groaned and sat back in his seat.

We're getting robbed. Dagnabbit. No wonder people are fed up with all the robberies along this route. Geesh, I'm gettin' fed up with it, and I used to be one of the fellas doin' all the robbin'.

He sat up straighter still, as the train finally came to a halt, and he peered out the window in hopes of catching sight of the men who were pulling the heist. Chances were good it was the Elk Mountain Gang, since this was their territory. He had to admit that curiosity and the opportunity to see the fellas again was tugging hard at him.

I wonder if Gus is still runnin' things.

Then he heard rifles being cocked and activity going on around him in the car. He looked over to see that most of the other men, who had been sitting quietly, minding their own business, were now on their feet and ready for action. The few who were not going for rifles were just as confused as Jack, but it didn't take long for them to follow the example of the majority, and they brought up their own weapons in a show of support.

Jack felt his blood turn to ice water in his veins.

Is this a trap? Deputy Schumacher comin' back here ta talk ta me, and askin' some pointed questions about why I'm on this train. Now that's got me wonderin'. Why is Deputy Schumacher on this train? And then an even worse thought hit Jack right between the eyes. *Is Morrison on this train? Oh crap! I gotta get outta here. I gotta warn them fellas.*

Jack was just about to his feet when the train car exploded with reports from numerous Winchester rifles discharging at once. Glass windows exploded with deadly shards, and the air filled with gun smoke. Jack dropped to the floor, covering his head.

Then all hell broke loose.

Armed men took positions on both sides of the car, ducking down beneath the shattered windows and firing at will at any target that presented itself. Bullets also came crashing into the car, sending more glass flying through the air and chipping away at the wooden interior. Lethal missiles shot out and embedded themselves into anything that got in their way.

Jack was on the floor beneath the seats, knowing it was too late to give warning, too late to help any of his friends out there in no man's land! He rolled himself into a ball, covering his head with his arms as the world exploded around him. He felt glass and wood splinters hit him, but his adrenaline was pumping so hard, he wouldn't notice that they were embedding themselves into his hands until later.

Right then, all he knew was the chaos, with the acrid smell of gun powder burning his nostrils, and the wild yells of men, both inside the car and outside, caught up in the frenzy of battle.

Jack prayed for it to end, for the cacophony of noise and fear to return to silence. Many men out there under attack where his friends and he wanted to scream out a warning; he wanted to jump up and return fire from within. But he couldn't. He lay on the floor, feeling like a coward, but even in the shock of this assault, he knew if he pulled his gun and started shooting the ambushers, he'd be dead in seconds.

Dammit. If Morrison is behind this, them fellas out there don't stand a chance.

***

After what seemed an eternity, though it was only ten minutes, the shooting began to ease off. The yelling of combatants and the screaming of dying horses quieted, and the armed men in the car began to stand up from behind their cover and breathe a collective sigh of relief. Then the adrenaline rush hit again and there were yells of exuberance, followed by cheerful laughter and victorious back-slapping.

"Woo hoo!"

"Yeah. We got 'em, boys. We got 'em."

"Finally. The Elk Mountain Gang! Whoopie."

"Ohh boy. Did ya see them two stragglers make a run for it? They're gonna fly straight back to their hideout—and won't they be in for a surprise then. Damn. Now I kinda wish I could be part of the posse that's gonna run 'em to ground, and them outlaws find out they got nowheres ta go."

"Hey, c'mon, Harry. You can't have all the fun. Let them fellas have their share. Besides, we got most of 'em right here. Yahoo. This is gonna be some payday."

Jack didn't move; he felt paralyzed with fear over the fate of his old gang. He shook with his own adrenaline rush, but he couldn't move. He remained rolled in a ball with his bloodied hands covering his head while he prayed that this couldn't be happening.

He felt hands grab him by his coat and drag him out from between the benches. He was hauled to his feet, his legs still shaking, and he had to grab hold of the back of a seat just to stand.

He looked at the faces surrounding him and—oh jeez—could this day get any worse? Morrison was standing there, sneering at him.

"Well, lookee here, boys," the marshal gloated, "we caught ourselves the biggest fish of them all. Too bad we gotta throw 'im back." Then Morrison grabbed Jack by his coat collar and dragged him toward the exit. "Ya might as well be of some use, Kiefer; you can help us identify the corpses."

***

Half an hour earlier

Gus Shaffer sat his horse just inside the copse of ponderosa pines. With him were two of his more experienced gang members.

Mukua, or Preacher, as some of his companions found easier to remember, was a tall and slender, hawk-nosed Shoshone Indian, who had earned his handle by spreading the word of the "Great Spirit" and living as close to a spiritual life as an outlaw could. It was rumored he'd killed an Indian Agent and was forced to leave his band and family behind. What the circumstances were, Gus didn't know and didn't ask. A man was entitled to his privacy.

Mukua generally dressed in buckskins and high, beaded moccasins, but for some reason, insisted on wearing a brightly colored shirt along with a feather in his battered black hat. It didn't matter what kind of feather; it could be anything from a chicken to an eagle, depending upon availability. But these wardrobe choices caused him to stand out from the crowd, and he was often teased that someone was going to shoot him one day, thinking he was a pheasant fit for the pot.

Gus's second companion was a man of Polish heritage, his pale, narrow eyes, set deep in his round face, marking him as a mean son-of-a-bitch. Only Napoleon Nash's iron grip on the gang's behavior, backed up by Kiefer's gun, had kept this outlaw in line, then only loyalty. And loyalty, as far as Lobo was concerned, only lasted as long as the money flowed.

Why Gus kept these two men around once he had taken over, was anyone's guess. It might have been that Mukua was a holy man, as such, though not like any Christian Gus had ever known, and he did help to keep the fellas' spirits up when things were dark. Gus also knew that Nash had liked that injun and wouldn't kick him out. But it wasn't until Nash's trial that the relationship between the two men became apparent.

Gus had always figured Nash was of mixed blood, but he didn't know what mix, nor did he care. But Shoshone Indian would not have been his first guess. Then to find out that Mukua was blood kin to their upstart-of-a-boy-genius leader, only served to irritate Gus more than he'd been already. He could have kicked the old injun out after Nash had been sent to the Big House, but some instinct told him this wasn't a good idea. So, playing it safe, Gus let him hang around on those occasions when the injun wanted to. It wasn't unusual for Mukua to head south for the winter months.

As for Lobo, at least he could be trusted to not be trusted, and all he had to do to cow any rowdy train passengers was to let his natural personality shine through. That was worth a lot now that they didn't have the Kid's gun anymore.

These were the three men waiting with gleeful anticipation, as the train of their choice piled on the brakes and ground to a halt before hitting the barrier of fallen logs. Henderson and Charlie had done a good job of setting up the barricade so that any engineer worth his salt would know that to try and run it would risk derailing his train. Yeah, Gus's boys were real good at their jobs.

***

Word had gotten to them that this train would be carrying a large payroll to make up for the ones that hadn't made it through during those devastating winter months. It should be a real good haul, and the gang needed it too, after the lean winter they had put in. Time to get the money flowing again, and this payroll was just the ticket.

Everyone knew their jobs, and everything was going like clockwork. The train screeched to a halt, and Gus gave the signal for the outlaws to break cover and make the charge. He knew Malachi, along with four of their new-hires, would be on the other side of the train with his trusty stash of dynamite, all set to blow that safe. Then the gang would be in tall cotton again. With his regular boys and the new fellas, the gang was fifteen strong, and even with the five that were left to guard the hide-out, the ten men who came on this job were enough to take this train, easy. And they wanted it.

Everybody put their horses into a full gallop and came at the train, whooping and hollering, and firing their guns into the air to intimidate any of the more adventurous passengers. This was their day; this was their train.

The rifle fire began streaking out at them from the windows of the passenger car, and the tables turned.

Before any of them could comprehend what was happening, Lobo's horse went down in a heap. There was no scream of pain, no thrashing of hooves; one second it was galloping, full speed ahead, and the next it was a crumpled mass of blood and shattered bone, plowing into the ground. Lobo flew over its head, hitting the dirt hard and sending a spray of it into the air as he did a flailing somersault to land heavy, face up and motionless.

Gus tried to pull his horse up, but the animal was spooked and ignored the bit hauling on its mouth. It saw the motionless form of its stablemate suddenly loom up in front of him, but still had the presence of mind to lift and jump over the obstacle rather than plow right into it. But then its forelegs came down hard, right on top of Lobo, breaking the outlaw's right arm and shoulder, and crushing the right side of his rib cage, before carrying on, running frantically to get away from the hot gashes that the rifle bullets left in its flanks.

Gus finally got the animal's head turned to the left, forcing it to slow down and follow the direction its nose was being pulled in.

The gang leader was shooting for real, now that his horse was under control. He aimed for the windows of the passenger cars, though chances were, the plunging of his still frantic animal made hitting a mark highly unlikely. All he could do was hope that by chance he would actually hit something, since all he could see was the deadly rifle fire coming at them.

Mukua was back where Lobo had fallen. He'd dismounted from his horse and was using Lobo's dead animal for cover and shooting back at the train, even though, like Gus, he couldn't see anything to shoot at. They were into it now; there was no turning back, no time to take cover. Bullets were everywhere, and the air reeked of gun smoke.

Mukua's appaloosa gelding shrieked and went down, legs thrashing and kicking wildly in its death agony, the innocent victim caught between fire. Even with its lungs punctured, the horse tried to get to its feet when another volley of bullets blew apart its skull and

Before any of them could comprehend what was happening,
Lobo's horse went down in a heap.

mercifully put the animal out of its misery.

Charlie and Henderson came galloping back from the head of the train, shooting and yelling loud enough to raise the devil. One would wonder why they didn't just hightail it outta there, but they couldn't believe it had been a set-up. Surely it was just a few passengers getting uppity. They'd had that happen before and all it took was a little show of force, and the insurgents would limp back to their seats and behave themselves. By the time the outlaws realized that this was more than just a minor resistance, it was too late, and they were into it.

Charlie had his rifle up and shooting at the train while at a full gallop, but that didn't save him. The fire from the train changed its focus from Gus and Mukua, over to the two newcomers, and Charlie took a full onslaught to the chest and fell without a sound.

Henderson tried to pull up and turn tail, but his horse was in a panic, and finding its all-out gallop being hindered, it lunged into the air and then started to buck. Henderson struggled to bring the animal under control, but the horse was so frantic, it fought against its rider even more, until it lost its footing and went over in an explosion of billowing dust and flailing hooves.

Panicking even more now that it was down, the horse began to kick wildly, frantically trying to get back onto its feet. It finally got halfway up, but then its forelegs became tangled in the reins and it went down again, this time landing on top of Henderson and pushing the horn of the saddle into his shoulder, breaking the outlaw's collar-bone.

Henderson tried desperately to get away from the thrashing animal, but luck wasn't with him on this day. The horse rolled over again, kicking out with its hind legs, trying to get into position so it could heave itself back up onto its feet. The hooves lashed out like a sledge hammer, striking the outlaw in the head, caving in his skull and breaking his neck.

Finally, and only then, did the animal scramble to its feet and take off in a panicked gallop to join up with its herd-mates.

By this time, Gus had had enough. He allowed the two loose horses to come up to his, then, reaching down, he grabbed the reins of Charlie's animal and somehow managed to strong-arm the small herd over to where Mukua was still taking pot shots at anything he could.

But even Mukua knew when it was time to call it quits. As Gus and the horses came close to him, he abandoned his hiding place, grabbed for Charlie's horse and swung himself aboard. The two men and three horses made a mad dash for the same copse of trees where all of this had started, praying that none of the bullets being fired after them would find their mark.

***

On the other side of the train, Malachi Cobb, and four of the relatively new gang members, didn't even have a chance to reach the baggage car. They had been waiting at a discreet distance for the train to be secured before Malachi, being the demolitions expert, would move in with the dynamite to blow the safe and collect their pay.

The first sounds of gunfire had caught their attention just in time for the youngest member, a lad by the name of Les Howard, to take a full rifle barrage in the chest.

Both his and Malachi's horses reared in fright, and Howard fell to the ground, choking out his life's blood before ever knowing the thrill of being a real-life, honest to goodness, outlaw. Running away from home hadn't been such a good idea after all.

The next volley of gunfire took out two more of the outlaws in one go. Black Henry Jackson took a direct hit to the head, and his horse took off at a gallop with the lifeless body eerily staying upright in the saddle for a good thirty feet. The torso swayed, and the arms flailed unnaturally, until it finally over-balanced and tumbled to the ground. The horse kicked at it, then galloped on, heading for home.

In the same instant, ole' Dan, who was new to the gang but a seasoned hand at outlawin', had begun to think he was invincible until he met his maker this day. The law got him with a vengeance to make up for previous lost opportunities, and he fell to the ground with a bullet through his throat, two in his left lung and the last going through his left eye.

Malachi knew when it was time to high-tail it. He pulled his horse around and put it into a very willing gallop back toward cover, when he felt himself get punched in the shoulder.

The small man knew he had been hit, but he leaned forward and hung on as he kicked his horse for more speed. Then, suddenly, there was no horse under him anymore, and he was airborne. He could see the ground coming at him at a terrific speed, then he hit hard, plowed into the dirt, tasting the grit in his mouth as it mixed with his chewing tobacco. The air and his plug were forced out of him as he did a flip and came crashing down on his back. He lost consciousness to lie in a limp and bleeding heap, not far from the body of his dead horse.

The final member of this group, George Carmon, had booted his own horse into a gallop the instant Howard went down. He took off in the opposite direction from the one Malachi had ultimately chosen, heading for the front of the train. Once he came level with the engine, he turned his horse to gallop away at an angle toward the bend in the tracks and disappeared around it.

He never did return to Elk Mountain, which turned out to be a wise—or lucky choice on his part, because it meant that he could go on living a while longer to rob and steal another day.

***

Back where they were again safely hidden in that copse of pines, Gus Shaffer and Mukua were finally able to bring their small herd of stressed horses to a halt. With jangled nerves, they turned around to survey their situation. All five fought to breathe as their bodies trembled with shock. Everyone was bleeding from more than one close call. With hearts pounding, they peered through the trees and back at the train, mainly to see if any others from the gang had made it out.

But all they saw was the scattered bodies of horses and men, and none of them were moving.

The next thing they saw were men coming out of the passenger cars: men with rifles and tin stars that glittered in the sunlight.

Gus cursed. Then he caught his breath, and he and Mukua exchanged looks.

"No," Mukua mumbled, "it cannot be."

"Yeah, it can't be," Gus snarled, his heavy moustache bristling, "but it is. I'd recognize that damn rigging anywhere."

"No. my nephew's nephew would not turn on us," Mukua insisted. "You know he would not."

"All I know is what I'm seein'," Gus countered, "and what I'm seein' is a yella'-bellied traitor."

"No, Gus. I will not believe—"

Then Gus caught his breath again and grabbing Mukua's arm, he gestured toward the second boxcar.

The doors had just slid open and a ramp was being pulled down until the one end of it landed on the ground. Horses were led out, and some of the men from the second passenger car mounted them and began to check over their firearms.

Gus and Mukua exchanged looks again.

"You got any ammunition left, Preacher-man?"

"By the Great Spirit, I do not."

"Time to leave," Gus ordered, needlessly. "You better pray to that great spirit a yours that these horses still have enough left in 'em ta get us back to the Elk!"

"Hiya!"

CHAPTER TWO
ASSAULT ON THE ELK

Elk Mountain hide-out
Earlier that same morning

The majority of the gang members had ridden out an hour ago to tackle their first train of the season. Everyone was relieved that winter had finally broken its hold on the outlaw hideout, as even with rationing, the food supplies for both men and horses now ran thin. There had even been some contemplation of killing off the last few chickens to tide everyone over, but then there would be no eggs until the hens could be replaced. Eggs were their mainstay during those bleak days, so the hens got to live another season.

The gang made do with scrambles and oatmeal and the horses ate straw, just so they could feel like their bellies were full. Everyone limped their way through to spring. When word of the over-sized payroll came through, they were all jubilant in anticipation of a good score, and therein lay the main difference between Nash and Shaffer.

For one thing, Leon would never have allowed the gang to head into winter without enough stores and money to see them all through. Even if there hadn't been much in the way of jobs to do, Leon was too good a poker player. He would have made sure there was enough for everyone. Also, he would have been very suspicious of such a good haul coming through right when they needed it the most.

Leon was reckless as a young man, and he had carried with him a buried anger that would sometimes cloud his vision. But as much as he had pretended to resent his uncle's meddling, Mukua's wise words still found their way into the gang leader's reasoning.

Nor was Leon adverse to listening to Jack. Stuck between the two of them: his uncle and his nephew, some of Leon's wildest schemes were taken down a notch. But only because he was willing to listen and consider all options. He would have done his research, taking control of the situation as he would a high-stakes poker game and made sure it was legit before sending his men into the fray. He wouldn't have cared how hungry they were; he had learned to be wary of traps.

But Gus could be arrogant and wouldn't have taken the time to think things through or take advice from anyone, including his buddy, Malachi. And certainly not from that old Injun renegade. Nor was he the poker player that Leon was. As far as he was concerned, this train was pay dirt. This train was gonna get them on their feet again. This train was gonna change everything.

The morning of the big day dawned cold and damp, but nobody cared about that; everyone woke up in good spirits and boisterous moods. The coffee tasted real good, and even the oatmeal was palatable. This was gonna be a good day.

Those fellas who stayed behind were just as excited as those going. Naturally, everyone wanted to be part of the heist, but there always had to be somebody staying to watch over the hide-out. It was an accepted reality and all part of being a member of this gang.

There were five men left behind that day. Tom and Chuck Ebner, brothers who joined the gang two years earlier, had drawn the look-out duty. Chuck had drawn the duty, and Tom had volunteered to be the second, since the two of them preferred to stick together. This arrangement suited everyone else just fine.

Curly Buchannan, who had come up from the Red Sash Gang, along with Black Henry Jackson, was a little ticked at having to stay behind. He was still recovering from a bad bout of the flu, but despite his disappointment, he had to admit that he was still not up to the physical exertions that a train heist demanded. So, he accepted his lot and settled in at the Elk for a day of rest and anticipation.

Most of the morning, Curly spent playing cards with Benny Larson, who's horse had fallen on him and he'd broken his collar-bone, so he was out of the heist.

Then there was Roger Cartless, who had joined up with his buddy, Les Howard. But Gus didn't want to have more than one young greenhorn on the same job at the same time, so the two had drawn straws, and Les had won. Gus assured a disappointed Roger that he could join them on the next job.

So, the three men, or should we say, the two men and the boy, played cards to help pass the time until the job was done and the celebrating could begin.

It couldn't have been much past noon when the quiet day suddenly took a turn for the worse. A loud dynamite blast from somewhere back of the hide-out, rent the air and shook the buildings, causing dust, dirt, and spiders to fall from the ceiling and land in their coffee cups and amongst their game. The dishes rattled and the wood stove shook. The three fellas sitting in the bunk house all stared at each other for a beat of time, their minds skipping in shock.

"Get out!" Curly yelled, as he shoved his chair back. "Grab your guns and get outta here!"

Two sets of saucer eyes jerked toward him. In an instant they were on the move, grabbing gun belts and rifles as they made a run out to the yard.

At first there was nothing to see, then three sets of eyes watched as another stick of dynamite came sailing through the air to land on the roof of the recently vacated bunkhouse.

"Oh crap!" It was Curly again. "Get under cover!"

The three outlaws dashed, with shoulders leaning forward and arms covering their heads to protect themselves, for the first structure they saw. Just as they made it behind the outhouse, another explosion shook the ground. Planks of splintered wood went flying in every direction, and then the bunkhouse trembled for a moment before what was left of the roof collapsed in upon itself.

Inside the structure, the table and chairs were strewn about and broken apart by the blast and the falling debris. The wood stove was knocked over, its contents scattering across the floor. Within seconds, the hot embers settled in amongst wood splinters and ratty rugs, and the entire wooden structure was very quickly engulfed in flames.

The three outlaws clustered behind the outhouse and tried to get themselves organized under short notice. They hurriedly strapped gunbelts around their waists as Curley shouted out orders.

"We gotta split up. And keep your eyes open. We's under attack, boys!"

"But how can that be?" Benny demanded as the roaring fire from the bunkhouse reflected in his eyes. "Elk Mountain is impregnable. Ain't nobody can get in here without us knowin' about it!"

"How the hell should I know? But somebody did get in, and now they're comin'! Git goin'!"

He gave Benny a shove just to get him moving, then turned to the teenager who was rooted to the spot.

Curly grabbed the wide-eyed boy by the lapels and shook him until his vision focused. "Run, ya fool!"

"Where?" Roger squeaked.

"How should I know?" Curly yelled as he absently noted the spreading wet spot on the crotch of Roger's trousers. He spun the boy around and shoved in the opposite direction from Benny "Find cover and stay there ifn ya value yer life!"

Acrid, black smoke filled the yard. Curly's eyes stung and started watering as he tried desperately to see what was going on. He thought he could hear the thundering of horses' hooves, but his senses were overwhelmed by the loud roar of the flames as they devoured the old, dry wood.

Then he saw them: horses and men bursting through the smoke. All Curly could hear was the thunder of the hooves and the yelling of men. It sounded like an army. Taking his own advice, he turned tail and headed for the barn. Once inside, he grabbed a bridle from its hook with the unlikely intention of catching a horse and high-tailing it outta there. He didn't have a chance.

Another explosion rocked the air as more dynamite hit the barn. Curly was instantly knocked to the floor when the explosion did its damage. He screamed as burning timbers fell on and around him, and he felt the heat of the flames singe the hair on his hands and arms as he tried to cover his head. Then his screams were ripped out of his parched throat, as what was left of the burning structure caved in on top of him. Mercifully his back broke and his skull was crushed before he could burn to death.

The horses in the paddock panicked. The dust from their pounding hooves filled the air and mingled with the heavy smoke as they ran circles around their enclosure, frantically looking for a way out. Finally, in a mindless rush, one animal ran into the railing of the fence, and its weight caused the wood to splinter and come apart. The other horses charged for it at once, knocking the first animal to the ground and trampling over it in their haste to escape.

More railings were pushed down and broken as the horses galloped through, leaving the fallen horse thrashing, and bellowing where it lay. He desperately wanted to join his stablemates, but was unable to get up.

Then the posse of lawmen came galloping through the smoke-filled dust and found themselves being assaulted by three of the half-wild, mangy curs that had decided to make Elk Mountain their home. The dogs didn't appreciate these intruders charging in and upsetting everything, and they were doing their best in the way of growling and yapping to let their feelings be known.

Unfortunately, their efforts were for naught, and three quick shots followed by dying yelps put an end to the protest.

The posse split up. Three or four riders headed off in different directions to cause confusion, and to lay waste to the remaining structures standing in the yard. Three of the lawmen followed the panicked horses down the main trail leading to the lookout post. Tom and Chuck were about to have company.

Benny had ducked in behind the chicken coop, and despite his broken collarbone, had been able to put his six-shooter to good use. With the structure itself, and the confusion of flapping hens and fluttering feathers creating decent cover, Benny had laid down a blanket of fire as he yelled obscenities at his attackers.

He brought down one of the posse men and two of their horses before he found himself surrounded and done for. He wasn't about to give up though; prison wasn't for him. So, even though he knew he didn't stand a chance, he kept firing at his assailants. He hit one of them in the leg and knocked another one out with a bullet clipping the man's temple. Once his six-shooter was empty, he flung it aside and tried to fire the rifle but his broken collar bone made that almost impossible

Giving up on the rifle, he pulled a knife from his boot, and with a snarl of defiance, he lunged at the closest horse. Leaping up and grabbing hold of the rider, Benny caused himself, the lawman, and the horse to overbalance and topple to the ground. Before the dust had even begun to settle, Benny plunged his knife into the man's torso and felt the blade slide in between the ribs. But the lawman still had enough wits about him to box the outlaw on the ears, then push the man away from him.

Both horse and rider scrambled into the clear, and then three rifles discharged at once, with Benny taking all three hits to the chest. He fell back into the dust, choking up blood and trying to keep breathing despite three punctures to his lungs.

Two men dismounted to tend to their wounded comrades and to stop the bleeding caused by Benny's knife thrust, but nobody bothered to tend to the fallen outlaw. Not that he could have been saved anyway.

So, Benny was left lying in the dust, gasping out his last breaths. The blood from his injuries seeped out from the exit wounds in his back and spread in a deep, dark, pool as it slowly soaked into the dirt.

It's better this way, he thought, as the calmness and euphoria of death washed over him, *so much better than what happened to Nash. Who'd want that? No . . . this was so much better . . .*

***

Roger's mind was in turmoil, his eyes and throat burning from the onslaught of ash and smoke. His best buddy, Les, had thought this was going to be a great big adventure. Yeah! Join up with the Elk Mountain Gang and have the time of their lives. But now, Roger ran for his life, and he was scared to death. He didn't think about where he was going, he was just looking for cover, and he ran to wherever his legs took him.

He charged up the steps and through the front door of the leader's cabin, looking around in a panic. His breath came in gasps, as sobs of terror overtook him. He started running again, bashing through another door and finding himself in one of the bedrooms. He grabbed the quilt off the bed and for some reason he didn't question or even try to understand, he wrapped the quilt around himself and backed into the far corner of the room facing the door.

His whole body trembled, and his teeth chattered in fear, as his legs gave way beneath him, and he sank to the floor. There he sat, with his knees drawn up and the quilt pulled tightly around himself.

"Oh, dear God," his very voice trembled in fear. "Please let me live, please, please. I just wanna go home. Mama, I just wanna come home . . ."

Outside, four of the posse members spied the lad running for the cabin and decided to go in after him, rather than simply burning him out. He hadn't fired a shot in their direction, and he looked no more than a terrified teenager, so they thought they'd give him a chance. All the same, though, they entered the cabin cautiously and with guns at the ready. Even a teenager can fight back when cornered, and nobody wanted to take a bullet for their kindness.

Within minutes, the lawmen had spied the trembling quilt in the corner of the bedroom and made a unified run at it. The quilt was ripped aside, then a screaming Roger was hauled to his feet and unceremoniously pushed face down onto the bed. His hands were roughly pulled backed and cuffed. He started to cry as he lay there shaking, but that didn't stop rough hands from giving him a thorough search, and what weapons he had on him were instantly confiscated. He was then hauled to his feet, manhandled out to the main room of the cabin, then shoved into a chair by the table and told to stay there.

Two of the men remained to guard the prisoner. The other two went back outside to help with the assessment and clean up whatever was left of this nest of rats that had been allowed to continue being pests of the territory for far too long.

Roger began to calm down, as he slowly came to realize that he was still alive and was more than likely to remain that way. *Just don't do nothin' stupid,* he told himself. *Keep your mouth shut and don't do nothin' stupid.*

***

Elk Mountain Lookout Post

Meanwhile, Tom and Chuck waited expectantly for the gang's return. They would have hit that train by now and be heading back toward the Elk, where they could all get their shares divvied up and then start making plans for a grand night on the town. Provided Shaffer didn't hold everybody back a day or two, to let things calm down, that is. Damn. That would be irritating. A fun night in Bear Creek would suit everybody right about now.

Then they heard the explosion.

The brothers locked eyes, and neither of them made a move for a good ten seconds, probably because they were each waiting for the other one to take charge and decide what they should do. Finally, Tom, who was after all, the oldest, figured he was the one to call the shots.

"Ah, maybe you better ride back up to the yard and see what that was."

"I know what that was," Chuck insisted. "Why don't you ride up and see?"

"'Cause I'm the oldest, and I'm sayin'," Tom insisted. "Besides, it's probably just Roger playin' with Malachi's dynamite. I mean, nobody can get into the Elk without us seein' 'em."

"Well, why don't we both go see, then?"

"'Cause one of us has gotta stay here and keep watch."

"But what if . . .?"

Another loud explosion coming from the yard drowned out Chuck's continued protesting, and again, both brothers stopped talking and stared at each other with open mouths. Then they heard the distant rifle fire coming from the same direction, and that got them really nervous.

"What the hell's goin' on up there?" came Chuck's anxious query. "I don't like the sound a that, at all."

"We should get up there and take a look," Tom suggested, though he didn't sound very enthusiastic about the idea. "You know—just to make sure everything's all right."

"I dunno," Chuck considered the options, his eyes wide with fear. "I think we should just high-tail it outta here."

A third explosion rent the air, and they heard the distant bellowing of injured and terrified horses, then more gunfire. Chuck got to his feet, preparing to run down to their own horses that were tethered in the little grove behind them.

Tom jumped up and grabbed him, stopping him in his tracks.

"We can't abandon our post! Shaffer's trustin' us. I'll stay here and you get up there and see what in tarnation is goin' on!"

"Yeah, and what if Shaffer ain't comin' back?" Chuck shouted back. "The only place I'm goin' is outta here. You go up and see what's goin' on. I ain't stickin' around!"

Tom wouldn't let him go, so Chuck started to fight against his brother with the full intention of grabbing his horse and vacating the premises.

The battle went on for a precious five minutes, with both brothers determined to have their own way. Then they stopped the struggle with each other and looked up the trail leading to the hideout. They could hear horses coming toward them at a full gallop.

Then, getting out of there became a moot point, when their own horses, already nervous from the explosions, began to panic. They pulled back on their tether lines and started to buck and fight against the restraints until the lines broke and they were free.

Just then, the herd of loose horses from the paddock came

barreling around the corner and didn't even acknowledge the two men running down the small incline in a futile attempt to grab their own animals. The two saddled horses were having none of it, and they jumped away from the men to join up with their stablemates. The whole herd galloped on past and headed downhill, toward open country.

"Dammit," Tom yelled, throwing his hat on the ground. "What are we gonna do now?"

A rifle shot cracked, the sound coming from the distant grove of trees in the direction from whence the loose horses had come. Before Tom could get an answer from his brother, Chuck's eyes flew wide open in surprise, as his head jerked to the side and blood splattered out from the suddenly gaping hole in his skull. Chuck dropped to the ground like a sack of flower, the look of disbelief still on what was left of his face.

Tom screamed in rage and pulled his six-shooter while spinning around toward the direction of the shot, but he never got a chance to pull the trigger. More rifle shots came at him and he took two direct hits to his chest, one to his right arm and one in the middle of his forehead. He dropped down to lay sprawled beside his brother, their life's blood seeping out of their open wounds, to mingle darkly together, before pooling and then sinking down into the damp, cold ground.

***

Four lawmen then emerged from the trees and loped their horses over to the fallen brothers. They all had their rifles out and ready just in case either of them was still alive and kicking. As they got closer though, it became apparent that caution was unnecessary, and the four men returned the rifles to their scabbards and dismounted.

One of the men had two scabbards, one on each side of his saddle. Having returned the Winchester to its resting place, he then took hold of the other and pulled a Sharps repeating rifle out from its place and set about readying it for use.

Meanwhile, the other three kicked the two corpses onto their backs, in the hopes that they could be identified.

"They look familiar to any of ya?"

"Kinda hard ta tell, ain't it?" one of the men answered. Then he

Departures

squatted and wiped blood from Tom's face. He stood up again and the lawmen gazed down upon the corpse.

"Nope. Still don't recognize 'im."

"No need ta bother with the other one. From what's left a his face, I wouldn't even recognize my own grandma."

They all chuckled at the joke, then went on about their business.

"John, you and Bill get these carcasses back up to the hideout. Maybe one of the other fellas will know who they are. It's time the rest of us got our little welcome home party organized."

More chuckles made the rounds as the two deputies looped ropes around the lifeless ankles, then remounted their horses and headed back up toward the yard, dragging the dead brothers along behind them.

The two remaining men tethered their horses in the gulley, grabbed their Winchesters again, and headed up the small incline to settle in at the lookout station. The Sharps rifle was prepped and ready to go, with the Winchesters taking on the role of backup. The two, well-armed men would wait there all afternoon if needs be, waiting, just in case any of the gang made it out of the ambush at the train and tried to head back to the safety of Elk Mountain.

***

Gus and Mukua rode as though the very hounds of Hell were on their trail. They whipped and spurred those poor horses into giving all they had, to get them back safely to the Elk—or die trying.

Henderson's horse still galloped along with the others, and though he was tired as well, he didn't have the extra weight of a person on his back, so he felt no need to leave his buddies. Besides, he wanted to get home, too.

The two men barely spoke to each other. They were focused more on the ground ahead of them to avoid pitfalls, and occasionally, sending nervous glances behind them to check on the progress of the posse. They knew the pursuers were there, and on fresh horses too, so why couldn't the outlaws see them? Why were they holding back? They must know that if the outlaws made it to their sanctuary, the race would be over; the outlaws would be safe. No one had ever been able to force their way into the Elk; it'd never been done. So, what was going on? It was almost as though the posse was letting them get away.

This situation was more nerve-wracking than having the posse right on their tail and shooting at them. It didn't make sense, and the closer the two men got to Elk Mountain, the more anxious they became.

Then two things happened almost simultaneously, causing the outlaws to pull up short and reconsider their options.

They were still a couple of miles away from the approach to their hideout when they came galloping up a hill and around a corner, and almost plowed, full force, into a group of loose horses that had stopped there to graze.

"Damn!" Gus cursed as he hauled on his horse's mouth. "Where the hell did they come from?"

All the horses reacted to the sudden intrusion, the loose ones dancing about, with heads and tails up, blowing their displeasure.

Mukua got his horse stopped, then pointed at the two saddled animals that were trotting around within the group, blowing with excitement.

"Aren't those Tom and Chuck's horses?"

Gus took a closer look as his horse continued to dance on the spot.

He frowned. "Bloody hell. Them two were on lookout duty." He shot a look toward the hideout, and the blood froze in his veins. Black smoke bellowed into the air, right above their hideout.

Mukua grunted. "Hmm, our home is on fire."

Gus glared at him. "Yeah, no shit!" He was about to snark even further when he saw real worry in the old Indian's eyes. "Let's get the hell outta here."

"We will be at risk in open country," Mukua called after his boss.

"We ain't got no choice. Now run!"

The two men galloped out across open country in the hope they could reach that other grove of trees before the posse showed up. Once there, they could get onto the lesser known tracks that were hidden in amongst those gullies and, hopefully, get their pursuers off their trail.

All the horses joined up then, and went for a race. But as Mukua had feared, the gamble they took did not pay off, and the race was destined to be short-lived.

They didn't hear the rifle-shot over the thundering sound of hooves pounding into the dirt, but they both saw Hamilton's horse stumble and then go down in a tangle of flailing legs and an explosion of dirt. The loose horse coming up behind, could not stop or maneuver out of the way in time. It plowed right into the mass at full gallop, causing it to do a somersault through the air, before crashing down heavily onto its back.

That was all the outlaws saw of that wreck as they galloped onward.

Then Gus felt a shock wave go through his own mount when the animal took a hit in the shoulder. The horse grunted, then crumpled to the ground. Rolling over onto its side, it kicked violently in its fear and anguish, with futile attempts to regain its feet. Gus was thrown clear, then scrambled to get out of the animal's range, nearly getting trampled by the other loose horses coming up from behind.

Mukua spun around and galloped back to his leader. The two men locked arms and Gus was hauled up behind Mukua's saddle, and they were off and running again.

Bullets struck the ground in front of the horses' feet, causing the animals to put on the brakes and pivot to get away from their invisible attackers. They headed back toward Elk Mountain, but there was nothing the outlaws could do about it—the posse, five-men strong, was onto them, pushing them in the direction they wanted the outlaws to go.

Mukua knew his horse could not keep up the fast pace while carrying two men. He was doing his best to maneuver them into position alongside one of the loose, but saddled horses, so that Gus could transfer over. A dangerous move to make while at a full gallop, but neither of them saw another choice; all stoppers were out, and they went for broke.

Surprisingly enough, they were able to get into position. Mukua reached out and grabbed hold of the loose horse's bridle. That horse laid its ears back and tried to kick at them, but Gus made the jump, and with a frantic grab for the saddle horn, he stayed on.

Once Gus was settled, Mukua hauled his horse's head around and again angled it away from the direction of the hideout. But by this time, they were in range of the lookout post, and even above the sound of pounding hooves and the wind in their ears, they heard the boom of the Sharps rifle letting fly.

Mukua's horse went down this time, the heavy bullet going right through Mukua's leg, shattering the bone, then carrying on through the horse's ribcage and blowing apart its lungs. The horse went down in a heap, and Mukua hit the dirt and rolled clear before trying to stand up.

Gus attempted to get back to him, to return the previous favor. Mukua struggled to his feet and made a desperate grab for Gus's arm, but the injured leg refused to hold him and the Indian collapsed to his knees.

"You must go!" Mukua shouted. "I die a warrior!"

"You goddamn Injun! Grab my hand!"

Mukua tried to follow orders but the Sharpe's spoke again, and Mukua's body jerked as the bullet zinged through his upper chest. He crumbled down beside his horse and lay where he fell.

Gus cursed again, and, hauling his horse around, he spurred it back to a gallop, racing across the open ground toward the copse of trees.

He found himself with the advantage for a change; he rode a relatively fresh horse and he knew the lay of the land like the back of his hand. The posse was closing the gap between them, and he could feel the whizz of bullets flying past his ears. He also suspected that whoever was wielding that Sharps rifle would be reloading it for another shot before the outlaw was out of range. But Gus knew he was going to make it—if he could just get to those trees before another lucky shot from the posse took either him or his horse down.

He wished the last of the loose horses would stop following him, as they were making it hard for him to disappear into the woodlands. The tracks they left, along with the noise they made would keep the posse right on his trail until they ran him into the ground. If he'd still had ammunition for his revolver, or a rifle with this saddle, he would shoot the horses just to be rid of them. But he had neither, so he had to keep going with the herd in tow.

He finally made the trees and pushed his horse along a steep and narrow trail that he knew led down into a gulley. From there, he could backtrack and find the head of another well-hidden trail that would take him across a creek and then into a small box canyon.

This particular canyon had a narrow entrance, and to anyone who didn't know the land, it would appear to simply be a dent in the rocks with a grown-over trail leading to a dead-end. But Gus knew better, and as the sound of pursuit fell further and further behind, he made for this canyon and the only chance he had left to get out of this alive.

He finally made the trees and pushed his horse along a steep and
narrow trail that he knew led down into a gulley.

CHAPTER THREE
PAST MISTAKES

Back at the train

Jack was still reeling from the shock when Morrison grabbed him by the coat and hauled him off the passenger car. He couldn't believe what was going on around him. This was insane. He felt completely abandoned, like a cat suddenly thrown in amongst a pack of wolves, and the wolves were all grinning over the thrill of the kill. Even the regular train passengers joined in on the good spirits, since once they realized what was going on, they were all for it. About time somebody did something about those damn outlaws.

Jack's nerves were so on edge, he jumped and quickly looked around as the baggage car door noisily slid open, and the wooden ramp was pulled out and dropped to the ground. He groaned at the sight of the horses being led out and a select group of men mounting up in preparation for chasing down the fugitives.

He had no idea who was down and who had gotten away. All he heard was that two of the outlaws had made a dash for the woods and were probably headed back to Elk Mountain. He was also able to pick up from the joshin' and jokin' that this plan of action was a good thing for the lawmen, but not such a good thing for the outlaws.

What's happened? No assault against the hide-out has ever been successful, so why are these men so cocky in their belief of success this time?

Jack stood in a daze, leaning against the side of the passenger car, shaking his head in disbelief—until the bodies began to show up.

Then there was no escaping it, and he felt like he was going to be sick. Morrison came over and, grabbing him by the arm, haul him to where the men were depositing the dead and wounded.

"C'mon Kiefer, this oughta be easy for you," Morrison chided him. "I know most of these fellas, but a second opinion is always welcome."

Jack hated every minute of this, but he forced himself to look. He needed to know as well, so he could tell Leon.

Ohh, Leon: this is gonna be hard news for him.

They may have stopped running with the gang years ago, but Leon still thought of them all as friends and, well—his gang.

Jack went over to the first bloody mess that was dragged over, and he looked into the dead face.

"Ahh, jeez. That's Charlie," Jack told the marshal.

"Charlie Hadden?"

"Yeah."

"What about this one?"

"I don't know him."

One of the local deputies stepped forward and looked at the dead outlaw.

"I think that's Henderson," he informed Morrison. "Kinda hard to tell with his face all stove in like that, but it sorta looks like it could be him. He used to be over Arizona way, but I heard that he joined up with Elk Mountain some time back."

Jack's brow creased as he took in the name.

"Matt Henderson?"

"Yeah, that's it."

"Ya know him now, Kiefer?" Morrison pushed him.

"No, I don't, but Nash would."

As they moved on to the next bloody body, Morrison smirked. "Oh, I know him. That's Maurice Lobinskie."

Kiefer frowned. *Maurice Lobinskie? No, that's . . . oh—Lobo!'* Funny, Jack had never thought about the fact that Lobo would have a legitimate name. Now that he was presented with it, it made sense; what mother would call her son "Lobo"? But then, what mother would call her son "Maurice"? No wonder the man was so mean. That was almost as bad as "Napoleon".

"Yeah, but he's still alive," Schumacher informed the group.

Jack perked up. "He's what?"

"Yep, believe it or not," Schumacher confirmed. "He's broke up bad, but he's still breathin'. Remains to be seen if he makes it to town though. The group was distracted by the commotion caused by more bodies being dragged through the train from the other side. More bloody, broken masses for Jack to identify. Oh, what a god-awful day this had turned out to be. Then a thought struck him, and he breathed a truly heartfelt sigh of relief.

Thank God Penny hadn't come on this trip. If this day coulda been made worse, that would have done it.

Jack carried on, willing his guts to not heave up on him as he peered at the next bloody corpse.

"Oh, jeez. That's ahh, what's his name," Jack struggled with this one. He knew the man, but not well, as he hadn't run with the Elk Mountain Gang during his and Leon's time. "OH! Ah, Black Henry Jackson," the name finally clicked. "But what was he doin' up here? He usually ran with the Red Sash Gang."

"That gang broke up about six months ago," Mike Schumacher informed him. "I heard that Black Henry and Curly Buchannan came this way. I guess this confirms it. Don't know where Del Starsky went though. Probably up into Montana."

Jack nodded, then moved on. He clenched his teeth when he found himself looking down at the fresh, youthful face of Les Howard. He groaned with sadness and disappointment, shaking his head in regret. He knelt beside the slim body and laid a hand on the bloodied shoulder.

"You know 'im?" Morrison asked.

"No," Jack admitted, 'but he's just a kid—a boy. Dammit! What's Gus thinkin', lettin' a youngster like this join the gang?"

"What does it matter?" Morrison commented. "He's dead now. What about this one over here?"

Jack stood up and followed the marshal over to the last body. It was a real mess, having been hit numerous times, and Jack had a hard time getting a good look at the face. All he could tell was it was an older man, and Jack didn't think he knew him.

"Oh, that's ole Dan Willoughby," one of the deputies announced with a laugh. "Man, you just never know what fish you're gonna catch when ya throw the net."

"Dan Willoughby?" Morrison queried. "I thought he'd up and died years ago. What do ya know."

Jack felt drained. He stood quietly for a few minutes, hands in his pockets, head down, trying to process all the emotions that were coming at him from every direction. The last thing he was expecting at that moment, was to hear a familiar voice.

"Kid?"

Jack swung around and found himself looking into the bright blue eyes of Malachi Cobb. But the expression coming through the blood on the outlaw's face was not one of pleasant surprise. It was more of disbelief and then anger.

"What did ya do, Kid?" Malachi asked him, his eyes filled with pain and disillusionment. "What did ya do to us?"

"What? Malachi . . ." Jack was taken aback by the accusation in the other man's tone and expression. "I didn't do nothin', Ky."

"Well, what you doin' here then?" Malachi asked him, still barely able to believe his own eyes. "You set us up?"

"No! Ky, I would never . . . I was just—"

His protest was interrupted when a deputy grabbed Malachi's uninjured arm, then half dragged, half pulled the wounded and dazed outlaw over to the baggage car. He would be spending the trip into Rawlins in the company of the corpses, and of Lobo, who might very well be a corpse by the time they bother getting him to a doctor.

Jack started to go after him, to try and explain that him being on this train was just a coincidence and that he hadn't known anything about this.

Morrison grabbed his arm and stopped him.

"Get back on board, Kiefer," the marshal told him.

"Look, how about if I ride the rest of the way in the baggage car?" Jack asked. "I need ta talk to him."

Morrison denied the request. "I want you where I can see ya. Besides, we got one more stop to make before gettin' into town, and I might just be needing your expert opinion again." Morrison was pleased at Jack's discomfort, and he smiled. "That's the problem with switchin' sides, Kiefer; ya can't help but make enemies outta old friends. Better get used to it."

Jack was of a mind to protest, but then he felt the presence of numerous deputies standing around him, just waiting for him to put up a fight. He thought better of it, and with a quick glance of regret toward the baggage car, he pulled himself up onto the landing of the passenger car and went inside.

***

It wasn't long after everyone got settled when the engineer sounded the whistle and the train began moving again.

Jack sat alone and stared out the window, trying to come to terms with this strange and tragic day. What had once been a relaxing and familiar landscape was now a battle scene dotted with dead horses. The animals had been stripped of their tack, since those items that were salvageable could be sold to help pay for the new prisoners' upkeep. The horses themselves were just left laying out there, waiting patiently for the scavengers to come around and do the cleaning up. It's an ill wind indeed that doesn't bring good to something.

Twenty minutes later, the train slowed down again and gradually came to a full stop. Jack was not in any hurry to get up because he knew what was coming, and he dreaded whose body he might be having to identify next. But then the other passengers in the car started moving over to the one side of the train to stare out the windows, and they began laughing and spreading more congratulations.

Oh no, Jack thought. *Anything these fellas are that pleased about could not bode well for me.*

A part of him didn't want to look at what all the excitement was about, but then curiosity got the better of him. He stood up and glanced out the windows along with everyone else. Sure enough, what everyone else on board was laughing and cheering about, brought a knot to Jack's stomach and a tightness to his throat.

Black smoke, billowing clouds of it, rising into the air above where he knew the outlaw hideout was located. Elk Mountain was burning. His home for how many years? It was going up in that thick, acrid, smoke. Then it hit Jack as surely as though it were a slap in his face; he was witnessing the end of an era: the closing of yet another chapter in his life, once and for all and forever more. It'd been a long time since he had felt this alone.

As the train eventually came to a stop, Jack could see more horsemen approaching the locomotive from the direction of the burning hideout. He sighed with disappointment; several riders led horses that were loaded down with motionless burdens that could only be more dead bodies. The only bright side to this group was that there was at least one uninjured outlaw who was being brought back in handcuffs instead of draped over the back of a horse.

Jack straightened and followed the other men outside to meet up with the new arrivals. There was no getting out of it, so might as well get it over with.

There were whoops and hollers from the two groups of men, as they met up alongside the train. Jack stood back from the celebration, feeling like the odd man out until he glanced at the youth sitting on the horse and looking forlorn. His wrists were cuffed behind him.

Jack sauntered over to him and laid a placating hand on his leg to get his attention.

The lad looked down at him with worried eyes.

Jack sighed to himself; this youngster was no older than the boy whose body was wrapped up in a tarp and laying inside the baggage car.

"What's your name, son?" Jack asked him.

"Roger Cartless, sir."

"How old are ya?"

"Fifteen, sir."

Jack shook his head, anger rising in him again at Gus for allowing such young boys to join the gang. Leon would never have done such a thing.

"What the hell were you thinkin'?" Jack mumbled, addressing the comment to the absent Gus, but young Roger thought it was directed at him.

"Me and my best buddy, Les," Roger explained, "we thought it would be an adventure. Join up with a real outlaw gang, you know. We thought it would be fun. Do you know where he is, sir? Les? He went with the gang to help on this job."

"Kiefer!" Morrison called him. "Get over here."

Jack glanced at the marshal, almost wishing he didn't have his pardon, so he wouldn't be disappointing anyone by pulling his gun and shooting the lawman through the head. As it was, he just nodded.

"Kiefer?" Roger asked, a slightly awed note to his tone. "You're the Kansas Kid?"

"Yeah," Jack answered absently, almost regretfully. Then he looked back up at the boy with sincere sadness in his expression. "I'm sorry, Roger, but your friend is dead. These men killed 'im."

"No," Roger denied the truth of it. Then his face broke apart, and he started to cry. "No! He can't be. This was supposed to be fun."

"Yeah," Jack sighed. He gave Roger another consoling pat on the knee, then turned and went back to the group now standing around the prone figures that had been laid out on the ground.

Jack looked down at the two brothers, Tom and Chuck.

"I don't know 'em," he answered listlessly. "They must have joined up after Nash and I left."

He moved on to another body and shook his head. "No, don't know 'im."

"That's Ben Larson," piped in one of the deputies. "He used to ride for the Widow Creek gang, until it broke up. I guess he came north and joined up here. Bad luck for him."

Jack took in this information without so much as a nod of acknowledgement. It was like he couldn't feel anything anymore. His nerves were so frazzled over who's would be the next body dead he'd recognize, who would be the next friend he would identify, that he was burned out on emotion. Or so he thought.

He walked over to the next body as the black hat with a hawk feather stuck in the band was flipped back from the dead face.

Jack's heart broke. "Aww no," he moaned and dropped down to his knees beside his dead friend.

Morrison smiled, knowing they'd hit pay dirt.

Jack gently touched the face of the dead man, then clutched the bloody shirt as he gulped down the burning tears through the tightening of his throat. He gripped the blood-stiffened material of the man's jacket and shook his head, wishing he could deny the truth of who lay before him.

"Aww no," he mumbled again. "Mukua—not Mukua. He usually winters down in New Mexico. What the hell was he doin' here?"

"I tell ya, Marshal," Deputy Alex Strode commented, "that new marksman you hired is even better than Layton. Jorgensen musta been close to a mile away when he made that shot, and it couldn'ta been a cleaner hit. Blew apart his heart right on the first try."

"Yeah," Morrison agreed with a satisfied smile. "Gettin' The Preacher is definitely a bonus. The reward on this murderin' bastard alone will be more than all the rest of these low-lifes put together." He snorted. "The family of the Indian Agent that bastard killed is sure gonna be happy to hear we finally got him. Shootin' a man just for trying to help out. But, what can ya expect from them damn Injuns? I always wondered what the hell Nash was thinkin' lettin' this murderous snake ride with his gang. Now we know. I guess it makes sense, them redskins stickin' together."

"There's more to it than that," Jack mumbled. "He only ever killed that one man, and he had good reason."

"Yeah, whatever," Morrison sniped. "Probably better he's dead; saves the territory payin' good money to have 'im hanged."

Jack picked up the feathered hat and, with quiet respect, placed it over the dead face. He sat there for a moment, staring down at it and saying his silent goodbyes. Just as Leon had decided, standing there on the Marsham's front porch, allowing tears to show in front of these lawmen was not going to happen. *Grieve for these friends later, when you're alone, or with Leon. Oh, this is gonna be hard on Leon.* Despite his reputation, everyone liked Mukua, and he and Leon had been more than friends; they had been family.

"Where's Gus Shaffer?" Morrison asked, looking around. "I don't see his body anywhere here. Don't tell me we missed 'im!"

"There's still two unaccounted for," Deputy Strode told him. "One up at the hideout got buried under a burning building, so we haven't dug him out yet. And Mukua was with someone who, unfortunately, got away from the trap. Hogan and his group are runnin' 'im down now."

"I doubt Shaffer would have stayed up at the hideout while a robbery was going on," Morrison surmised. "He must be the one making a run for it. Dammit! Why can't anything go smoothly? The deal with the governor was that we get every last low-life, thieving one of 'em. Shaffer may not be the leader that Nash was, but he was still the leader, so Hogan damn well better get 'im."

This outburst was met by silence from the group of men milling about. Everybody had been feeling pretty good about the way things turned out, but the reprimand from their boss put a damper on it. Obviously, nothing short of perfect was going to be acceptable.

Jack glanced up from his own mourning as a still sobbing Roger was dragged past him to be incarcerated inside the baggage car. He'd be making the trip to Rawlins alongside Malachi and the bodies of all his compatriots, including his best buddy, Les.

Jack sadly shook his head; all of this, for what? The only one in this group who was worth anything substantial was Mukua, but even at that, once the rewards were divvied up between all these men, it would hardly be worth their while. Why bother? Jack couldn't understand it.

"Okay!" Morrison announced. "Let's get these bodies loaded up.

And you fellas—get these horses back into that second baggage car. C'mon. Let's get moving. C'mon, Kiefer," he grabbed Jack by the back of his coat and hauled him to his feet. "You've said your goodbyes, so get on board."

***

The rest of the trip to Morrison's hometown of Rawlins was completed in painful silence for the ex-outlaw. Everybody else around him chatted away in quiet comradery, pleased with a dangerous job well executed. Even the regular passengers who, like Jack, had been aboard this train by mere coincidence, joined in on the light-hearted celebration.

Jack now wished he had disembarked this train in Laramie, as was his usual practice. If only Taggard hadn't requested he stop by Medicine Bow first, he could have avoided this whole unfortunate situation. Now, the question presented itself to Jack's mind.

Why had Taggard requested Jack come see him? Did he know about this? Had he known, and not said anything—not warned him?

Anger filled his thoughts. Now, more than ever, he was eager to have a visit with their old friend, Sheriff Taggard Murphy.

***

Elk Mountain
Wyoming Territory

Late afternoon shadows settled over the landscape by the time Gus Shaffer finally felt he had covered his trail enough so the posse would not be able to track him further that night. He trotted his horse through the creek, up the far bank and then led his small herd toward the narrow canyon entrance.

That night, inside his hideaway, Gus felt safe enough to stop for a few hours' rest. He didn't dare make a fire, but he untacked the two horses that had been wearing saddles and turned them all loose to graze. He used the underside of the saddles as a seat and backrest, then wrapped himself up in the two saddle blankets and got comfortable. He was hungry and exhausted, but at least he was warm. And it wasn't raining—thank God.

Sitting there, all bundled up, he assessed his situation. He had no food, no rifle and no ammunition for his revolver. Nor did he have any money to purchase any of the above items. Elk Mountain was no longer a safe hold-out, and he had no idea how many, if any, of his gang were still at liberty, or even alive. He had four horses with him, and two saddles, so he could sell most of them. He needed money, for sure, and fast. And he'd need a place to hole up for a while and wait for things to settle down.

Then he needed a plan. His dark eyes narrowed, and his jaw tightened as anger once again took over his thoughts.

Damn that Kiefer. That bloody, no-good, back-stabbing, son-of-a-bitch. I'm gonna kill that bastard. I don't know how, but somehow I'll find a way. I'm gonna get him for this, if it's the last thing I do.

***

Rawlins, Wyoming

It was late evening by the time the train stopped at the posse's destination. Everyone working for Morrison disembarked to help unload bodies and horses, then get the two uninjured prisoners to the jailhouse.

Jack tried to get to Malachi Cobb, to tell his friend that he hadn't been a part of this, but Morrison wouldn't let Jack get near the prisoners.

He saw the disheveled Malachi look at him with a hurt expression on his face; the scruffy outlaw tried to cover his pain but Jack knew him too well to be fooled. Jack shook his head at him, trying desperately to get the message across. But Malachi just looked away and then was gone, out of the lighted platform of the train depot and into the darkness of the street, heading to the jailhouse.

Roger Cartless wasn't far behind Malachi, but his concerns were more juvenile.

"I gotta get word to my folks," he protested to the deputy escorting him. "Maybe we should stop at the telegraph office first."

"We'll get word to your folks." The deputy sounded tired and bored. Looking after some scared teenager wasn't what he'd had in mind.

"Yeah but, I really wanna see my ma," Roger continued as they left the platform. "I know I'm gonna get grounded, but I wanna see my ma."

"I'm sure your ma will come get ya."

"Yeah, but . . ."

And his voice trailed off, as both he and the deputy disappeared into the street. Soon, one of the street lamps illuminated them again before they entered the sheriff's office, with Roger's voice still seeking reassurance.

Next, Lobo was hauled out of the baggage car and carried to the doctor's office. Jack felt relief; at least Lobo was still alive—for now, anyway. And Lobo was tough. If anybody could pull through something like this, he could.

Jack found himself wondering where Gus was and hoping the craggy outlaw was still on the loose, and, if he was smart, heading for parts unknown. He better not try anything stupid like breaking Malachi out of jail. Not with Morrison in charge. Gus would only succeed in getting himself killed.

The train whistled in preparation for pulling out of the station, and Jack knew he better get on board or be left behind. This was the last town he wanted to be stranded in. He was just about to turn toward the train when he caught Morrison's eye. The marshal smiled at him, nodded, then tipped his hat.

Jack's jaw tightened and his right hand, developing a mind of its own, was trying, oh so very hard, to go for his gun. But Jack controlled it, and with tight lips and a burning in his heart, he ignored the marshal's jibe and stepped on board the train just as it was chugging into motion.

***

Usually, Jack did not have trouble sleeping, even on a moving, rocking passenger train, but this night was not usual, and sleep did not come. Every time he closed his eyes, all he would hear was gunfire, screaming horses, and yelling men. All he'd see was blood, and billowing black smoke, and Mukua's dead face lying there in the dirt. A young boy crying: *He can't be dead. This was supposed to be fun.*

So, Jack spent the night, his head leaning against the back rest of the seat, wrapped up warmly in his winter coat. He stared out the window, seeing only darkness and his own reflection, and just as Leon had done, almost two years ago, he reflected on his life and how he'd come to all of this. He felt, now more than ever, that he was just as much a prisoner of his past mistakes as his partner was a prisoner in his cell. Only goodness knew if either one of them would ever be free again.

***

The following morning dawned gray and chilly, just like the day before, and Jack didn't feel at all like getting out of his warm cocoon, even though the urge for coffee was making itself known. Eventually, the call became too persistent, and he joined the other passengers in rousing himself and heading for the dining car.

Most of the talk going on around him was about the excitement of the previous day. The passengers who had been on the train for the event were all quite happy to describe everything in great detail to the new arrivals. Jack tried to ignore it as be sipped his coffee and did his best to eat a plateful of scrambled eggs and ham, but he couldn't help notice the occasional comment made in his direction, and eyes looking at him, curiously. If there was anyone in the dining car who hadn't known who he was, they were quickly informed.

Finally, at 10:35 a.m., the train pulled into Medicine Bow. Jack was quick to disembark and get away from the curious looks and whispered comments of his fellow passengers. He might not be an outlaw anymore, but he was still a celebrity of sorts, still someone worth gossiping about. He sighed dolefully; was that ever going to go away?

The walk along the boardwalk from the train depot to the sheriff's office was completed in a daze. Jack was exhausted, emotionally and physically. He was worn out. But he had to talk to Taggard. He had to find out what was going on.

He walked into the office to find Taggard Murphy in deep conversation with a large, rather clumsy looking man who turned out to be Taggard's regular deputy, Ottus Gilmore. Both men looked up at the sound of the door opening, and then a heavy silence ensued when they recognized their visitor.

Jack stood at the door, holding onto the knob and staring at his friend with what could be described as an accusing look in his eyes. His exhaustion was apparent.

Ottus's eyes narrowed. He was aware of his sheriff's past and the friendship he shared with the outlaw, but that didn't mean he had to go along with that trust. His loyalty to the sheriff was undying, and he had every intention of ensuring that his boss didn't wind up being betrayed by those hoot owls. The look in the gunfighter's eye was enough to convince Ottus that now was not the time to leave for his morning rounds.

Taggard broke the silence. He knew the animosity that lingered under the surface of his deputy and felt it would be best to keep these two men apart.

"You best go make the rounds without me this time, Ottus. Kiefer and me got some things to discuss."

Ottus huffed, but complied. "Oh well. If that's what you think best, Sheriff." But he kept his eye fixed on their visitor. "I'll just go do the rounds on my own then."

Nobody moved. Ottus and Jack stared at each other.

"Off you go then, Ottus," Taggard reminded him.

Ottus jumped. "Oh, yessir, Sheriff. I'll just ah . . . just go do the rounds then . . ."

The deputy headed for the door, and Jack wisely stepped out of his way to give him room to pass. Closing the door after the deputy had left, Jack continued to stand on the threshold, looking sadly at the lawman.

"C'mon, Kid," Taggard offered, as he moved to his desk. "Sit down and have some coffee."

"No," came the cold reply.

Taggard looked up, taking note of the tone in Jack's voice and wondering if he'd have enough time to grab the rifle lying on his desk, if the gunman turned mean. Then he relaxed and tried to have some faith in the level of the other man's common sense. He was hurting, confused, and maybe even angry, but he wasn't lethal—that much Taggard was sure of.

"Don't tell me you were on that train," Taggard stated, by way of opening the conversation.

"Did you know about this?" Jack asked him.

Taggard nodded. "Yeah, I knew about it."

Jack's nerves exploded. "And you didn't tell me?"

"That's right, Kid, I didn't tell ya."

Jack's temper took hold and he came at the sheriff in an angry

Departures

charge. Taggard used all his self-control to not back off, nor to make a grab for the rifle, knowing that either action would only ignite more anger.

"Why not?" Jack yelled at him, as he came up to the desk. "Those weren't just my friends who got butchered up there. Some of 'em were yours."

"Don't you think I know that?" Taggard asked him, forcing himself to look squarely into those icy blue daggers. "Do you really think this was easy for me? But I made my choice years ago, Jack. Just like you and Leon did. Ya can't stand on the fence forever. Ya gotta decide which side you're on!"

"We never turned on our friends!" Jack stabbed the desk top with his finger to emphasize his point. "One of the reasons Leon is in prison now is because he wouldn't turn on his friends."

"That's a very fine line you're walkin'."

"But it's still a line we won't cross." Jack's anger was in a slow burn. "You shoulda told me, Taggard. I coulda warned 'em."

"And that's exactly why I didn't tell ya," Taggard scowled back, getting angry himself now in his own defense. "I knew that's exactly what you would do. Throw away everything you and Leon worked so hard for. And for what? Those fellas made their choices, Jack, just like we did. Sometimes that's the price ya gotta pay.

"Dammit, Jack, you weren't even supposed to be on that train. I wasn't expectin' ya until the weekend. I was gonna tell ya about it then, after the fact. I guess ya found out about it the hard way though, didn't ya."

"I sure as hell did! And why?" Jack was back up to yelling strength. "The rewards for that whole gang won't even come close to covering the expenses of this venture. What was the point?"

"Sit down, Jack."

"No!"

"Sit down," Taggard insisted. "That's not a request!"

The two men locked into a silent contest of wills until Jack finally sighed and relented. He knew Taggard wasn't going to tell him what it was all about unless he complied, and right now, information was what he wanted more than anything else. He looked around for a chair, then slid it over to the desk and grudgingly sat down.

Taggard relaxed, then pulling open the top drawer of his desk, he took out the inevitable bottle of whiskey and two shot glasses. He

58

filled both and slid one over to his companion.

"Drink this."

"No."

Taggard gave him a look that didn't need words to back it up. Again, it was not a request.

Jack hesitated a moment, then picked up the glass and downed the contents in one swig. Taggard did the same, then re-filled both glasses and put the bottle away.

Tensions eased.

Taggard sat down himself and gave a heavy sigh.

"Outlaws have had their day, Jack. This was bound to happen sooner or later, you know that. You and Leon saw the writing on the wall seven years ago, and thank goodness, you got out of it while you could."

"That didn't help Leon much, did it?" Jack snarled, bitterly.

"I know," Taggard conceded, "but if you'd stayed with Elk Mountain, you'd both be dead, and you know it. It was a losing game, now more than ever."

"Why?" Jack asked him. "What's so different about 'now'?"

"I know you don't follow politics too much," Taggard explained, "but Wyoming is heading, full steam, toward statehood, but that isn't gonna come about so long as the territory is still being strangled by gangs of outlaws. In order to show that Wyoming has enough population, enough industry, and enough maturity to warrant statehood, Governor Moonlight had to find a way to clean up the gangs and get rid of the strongholds."

Taggard paused here for a moment to let this sink in; he took a sip of whiskey from his glass.

Jack just stared at the desk in front of him and basically forgot about the shot glass he held.

"So," Taggard continued, "Moonlight had been impressed with how Morrison handled bringing in you and Leon, and he offered the marshal a large sum of money to hire as many men as he felt he would need, and gave him access to all the resources he'd want, to ensure bringing down the Elk Mountain Gang—among others."

Jack's jaw clenched in anger. "So, Morrison had a lot more at stake than just the reward money."

"That's right. The reward money on most of those fellas was just an extra tidbit compared to what Moonlight is payin' 'em to get the job done."

"Morrison is gonna get himself shot one a these days," Jack growled, "and I just might be the one who does it!"

"Now you're talkin' stupid." Taggard said. "And if I didn't know it's just 'cause you're hurtin' right now, I'd lock ya up for makin' threats against a law officer."

"The guy's a bastard!" Jack insisted.

"Only 'cause you're lookin' at 'im from the wrong side of the fence, Jack!" Taggard pointed out. "To the honest, hard-workin' citizens of this territory, Morrison is quickly becomin' a hero. He's the one who is finally gettin' the job done. Finally, clearin' out that nest of thieves who have been runnin' rough-shod over the territory for years. People have gotten fed up with it. Now, maybe you and Leon held some favor with folks, 'cause you focused on the larger corporations and showed a bit of class when it came to dealin' with the average citizen. But even so, people just aren't gonna put up with it anymore."

Jack sat back in his chair. He finally remembered the shot glass he was holding, and bringing it up to his mouth, he downed the contents.

"But how?" Jack asked. "Elk Mountain has always been secure. How did they get in?"

Taggard sat back in his chair and looked into the middle distance before locking eyes with his companion.

"You remember Seth Flannigan?" he asked.

Jack creased his brow in thought. "Ahh, Flannigan . . . the name sounds familiar, but . . ."

"He was up at the Elk the same time as we were," Taggard reminded him. "When Cortez was still runnin' things."

Jack shook his head, still at a loss to place the man.

"Young fella," Taggard continued, "a little older than Leon, but acted younger. Tall, skinny with that long stringy black hair."

"Oh!" the penny finally dropped, and Jack remembered him, "Oh yeah. He was always pushin' me for a fight."

"Right," Taggard agreed. "Cortez finally got tired of him pushin' his weight around and kicked him out."

"Yeah, okay," Jack said. "I got 'im now. What about him?"

"It seems he got himself into a lot of trouble down in Utah. He went and killed somebody, and they locked him up for life."

"Well, that don't surprise me," Jack commented, dryly. "What's that got to do with Elk Mountain?"

"I'm comin' to that. It seems he was willin' ta do what you and Leon won't. He got tired of sittin' in prison, so he started makin' noises, like he knew a back way into the Elk Mountain hideout, stuff like that. The law ignored him for the most part. These guys are always talkin' big but end up with nothin' to offer. Then Morrison found out about it and he went and had a talk with ole Mister Flannigan."

"Back way?" Jack asked. "The only back way that I know of was that winding little track that went through the rock face. That thing wasn't even wide enough for a pack mule to get through, and even at that, Cortez had us dynamite it, so it was blocked completely. Then, he still insisted on havin' a sentry on it through the dry months. So did Leon, for that matter."

"Yeah, I know," Taggard nodded. "I remember pullin' that duty sometimes; what a pain—eight hours of sittin' there, lookin' at nothin'."

Jack snorted. "Yeah. You're not the only one who hated it. None of us were excluded from it. Worse duty you could pull. The only good thing about winter was that the snow was so deep back in there a snowshoe rabbit couldn't get through, so we didn't have to watch it."

"Yeah, well," Taggard shook his head with regret, "unfortunately, Gus got sloppy and he stopped puttin' sentries on that back trail, even during the summer months. I guess he figured it was blocked up solid, so there was no need to keep watchin' it."

Jack groaned. "Oh no. What the hell was he thinkin'?"

"He was thinkin' that he was secure," Taggard said, "Then, there's ole Flannigan, carryin' a grudge and thinkin' that he just found his way out of a life sentence. And he was right. Morrison and Moonlight made a deal with the governor of Utah, statin' that if the information Flannigan gave them led to the downfall of the Elk Mountain Gang, then Flannigan would receive a full pardon and be a free man.

"Then, as the snows started to melt away, Morrison began sendin' reconnaissance up into those hills. They found that back trail and started hangin' around, just to see if anyone up in the hideout noticed them. Nobody did. So, that's when they started formulatin' a plan.

"They sent word out that a large payroll was comin' through on that train, knowin' the gang would be desperate for a good score right around now. Get most the gang out of the hideout, and then blow open that back trail and take it by storm. They were met with very little resistance."

Heavy silence settled in over the sheriff's office. Jack didn't know whether to be angry or sad—and angry at whom? Gus or Flannigan? Or both. Gus, for being an idiot, and Flannigan for being a traitor, selling out the whole gang for the price of his freedom. Well, he'll be spending the rest of his life looking over his shoulder. Even outlaws who weren't part of the Elk Mountain gang will be watching out for him.

"Now Malachi and probably Gus too, think I turned traitor. That I did the one thing me and Leon swore we'd never . . .." Jack gave a big sigh and brought himself back to the present. "So, the new governor is the one behind this sneak attack," he asked quietly, almost making it a statement. "He's the one who put up the money to hire Morrison ta get it done?"

"Yeah, that's right, Jack,' Taggard said, knowing exactly what the next words out of Jack's mouth were going to be.

"And this is the same governor we've got an appointment to go see in ten days, with the intention of askin' him if he would please give Napoleon Nash a pardon."

"Yeah, that's right."

"Aww Jeez."

"Don't give up on it," Taggard tried to sound optimistic. "We've got a good case."

"Yeah, right." Jack's tone dripped with sarcasm. "He's gonna laugh us right out of his office. That's if we can even get into his office in the first place." Jack's fist came down onto Taggard's desk, then he was up on his feet and pacing, frustration written all over his countenance. "Dammit!"

"Jack, calm—"

"Don't tell me to calm down, Taggard," Jack snarled at him. "That's my best friend locked up in there. I promised him I'd get him out. I promised him. 'Hang on, Leon, we'll get ya outta there, just hang on a little bit longer'. Dammit!"

Taggard sighed and didn't say anything more. He could understand Jack's frustration, because he felt frustrated too. Leon seemed to be adjusting better to prison life lately, but even Taggard knew he couldn't hold on forever, and for what? If every hope they had kept getting squashed under their feet, what was there left to hold on for? His biggest concern now was that Jack was going to do something rash. Something he wouldn't be able to walk away from.

Gradually, Jack calmed down again, and with one last hand through his blonde curls, he came and sat in his chair. He stared at the desk for a few minutes, then came to a decision. He looked Taggard straight in the eye.

"I wanna go up to the hideout."

"What?" Taggard asked, not sure he had heard right.

"I wanna see the hideout. I gotta . . . I gotta see how it is."

"I don't think that's a good idea."

"Taggard, I'm goin' up to the hideout. You can either come with me or not, but I'm goin'."

Taggard sighed and nodded, recognizing Jack's tone and hard look, and knowing there was no arguing with him.

"All right, Jack," he agreed. "I'll come with you. I should probably see it, too. You aren't the only one who called that place home. I suppose Ottus can look after the town for a few days. I've got some things to look after tomorrow, so we can head up there on Sunday. How's that?"

"Yeah, okay."

"In the meantime, you can stay at my place; give ya a chance to rest up a bit. Ya look like hell."

Jack nodded. He felt like hell. Then he groaned as he remembered something. "Ohh, Leon."

"What about him?"

"He was expectin' ta see me this weekend," Jack admitted. "Ahh, I better send him a telegram, let him know I'll be delayed a week. Jeez, our first visit since the fall, and all I have ta bring him is bad news."

CHAPTER FOUR
RETURN TO ELK MOUNTAIN

Elk Mountain, Wyoming
Spring 1887

Taggard and Jack, along with their two horses and a pack mule, headed up toward what was left of the Elk Mountain hideout. It wasn't a short ride, and they knew they would be camping out for two nights at least, before making it to the old stomping grounds. The weather was still chilly and damp, and the nights spent under the clouds were not pleasant, but Jack felt the need to see it, so they went.

The third day on the trail, they saw another group of riders coming down the side of the mountain ridge and heading toward them. This group was leading two pack mules; one for carrying supplies and the other carrying a grislier package. As the second group got closer to the two men, they could smell the pungent odor of smoke and burnt flesh, and knew they were carrying back the body of the outlaw who had died in the barn.

The two parties stopped and acknowledged one another. Jack nodded to the one man in the group whom he recognized.

"Deputy Strode."

"Hey, Kiefer," Strode responded, then nodded at the sheriff. "Sheriff Murphy."

"Deputy," Taggard greeted him. "You fellas been up at the hideout?"

"Yeah," Strode said, looking regretful. "Morrison wanted us to dig this one out and bring 'im back for identification. Though, if ya ask me, it's a waste of time. He got burnt up so bad, there's nothin' recognizable about 'im. A simple count would suggest that it's Curly Red Johnston, and I would have been just as happy to leave it at that."

He swallowed. His complexion was still pallid at the morbid job that had been handed down to him.

"What do ya mean, a simple count?" Jack asked.

"Well, that kid, Cartless, said that Ben Jackson and Curly Red Johnston were the only fellas with him at the Elk when they got hit," Strode explained. "The two Bishop brothers were on lookout and they're accounted for, so the only one who wasn't accounted for was Johnston." Strode shrugged his shoulders, "so, process of elimination."

Jack and Taggard both nodded silently, feeling the need to show some respect to the dead man, outlaw or not.

"What's gonna happen to Cartless?" Jack finally asked.

"Nothin'," Strode assured them. "He's just a kid, hadn't broken any laws yet, except he was hangin' out with known outlaws, but that don't matter. Morrison got in touch with his folks and they're comin' ta get 'im."

Jack nodded, relieved. "Good."

"Yeah," Strode agreed. "I guess the other one, Howard, his folks are comin' up as well, to claim the body and take it home for burial. It's a shame, that. A real hard lesson for Cartless, and I just hope he takes it serious and don't go off playin' outlaw again."

"I think he's had enough of the outlaw life," Jack said. "He was pretty cut up over losin' his friend."

"Yup, I guess," Strode agreed. "Well, we best be movin' on here. The sooner I can get away from this body, the better I'll like it."

"Yeah, okay, Deputy." Jack tipped his hat.

"We'll see ya later, gentlemen," Taggard commented.

They all started to move off, when Jack pulled up his horse as he remembered something.

"Oh, Deputy?"

"Yeah?"

"Any sign of Shaffer?"

"Nope," Strode informed him. "That outlaw done disappeared in a wisp of smoke. And Morrison's none too pleased about it either, I can tell ya."

"Yeah, I bet. What about Lobo?"

"Still breathin'."

The Kid nodded acknowledgment, and the two groups parted

company and carried on their separate ways.

***

Five hours later, the two friends could tell they were approaching the entrance to the Elk, even if they hadn't been able to recognize the landscape. The acrid smell of wood smoke was so heavy on the breeze that even the horses tossed their heads and snorted in irritation.

Jack began to feel sick even before they entered the yard, and by the time they pulled their horses up and dismounted, he was thinking that maybe it hadn't been such a good idea to come up here, after all. But now that he was here, he was determined to see it through. He had to know for sure that this chapter of his life was truly gone. He had to see it for himself.

What he saw was devastation. Even after the time that had passed, smoke still lifted from the blackened ash-covered remnants of what was once a collection of sturdy buildings. Jack walked forward, looking around and trying to get his bearings, but with no buildings or other structures around, it was hard to know exactly where he was in the yard.

Then he saw what was left of one of the rocking chairs that normally sat on the front porch of the leader's cabin. Then, yeah, there were a couple of the posts and some of the steps that led up to the front door. This was all that was left of the structure that was recognizable, other than the solid stone cooking stove with the blackened tin coffee pot still setting on it. And some of the pots and plates and utensils scattered in amongst the pile of smoking, blackened pieces of wood.

Jack stopped and stared at the debris, thinking how odd and out of place those items appeared now. He looked again, upon the blackened rocking chairs. How many times had he and Leon sat right there, on that porch, drinking coffee, or something stronger, and discussing a new plan? Or going over a job and thinking about how they could do it better next time. Or just sitting, not discussing anything and smoking cigars and drinking whiskey, and quietly appreciating a peaceful evening.

Those had been good times. He'd forgotten how good they had been until now, standing there in the middle of this destruction and reminiscing about it. He sighed and moved on.

There was the barn, or what used to be the barn. The paddock fence was still standing, for the most part, though definitely blackened by fire. Some of the railings and posts had been splintered and knocked down, probably by horses trying to get out and away from the flames. What a mess.

Over there was the bunkhouse, and again, the only thing left intact was the old black cast iron cooking stove, tipped over onto its side, surrounded by more of the same ash-covered debris.

Then, oddly enough, the outhouse which hadn't been touched by fire and still stood, keeping a solemn watch over its fallen neighbors.

Jack turned and saw the chicken coop, and his heart took a hit. He went back to that day, oh so many years ago, when he had returned to the Elk with a box full of hens and a rooster, because he wanted fresh eggs for breakfast. Can't have fresh eggs without chickens.

Leon had laughed, *What are ya gonna do with a bunch of chickens?*

But Jack had been determined, and he set about banging and hammering to put together a chicken coop.

Leon had finally taken pity on his nephew and came over to help, just as Jack knew he would, and together, they planned and built the best chicken coop Elk Mountain had ever seen.

Now, it was a blackened skeleton of its former self. Once large and sturdy, with wire meshing and a safe, warm house lined with laying boxes to keep out the feral dogs and cats, it had been Jack's pride and joy. Having those fresh eggs didn't hurt either.

Jack couldn't help but smile at the memory that always made him smile, even when he was sad, the memory of Leon walking in amongst the chickens and spreading the grain around for them. *Here, chick, chick, chick.*! And clucking away to them just like old times.

It was so unlike the adult Leon to be in there, feeding the chickens, and yet, so much like the child, Napoleon, whom Jack so clearly remembered out there in the back yard of the Nash's homestead, feeding the chickens.

Jack furrowed his brow as he thought about it. It was two jumps back in time, him standing here now and thinking back to the outlaw leader feeding the chickens, and himself then, watching him and thinking back to the child, Napoleon, feeding the chickens.

This stuff could get weird.

Jack sighed and, shaking his head, turned away from the blackened, charred chicken coop and walked further out into the open yard. He caught sight of the foul heap of burnt carcasses where the posse men had dragged the dead bodies of horses, dogs and chickens that had been unfortunate enough to get caught up in the middle of this cruel slaughtering.

Jack noted there were no cat remains in that pile. There had been several cats taking up residence in the barn, but, cats being cats, Jack figured they'd all lit out for new digs at the first sign of trouble. Odd how the mind works at times like this. Why would he even be concerned about a bunch of feral cats?

A slight breeze came up, and it was enough to assault his senses, full force, with the strong, pungent smell of burnt wood and flesh mingling together. That odor had been with them all along, but the sudden assault the wind had kicked up, brought with it a rush of memories that Jack had not expected, and had been in no way prepared for. He grabbed onto the side of the outhouse and vomited.

Taggard, who had been holding back and letting Jack make his rounds and come to peace with this devastation on his own, started to come forward. But he stopped after only a few steps, knowing that his friend would rather be left in privacy right now, and so he waited, and held the horses and mule.

He found the odor that permeated the hideout to be sickening as well, but not so much as to cause him to lose his breakfast. Being here again certainly brought back his own rush of memories, but he knew this must be much harder on the Kid. He waited patiently for him to gain control again, then walked over to him, leading the horses.

"You all right, Jack?"

"Yeah," Jack answered, though still sounding strangled.

He went over to his horse and taking the canteen from the saddle, he took a drink, swished the water around in his mouth, then spit it out. He took another drink and swallowed it. He poured more water into his cupped hand and splashed it over his face. Finally, he took another, longer drink.

Taggard waited.

"Sorry," Jack said, once he got his breath. "It's just that smell. It took me by surprise."

"Yeah. It's strong, all right."

"No, it's not that," Jack told him. "It's just . . . it's the same smell, after those raiders attacked our farm. That same mix of burnin' wood and animal flesh." Jack retched again, but he had nothing left in his stomach to bring up. "Oh jeez. I gotta get outta here. Let's go, Taggard."

"Okay. You've seen enough?"

"Yeah. Everything's gone. There's nothin' left here for me now, it's all gone. Let's go."

The ride back to Medicine Bow was a quiet and solemn one. Jack Kiefer was in mourning and Taggard Murphy was wise enough to leave him alone.

***

Laramie, Wyoming
The Territorial Prison

Nash sat, staring silently at nothing over Jack's left shoulder. Finally, he gave a little cough and swallowed.

"Charlie Hadden's dead?" He needed confirmation, still not looking Jack in the eye.

"Yeah, Leon."

"And Matt Hamilton too—well, that's no great loss," Leon mumbled more to himself than to his nephew. "Too bad about the Red Sash fellas though, they seemed all right."

"Yeah."

"So . . . ahh . . . Malachi and Lobo are in custody," he reiterated, as though repeating the information over to himself would help his brain to work its way through the shock and allow him to accept the truth of it all. "And Gus is on the run."

"Yeah," Jack confirmed again, "at least that's how things stood when I left Medicine Bow yesterday. I don't know what Lobo's chances are of pullin' through; he was pretty badly broke up."

"Hmm. Might be better off if he just died," Leon mumbled. "Better than coming here."

Jack made no comment. He knew Leon was hurting and that he was struggling to come to terms with it. He also knew that Leon had yet to confirm the one death that was the hardest of all, that maybe if he didn't ask for confirmation, he could convince himself that he simply hadn't heard it. But if nothing else, Leon was a realist, and finally, through the hurt and the bitterness, he swallowed again and shifted anxiously in his chair.

"And Mukua? He's dead?" He forced himself to look over and meet his nephew's eyes. The pain he saw there answered his question even before Jack nodded.

"Yeah, Leon. Mukua too."

Leon nodded. "*Ata-i.*" It was barely more than a whisper.

Jack didn't respond.

"What was he doing at Elk Mountain?" Leon asked softly. "He usually winters down in New Mexico."

"Yeah, I know." Jack shrugged, "I dunno."

Leon sighed. "He told me once he'd rather die a warrior in battle than as an old, sick man in bed."

"He did?"

"Yeah." Silence again, then, "Elk Mountain's gone," Leon stated, matter-of-factly. "Well . . ."

The two friends sat in quiet reflection for a few minutes, both in mourning over the loss.

"I'm sorry, Leon," Jack finally said. "Not much of a reunion, bringin' ya news like this."

"Yeah . . . not your fault, Jack," Leon assured him. "I'm glad you told me. Better than having Carson rub it in my face. He would have loved that. It must have stuck in his craw, not being able to say anything."

Jack gave a little smirk. "Yeah, I'm sure." He looked at his friend, concern creeping into his eyes. "You gonna be okay, Leon? Not gonna go off and do somethin' stupid, are ya? Kenny was concerned about that. Well, we both were. You've been doin' so much better lately, stayin' outta trouble an' all. You're not gonna give Carson a reason to start beaten' on ya again, are ya?"

Leon sent Jack a sad smile. "No, Jack, I'm not going do anything stupid."

"Okay, good." Jack nodded, but he still needed more of an assurance. "You gonna be okay, Leon?"

Leon gave his friend the benefit of a full-dimpled smile.

"Yeah, Jack. I'm going to be okay. Don't worry about me." Then he dropped the smile and sent his own look of concern to his nephew. "You going to be okay?"

Jack smiled. "Yeah, Leon. I'll be okay."

***

Later that day, Kenny took a quiet stroll past Nash's cell with the intention of a quick, walk-by check on the inmate. The guard noticed the convict being escorted back into the cell block after his visit with Jack, and he looked wrung out. Just staring ahead and focusing on nothing—like he was in shock. Kenny knew he wouldn't feel right, heading for home that night, if he didn't make sure the inmate was okay.

The guard came level with the cell door, but what he saw Nash doing while he sat on his cot, leaning over his small table in concentration, caused Kenny to suddenly change direction and cross the threshold.

Leon glanced up, startled. Then, seeing that it was a guard, even Officer Reece, he instantly dropped his gaze and sat back, away from the table.

"No, it's all right, Nash," Kenny assured him. "There's no problem."

Leon nodded and visibly relaxed, but still didn't look up.

"I've noticed you playing with this deck of cards before," Kenny explained. "I'm curious about what you're doing."

No response from the inmate.

Kenny rephrased the sentence. "Show me what you're doing with the cards."

A ghost of a smile played across Leon's lips, and he sat back up again and pulled the cards into a deck.

Kenny stepped forward, watching intently. He'd never really noticed Leon's hands before, and it surprised him to see how delicate they were. Not feminine in any way, most definitely masculine, but lithe and graceful, with long, slender fingers dancing over the cards, apparently seducing them without touching them, into doing what he wanted them to do. It was amazing just to watch.

Leon picked up the deck of cards and shuffled them, the smile on his face becoming broader as he warmed to his audience.

"The object of this game," he explained as he dealt out the cards, "is to deal out twenty-five cards, then try to make five pat hands out of them."

Kenny creased his brow. "You can do that?"

"Hmm," Leon hummed. "Nine times out of ten—usually."

Kenny smiled. "Show me."

***

After Kenny left, Leon put away his deck of cards. He pushed himself onto the bunk and settled into a cross-legged position. Resting his hands on his knees, he leaned back against the wall and closed his eyes.

Ata-i. How can you be gone? You were my last link. You were all I had left of my mother. The last connection to my Shoshone family. How can you be gone?

I am not gone. I will always stand by you, Napai'aishe. Your mother and I will always be with you. Stay true to the Spirits and you will find your strength.

Leon's eyes snapped open. He looked around his cell, expecting to see Mukua standing there, smiling at him with the wisdom that he held.

But the cell was empty.

Leon sighed and stretched out. Funny how the mind can play such tricks on you.

***

"Jack," Kenny greeted his visitor at the front door. "Come on in."

Jack felt awkward at first, stepping into the front hallway of Kenny's home, but Kenny ushered him forward, showed him where to hang his coat and hat along with his gun belt, then led the way into the well-lit and homey kitchen.

A motherly woman turned to greet him, her dark blue eyes sending him a warm smile. Her brown hair streaked with gray was pulled back into a bun, neatly highlighting her round and pleasant face. Like Jean, she had a way of making a stranger feel right at home.

"This is my wife, Sarah," Kenny introduced them. "Sarah, this is Jack Kiefer."

"Ma'am," Jack nodded.

"Mr. Kiefer." Sarah came forward and shook his hand. "Finally, I get to meet one half of the partnership that's been giving my husband so many sleepless nights."

"Ahh, ma'am?" Jack asked, feeling confused.

Kenny cocked a brow and sent his wife a teasing reprimand.

"Later," he said. "We can get into that after supper. OH! Here come the kids. Behave yourselves now, we have company."

Two well-grown lads had heard voices in the kitchen and knowing who was expected, they quickly made their way into the room to join them and meet their infamous visitor. Both boys were awe-struck and nervous, but also grinning with excited anticipation.

"Jack, these are two of my boys," Kenny introduced them. "The older one there is Charlie, he's sixteen, and the one hiding behind him is Alexander. He just had his fourteenth birthday. Boys, say hello to Mr. Kiefer."

Jack shook hands with both boys, who responded with slack jaws and wide eyes.

"Howdy Charlie, Alexander."

"Hello Mr. Kiefer," came Charlie's response, but Alex just stared, not sure what to do with his hands.

"Our oldest boy, Conner, is back East in college," Kenny explained, "though I could have sworn we usually have one more offspring underfoot at dinner time."

Sarah rolled her eyes. "I think Evelyn is a little shy about meeting you, Mr. Kiefer. Give her a moment and she'll show up."

Jack smiled. "No need for her to be shy, ma'am. I won't bite. How old is she?"

"She's six," Sarah stated with a mixture of pride and exasperation, "and quite the little tomboy."

Jack's smile widened into a grin. "Oh, I wouldn't worry about that, ma'am, I seem to recall knowin' a couple of other young tomboys who have managed to grow up inta fine young ladies. One of 'em is gettin' married this summer."

"Well, that's reassuring!" Sarah admitted with a laugh. "Not a lost cause then?"

"No, ma'am."

"Please, call me Sarah," she told him. "Kenny has spoken about you and your partner so often, I feel like I've known you for years."

"Oh. Yes ma'am . . . ah, Sarah." Jack smiled. He always had trouble switching over to the more casual address, when it came to the older ladies. It made him feel as though he wasn't showing them proper respect.

Sarah smiled at his discomfort but was confident he would get over it.

"Dinner will be ready in half an hour," she announced. "If you gentlemen will excuse me." She creased her brow as she turned back to the stove. "Where is that girl? She's supposed to be helping me here. Boys, go find your sister."

"Aww, Ma!" came the unified complaint, but they were shooed out of the kitchen anyway, to go and accomplish their mission.

"Come on, Jack," Kenny suggested, "let's get out from underfoot."

***

The two men headed into the sitting room and while Jack settled into one of the comfortable armchairs, Kenny poured out two glasses of brandy and passed one over to him. He tapped Jack's glass in a silent salute, then sat down himself and took a sip.

He sighed into relaxation. "Ohh, it's good to get home."

"It's a nice home ta get home to," Jack agreed.

Kenny nodded, looking pleased. "Yes. I'm lucky. I know that. I see some of those young men who end up at the prison, and I thank my lucky stars that my boys seem to be getting off on the right track."

"Well, a good solid home life, decent parents, that can make all the difference," Jack observed, then added, almost to himself, "if me and Leon had . . ." He stopped and sighed apologetically. He hadn't meant to go there.

Kenny studied the man sitting across from him.

"Did Nash get the chance to tell you about the orphans?" he finally asked.

Jack cocked a brow. "Orphans? No."

Kenny smiled with the memory. "That's a shame. He was excited about it and was looking forward to telling you. I guess that other news got in the way."

"Yeah," Jack agreed and looked at his drink. "How was he after I left? Was he okay?"

"I think so. I went by to check on him and he was playing with that deck of cards you gave him. He seemed all right."

Jack nodded. "Good. That's a good sign. He'll do that when he's workin' somethin' out in his mind, workin' through things. That's good. It's when he stops doin' somethin', just sits and stares, that's when ya gotta watch out."

"Was it bad?" Kenny asked. "What happened?"

"Yeah, it was." A hint of sadness settled over Jack. "I was right there, and that marshal in charge of it, Morrison, well, me and Leon have had dealings with him before and he made me look at all the bodies, wantin' me to identify 'em. He already knew most of 'em, but he wanted to rub my nose in it."

Kenny frowned. "Not very diplomatic. I guess you did know most of them?"

"Yeah," Jack conceded. "A few of 'em were friends. And it's likely you're gonna be meetin' a couple of 'em at some point, if things go as planned."

"Okay. I'll get the rundown on them when the time comes."

"Yeah," Jack said again. He became quiet, contemplative, and Kenny knew there was something more coming, something that was obviously bothering him. Finally, Jack looked up with a sigh and smiled sadly at his host. "I see your sons and think 'thank goodness they've got a decent home and a decent start'. Me and Leon were younger than they are when we got started on the wrong foot—just, nobody to show us different. Then, on that train, I saw history repeatin' itself, but things worked out better for one and worse for the other."

"What do you mean?"

"There were two young fellas, who'd just joined up with the gang," Jack explained. "Fifteen years old, best friends and, apparently, from pretty decent families too. But they got the idea that it would be 'fun' to run away from home and join an outlaw gang."

Kenny groaned.

"Yeah," Jack continued. "One of them young fellas got shot dead, right outta the saddle. The other one, well, hopefully he's back home by now, but he's taken a hard lesson back with 'im. Had to lose his best friend ta find out that bein' an outlaw ain't quite so glamorous, after all."

"That's sad to hear," Kenny admitted, instantly thinking of his own sons. "But, in a way, this takes us back to something Nash was going to ask you. Ha! Now, since he didn't get the chance, I suppose it's up to me. Somehow, I had a feeling it would be."

"Oh yeah?" Jack asked. "What's that?"

"The orphans."

"Right," Jack commented. "You mentioned that before. What's it all about?"

Kenny smiled. "Dr. Mariam asked Nash if he would go to the orphanage and spend some time talking with the children there. You know, answer their questions about life as an outlaw, that sort of thing. Ohh, he didn't want to go at first; he was scared to death."

"What?" Jack was incredulous. "Leon scared ta talk about himself? I don't believe it."

"Umm hmm," Kenny nodded. "Put out every excuse he could think of. But Mariam finally convinced him to do it, and not surprisingly, once he found his footing, he kind of enjoyed himself."

"Now that sounds more like it. He had a good time?"

"Yes, I think so."

"Good," Jack emphasized. "Leon needs some good times these days."

"Yes," Kenny agreed, then sent Jack a scrutinizing look. "The children enjoyed it too; so much so, that they became quite enthusiastic when Nash suggested that you should come out and spend time with them as well."

Jack paled. "Me?"

"Hmm."

"Aww, no," Jack backtracked. "Leon is the talker, not me. I'd be no good at that."

"Well, just think about it," Kenny suggested. "A couple of the boys there would be close in age to the ones who got themselves mixed up with your gang. A word of caution from you would go a whole lot further than anything the Sisters might have to say."

"Yeah. I suppose . . ." Still, Jack was not enthusiastic.

Then a small voice at the threshold caught their attention and both men looked over in that direction.

"Papa."

"There she is!" Kenny announced, his whole face lighting up with paternal pride. He stretched out his arm to beckon her over. "Come on in, sweetheart, and say 'hello' to Mr. Kiefer."

Rushing footsteps filled the sitting room as the young girl ran to her father's protective arms. Once there, she stood, snuggled up beside him, then turned to shyly acknowledge their visitor.

Jack sent her his most reassuring smile.

She was a pretty little thing, with her mother's brown hair and dark lashes nicely contrasting with the gray eyes that were so much like her father's, Her features were unusual—and striking. She was going to be a looker, that was for sure.

"Evenin' Miss . . . Evelyn, ain't it?" Jack greeted her.

"Yessir," came the very quiet response, and she turned and hid her face in her father's shoulder.

Kenny laughed and gave her a reassuring pat on the back. "Is supper ready?" he asked her.

She nodded silently.

"Good!" Kenny stated. "Come on, Jack. Let's go eat. We'll discuss that other matter after supper."

***

The mood around the supper table became light and amiable as the two boys got over their shyness. The inevitable questions started coming at Jack faster than his shootin' arm could have stopped them.

"Are you as good as your reputation?" Charlie asked over a mouthful of biscuit. "I mean, they say you're so fast, ya can't even see it."

"I don't know," Jack admitted. "I injured my shoulder a while back and it's takin' time to get it workin' right again."

"What happened?" asked Alex. "Did it get broke?"

"Broken," Kenny corrected his youngest son. "And I'm not so sure that Mr. Kiefer wants to discuss that right now."

"No, that's okay, Kenny," Jack assured him. "I don't mind answerin' their questions."

Kenny acquiesced and turned the floor over to Jack.

"That's right," Jack answered the question. "It got broken real bad, and it has taken time ta heal up proper."

"Ohh," came the unified response.

"But you're still fast, ain't ya?" Alex held the floor.

"Aren't you," Kenny piped in, though he felt he was fighting a losing battle.

"Yeah, I'm still fast," Jack assured them.

Both boys smiled broadly. It wouldn't be right at all, if the Kansas Kid was no longer the fastest gun in the West.

"Can we see it?" Charlie asked.

"Yeah, can we?"

"Ahh . . ."

"Not tonight, boys," Kenny stepped in. "Maybe another time."
"Aww!"

"How come your eyes are so blue?" came the quiet, tentative question from little Evelyn.

Kenny and Sarah were doing their best to stifle a laugh.

Jack was caught flat-footed and just stared at her, with his mouth open, for a couple of beats. The inquisitive gray eyes gazed back at him, awaiting an answer.

"Ah, well . . ." Jack couldn't help but laugh out loud. "Well, I suppose you'll have ta blame my ma for that. She was real pretty, with long blond, curly hair and the most brilliant blue eyes you would ever wish ta see. Like lookin' into a clear mountain pool with the summer sun shinin' on it."

Evelyn smiled and was instantly in love.

Kenny's brows went up at the look that came over his daughter's face, then he sent what could only be called a teasing smile to their guest.

The two boys rolled their eyes and groaned. Girls are so silly.

Sarah was still smiling as she pushed herself away from the table. "Come along, Evelyn, help me get the desserts. No, no, Jack. You stay put; you're our guest tonight."

"Oh. Yes, ma'am."

Evelyn grinned openly at her new "boyfriend", then quickly climbed down from her chair and scurried after her mother.

"Boys, clear up the plates," Kenny told them. "Help your mother."

"Yes, Pa."

Once the two men were left alone at the table for those few moments, Kenny sent a humorous look to Jack.

"I can't see you having any trouble at all impressing a room full of orphans," he noted. "And I thought you said Nash is the only one with the 'silver tongue'."

Jack simply rolled his eyes, feeling uncomfortable.

***

After supper was dispensed with, Jack and Kenny retreated to the sitting room and settled into the comfortable armchairs, their second cups of coffee placed upon the convenient side tables.

It was time to get down to the real reason for the social call. Kenny had plenty of time to think about the request, and he knew how important it was, but he was still struggling with just how much he would be willing to stick his neck out.

"I agree that it's an important issue," Kenny stated. "The prison system really does need fixing, especially with Wyoming trying to attain statehood. But I must be very careful here."

"I know," Jack agreed. "That's why I don't wanna pressure you or Dr. Palin to give us any more than you're willin' to. I don't wanna see anybody losin' their jobs over this—or worse."

Kenny looked off into the middle distance for a moment, struggling with himself.

"Yes," he finally concurred. "It could be dangerous, and I have my family to consider. With the boys all coming of age now, it would not be a good time to be out of work. Conner is already in his second year at college, and of course, Charlie is eighteen and champing at the bit to join him there. Alex will probably be right behind him." Kenny sighed and ran a hand through his hair in what seemed to be a universal indication of stress. "Even with there being some benefits with my job, it's still an expensive undertaking."

Jack nodded, thinking that was the end of it.

"But," Kenny continued. "I've always told my boys to stand up for what they think is right, even if it means going against the popular belief. What kind of father would I be if I didn't live by my own teachings? What I see in that prison on a day-to-day basis is enough to make one reconsider the options." Jack looked up, feeling hopeful. "It's not just the excessive physical punishments inflicted upon the inmates, but I have begun to doubt the legitimacy of the very structure of the prison system itself."

"In what way?" Jack asked, not wanting to reveal just yet that their lawyer had already mentioned the possibility of presenting their case in a hearing based upon that very topic. He also knew the guard was sticking his neck out just making the statement, and Jack wanted to be sure that Kenny would look at this as his idea, not Jack trying to pressure him into anything.

"This dictum that it's for the inmates' social well-being that they are not permitted to speak," Kenny carried on. He was unsure of his footing, but now that he had opened the topic, he was determined to have his say. "The idea being that if the inmate is silent, it will give him time to reflect on his crimes and wish to attain absolution."

Jack gave a sardonic snort.

"Yes," Kenny agreed with a nod. "I've seen it happen, repeatedly. Rather than the inmate becoming reflective and appreciative, many of them slide away in the opposite direction. A new convict who comes into the system being quiet and unassuming, will often, over time, become aggressive and volatile. Then, depending on their personalities, they either continue with the aggressive behavior until they need to be put in chains, or they sink into a depression and kill themselves.

"Oh jeez," Jack groaned, running a hand over his eyes. "That's worse than I thought."

"I'm talking about the long-term inmates, now," Kenny pointed out. "Not the fellas who are in for five years or less. A five-year sentence is doable. An inmate can see the end of it and they can usually hold on until they are released. It's the fellas who are looking at a ten to twenty-year sentence, or life. They're the ones who, for lack of a better term, can end up insane."

"Yeah," Jack reiterated. "The fellas who are lookin' at twenty years ta life."

"Yes," Kenny agreed, knowing exactly where Jack's thoughts were going. "That's why I've tried to keep Nash occupied with— anything. Keep his mind active, keep him from sinking. I mean, Nash came into the system already kicking and fighting, already volatile and unpredictable, already angry. It didn't take much for Carson to push his buttons."

Jack simply nodded. He knew Kenny was right. Leon hadn't done himself any favors with his aggressive behavior, and it was mainly due to Kenny's diligence that the convict had been able to adjust at all.

"I know you're doin' a lot for him," Jack finally commented, "and believe me, we all very much appreciate it."

Kenny smiled. "Yes. Your friend, Miss Marsham has already expressed her thanks on that account."

Jack perked up with a raised eyebrow.

"Penny?" he queried. "Oh yes! She mentioned that she had met you. She was very impressed."

"Likewise," Kenny responded. "Not too many young ladies will stand up to two men with billy clubs, even if it is to protect a friend."

Departures

Jack stared at Kenny for a moment, not quite sure he'd heard that right.

"She did what?" he finally asked.

Now it was Kenny's turn to be surprised. "She didn't tell you?"

"No!"

"Well, the beating Nash took in the infirmary, that day, would have been a lot worse if Miss Marsham hadn't gotten in between him, and Carson and Thompson. I think they stopped more out of surprise than any feelings of intimidation, but it still did the trick. And it took a lot of courage on her part. She's quite the young lady."

Jack sat back with a sigh. "Yeah, well now that you mention it, I guess it's not so out of character for her. She's put herself between me and a deputy's rifle on a couple of occasions, and probably saved my life by doin' it that last time."

Again, it was Kenny's turn to stare back at Jack in a moment of surprised silence. Then he whistled softly and shook his head.

"Yeah," Jack commented dryly. "I don't know whether she's courageous or just naïve. Probably both! I'm afraid that one of these times, she gonna get herself hurt, or killed." Jack's voice caught a little bit with that last word. "She's so headstrong. Her and her sister, both."

Kenny cocked a brow at his friend's obvious emotion. "Or fiercely loyal," he suggested. "I think once she develops better judgment, she'll be a real force to reckon with. I'm glad she's on our side."

"Yeah," Jack smiled. "If—when we get Leon outta prison, a lot of it will be due to those two young ladies, that's for sure."

Silence reigned again for a few moments, while both men sipped their coffee and disappeared into their own thoughts.

"Which way do ya think Leon is likely to go?" Jack eventually asked.

Kenny creased his brow, not sure what Jack meant by that.

Jack met his eyes, a worried expression settling over his features. "Extreme aggression or suicidal?"

"Oh," Kenny muttered, then thought about it. "I don't know," he admitted. "It's hard to predict. Someone who's quiet and seems well adjusted, will suddenly explode one day and go on a rampage. It's hard to know. Some of the warning signs for a suicide are, of course: ongoing depression, lack of appetite, or when they do eat, it's usually by themselves in their cell."

"Nash was displaying a lot of those tendencies during his first year here, along with the aggression, which is why I tried to get him involved with other things. Like you said, keep his mind active and challenged, and we might just keep him sane. If we can keep him busy, hopefully he'll get through it all right."

"Is it working?"

Kenny nodded. "For now, yes. This past winter he has done very well, helping in the infirmary. Dr. Palin is certainly impressed with him. And it looks as though he is dealing with the bad news you had to bring him. I'll still keep a close eye on him though. Sometimes the shock of news like that can take a few days to sink in."

"Dammit!" Jack said, as he punched the arm of his chair. "I gotta get him outta there. I just don't know what else to do at this point."

Kenny nodded. Though he was surprised by Jack's sudden outburst, he could understand it and tried to be a bit more optimistic.

"The two extremes are not always the case," he pointed out. "Many long-term inmates adjust to their lives in the prison and end up being role-models for the others. It wouldn't surprise me if Nash goes that route. He's back to enjoying Dr. Mariam's sermons, and the little word challenges she gives him certainly keep his mind occupied."

Kenny's deliberate attempt to change the mood of the conversation worked, and Jack laughed. Being reminded of that game lifted him out of his slump.

"I don't know whether to thank ya or curse ya for givin' him that dictionary," Jack admitted. "Now he's got me playin' word games too."

Kenny chuckled. "We're not really supposed to give gifts to the inmates, but I thought that would be a worthwhile exception."

"Yeah, well he certainly latched onto it," Jack concurred, "and I suppose it is kinda fun." He laughed again as he remembered his partner's enthusiasm at the start of it. "He loves to throw words at me that he knows I won't understand. But I guess it's just his way a gettin' me involved with it too. So, that's all right."

Kenny nodded. "And this brings us back to something else I think will be good for Nash. It's something you could both be involved with, and I'm sure it will help your partner deal better with his life as he knows it now."

Jack looked at Kenny suspiciously, knowing he'd walked right into that one.

"The orphanage," Jack stated.

Kenny nodded. "It'll not only help Nash to know that he's doing something worthwhile, but it'll be helping those kids too. Hearing it right from the 'horse's mouth', will do a lot more to deter them from the outlaw life, than any pleading or threats of punishment are going to do."

"I suppose it would, wouldn't it?" Jack commented, thinking back to the two young men who had both paid a heavy price for a bad decision.

"Umm hmm," Kenny agreed.

"Well, give me a heads up when he's gonna go back, and I'll see what I can do."

"Good!" Kenny responded, then turned serious again. "As for our other topic of conversation, do you have anything in the works now?"

"Yeah," Jack admitted. "We have that appointment to see Governor Moonlight to discuss the possibility of a pardon. But after this latest event, I ain't holdin' my breath on it. I'm beginnin' ta think we're gonna have ta hit the prison board ta make them aware of what is going on behind closed doors. Steven, our lawyer, is also filing an appeal with the Wyoming Supreme Court in the hopes of gettin' Leon's sentence overturned."

"Well," Kenny sighed, "if it comes to that, I'll submit my records for consideration to the prison board, and I'll see if Palin is willing to do the same. I'd rather not appear in person though. After all, the Auburn Prison System is the one paying my wage and helping me to send my boys to college. I won't be able to help you out with the Supreme Court, even if you are lucky enough to be heard. I don't have any say over Nash's sentencing."

"I know, Kenny," Jack conceded. "Anything you feel comfortable submittin' will be appreciated. Thank you."

The now familiar thumping of running feet upon the floor interrupted their conversation, and little Evelyn came charging in to give her papa a kiss on the cheek.

"Time for bed, little one?" he asked her.

"Yes, Papa," she admitted, as she shyly peeked at Jack. "Mama said to come in and wish everyone a good night, and to say goodbye to our guest."

"Goodnight, sweetheart," Kenny said to her and gave her a big hug and a kiss on the forehead. "Say goodnight to Mr. Kiefer."

Having been given permission, Evelyn ran to Jack and gave him a big hug around the neck and a kiss on the cheek, as well.

"Goodnight, Mr. Kiefer."

Jack couldn't help but feel flattered and he grinned broadly to be so honored.

"Goodnight, darlin'," he said. "It's been a real pleasure to meet ya."

Evelyn blushed sweetly and was in no hurry to release her hold, but Sarah was waiting by the threshold and soon stepped in to break it up.

"Come along, little one," she said as she came up and took her daughter's hand. "You've said your goodnights, now it's time for bed."

Evelyn let go of Jack's neck but smiled up at him and gave him a little wave as her mother ushered her away.

Jack chuckled as he watched her go. Then he settled back again and met the amused eyes of her father.

"You got a real nice family here, Kenny," Jack said, and Kenny again beamed with pride. "I can only hope ta be so lucky one day."

"I wouldn't be surprised if it comes to you too, eventually," Kenny assured him. "More coffee?"

***

Later that night, Jack was in his hotel room, lying in bed and staring at the ceiling, thinking about all the turmoil of the past week. It had been a real doozy, and it wasn't over yet.

Malachi would be going to trial soon, the only question being how long he would get. Certainly, not the same sentence that Leon had received; that was pretty much a given. But still, up in the air as to what exactly the court would feel an outlaw of Malachi's duration would be deserving of.

Jack worried about how Malachi would handle prison; he was none too bright, but he was a gentle soul and might not be able to stand up for himself. Of course, Leon would be there to watch out for him, but then that could bring trouble of its own.

Jack sighed. He was going to be having more than one inmate to come visit, if things went the way it was expected. At least they'd all be in the same place. Two birds with one stone—maybe three.

And that brought up the question of Lobo. Jack wasn't sure what he hoped would happen with this. Part of him wanted the outlaw to recover from his injuries; there'd been so many deaths already. But another part of him agreed with Leon's morbid comment: that Lobo would be better off dead than ending up in prison.

But still, Lobo might not get too long a sentence. It was hard to tell. And he was just mean enough to survive his injuries and get through his sentence just to spite everybody. At that time, he would get out and probably return to outlawin'. He didn't have anything else to fall back on.

For that matter, neither did Malachi.

And what about Gus? Where was he? Did he take off for parts unknown, or was he lying low, hoping for a chance to spring Malachi? Secretly, Jack hoped Gus had done the smart thing and headed away from the usual haunts: someplace like Washington or Idaho, or maybe even Canada. Just go where nobody knew him, and he could start over. With Morrison on his trail, he didn't stand a chance if he stayed around these parts. But then, Gus never was all that smart.

Then there were four. Jack mused. *Oh brother. Leon could go ahead and reestablish his old gang right there inside the prison. Wouldn't that be fun. Well, at least they could all look out for each other, and Carson wouldn't stand a chance. Yeah, that would kinda turn the tables a bit.*

Next on the agenda, Jack started thinking about the meeting they had set up with the governor, and he gave a sardonic snort even though there was nobody else in the room to hear him.

Fat chance that was going to do them any good. Obviously, Moonlight wasn't going to be interested in giving Napoleon Nash a pardon, not if he was willing to offer Morrison even more money than the official rewards would bring, to ensure the end of the Elk Mountain Gang.

Jack sighed into the darkness and ran both hands through his hair. This was getting to be too much. How had it become so complicated? All they wanted was a clean slate; a chance to start over again. Was that too much to ask? Apparently so.

Damn, he missed his uncle. He felt like they were drifting away from each other; their lives heading down two different paths that were taking them further and further apart as time went on. But neither of them could stop their individual journeys, nor turn around and join up with the other. This wasn't the way it was supposed to be.

All these thoughts and questions whirled around in Jack's head, making it impossible for him to settle into sleep.

Geesh! he rolled onto his side. *I'm turnin' into another Leon. Thinkin' and worryin' about stuff I can't do nothin' about. Dammit.*

He flung the covers off and got out of bed. There was no point in whipping a dead horse, so he may as well go out and do something about it. He got dressed and headed outside, making his way to the lit and obviously still busy saloon.

Stepping into the bright and noisy establishment, he headed to the bar and ordered a whiskey, then taking the shot glass in his hand, he turned to survey the room. There were the usual card games going on, but Jack wasn't interested in them. He noted other fellas talking with friends, or spending time and money on the saloon gals, but he wasn't interested in that either. He wasn't going to waste time and coinage flirting with a downstairs girl, and he scanned the busy floor, until his eyes lit upon a particular upstairs gal who had become his regular.

He smiled and summoned her over. Her eyes lit up, and it wasn't just an act for the paying patron either. Though she knew she would be getting paid for her services, Jack Kiefer was one of her favorite customers. Not only was he painfully handsome, but he was a generous and versatile lover as well. Getting paid for it was an added benefit.

She turned her back on the drunk idiot who was doing a miserable job of flirting with her and sashayed over to the bar to snuggle up to the blonde ex-outlaw.

"Why, good evenin', Jack," she cooed at him. "I was beginnin' to think I wasn't gonna be seein' ya this trip."

"I know Marla, I know," Jack smiled at her, "but I got ta thinkin' about how pretty you are, and I knew I just couldn't leave town without a visit to my favorite gal."

"Uh huh," Marla responded with a laugh. She knew a line of bullshit when she heard it, but that was okay; it was all part of the game. She discreetly placed her hand on his hip, then slid it down to nestle comfortably against his groin. "You feelin' restless tonight, sweetheart?"

"When ya ask it like that, how can a man say 'no'?" Jack caressed her arm and leaned in for a kiss. She met him halfway and at the same time, gave a slight squeeze with her hand, right where it counted. A groaned escaped him. "Upstairs," he breathed into her ear. "Help me forget my worries."

Marla smiled as she and the bartender exchanged a knowing nod. She then took her project for the evening by the hand and led him over toward the staircase.

Jack followed very willingly, and by the time they were halfway up, he was the one in the lead, 'cause he knew the way so well . . .

CHAPTER FIVE
FALL BACK AND REGROUP

Cheyenne, Wyoming
Spring 1887

Jack Kiefer was seething.

He was angry with himself afterward, because he really should have been prepared for the outcome; indeed, he had predicted as much after the raid on Elk Mountain. Still, he had allowed himself to hope, and that hope had set him up for disappointment.

He got a hint of what was to come right at the beginning of the meeting. Governor Moonlight had given Steven a hearty handshake, Taggard an average one, and to Jack, he had barely clasped his hand and did not even pretend to make steady eye contact. There was a time when Jack would have felt intimidated by such an acknowledgment from a high-up official, now all it did was tick him off.

"Well, Mr. Granger, I can certainly see that you have done your homework," Moonlight commented while he flipped, once again, through the paperwork that Steven had presented him with. "But I really don't see anything here that would suggest Mr. Nash is deserving of a pardon, or even a reduction in his sentence, for that matter."

"Surely, Governor Moonlight, you must see the travesty of justice in this case," Steven pushed. "For a man who has never committed murder, or even assault, for that matter, for him to be sentenced to life in prison, is extreme to say the least."

"On the contrary, Mr. Granger," Moonlight countered him, ignoring the fact that one of the individuals to whom he would be referring, sat right in front of him. "Napoleon Nash and the Kansas Kid created havoc amongst the honest, hard-working citizens of this territory, and they did it for years. Now, perhaps Mr. Nash never killed or 'assaulted' anyone in the most basic meaning of the terms, but he and his partner still caused a great deal of harm, undermining the very structure of the territory's financial base."

"No more than any number of other outlaws who have gone through the court system and received far less stringent sentences," Steven pointed out. "Why should Mr. Nash—"

"I have gone over the testimonies from the trial," Moonlight persisted. "I have read the statements made by witnesses, along with comments and observations made by Judge Lacey. Mr. Nash was disrespectful to the court, right from the beginning, and even behaved in a threatening manner toward at least one of the witnesses brought forward to testify. He was given numerous warnings to conduct himself in a more respectful manner, and yet, declined to do so. The man is a scoundrel and showed no respect for the law, whatsoever."

"That's not the true situation at all," Jack jumped in, much to Steven's chagrin.

Taggard groaned.

Jack ignored them. "Nash and I tried for five years to earn those pardons that this office promised us. We worked hard for 'em, because we knew how important they were. Nash's disrespect wasn't toward the law or the court, but toward a man who was willin' ta knife his friends in the back in order ta save himself!"

For the first time during this meeting, Governor Moonlight acknowledged the ex-outlaw with a direct look in the eye. But the look was hard and unconditional, showing nothing but disdain for the man sitting before him.

"From what I can see, Mr. Nash was simply attempting to pull another 'con'," Moonlight growled quietly, his thick, black beard bristling. "Only this time he attempted to hoodwink the legal system of this territory. It had become obvious, even to him, that the day of the outlaw was coming to an end—he even states as much in his own testimony. His attempts to gain a pardon were based more on his desire to avoid prison time than any new-found respect for the laws of this country."

Jack did not back down. "With all due respect—"

"Don't insult me by even pretending to have 'respect' for this office, Mr. Kiefer! Why Mr. Hoyt would make a supposed deal with outlaws as prolific as you, in the first place, is beyond me. And I was appalled by Mr. Warren, allowing himself to be pressured by public opinion into granting you a pardon. But I suppose I should have expected as much. After all, what else can one expect from a bloody Republican? If it was within my power to do so, I would rescind that damned pardon, have you thrown in irons and taken directly from here to the Territorial Prison, where you could re-join your partner until hell freezes over!"

And this is when Jack Kiefer started to seethe.

"Governor Moonlight!" Steven interjected, before his client did something he would later regret. "I remind you that we came to this meeting in good faith. That you would honor the legal standing of my client and respect his status as a citizen of this country. You have no right to make such a threat against him."

"That is the only reason he is still seated in my office as a free man," Moonlight bellowed. "If the law, as it stands now, protects this man from being sent to prison, then there's not too much I can do about it. But to expect me to grant a pardon to Napoleon Nash after he has been fairly tried and sentenced, is utterly ridiculous!"

"I believe the point we are trying to make here, Governor, is that it was NOT a fair trial," Steven threw back. "That a twenty-years-to-life sentence far exceeds what was fair, considering the nature of the crimes Mr. Nash was tried for."

"Matter of opinion, Mr. Granger," Moonlight pointed out. "Mr. Nash lied continually throughout his trial, claiming to have gone straight, only for it to be revealed, through the testimonies of others, that he had done no such thing. Indeed, he was using the trust that had been given to him by his friends as the very tool he needed to deceive them. Hardly someone who would be worthy of that type of trust again."

"Considering that I am one of those friends whom he deceived," Taggard spoke up for the first time, "and I have forgiven him that deception, once I came to understand the justification for it—"

"Then you are a fool, Sheriff Murphy," Moonlight accused him, "and for a lawman of your standing, that is a sorry thing to see. I am a busy man, gentlemen. I have given you my answer to your request and that is the end of it. Good day."

***

The three men sat at a table in the café, drinking coffee and discussing the meeting and its repercussions. Or perhaps, it would be more accurate to say that two sat and discussed the meeting. One sat, tight-lipped and silent, staring into nothing and strangling his coffee cup.

"I guess that settles it," Steven commented. "The next step is to take it to the Prison Commission and then the Supreme Court. Moonlight can't just arbitrarily brush away a formal appeal. If the evidence is strong enough, he must respond to it."

"Yeah, but is the evidence strong enough?" Taggard questioned with doubt in his tone. "What else have we really got that wasn't presented to him here?"

Steven glanced at the third member of their party. "What do you think, Jack?" he asked his friend. "Is it likely that Officer Reece and Doctor Palin will testify at a hearing on Nash's behalf?"

"No," was Jack's curt and angry response.

"No?" Steven reiterated. "Not at all?"

Jack sighed and relaxed a little, realizing that remaining in a snit wasn't going to help their situation.

"They're both willin' to submit their records, but not appear in person," Jack filled in the blanks. "They're concerned that they could lose their jobs if they do any more than that."

"That's understandable," Steven nodded. "It would be putting them on the spot. Hopefully the records of unwarranted abuses will be enough. Then we have Penny's eyewitness account, and if Dr. Mariam Soames is willing to testify, that would help, too."

"To be quite honest, Steven," Jack said, "I can see this plan helpin' us if all we wanted ta accomplish was ta question the Auburn Prison System. But I don't see how it is gonna help Leon get outta there. It might change the way he's bein' treated, which is certainly better than nothin', but how is it gonna affect his sentence?"

"That is the issue we will take to the Supreme Court. We will continue to question the legitimacy of that sentence and suggest that he has been wrongfully incarcerated for over a year and has suffered enough punishment so, therefore, is deserving of a pardon. Especially if he continues to behave himself and stays out of trouble. That could only be to his benefit."

Jack and Taggard exchanged glances. It's true that Leon had done well through the winter, but how long could he keep that up? Or was he going to behave in a manner similar to what Kenny had described to Jack: put on an act of acceptance and cooperation until one day, something lights the fuse and he explodes.

Then Betsy came over with the coffee pot to refill cups and take their dinner orders.

"It sure is nice to see you again, Steven," Betsy commented as she filled their cups. "It's been a long time. I hear you're betrothed."

Steven smiled. "Yes. A young lady in Colorado."

"That's nice," she congratulated him sincerely. "When is the big day?"

"Oh, ah—end of July." Steven had to think about it, as his mind had recently been filled with other matters.

Betsy smiled. "She's a lucky lady." Then she acknowledged the other two patrons.

"Hello, Sheriff."

"Ma'am," Taggard nodded a greeting and left it at that, since he knew her attention had already moved on to his companion.

"Evening, Mr. Kiefer."

"Evenin', Betsy," Jack greeted her. "Still workin' here, I see."

"Considerin' I'm part owner now, I guess I'll be workin' here for a while," she announced with a proud smile. "You tend to put more effort into a place that's your own."

"Congratulations," all three men responded.

"That's quite an accomplishment."

"Good for you."

Betsy beamed, and her smile twinkled at Jack.

Taggard rolled his eyes, and Steven just observed the interchange with a humorous smile.

There was something about both partners that the ladies found irresistible. Something in the bloodline that had blessed them with a natural charm and charisma; something that was indefinable. Taggard surmised that Nash could probably be sitting here, with shaven head and sunken cheekbones, and still command the majority of the feminine attention.

"So," Betsy continued, trying to pull herself out of those enchanting blue eyes and return to the matter at hand, "are you gentlemen havin' supper tonight?"

"Oh yes!"

"Uh huh."

"I suppose."

Departures

"We have some real nice venison steaks with all the fixin's, then berry cobbler for dessert. How does that sound?"

Everyone perked up at the sound of this, and Jack realized that he was hungry after all, despite his bitter disappointment at the outcome of the meeting.

***

Laramie, Wyoming

Three weeks later, Leon was in the warehouse, going through the old routine of making a broom while trying to stay out of trouble. It was a good thing that this duty was down to basic motor skills now, because Leon had his mind on other things and yet was able to accomplish his tasks without reprimand from any of the guards.

He still found it hard to accept the fact that his old hideout was gone. It didn't seem possible, and he was surprised at how empty he felt inside, knowing that the one place he called home no longer existed. He'd always felt that if, for some reason, the pardons didn't come through, well he and Jack could always go back, even if it was just to lay low for a while and make a new game plan. The fact that their lives had inadvertently taken paths that led them in a different direction from that, was irrelevant, he still felt vulnerable now that The Elk and its gang members, were no longer there for them.

And Mukua: *Ata-i.* Leon felt his heart tighten. A holy man in his culture, and a gentle councel to others, he brought peace and guidance to those who cared to listen yet could find none for himself. As a child, Leon worshipped Mukua and was proud to be the holy man's nephew. He remembered the bite of disappointment when, upon his return to his mother's people, Mukua was no longer with them. So, when the displaced Shoshone arrived at the Elk Mountain hideout, looking for *Napai'aishe*, his kin, Leon wasn't about to turn him away. Mukua found sanctuary within the gang, but absolution eluded him, and now he was dead, his life blown apart by Morrison and his posse.

Leon was still struggling with this loss, when more bad news came to him.

Jack, Steven and Taggard had all come by after their visit with Governor Moonlight to let him know how things had gone. Leon really hadn't expected anything other than what had happened, but he was still disappointed. Their only hope now was that the current trend of Wyoming governors, coming and going within a short time, would continue, and Moonlight would soon find himself replaced by somebody named Moonbeam, or Sun Shadow, or Starlight, or . . .

Oh well. Leon had begun to settle into life at the prison. It's not that he no longer held any hope of release, he just wasn't hanging on a hook expecting it to happen overnight. He had adjusted, as Kenny suspected he would, if he just gave himself the chance and stopped fighting it. Life went on, dull and mundane for the most part, but still punctuated with highlights and accomplishments, and he'd developed a way to find pleasure in the smallest of undertakings.

He was busy in his own mind, musing over life as he knew it now, when he became aware of a guard's uniform moving into his peripheral vision. He glanced up, then instantly dropped his gaze. He felt a tingle of apprehension tighten his shoulders, as he recognized Carson standing beside him.

"Convict 312, follow me."

Oh crap. Now what?

Leon put his work tools down and followed the senior guard out of the warehouse and across the yard to the main building. Once inside the prison proper, he was taken directly to the "pat down" room, as Leon referred to it, and Carson opened the door and hustled the convict inside. Then, none too gently, the guard shoved him up against the wall for the usual frisking.

The guard wasn't respectful in his head-to-foot search of the inmate, and upon reaching Leon's privates, made sure to be as harsh and probing as possible without being obscene.

Leon winched and sucked his teeth at the intrusion, then his upper lip curled in a silent snarl, knowing full well that Carson was deliberately being an ass by asserting his dominance in this manner.

The belt was cinched around Leon's waist, then he was pulled around and his hands snapped into the cuffs. The whole time this was going on, Carson was staring at him, trying to intimidate him into squirming, and though Leon could feel the intensity of it, he refused to comply. He stood stock still while being shackled and kept his eyes diverted, with his expression blank. He didn't know what was going on, but he wasn't going to give Carson any excuse to turn him into a punching bag for the rest of the afternoon.

Carson dragged out this procedure for as long as he could, then the inmate was taken from the common room and over to the stairs heading down to the main level.

Leon's heart sank when he realized he was being escorted to the warden's office again.

Damn.

He had gotten used to not having to deal with Warden Mitchell and the little game he insisted on playing. Now, here they were, heading right back into it. Leon sighed.

Damn.

***

They entered the warden's office and stood in front of the desk, waiting for acknowledgment. Warden Mitchell sat quietly, flipping through a folder of papers, not bothering to look up at his company. He knew who was there.

"So, Mr. Nash," Mitchell still did not look up. "It appears we will be having a couple of your compatriots coming to join us soon."

Silence. Leon hadn't heard a question in that run of words.

Mitchell looked closely at the title page of one of the folders.

"Mr. Malachi Cobb." He pressed a finger upon the written name. "Apparently, his wound was not too bad, after all, and he went to trial quickly. Obviously not much of an outlaw, since he only garnered two years with us. Probably get out after eighteen months, if he behaves himself." Mitchell tossed that folder aside and opened the other one. His lips pursed in concentration. "Maurice Lobinskie. Still recovering from his injuries, so hasn't gone to trial yet. Nevertheless, I'm sure he'll be along soon." Mitchell condescended to look at Leon. "What can you tell me about these two men, Mr. Nash?"

"Umm, I don't know a Maurice Lobinskie."

Mitchell opened the folder again and re-read the statistics.

"Nickname 'Lobo'. Ran with the Elk Mountain Gang for the last fifteen years. That would put him there during your reign, Mr. Nash. How could you not know him?"

"Ohh," Leon was enlightened. "Yes, I know Lobo. Didn't know his legal name, is all."

Silence. Mitchell sighed. This inmate could be so trying sometimes.

"What do you know about them, Mr. Nash?" Mitchell reiterated.

"Oh. Umm . . . well, they're both good outlaws, sir."

Carson's billy club snapped Leon's right leg out from under him, and in a shower of déjà vu, the inmate found himself collapsed on the floor, wondering if he should bother getting to his feet or not. The question got answered when Carson grabbed him by an arm and hauled him back up.

Mitchell looked at him like a parent coming to the end of their patience with a misbehaving child.

"I'm getting tired of this game we are playing, Mr. Nash," Mitchell admitted. "And I am particularly getting tired of your flippant answers. You like to play the fool, but I'm well aware that you are far from it. When I ask you a question, I expect a reasonable answer. Now, again, what do you know about these two men?"

Leon's lips tightened, but he was also very much aware of Carson's proximity behind him, and that guard's willingness to do him harm. He sighed, and doing his best to relax his demeanor, and putting on his best poker face, he became complacent.

"Ah, both those men were kind of at the bottom of the barrel when it came to the gang members. I seem to recall that Cobb was good with dynamite, as long as you didn't leave him alone with it for too long. And Lobo . . . ah," Leon shrugged, "he was there for fifteen years?"

Mitchell nodded.

"I guess he was good at following orders," Leon surmised. "He must of spent most of his time in the bunkhouse and wasn't all that noticeable in any way, because I don't really remember anything remarkable about him."

"Really," Mitchell commented, dryly.

"Hmm."

"I realize you have friends on the outside, Mr. Nash," Mitchell informed the inmate, suddenly changing the subject. "Indeed, they are making their presence well known. Your lawyer seems to enjoy keeping me informed of all the things I'm doing that are not acceptable. However, just this morning, I received an interesting letter from our governor. I'm sure you must feel honored that the governor of the territory takes time out of his busy schedule to notice you." Mitchell stopped and sat quietly for a moment while he watched the inmate for some reaction to this.

Leon remained neutral, and, truth be known, did not feel honored at all.

Departures

Mitchell continued. "Apparently, Governor Moonlight has also had to deal with some harassment from your friends. He sent them packing when they had the audacity to suggest that he grant you a pardon. Still, I'm sure you're already aware of these developments, but what you may not be aware of is the extent to which Governor Moonlight is in support of how I conduct affairs here at the prison."

Leon's heart sank. The hope of getting a governor in office who might be reasonable was being repeatedly squashed beneath the inmate's feet. Now, if Moonlight was openly lending his support to Mitchell and his regime, then Leon didn't stand a chance. Hearing or no hearing, the door leading to his freedom had just been slammed in his face. Again.

The inmate couldn't help but show his disappointment.

Mitchell smiled, knowing he had won the day.

"So," the warden summarized, "it doesn't really matter how much your friends want to shout and wave their fists, if the governor of the territory is not interested in their complaints, then there is no reason why I should be concerned about them either.

"Now, having said that, I will inform you that I am aware of your duplicity concerning our previous agreement. Over these past eighteen months, you really haven't brought me any information of value, whatsoever. And, I must admit that, at this point, any information you might see fit to pass on to me would be highly suspect."

Again, Mitchell smiled at the inmate, looking for a reaction.

Leon was working his poker face for all it was worth.

"You will be allowed to carry on with your privileges," Mitchell continued. "Hell, you can even go visit the little orphan children if you want to. But be warned, Mr. Nash, I am watching you. Any deviation from the rules, any misconduct, or lack of respect toward the guards, will be met with most harshly. Your friends can rant and rave, and carry on about abusive treatment and unfair conditions all they want to, but it's not going to do them, or you, a lick of good. You're mine now, Prisoner 312, and I will do with you as I choose. Do we understand one another?"

Leon stood silently. The disdain that he usually felt for this man doubled in its intensity, but now, added to it, the convict also felt real fear. He hated it. It was not an emotion he was accustomed to feeling, and yet, it was one that seemed to be attacking him, more and more, since his arrest nearly two years ago. Before that, he had always felt confident that he could talk himself out of any tight corner he got into.

Then, he'd come up against Tom Morrison, and the rules had changed. Slowly but surely, he had been pulled deeper and deeper into the quagmire, and any semblance of free-will had been stripped away from him. He was well and truly trapped.

Being preoccupied with this new revelation, Leon did not answer the question fast enough, and Carson gave him a sharp whack on the back of his thigh as a reminder.

"Yessir," came out as a forced breath, "we understand one another."

"Good. You may return to your duties."

***

Leon did return to his duties for the hour that was left of the working day, and though he got through it all right, again his mind was not on it. The sting from the two billy club smacks still lingered but those developing bruises paled compared to his emotional turmoil.

Carson smirked at the distracted and slightly worried expression that stayed with the convict for the rest of the shift. He noted that even over supper, Leon was distant and his appetite practically non-existent.

Indeed, Leon was so wrapped up in his own concerns, that on his way back to his cell with his usual cup of coffee, he started up the stairway to his level without paying much attention to his surroundings. Quite unexpectedly, one of the numerous prison cats became entangled in his feet upon the stairs, and amongst the loud yowling of the indignant feline, and the clatter and clang of his dropped coffee cup, Leon found himself making a wild grab for the hand railing to prevent himself from a nasty tumble.

The cat took off in leaps and bounds down the steps, ears back and tail high, heading for some dark corner to hide in. It reached the ground level, made a wild skid on the concrete floor while turning a corner, then charged down the hallway and out of sight.

Leon sat on the steps, holding onto the railing until his legs stopped shaking. Dammit. Now he was going to have to get a rag from the kitchen and clean up the spilled coffee. Then get himself another cup. He really did need Jack in here to watch his back, and, apparently, his feet.

The loud racket had caught the attention of the other inmates and guards in the area, and everyone seemed to think it had been quite a humorous sight. Leon was not laughing. He hauled himself to his feet, and with a scowl upon his face, he thought about how much he disliked cats. Bloody vermin! They belonged in the barn with the rats, and not laid out on the steps just waiting to trip people up!

***

The next morning, Leon was working the laundry room again and was more than happy to be doing so. He didn't feel like having to deal with the snickering looks from the other inmates over the "cat on the steps" incident, and hopefully, by the time he was back working the floor, the whole thing will have been forgotten.

Around mid-afternoon, some movement by the door caught Leon's eye. He glanced over at floor level and found himself staring into the intense yellow eyes of the black and white feline. Both parties bristled with indignant self-righteousness, and Leon felt his fists clench. The cat flattened its ears while growling softly and lashing its tail back and forth.

After thirty seconds of this stand-off, the cat's attention was diverted by something happening out in the aisle and made the mistake of taking its eyes off the inmate. Leon made a quick grab for the handy bar of soap and sent it skimming across the floor.

The cat saw it coming, and, with an angry hiss and a scramble of claws on concrete, it scampered out of the way, just in time for the bar of soap to whack into a guard's uniform, right at ankle level.

Oh crap! Dammit all to hell. Bloody cats. They should all be roasted on a spit and made into stew!

Leon and Kenny locked eyes, just for an instant; just long enough for Leon to see the look of surprised amusement coming back at him. The inmate dropped his gaze and stood passive and repentant on the other side of the laundry table, not quite sure what to expect for his excellent aim.

"No more convicts looking for a fight, so you thought you'd start in on the cats?" Kenny asked him through his smile.

"No sir, Mr. Reece," Leon mumbled an apology. "Sorry. I didn't intend to hit you."

Kenny nodded and made his way deeper into the laundry room.

"I heard about your encounter with that particular tom. I can understand you wanting to retaliate."

Leon's shoulders slumped, and he made a brief attempt to subdue an eye-roll. Was everybody going to hear about that?

"Be careful though," Kenny cautioned. "Those toms can play dirty if they decide they don't like you." Then the guard got down to business. "I wanted to talk to you about the two prisoners who will be joining us soon. As you know, I like to get some background on the new inmates, so I'll have a better idea of what to expect."

Leon glanced up, surprised, then dropped his eyes again and didn't say anything.

"What?" Kenny asked him. "You were about to say something. What was it?"

Leon hesitated, not sure how much to admit, then decided, if any of the guards were on his side, it was Kenny. "The warden already asked me about this."

Now it was Kenny's turn to look surprised. "That's odd. The warden doesn't usually bother himself with new inmates—other than the usual 'welcome to the prison' speech. He doesn't generally deal with them on a day-to-day basis, so . . . was anyone else with you?"

"Officer Carson," Leon informed him.

"Carson. Hmm." Kenny pursed his lips. "I wonder what that was all about. What did you tell them?"

"Not much."

Kenny smiled. "I bet," he then turned serious again. "Would you be willing to tell me more?"

"Yes."

"Good. Ah, Mr. Cobb is expected here tomorrow afternoon. Mr. Lobinskie hasn't gone to trial yet, due to his injuries, which were considerable."

Kenny flipped open one of the two folders he had with him and began to read some of the passages to himself as a reminder.

"Crushed arm, broken shoulder, and numerous broken ribs. The right lung seems to have been damaged as well, so even if he does recover, he's going to be weak in that area. We'll have to watch him carefully for signs of pneumonia and other lung ailments during the first winter. I doubt he would survive a bad infection like that." He closed the folder and looked at the inmate. "What else can you tell me about him?"

"Well, for one thing," Leon stated, as he started folding sheets, "don't call him Mr. Lobinskie. I don't think even he would respond to that name. We always called him 'Lobo'."

"'Lobo'. Yes, I did notice that mentioned in his file. What else?"

Leon hesitated again, continuing to fold sheets while he thought about his answer.

"Lobo was always good in a fight. He was loyal to the gang, but not necessarily to the leader—he'd pick and choose whose side he was going to be on, depending on who was most likely to win. On the job, you could count on him to do what you needed him to do, and to be there in a pinch. But he has a mean streak—don't ever turn your back on him. I never did."

"Okay," Kenny took all this in. "That'll help. Thanks. What about the other one: Cobb?"

Leon grinned. "Good ole Malachi. Ky is . . . one puppy short of a litter, if you get my meaning. He's always so eager to help, to be a part of what's going on, then tripping over his own feet in the process. He's like a boy in a man's body. A small man." Leon stopped smiling and became reflective. "I'm worried about how he'll make it in here. Carson and Boeman—they'll figure out that he's an easy target. Ky's not a fighter; he won't know how to stand up for himself."

"All right," Kenny responded. "I'll keep an eye on him until he finds his footing. I know you'll be doing the same."

"Yes."

"And watch your back."

"I try."

"And no more throwing the soap around," Kenny reprimanded him. "We have plenty of cats here, but soap costs money."

Leon rolled his eyes and went back to his laundry duties.

CHAPTER SIX
NEW ARRIVALS

The next day, Leon was in the infirmary so he missed Malachi's introduction to the prison. If things went the same way for him as they had for Leon, then the new inmate would not be on the work floor his first day, so he would have a chance to settle in. Still, Leon was anxious, knowing that Malachi would be in for a hard time, even just getting used to the idea of actually being here.

The end of the workday finally arrived, and Pearson came to escort Leon to the common area for supper. Leon entered the large room slowly, scanning the various tables and looking for the familiar figure. It didn't take long for the seasoned inmate to spot the new one; there was always something about the demeanor of a new arrival that made them stick out like a pinto horse amongst thoroughbreds.

But Malachi was doing more than just sticking out. He looked like a nervous, bald chicken with one wing in a sling, and his eyes wide as saucers. He sat, staring around at the guards and other inmates in anticipation of an attack from all sides.

Leon got his own plate of food, then started to walk over to the table where Malachi was sitting. It was then that he noticed Harris, making his move to sit next to the newbie, with the intentions of starting early on with the pecking order dictate.

Malachi was uncomfortably aware of the larger man sitting down too close to him for it to be a casual encounter. He nervously sent Harris a glance, and the convict smiled like a jackal, then reached over and snatched the piece of bread off the newbie's plate. Malachi was about to protest, but then thought better of it, and hung his head as he tried to disappear into the floorboards.

Still ginning, Harris picked up his spoon and was just about to help himself to some of Malachi's stew when he caught sight of Leon in his peripheral vision. The seasoned con quickly changed his mind as to how hungry he was and returned his empty spoon to his own plate.

Leon continued to stand behind him, glaring at him, and unlike Carson, he was successful at making his target squirm. Harris picked up the stolen piece of bread, returned it to its original owner, then, without daring to make eye contact with Leon, he picked up his plate and moved on, to sit at another table.

Leon sat down next to his friend, keeping an eye on Harris just to make sure he kept going and stayed away. Once satisfied, Leon smiled a quiet greeting at his ex-gang member. The look that came back to him froze the smile on his face, and turned his expression to one of confusion.

Why is Malachi so angry with me?

It had always struck Leon as funny that Malachi had eyes that were just as big and blue and innocent as Jack's were—until Jack got mad, then they weren't so innocent anymore. But Leon had never really seen Malachi angry. Icy blue daggers pierced his heart and put a knot in his stomach. His feelings were hurt; he thought Malachi would be relieved to see him, maybe even happy, so that glare of reproach was a blow, indeed.

Leon got over his surprise and sent his friend a questioning look, then silently mouthed the word *What?*

Malachi pursed his lips and looked back at his food but showed no interest in eating it.

Leon's jaw tightened, and his expression darkened. He gave Malachi a sharp jab in the thigh with his knuckle to get his attention again. When the blue eyes turned to him, he put more emphasis on the silent inquiry. *WHAT?*

Malachi did a quick glance around, already cautious of the guards. Not seeing any looking their way, he turned back to his ex-leader and whispered his accusation.

"Kid betrayed us."

"No," Leon breathed back.

"Yeah, he did!"

"No, Ky. Jack didn't know—"

The billy club hit the table between them so hard that the dishes rattled, and water splashed out of their cups. Both inmates looked away and became passive.

"I can't believe that I'm seeing you two talkin' here like it's and old-time family reunion," came Thompson's incredulous tone. "You already bein' a bad influence on the new inmate, Nash? Don't you think he's got enough to learn without you leadin' 'im astray so soon?"

Leon remained silent, not sure whether he should answer with a negative or a positive. Fortunately, the guard didn't seem to expect any answer at all.

"The only movin' your jaws should be doin' is chewin' on supper. You understand?"

"Yes sir, Mr. Thompson," Leon answered quickly.

"How about you, newbie?" Thompson asked Malachi, as he tapped the inmate on the shoulder with the billy club. "You understand?"

Malachi cringed, then sent a nervous glance over to his 'boss'. Leon gave him a subtle nod of affirmation.

"Yessir," came the quiet squeak.

"Good," Thompson continued. "That's good to hear. Seems you're a mite smarter than your friend here, who's had a hard time learnin' the rules. But you seem to be picking them up quick enough. Now finish your supper and get back to your cells. I don't wanna have to be keepin' an eye on you two."

Leon watched the guard move off and once he knew they were in the clear, he picked up his spoon and started to eat.

Malachi sat like a lump, his left hand cradling his right arm that was still in a sling. He stared dully at the table in front of him.

Leon nudged him again, then pointed at his plate. Malachi shook his head. Leon's anger flared a second time, and his upper lip tightened, as he slammed his open palm down on the table with a resounding 'whack'. Everyone else at the table jumped and looked at him, but Leon was only interested in his companion. He picked up the idle spoon and plunked it into the bowl of stew in front of Malachi and pointed harshly at the utensil. He waited to be obeyed.

Malachi sighed and, picking up the spoon, slowly began to pick his way through the stew. He wasn't hungry. Why was Leon being so mean?

But Leon was making a point, not only to Malachi, as to who was still 'boss', but to the other inmates, as well. Malachi was under his protection and anyone messing with the new inmate would find themselves messing with Napoleon Nash.

The message was clear. Malachi would be left alone.

***

A month later, Lobo showed up. He still looked sickly and underweight but toted a menacing look to his eyes that kept the lower-end inmates at bay. Lobo acknowledged Leon, but kept his distance, preferring to stand alone and make his own way than appear to be kowtowing to his ex-boss. Leon respected the man's space, but kept a watchful eye on him, hoping that the mean-tempered outlaw wouldn't get himself into too much trouble.

Leon was disappointed when Kenny informed him of Lobo's sentence. The outlaw had warranted eight years, and knowing Lobo, he wasn't likely to get out early for good behavior. With a bit of support, Malachi should be able to do his time and be a free man. But Lobo carried anger around with him like a shield, and Leon wondered how long it would take before he started making enemies.

Sure enough, within the first week, Lobo ended up spending a day in the dark cell for starting a fight with another inmate. Ten days after that, Kenny had to lay down the law to him for talking back and coming at the guard in a threatening manner.

If Leon had thought about it at all, he would have recognized his own behavior repeating itself, but though Lobo was devious in his own right, he did not have Leon's intellect. He didn't bother taking the time to learn how to circumnavigate the rules, but simply plowed right through them, thereby causing himself a lot of unnecessary pain and suffering.

Leon didn't know what support he could give him, other than to watch out for him and try to back him up if he got into something too deep. The new inmate was obviously not fully recovered from his injuries and chances were he never really would be. Any exertion caused him to start coughing and gasping for air, and he always seemed to be in pain, which didn't do much for his already volatile temper. Leon watched him from a distance and worried, knowing that only time would tell if Lobo adjusted to prison life or not.

***

Arvada, Colorado

May 1887

It was springtime on the Rocking M Ranch, and up on the northern pastures, the new foals and calves were showing up, one right after another. It was a wondrous time of year for Penny, as she loved to see the new babies arrive, all full of life and playful high spirits.

In the barnyard pasture, Karma, Midnight and another mare with a new foal at foot, contentedly grazed in a group, enjoying the warm sunny day and each other's company.

Midnight was kept in this field for two reasons, one was to have him easily accessible for his human to catch whenever he needed to ride into town or out to check on livestock. The other was to keep Karma company. The big gelding had a calming effect on the otherwise high-strung mare, and Cameron had good reason for wanting to keep her at ease.

The cargo she carried in her ever-expanding belly was too precious to be left out on the range with the herd of other brood mares. Indeed, her coming foal could be the beginning of a whole new line for the Rocking M Ranch, and that made it more precious than gold.

Karma herself didn't understand what was going on with her body. She just knew that, as time wore on, she became heavier and more sluggish, and her appetite raged. If she ever stopped eating to think about it, she was relieved that nobody was putting a saddle on her and expecting her to go for a gallop across the landscape. That was something she would normally enjoy, but not now. All she wanted to do now was eat, sleep, and swish her tail at the flies.

The other mare and foal were there so that Karma's baby, once it arrived, would have a playmate. It's important for young foals to be able to associate with one another, as they learn a lot about etiquette and socializing from each other, not to mention, it's just plain fun to run and buck and play with someone your own age.

On this one particular spring morning, Cameron and Penny were leaning up against the pasture fence, studying the bulging mare.

"How was she in her stall last night?" Cameron asked his daughter. "Was she restless at all?"

"No," Penny assured her father. "She was the same as always, content and hungry."

"Good." Cameron smiled. "Are you still checking her udder every morning?"

"Yes," she answered with some exasperation. "It's bagged up and ready. I have done this before, you know."

"I know," Cameron assured her. "I guess I am behaving like an old mother hen. David would be proud of me. And I keep forgetting that you're not a little girl anymore. You've been a great help on this ranch, Penny. I'm proud of you."

Penny smiled and gave her father a kiss on the cheek.

"Thank you," she said. "And you can trust me, you know. I'll know when her udder has changed, and I'll let you know, right away. I'm just as excited about this baby as you are. I know it's going to be perfect."

Jack came out of the house, and seeing them at the fence, strode over to join in on the conversation. He would be going to visit Leon again soon, and he hoped that the foal would hurry up and get here, so he could give his uncle some good news for a change. Leon needed some good news right about now.

He arrived at the fence and casually draped an arm across Penny's shoulders, and she absently reached up and held the hand that dangled down in front of her.

Cameron smiled. For a couple who were not officially courting and indeed, continued to insist that they were just friends, Jack and Penny were awfully comfortable in each other's company. As long as they didn't get too comfortable too soon.

"How is she today?" Jack asked. "Still pregnant?"

"I certainly hope so!" Penny laughed. "Otherwise, she better back off all that grass or she's going to explode."

Jack smirked. "We can't have that." Then, with a quick glance back to the house, added the comment; "Oh, oh, here comes trouble."

The other two people followed his gaze, and both smiled.

Two-year-old Eli had run out onto the porch and stopped to contemplate the steps in front of him. He absolutely adored his Uncle Jack, and upon seeing that personage walk out the front door, had then been determined to join him wherever he was going. But the porch steps had always been a stumbling block for him and normally, he insisted on enticing an adult to pick him up and carry him down to ground level.

Unfortunately, as it happened on this morning, all the adults were busy elsewhere, and Eli was determined to get to where he wanted to go. The people standing by the fence watched with curiosity to see what the little fella would do.

Eli stood with one pudgy hand on the post and looked at the steps for a moment, considering his options. Then, hardly missing a beat, he turned himself around and with feet first and hands following, he toddled his way down backwards on all fours.

Once he felt dirt under his feet, he straightened and, turning again, he laughed excitedly at his success. He started to run toward his target, then promptly tripped over his own feet and went down face first, with a thump and a puff of dust. Everyone at the fence cringed and expected to hear a bellow of tears, but much to their surprise, it didn't happen. Instead, Eli picked himself up, and shrieking with laughter, continued his run until he made his destination.

Once there, he tugged on Jack's pant leg, then reached his arms up.

"Unca' 'ak. Up."

Jack couldn't help but laugh. This was a game they played over and over again. "What do you want, little man?"

"Up."

"What? Up here?"

Eli gave him a manly punch on the knee. "Up!"

"Ohh. Well, why didn't you say so?"

"UP!"

Jack smiled into those determined brown eyes, then ruffled the boy's long, white-blond hair.

"Okay, up ya come."

Jack reached down and lifted the youngster up onto his knee that he had raised with a foot on the lower plank of the fence.

Eli was in heaven; he laughed and giggled, and hung onto the upper plank while Jack bounced his knee and gave the little boy a "pony ride".

Cameron smiled while he watched his son.

"I don't know why that boy likes you so much, Jack. You tease him no end, and he keeps coming back for more."

"He's a glutton for punishment," Jack explained. "I have an uncle just like 'im."

"Mid'i. Wide!" Eli called out, pointing a little finger at Jack's big gelding.

"No, we can't ride Midnight today," Jack told him. "He's not feeling well."

"Aww."

"Maybe tomorrow, okay?"

"'Kay."

"Midnight's not feeling well?" Cameron repeated. "What's wrong?"

"Ah, it's just that same ole tendon," Jack explained. "After our ride into town yesterday, he came up lame again. I don't know what's wrong."

"How many times is that now?" Cameron asked.

"Just twice. I'll rest him a bit longer this time. Probably didn't give it enough time ta heal when he first pulled it. He'll be fine."

Cameron made no comment, but his expression remained thoughtful. Then he pushed himself off the fence and dusted off his hands.

"Well, chores aren't going to get done on their own," he theorized. "Time we get on with them."

***

Early the next day, Penny was in the barn to check up on her special project, while Sam was busy getting the breakfast feed ready. She slipped into Karma's stall with a good morning greeting and a pat on her neck. Karma turned her head and nuzzled her young human friend, then turned her attention back to what Sam was doing.

Penny stroked her neck and quietly ran her hand down along the mare's shoulder and around her huge belly, then down along her flanks. She continued to speak quietly to her, then bent over and took a quick look at the bagged-up udder that was tucked neatly between the mare's hind legs. It was full and round, and ready for the new arrival.

Penny smiled, and her eyes sparkled with excitement as she stood up.

"It's different," she mumbled to herself.

"What?" asked Sam from the feed room.

"It's different," she said louder. "Karma's bag is different."

Giving the mare one more pat upon the neck, Penny left the stall and headed out of the barn. As soon as she was clear of the building, she couldn't help but break into an excited run as she made a beeline for the house. Though she had witnessed many a foal and calf being born, this foal was special, and she was laughing in her excitement as she charged up the porch steps, two at a time, and made a grand entrance into the house.

Her mother was just dishing out the oatmeal for breakfast while her father enjoyed his first morning cup of the coffee, when her sudden appearance surprised them both.

Penny stopped to catch her breath, her eyes dancing with delight.

"It's different," she announced. "As usual, I don't know how it's different—but it's different."

Cameron looked at his wife, and they both smiled.

"Good," he stated matter-of-factly. "She's getting close."

"Oh, I hope she has the foal today," Penny declared as she plunked herself down at the table. "This is always the hardest part. We're so close now."

"Well, she could," Cameron agreed. "I doubt it though; more likely tomorrow or even the next day."

"Don't say that," Penny scolded her father. "I could probably manage until tomorrow—but the next day? Surely Karma wouldn't make me wait so long."

"You need to learn to be patient, Penny," her mother reminded her. "You know as well as anyone, these babies come along when they're darn good and ready."

"Yes," Penny agreed, as she poured milk onto her oatmeal, "I know."

"Put her out in the field with Midnight, as usual," Cameron suggested, "but keep a close eye on her. If she starts swishing her tail more than usual, or looks at all uncomfortable, you bring her back into her stall, then come get me."

Penny sent her father an exasperated look.

"Yes, Papa, I know," she insisted. "And I will make sure her stall is spotless—and I will put extra straw in it."

Cameron smiled and kept his mouth shut. He knew when he was being reprimanded.

***

That night, Penny insisted on sleeping in the barn. She often did when a birthing was imminent, but the premonition in her heart for this new arrival was stronger than usual, and she had no intention of ignoring it.

Cameron and Jean, who had both learned not to argue when these feelings came over her, went to bed with the anticipation of a less than peaceful night. The coffee pot was made ready and set aside for quick brewing, and the stove prepared, so all it would need was lighting to get things heated up. Cameron made sure his trousers, coat, and boots were handy for finding in the dark, and everyone settled for the night.

In the barn, Penny wrapped herself in blankets and nestled into a thick, straw-padded corner of Karma's stall. The lantern hung from its hook, sending a soft light over the area. Penny was determined to stay awake the whole night to keep her favorite mare company and brought a book out with her to read for that very purpose.

Two o'clock in the morning, she was awakened from a deep sleep by rustling noises close by her. She jerked her eyes open, afraid that she might have missed the whole thing. With her blankets still wrapped around her against the chill, she stood up and reached for the lantern. Turning up the light, she was relieved to see that Karma was still the only horse in the stall with her. But the mare was up and circling, with her head down and a distracted look to her eye.

Penny came to the mare and tried to give her a head hug.

"It's all right, Karma."

But Karma was too distracted, and though she took comfort from her human's company, she continued to pace around the stall and occasionally emitted a quiet groan.

Penny tried to stay calm for the mare's sake, but her excitement was growing with each passing moment. This was it, this was the time they had all been waiting for.

Giving the mare one more reassuring pat, she left the stall and made a dash for the house. She was up the stairs to the second floor in a flash and started pounding on the door to her parents' room.

"Papa!" she called. "Papa, it's time."

"What . . ." came the sleepy grumble from inside.

"It's time," Penny repeated. "Karma's in labor."

"Oh, all right," came a more alert response. "I'll be out there in a minute."

Penny turned and charged back down the stairs. She didn't want to leave Karma alone any longer than necessary because now that labor had started, the foal could arrive at any time.

Twenty minutes later, Cameron, Jack, and Penny were in the

barn, getting the mare prepared for the big event. Cameron had wrapped up her tail in cloth to keep it out of the way and the pitchfork was handy to make sure the stall stayed clean for the new arrival.

The other horses in the barn were all awake and watchful, especially the other brood mare, who stood sentinel in the stall next to Karma's, sending out calm vibes and reassurance. Midnight stood quietly in his stall across the aisle. He was a wise old boy, and he knew exactly what was going on.

Karma continued to circle her stall, head lowered, and eyes half closed. She was uncomfortable and didn't know why, but the humans, whom she had come to know and trust, were there with her, and nobody seemed too concerned. But there was an atmosphere of expectation, so she knew something was coming. But what? Her friend, Midnight, stood quietly, sending her silent but comforting images. She tossed her head and snorted, then continued to circle.

The muscles around her barrel tensed, and she tossed her head again, with the pain that racked through her. Her nostrils flared, and the whites of her eyes showed as her body broke out into a layer of sweat. She didn't know what was going on, and she was getting scared.

Then the boss human stroked her neck and spoke quietly to her.

"It's all right, Karma. I know this is your first; I know you're scared. But we'll look after you. Don't worry."

Although Karma could not understand the words, she understood the tone and the intentions behind it, and she began to calm down. Then her muscles tensed again, and she tossed her head and blew out a snort, followed by a groan.

Jack stood quietly outside the stall, not wanting to get in anybody's way. As a child, he had witnessed many calves being born on their farm, and had always been fascinated by it. But just as it was with Penny, this birth was special, and he had no intention of going anywhere. He smiled as he watched Penny soothe the mare and encourage her to be brave. They made a good pair. He thought of his partner and wished he could be here for this. Jack was going to watch everything and then he could let Leon know how it all went. Not quite as good as being here himself, but the next best thing.

Then Karma lifted her tail and a great gushing of fluid splashed onto the straw. Her nerves were so on edge, she jumped with the noise it made as it hit the bedding.

"There goes her water," Cameron commented, as he moved in with the pitchfork to clear out as much of the wet bedding as he could. "It won't be long now."

Penny smiled at her father. She had never felt this excited, or nervous, at the other birthings she had attended, and she prayed that everything would go smoothly.

Karma circled one more time, then with another groan of pain, she slowly lowered herself onto her knees and her huge belly followed. Then with a grunt, she lay down on her side. She stretched out, trying to relieve the cramping as the contractions started in earnest. Nostrils flaring and eyes wide with pain, she grunted and tossed her head. She shifted, still trying to ease the cramping, but not having any luck. Her breathing was heavy, and her body was now covered in a heavy sweat from the strain and anxiety.

Penny sat by her head, stroking her and whispering gentle assurances, and Karma did her best to stay calm.

Cameron squatted down by Karma's tail, caressing her flank and saying words of soft encouragement.

Jack continued to watch the proceedings with a smile slowly growing across his lips. He'd never seen Cameron so gentle and reassuring, in his words and touch, as he was with this mare. Jack knew he was seeing another side to this strong but quiet rancher, and he truly believed that there was nothing this man couldn't handle and handle with quiet dignity.

And Penny. Jack's heart melted. Her face was aglow with such maternal pleasure, one would think it was her own child coming into the world. Her love for this unborn foal was so obvious that Jack knew there was going to be a special bond between them, no matter what the gender.

Karma groaned again, as the muscles along her abdomen and flanks rippled, and another strong contraction assaulted her. She strained for all she was worth as Jack gently stroked her face.

Cameron smiled.

"I'm seeing little pink baby hooves," he announced.

"Really, Papa?" Penny's excitement intensified.

Jack quietly came into the stall and sat down by Karma's head.

"You go down and help your pa," he told Penny. "I'll stay by her."

Penny hesitated. She wasn't sure if she should leave Karma's head, but she so wanted to see this foal being born.

"Go ahead," Jack repeated. "She'll be fine."

Penny smiled and went down to squat beside her father. Her face was radiant, her smile unforgettable.

Another contraction—Karma heaved and pushed again. Her nostrils flaring and eyes wide, she strained and pushed, and silently endured.

"The front legs are out," Cameron announced, and he took hold of them and pulled with Karma's contractions, trying to help her. It was coming.

"I see a nose!" Penny exclaimed. "A pink little nose."

"What color are the legs?" Jack asked.

"I don't know, it's hard to tell," Penny admitted. "Cream, I think—or white."

Karma gave one more huge push as another contraction hit her. Then suddenly, with a rush of fluids and the joyous thrill of new life, a large and confused, cream-colored foal lay sprawled in the straw.

"Oh, Papa, look! It's a palomino. It is, isn't it?"

"I'd say that's a pretty fair assessment," Cameron agreed.

Penny sparkled. "Isn't it beautiful, Mathew?"

Jack's grin almost hurt; it was so wide. He couldn't help it.

Karma heaved herself onto her belly and tried to reach her new baby. She couldn't quite do it, so she stretched out her front legs, almost knocking Jack over in the process, and proceeded to lumber her way to her feet. She turned and went to her foal, instantly beginning to lick it.

The umbilical cord had still been attached, but Karma's movement pulled it away from the baby. Cameron quickly clamped the end of it, so it wouldn't bleed out, then he used a handy piece of burlap to wipe the sack and mucus away from the tiny nostrils. Once sure the foal was breathing, he stood to let the mare tend to her newborn.

Penny wasn't quite ready to leave, and with shining eyes and a smile that wouldn't quit, she sat by the baby, petting and stroking it while giving congratulations to the new mother.

Karma continued to lick her foal.

"Well, Cameron," asked Jack, as he stood up, "is it a colt or a filly?"

Cameron sighed with just a hint of disappointment.

"No, it's a filly. But that's all right. I can see that I chose the right stallion, because the quality is undeniable. I'll breed Karma back to Pine Knot again, and then next year, we'll get the colt."

Cameron gently stroked the mare, as she continued to clean her baby. She was still having minor contractions and hadn't passed the afterbirth yet, so they would be in the barn with her for a while. It didn't really matter though, because Penny didn't look as though she intended to go anywhere, anyway.

"So, what do you think, Penny?" Cameron asked her as he passed her a larger piece of burlap. "Do you already have a name picked out for her, or do you need time to think about it?"

"She's so pretty. I can already tell what a lovely golden coat she will have once her baby fuzz grows out." Penny used the burlap to help Karma dry the damp, tawny coat. Her face glowed with love. "As soon as I saw her, she reminded me of the meadow up by Sutter's Creek, where the willow tree stands. That meadow gets so covered with daisies in the summertime, all you can see, as far as the horizon, is gold and white. So, that's what I'm going to name her: Daisy."

Jack smiled. "Well, that sounds like a real good name, Penny."

Then Jack frowned as he looked at the new-born. "What's the matter with its feet?"

Cameron followed Jack's gaze, then smiled. "Nothing. Those fleshy feathers covering the hooves are called capsules. They protect the uterus and birthing canal from those sharp edges. They start to degrade as soon as they hit the air and they'll be worn off as the foal walks around. It'll only take a few minutes and they'll be gone."

"Oh." Jack still looked concerned. "They don't look normal."

"Believe me, they are."

"Okay." Taking Cameron's word on the matter, Jack let it go and instead, focused on the young woman still sitting in the straw.

Penny continued to smile as she took turns stroking the mare and then the foal. This was going to be a night she would never forget. The joy and magic of it would stay with her for the rest of her life.

All heads turned as the barn door was pushed open and Jean entered, bringing with her a tray laden with coffee cups and some pastries. Cameron came over to help her, stepping over the three lounging dogs in the process.

"Thank you, dear," Jean said as Cameron took the tray and put it on a bale of hay. "I thought everyone could do with some refreshment. Has the new arrival arrived yet?"

"Yes," her husband told her. "A very nice filly. I don't think we're going to be able to get Penny to sleep in the house for at least a month."

Jean smiled in agreement, and as the cups were handed out, she went over to the stall to view the new foal.

"Oh my," she exclaimed, and her smile broadened. "She is lovely. Does she have a name yet?"

"I'm calling her Daisy," Penny announced as she came over to get her coffee. "I think it's perfect."

"Daisy," Jean repeated. "Yes. Very appropriate."

Jack was silent as he sipped his coffee. A slight smile still lingered upon his lips, but his eyes held a hint of sadness. He felt badly that Leon couldn't be here for this. Karma was his pride and joy, and being able to witness the birth of her first foal would have meant so much to him.

Jean came up to Jack and intuitively knew what he was feeling, and why. She put an arm around his waist and gave him a hug.

"It's all right, Mathew," she assured him. "He'll still be happy to hear about it from you."

Jack nodded but didn't say anything. He smiled, and putting an arm across Jean's shoulders, he returned the hug and gave her an affectionate kiss on the forehead.

Then his sad smile broadened into a wide grin as Daisy tried to stand up.

She stretched out her long and knobby-kneed front legs and then sat there, swaying, with limbs trembling, and wondered what the next step was supposed to be. Then she tucked her hind legs under herself and gave a heave, but as her hind legs lifted her bum up, her front legs gave out and she did a nose-dive into the straw, then found herself stretched out on her side again.

Everyone chuckled at the antics, but Daisy didn't think it was funny at all. She pushed herself back up onto her belly and lay there for a few moments while, with both ears flicking back and forth, she thought about her next strategic move. If at first . . . The front legs got into position once more, and she heaved again. This time she was a little bit more successful. A little. She managed to get up on all four legs, but they shook and wobbled, then—oops! She over-balanced and took a couple of desperate steps, but everything crumpled, and she toppled down into the straw and lay there, trembling and frustrated.

Daisy tossed her head and snorted but continued to lay where she'd fallen to give her new little body a chance to recuperate.

"How soon should they be able to get to their feet?" Jack asked. "I mean, she's not even half an hour old, and she's already tryin'."

"They need to get up fairly quickly," Cameron said. "For one thing, out on the open range, they're vulnerable to predators, so instinctively, they know they have to be up and moving as soon as possible. Also, it's vital that they start to nurse right away. There's a certain nutrient that precedes the milk, called colostrum, and the foal must get within the first few hours of birth, or they probably won't survive."

"Oh yeah. I kinda recall my pa sayin' something about that." He smiled and shrugged. "I guess I weren't really payin' much attention to that part of it."

"Hmm," Cameron nodded. "Well, just like with a calf, this filly will need to get on her feet quickly. If she doesn't start to nurse soon, we'll have to milk the mare and then bottle feed the baby to make sure she gets it." Then he smiled. "But judging by the way things are going,

I don't think it's going to be a problem."

Everybody looked back into the stall again, and sure enough, Daisy was once more struggling to her feet. She got up onto all four wobbling pegs and just stood there, swaying for a bit, almost afraid to move. Then she licked her lips and flapped her tail and took a couple of awkward but successful steps.

Karma brought her head around to lick and nuzzle her baby again. This act, in itself, caused Daisy to lose balance, and she staggered and swayed, but she was getting stronger with every attempt, and she was able to stay up on her unsteady limbs. She looked around her, blinking and still feeling a little dazed. This was all so new, so many smells and sensations, and little instincts tugging at her; it was all overwhelming.

She could smell her mother and feel the warm tongue caressing her; she felt secure and safe, leaning up against the warm shoulder. But there was another smell attracting her, and her little nostrils quivered as she tossed her head again and started to move around, back to her mother's flanks. The smell was stronger here; a warm sweetness that beckoned her, and she started to push her little nose against her mother's belly, searching, seeking out the source of that enticing scent.

Unable to stand by any longer and watch the foal trying desperately to find nourishment, Penny came forward to assist. She spoke softly to Daisy, saying her name as she caressed her body, running her hands along the soft neck and then stroking her face. Penny leaned down and with her hands, directed the soft muzzle over to a teat. Daisy butted it, investigated it, then latched on and began to nurse.

Penny straightened up with a triumphant grin and continued to caress the foal. Then she noticed that all eyes were upon her and she smiled, sheepishly.

"You all probably think I'm being silly, dotting on her like this. We all know Karma can take care of her, but I can't help it. I want to touch her."

"No, Penny," her father assured her, "What you're doing is a good thing. You touching her and helping Karma to dry her off and clean her up is going to have a life-long affect upon this filly. You're creating a connection with her, just as Karma is doing.

"Little Daisy is never going to forget the sound of your voice or the touch of your hand, and she will always associate it with food and security. She'll feel safe and content with you after this."

"Really?" Penny's face shone with pleasure as she turned loving eyes back to the filly. "I hope you're right. We're going to have so much fun together."

Daisy suckled contentedly, unaware of her future already being decided. Her little white tail flapped rapidly up and down, back and forth, as the warm, strength-giving formula flowed into her body, preparing her for a life just beginning.

Daisy continued to suckle, until her small belly was full and round, then her long legs began to shake again, and her eyelids became heavy. She barely had time to take two steps away from her mother when, as the sun came up, Daisy went down and was instantly asleep.

Everyone smiled and released sighs of contentment. Despite the gender of the foal, Cameron was pleased with the outcome of the breeding, and now that Daisy had done everything exactly the way she was supposed to, he felt confident that all was good.

"Well," Jean sighed, "that was quite a start to the day. I don't know about the rest of you, but I'm ready for breakfast. And—OH MY! Eli is probably hollering by now, and I completely forgot about him."

The others laughed as Jean excused herself from the barn and made her way back to the house. Jack went around and threw flakes of hay into everybody's stalls while Cameron made sure Karma had everything she needed for the next couple of hours. He would probably leave Karma and the baby inside for the day, since both were exhausted from their ordeal, and good ole Midnight could stay in as well, to keep the new mother company.

Jack gave his gelding a rub on the neck, then everyone headed back to the house to help with breakfast preparations.

CHAPTER SEVEN
GAINS AND LOSSES

Just as breakfast was being prepared, a buggy was heard pulling into the yard, and Jack went out on the porch to see who their visitor was. He smiled when he recognized the driver, but then his expression changed to concern as he noticed the man's condition.

"Jeez, David, you look like you've been up all night."

"Yeah, just about," the good doctor admitted, as he climbed wearily down from the buggy and came forward to tie his horse to the hitching rail by the porch. "I was hoping I could grab a cup of coffee off Jean before tackling the drive home. I'm exhausted."

"I don't suppose that'll be a problem," Jack assured him. "C'mon in."

The two men entered the house and made their way to the table that was set for breakfast. Jean came in already carrying a fresh cup of coffee, and with one look at the doctor, instantly ushered him to a chair.

"Oh, for goodness sake, David, sit down, before you fall down."

David nodded his thanks as he accepted the coffee and settled in. Jack sat down next to him and looked at his friend with concern. Penny set another place in front of him and everyone tucked into oatmeal and scrambled eggs. And more coffee.

"Just coffee is fine for me, Jean," David lamely insisted, knowing as soon as he'd said it, that it wouldn't wash.

"Don't be silly." Jean patted his shoulder. "You're here and it's breakfast time. Besides, you look like death warmed over. What in the world have you been up to?"

David sighed and took another sip of caffeine.

"I've spent most of the night with Sam and Maribelle Jefferies," he admitted.

Jean paled. "Oh dear," she mumbled.

"Is everything all right?" Cameron asked.

"No," David shook his head. "Unfortunately, they've lost their baby.

"Oh no." Jean's disappointment and concern clouded her face. "Is Maribelle all right?"

"Yes." David brightened as he confirmed this. "I was afraid it was going to be a repeat of the Robertson incident, but fortunately, Maribelle is doing fine. She lost a lot of blood and will need to stay bedridden for a while, but she's fine. Of course, they're both heartbroken. Naturally they were looking forward to welcoming a new baby into their lives."

Cameron and Jean quickly exchanged a sad glance, then carried on with the current conversation.

"I'll drop by and see her tomorrow," Jean offered. "I'm sure she's all done in for today."

David nodded over a mouthful of oatmeal.

He swallowed, then continued, "Sam's mother is here, thank goodness, and will be helping out. Fortunately, she and Maribelle seem to get along quite well, and another woman's support through this will be invaluable. Maribelle is strong and healthy. Once she's had time to recover, they can try again." David sighed and his voice drifted into a soft mumble, speaking more to himself than to anyone else as the table. It was as though he was trying to give himself encouragement that not everything was bleak and bad news. "It's not uncommon to lose a new-born, it doesn't necessarily mean they can't go on to have other children."

Jean smiled, seeing the pained look seep through the weariness in David's expression. This young man took every failure so personally.

"I'm sure she'll be fine," Jean commented. "They're young. They have lots of time."

David smiled and nodded, then glanced at Cameron.

"Don't expect to see Sam today," he predicted. "He's pretty done in himself, and probably isn't ready to leave his wife just yet."

"No, I wouldn't expect to see him," Cameron confirmed. "He can take as long as he likes. We'll manage until he's ready to come back to work."

David nodded, then the rest of the breakfast conversation naturally switched over to the new arrival in the barn. Penny was so full of exuberance and high energy that David couldn't help but be affected by it. When breakfast was over, he allowed himself to be dragged out the door to go view the sure-to-be-sleeping, foal.

Jean looked after her daughter, feeling disappointed that her kitchen helper was disappearing.

Jack stood up and started gathering dishes.

"I'll help ya clean up, Jean," he offered. "Penny is so distracted, she'd probably break everything anyway."

Jean smiled. "Thank you, Mathew."

"Well," Cameron stood and helped his son get down from his breakfast perch. "I'll get started on the morning chores. I'll see you outside when you're done, Jack."

Jack nodded and carried on into the kitchen.

***

"What's on your mind, Mathew?" Jean asked, as they got busy washing and drying.

"What?" Jack jerked out of his inner musings. "What makes ya think there's somethin' on my mind?"

Jean sent him a knowing smile. "You offer to help with the dishes, then stand here silent as a mouse, and yet, I can hear you thinking. Come on," she encouraged him. "I know you want to talk about something, or you wouldn't be here."

"Yeah, all right," he conceded the point. "It's just . . . life is so precious, ain't it?"

Jean's brows went up; this comment surprised her.

"Yes, it is."

"I never realized," Jack continued. "I mean, a course, I know that people get married and start families and all that, but I never thought about how fragile it all is. How dangerous, really. Geesh, a woman is literally takin' her life in her hands by havin' young'uns."

"Yes," Jean agreed again. "Dangerous and glorious, all at the same time."

"But why would ya take the risk?" Jack asked, truly confused on this issue. "It seems, that for every child that comes into the world, there's another that don't make it, and the mother just might not make it either. Why take the risk?"

Jean was silent for a moment as she formulated a constructive answer.

"Well, first of all, we really don't have much choice. It's the natural course of things," she said. "You meet that person whom you hope will be your partner through life, and well, children just happen. You don't think about the risks, it just happens, and then you pray that all will be well." She smiled brightly. "And it's a wonderful thing, Mathew, when you welcome new life into your world. Children are precious and well worth the risk. Even if, later, you sometimes feel like strangling them."

Jack laughed out loud. "Yep. I can understand that."

Then he went quiet again, and Jean knew there was more to come. "What is it, Mathew?"

"Life is precious," he repeated, quietly.

"Yes, it is. It's never to be taken for granted." She hesitated as she washed the dishes, knowing that it wasn't considered proper for a woman to discuss such personal matters with a man, but Mathew was family, and he was questioning this issue. She decided to let etiquette slide in favor of helping him to understand. "We don't talk about it much," she continued, "but Cameron and I know what Sam and Maribelle are going through right now. Through our life together, we've had five children."

"Five?" Jack was surprised.

"Yes," Jean confirmed. "My first confinement went the same way as Maribelle's has. It was heartbreaking. Being young and inexperienced, we were positive that we would never be able to have children after that. Then, the following year, I became in the family way with Caroline, and everything was fine. Eighteen months later, Penelope came along, and we couldn't have been happier.

"Two years after that, it happened again, and everything seemed fine for the first six months, then problems started showing themselves, and the baby arrived too early. Cameron Junior. We had him in our lives for five days, and then he was gone."

"Oh." Jack felt awkward with Jean speaking so candidly with him on this very personal subject, but he felt honored as well, knowing this could not be easy for her.

"As time went on, Cameron and I came to accept that our family was complete," Jean continued, "and then fifteen years later—what do you know?" She laughed and smiled up at her friend. "I have been blessed with a wonderful husband and three beautiful children, and every day I thank the good Lord for the joys they have brought me.

"On the other hand," Jean cocked a brow as she handed Jack a wet plate. "Some might say that I was doubly blessed."

Jack frowned as he dried the plate and set it on the counter. "Doubly blessed? How do you mean?"

"We had sixteen years between Penny and Elijah so when Eli did come along, it was almost like having our first again. Some women have a new baby every two years or so, and that must be terribly hard on them. Although, of course, the older children help to care for the younger ones, just as Penny does with Eli. Thank goodness!" She laughed at herself. "He is such a handful. Anyway, it is hard on a woman, having a baby, year after year, and the odds are, just like with me and Cameron, not all will survive. But that isn't up to us. The good Lord provided me with three healthy children, and I am content."

Jack was silent for a few moments and Jean could tell he was processing this information.

When he looked up and met her eyes, the pain she saw there caused her to place a consoling hand on his arm, and her own eyes silently asked him the question.

"I killed four people," Jack whispered, then he swallowed and looked away from her, feeling ashamed of himself all over again. "I was young and stupid, and so full of anger, and I didn't realize how precious and fragile life is." He shook his head, creasing his brow in thought. "I look back on what me and Leon got up to, and I cringe now, at the risks we used to take. But we never even thought about it, it was just fun. I mean, even being chased by a posse, being shot at; it was all a big joke. We'd get back to the hideout laughin' and carryin' on with never a thought as to how dangerous our lives were. It took losin' friends, and then, both of us gettin' seriously injured, before we even started ta question our choices.

"Now! Jeez Jean, I'm scared all the time. I'm scared Leon ain't gonna make it. That with all these setbacks, he's just gonna give up on us, and that will be another life gone. He don't see how valuable his life is; just the fact that we all survived bein' born is a miracle in itself.

"Then I turn around and snuff out four lives. I know it's easy for me ta justify that one was an accident and one was self-defense. But two of 'em, I went lookin' for revenge for what they done to my family, but that weren't right; ta take their lives away from 'em. That weren't my decision ta make."

Jean smiled sadly and squeezed his arm. "I know," she said. "But that's just it, isn't it? You were young and foolish, and you didn't realize. I know that it is a burden you will carry with you for the rest of your life. But you must find some way to forgive yourself, Mathew—forgive yourself and move on. Because if you don't, the guilt of it will eat you alive and cause you so much misery that your life will end up being wasted as well, and there's no point in that."

"No, I don't suppose so," Jack agreed.

"And don't give up on Peter," Jean encouraged him. "I know this is a difficult time for both of you, but he does have support there, people who are looking out for him. Didn't you say he was doing better these days?"

Jack nodded. "Yeah."

"Have faith, Jack," Jean said, then she hesitated, not sure if she should suggest this or not, then decided that there was no harm in offering. "You know you're welcome to join me for Sunday Services."

Jack grimaced slightly and became a little defensive. "That's not really my thing, Jean."

"I know," Jean admitted, "but it might help you to deal with all of this; to offer you another way of looking at things." She smiled at his discomfort. "I'm not suggesting you devote your life to Christ, or anything like that," she assured him. "Just take from it what you need to help you get through these difficult times. It might help."

Jack continued to silently dry the dishes, not knowing how to respond.

Jean attempted to put him at his ease.

"I don't get into town for services as often as I would like, but the offer is there," she told him. "If you decide you would like to join me at some point, just say so, and we'll go. No pressure. I leave it up to you. How's that?"

Jack nodded, then smiled, and giving Jean a big hug, he kissed her on the cheek.

"Thank you. I will think about it. You're right, though, in that I do need ta find a way to deal with this stuff. And I know Leon is goin' to services at the prison and is gettin' a lot out of it. It's kinda helpin' him to stay sane, if you know what I mean."

"I think the lady preacher has a lot to do with that!" Jean

commented, wisely.

Jack laughed. "Yeah, I think you're right. She's done a lot ta keep him interested."

"And that's exactly what I'm talking about," Jean explained. "I'm sure that once Peter is released, he will no longer attend Sunday Services, because he will feel that he no longer needs it. It often takes a woman to bring a man to the church. On the other hand, he may find it very helpful throughout his life. Either way it is giving him something he needs for now, and that is what matters. Do you understand?"

"Yeah, I do. I'll think about it," he agreed, then became reflective again. "I guess seein' that foal born this mornin', then Sam and Maribelle losin' their child, it just got me thinkin' about it again, is all."

"Well, that's all right," Jean assured him with a laugh. "If you never thought about things, you would never figure anything out. You'd just go through life like a lump on a log. Just don't get so bogged down in your thoughts that you can't get out of them."

"I'll keep that in mind."

Then David and Penny came into the kitchen and interrupted the discussion.

"Ohh, Mama. I'm sorry," Penny was truly contrite. "Here, I'll finish up, Mathew. I know Papa will need your help today if Sam's not coming in."

"Okay, fine," Jack agreed and handed the towel over to her.

He and David made a discreet exit through the front door.

***

"That is certainly a fine filly," David commented. "I'm glad Penny showed her to me, today of all days. It helps to end things on a more positive note."

"That's good, David," Jack grinned, as he clapped his friend on the shoulder. "Are you sure you're gonna be all right ta drive home? You look like you're about to collapse. I could always saddle Spike and ride in with ya."

"No, that's all right. Rudy knows the way." David yawned and rubbed his eyes. "Will you be going to see Napoleon again soon?"

"Yeah. I wanna tell him about the new arrival. And I wanna check up on those other two fellas who are there now." He smiled. "It seems I have more friends inside the prison than out."

David nodded. "Um hmm. Well, I don't know the other two, but I would appreciate you passing on my greetings to Napoleon. Tell him I'll write when I can. It's just that lately, keeping up with the practice and having a new baby at home ourselves, well, there just doesn't seem to be enough time in the day."

"Yeah, I'll let him know," Jack assured him. "He'll appreciate it, and he'll understand, too."

"Thanks."

They stopped by the buggy and the two friends said their goodbyes.

David hauled himself into the driver's seat and turned Rudy's head toward home. The little horse, ready for breakfast himself, set off at a steady trot and got him and his human back to town safely.

***

The following morning promised to be just as warm and pleasant a spring day as the previous one had been. With that in mind, Cameron decided that a couple of hours out on the pasture would be good for Karma and her foal. The other mare and foal, as well as Midnight, had already been out for a while, when Cameron entered the barn and slipped a halter onto the new mother.

He led Karma out of the barn, with Daisy glued to her dam's side, curious about what was going on, but not, in any way, ready to lose the security of her mother. She moved quickly to keep up, her head held high and her tail flapping, trying to take in all the new sights and sounds that assaulted her, and finding it all very over-whelming.

Rufus and the two little dogs trotted lazily along behind them, and Daisy decided that she didn't like that at all. She kept looking back at them, snorting and arching her neck indignantly, knowing instinctively that they were predators, and therefore, not to be trusted.

Then they reached the pasture gate, and Cameron slid the halter off Karma's head and turned the mare loose. Karma snorted and set off at a trot to get out to her favorite patch of grass before the others ate it all up.

Taken by surprise, Daisy gave a little high-pitched squeal of anxiety that she was going to be left behind. She jumped forward and almost tripped over her own hooves in her hurry to keep up with mom. She just didn't know how to keep her long legs moving co-operatively, so that she could stay upright and move forward, all at the same time.

Once she caught up to her mother, the new baby could not believe her eyes, or her nose, or her ears! All three of those senses were on high alert, and then a soft breeze picked up and gently played with her tuft of forelock, and the sense of touch kicked in as well. She stood by her mother's side, making sure to be in constant contact with her, while she held her head high, and with nostrils quivering and ears flicking back and forth, she surveyed her new domain.

"Papa!"

Cameron turned to see his youngest daughter trot down the porch steps while drying her hands from kitchen duty.

She then pointed an admonishing finger in his direction.

"Why didn't you tell me you were going to put them out? You know I wanted to watch her first visit to the field."

Cameron smiled as she approached the fence. "I knew you'd be out here for it. There is nothing that filly does that you don't seem to know about, no matter where you are."

Penny beamed a smile and, with a contented sigh, she leaned her arms and then her chin upon the top rail of the fence.

"It looks like she and Spade have noticed one another."

The sturdy black colt, who was a week older than Daisy, stood by his mother with ears and tail up, and locked eyes with the pretty little girl. Everything about his attentive posture showed how desperately he wanted to come over and introduce himself—and to play!

He sent a quick glance back to his mother, who was of course, grazing, then returned his attention to the filly. Finally, he gave a little snort and, with arched neck and his tail still standing at attention, he came trotting over to say "hello".

Cameron straightened up to watch this encounter, then relaxed.

"Karma's not concerned. Good. Sometimes a new mother will chase off another foal."

"Yes, Papa, I know. But having Molly and her foal in the stall right next to Karma has let them get acquainted. I didn't think there'd be a problem."

Cameron chuckled. "Maybe you need to tell Daisy that. She's not at all sure about this."

Daisy's expression of concern was comical, while she tried to process what to do.

As Spade got closer to her, her nerve broke and she scampered around to her mother's other side, then shyly peeked out from under Karma's tail, not too sure about this at all.

Spade was quite a brave fellow, and he came right up to Karma and stretched out his nose to the filly, wanting to get acquainted. Daisy hesitated and stood, hiding behind her mother's tail, until finally, curiosity won over and she tentatively stretched out her neck, and the two babies touched noses. Then Spade gave a little squeal and with a buck and a kick of exuberance, took off at a long-legged gallop to the other side of the pasture.

Once he reached the fence, he stopped and turned to look back at the filly, inviting her to come join him.

Daisy still wasn't sure about that, but she did move out from under the tail covering and kept her eyes and ears on that colt. She could not deny that the temptation to go play was growing stronger with every passing minute.

Spade snorted once more, then came trotting back.

They touched noses again.

Spade nuzzled her face, then her neck, then he gave her a gentle nip on the withers and spun on his little hind quarters and jumped away. But this time, he stopped about three yards off and turned to face Daisy again, tossing his head and giving a little rear.

Well, that did it! Daisy, tentatively at first, moved away from her mother. She gathered courage as she went, and before too long, the two foals were playing together, and all worries were forgotten.

Daisy learned how to use her legs, and only ended up face first in the grass four or five times before she finally had it figured out. Bucking ended up being another challenge. She had no trouble with the take-off, but the landings left a lot to be desired, often coming down and losing her balance as her legs would go off in different directions, and she'd end up toppling over, yet again.

"Oh dear," Penny laughed. "It's sad but funny all at the same time. She's trying so hard to keep up with him."

"Practice makes perfect," Cameron said, then laughed. "Whoops. Spade was even clumsier than her on his first day out."

"Yes, he certainly was. Daisy is already so graceful, even when she's falling over. She's going to be running circles around him before we know it."

Then, when play was done, both foals returned to their respective mothers to nurse and replenish their energy supply. Once this was accomplished, Daisy's legs literally collapsed out from under her, and she stretched out in the warm grass to instantly fall asleep.

The sun was shining, a soft breeze whispered across her baby fuzz, and with the reassuring sound of her mother grazing close by, Daisy was content, and life was grand.

***

The next day, Penny led Karma out to the field with Daisy trotting confidently along beside them. As soon as they were turned loose, Karma went off to graze, but Daisy squealed, gave a little buck, then galloped over to her new friend to spend the morning frolicking.

As much as Penny wanted to stay and watch the antics, she knew she had her own chores to do in the house. With a quick smile to the playing foals, she made herself walk away and get on with her day.

But as soon as the evening meal was well along in preparation, and Penny found herself with a few moments to spare, she again made her way out to the pasture fence to see how the filly was getting on.

Jack came over to join her and together, they smiled and chuckled at the antics of the two foals.

"Hmm, this ought to be interestin'," Jack straightened up from the fence as Spade tried to include the gelding, Midnight, into their play.

Daisy held back, not sure about the old fellow, but Spade seemed comfortable enough and began to buck and play around him, even going so far as to nibble on his tail. But the gelding paid him no mind and patiently continued to graze.

"Aww," Penny nudged Jack in the ribs. "It looks like Midnight likes the babies."

"That don't seem right," Jack put on an indignant act. "He's an outlaw horse. He's rough and tough. He's spent a life-time running from possies and dodging bullets. He's not some soft-hearted mush who can be pushed around by foals."

"You mean just like his owner?"

"Yeah!"

Penny huffed. "I think you're going to be in for a surprise. Look at how gentle he is."

Jack stood amazed as he watched his horse.

Midnight had realized that the filly was curious and his countenance encouraged her to approach him. She came in and stretched out her nose to meet his. Then Daisy began to move her mouth in a semblance of a sucking motion, indicating her vulnerability, but willingness to accept him as dominatef so long as he, please, didn't hurt her.

They touched noses and blew into the other's nostrils and the introduction was complete.

Karma continued to graze throughout this exchange, but had kept a close eye on the proceedings just in case Midnight tried to hurt her baby. But it soon became apparent that the old gelding had no intentions of doing harm and the new mother relaxed.

Karma snorted, and tossing her head, she walked over to join them. Pride of motherhood now shone through her gaze as she nuzzled her filly. Then, with arched necks and flaring nostrils, the mare and the gelding rubbed each other's cheeks and Midnight was accepted.

Considering how often, throughout their lives together, Karma had depended upon Midnight's calm and steady demeanor to help her through a stressful situation, the only surprise at this outcome was Karma's initial doubt of his fidelity.

But Midnight didn't seem to mind the flighty mare's concern and was just as patient with her insecurities as he was with the foals'. Once everything was settled, the gelding gave a sigh and sat down on a back hoof to snooze away the late afternoon.

"Wow. That's amazing," Jack said as he watched his horse calmly tolerate the antics of the foals. "I never woulda thought that old horse would take to them babies like that."

"Despite his detachment, he actually does seem to be enjoying them." Penny sighed and became reflective as she watched the dynamics of the small herd.

"Have you noticed that Karma has changed?"

"Changed?" Jack frowned and scrutinized the mare. "Well, she seems kinda proud of herself. But then she always was a princess in her own mind."

Penny chuckled. "Yes, she is. But it's something more than that. I noticed Karma the instant she walked onto this ranch. She had a natural charisma that draws your eyes to her. It's no wonder Napoleon loves her so much."

"Yeah, maybe too much," Jack grumbled. "I told Leon that she was too flashy for an outlaw horse, but he didn't listen. That mare drew far too much attention our way—"

"Ha!" Penny couldn't help herself. "I have a feeling that wasn't just Karma. You and Napoleon are equally as guilty of drawing attention."

"Yeah, well, I suppose."

"But my point is," Penny pulled the conversation back, "when Napoleon left and didn't come back, she lost that sparkle. Oh, she was still the princess and expected to be treated as such, but that glow was missing."

"Glow?" Jack looked out at the mare. "She looks like she's glowin' now. I swear she's got a smile on her face."

"Exactly," Penny said. "Oh, she's always been healthy and eager to go for a ride, and I think she likes me well enough, but nobody could take the place of Napoleon." She chuckled as she watched Karma dote on her baby. "Until now. She's glowing again, just like she used to. She's happy and content. Maybe after this, she won't miss Napoleon quite so much."

Jack looked at his young friend, then shook his head. "You amaze me."

"I do?" Penny turned sparkling eyes to meet his. "In what way?"

"Only you can look at a horse and see that deep into her soul. I never noticed nothin' different about her, until now. Now that you've pointed it out."

"You've had other things on your mind." Penny patted his arm. "I was worried about her, worried that she would never get over that loss. But I'm not worried anymore. Becoming a mother has been good for her."

"Penny!" Jean called over from the porch. "Come help me put supper on the table."

"Oh dear, I've lost track of time again." Penny waved to her mother. "Coming, Mama!" She turned a radiant smile to Jack. "Better get cleaned up and let Papa know it's suppertime."

***

Departures

The next morning, Jack was up early to get a good start on the day. It was his intention to feed the horses their breakfast, then walk up the hill at the back of the house to do his daily target practice before the barn chores distracted him from it. When Sam was there, Jack often found time in the mid-afternoon for his shooting but these days, the schedule had to be altered, so he found a way to fit in a half hour of practice before settling down to his own breakfast.

Not surprisingly, Jack came out of his bedroom, strapping on his holster, to find Penny already up and with the coffee brewing. She was eager to get out to the barn to help with the feeding, and to say a good morning to the foal. It was going to be a long time before this got old.

Penny was cheerful as she smiled at her friend and handed him a cup of coffee.

"I was wondering when you were going to finally get out of bed," she scolded him.

Jack's brows went up. It was an hour earlier than his usual rising time, and the sun had hardly put in an appearance. There was still a night chill in the air.

"You're in an awful hurry," he commented. "That filly ain't goin' nowhere, ya know."

"I know," Penny conceded with a smile. "But I figure you're going to want to practice your shooting before breakfast, and you know that I enjoy watching you do that when I can."

Jack smiled and nodded. "Yup," he agreed. "All right, c'mon then. Let's get those horses fed."

They headed down the front steps and walked to the first barn just as the sun was chasing away the night shadows. It was going to be another lovely spring morning, and the birds were already welcoming the day with their loud chirps and restless fluttering.

"When are you going to see Napoleon again?" Penny asked, as she followed him.

"I was gonna go this weekend, but with Sam away, I don't know if your pa would be too happy with that. Why? You wanna come this time?"

"Yes!" Penny was adamant. "You keep saying 'next time', then the next time comes and there's another reason why I can't go with you."

"I know, Penny. I'm sorry," Jack apologized. "Things just kinda got busy there for a bit, you know that."

"I know. But do you think this timeg I can actually go with you?"

"Yeah," Jack nodded. "I think it would be good. This way you can tell Leon all about Daisy, rather than just writin' it to 'im in a letter. I think he'd like that."

Penny smiled. "Yes. That's what I was thinking too."

"But only if Josephine can come along as a chaperone. You know how your folks feel about that."

Penny sighed with well-practiced drama. "Yes, all right. But Josephine will come, I'm sure of it. She wants to see Napoleon, too."

They walked into the barn, and the first thing Jack noticed was that there was no nickering from the occupants, demanding their breakfast. The second thing was that every horse in the barn was tense, letting it be known that something in their domain wasn't as it should be.

Jack then felt rather than heard a slight rustling behind him, followed by a gasp from Penny that was cut off in midstream. He spun, his gun whisking into his hand of its own accord and pointing toward the source of the sound.

The first things he saw were Penny's brown eyes, wide with fear and shock, then the grimy masculine hand covering her mouth, and the arm that came across her left shoulder from behind, pressing her back against the man holding her. He saw the gun pointed directly at him, and his own gun pointing back. The two men locked eyes.

"Let her go, Gus," Jack growled, his gun steady and aimed directly at the other man's forehead. "Let her go."

"Not on your life, Kid," Gus snarled back. "I need to talk ta you but I ain't doin' it without an edge."

"You ain't got no edge, Gus. You let her go or I'll drop you right now—and you know I won't miss."

Penny stood perfectly still, looking into her friend's blue eyes— like death turned to ice, and she knew the difference then, the difference between Mathew White practicing shooting at tin cans, and the Kansas Kid drawing his gun for real and meaning it. She felt a shiver of fear go through her, but the fear wasn't for herself, it was for the man standing behind her, because she knew he was walking a fine line, right now. The fine line between life and death, and if he did not make the right choice, and make it soon, his next step would be into oblivion.

She felt it; the doubt go through the man holding her. And Gus knew it too, he knew that even though he had a hostage and his gun was aimed directly at Jack, he knew he held the losing hand. Penny felt the smothering grip across her mouth loosen, and the arm release its hold on her. She gasped in a breath of air, and quickly stepping away from him, moved in behind her friend.

The two men continued to glare at each other, neither one dropping their aim or relaxing their stance.

Jack reached behind him and catching hold of Penny's sleeve, pressured her toward the open barn door.

Gus's stress level rose. "No. She ain't goin' nowhere."

"She ain't a part a this," Jack growled, his gun still aimed unerringly at the ex-gang leader. "I just want her out of harm's way."

"And how do I know she won't go runnin' up ta that house and spread the alarm?"

"She won't." Jack's eyes remained fixed on the intruder. "Will ya', Penny?"

Penny gulped; her eyes wide with fear as she glanced from one man to the other.

"No," she finally said in a small voice. "No, I won't. I promise."

Jack didn't wait for Gus to give permission. He pushed Penny away from him, and she backed up and slipped out the open door.

She kept her word though, probably more than Jack would have wanted, and did not run to the house. Instead, she stepped aside of the threshold and made herself as small as possible. She had no intention of missing any of this, and leaning in against the solid wood structure, she listened in on the conversation.

"Drop your gun, Gus," Jack ordered. "Put it away."

"If I do that, how do I know you won't just shoot me where I stand?" Gus threw back at him.

"You come in here and you grab my gal, then you accuse me of being the threat?"

Penny gasped at this announcement, then covered her mouth, afraid that the men might have heard her. But aside from a barely noticeable beat of silence, the adversaries were too intent upon their own agenda to notice the young lady's quickened heartbeat.

"You betrayed us," Gus hissed at him in a voice pitched high with stress. "You set us up."

"I didn't!" Jack practically yelled at him. "Now I ain't talkin' no more about this until you drop your gun. I ain't askin' ya, Gus—I'm tellin' ya. Drop it. Now."

Gus hesitated for a beat, then he tipped the muzzle of his gun upward, and releasing the hammer, he slipped it back into his holster.

"All right, Kid, we'll play it your way. But you better have a real good reason why you was on that train!"

Jack breathed out his tension. The last thing he wanted to do was shoot Gus; the last thing he needed was another death on his conscience. He relaxed, just a bit, then releasing the hammer on his own gun, he also returned it to its holster.

"I'm tellin' ya, Gus, I was on that train goin' ta see Taggard and then Nash. You know that was the first train of the season that was sure to get through."

"Why should I believe that?" Gus questioned him, anger still edging his voice.

"Why would I betray you?" Jack pleaded with him. "Why would I do that?"

"You'd do it if it meant gettin' Nash outta prison sooner," Gus insisted. "Nash, now he wouldn't do that. But you? I never trusted you. The only person in our gang you were loyal to was Nash. How many times did you threaten me if I so much as questioned anything he said? How many times did you pull a gun on any of us if we didn't fall in line? No, I never trusted you, Kid, and I wouldn't put it past you at all to turn on every one of us if it meant gettin' Nash outta prison sooner."

Jack stood silently, allowing the harsh accusations to sink in. He'd never thought of things that way; it never occurred to him that the other members of the gang only saw him as a threat, as Leon's hired gunman. Then he recalled that Gus tended to project his own view onto the whole gang, when, in fact, it was only Gus himself, who felt the threat. And yet, the fact that Gus now stood before him, accusing him of the ultimate betrayal, still cut him to the quick.

"I wouldn't do that, Gus," Jack quietly insisted. "I'd never do that. Jeez, that was one of the worst days of my life, Morrison forcin' me ta go out and identify . . ." Jack's voice caught as he remembered those terrible events.

The Kid's obvious hurt and distress over the accusation, and the memories it brought back, did more than anything else to convince Gus that maybe the ex-leader was telling the truth. The outlaw relaxed his stance a little bit more, then sighed, shaking his head at the deplorable turn of events.

"Okay, all right, maybe you didn't have nothin' ta do with it. But ya gotta see how it looked that way."

Jack nodded. "Yeah, I suppose. But I give ya my word, Gus, I was just as surprised as you fellas."

"So, what's goin' on, Kid? I know Malachi is doin' time, but did Lobo make it?"

"Yeah, he pulled through," Jack informed him. "He got eight years, though."

"Ahh jeez," Gus moaned.

"Nash is watchin' out for 'em," Jack said. "He'll look after 'em."

"Yeah, well that's fine for Malachi," Gus complained, "but Lobo don't like nobody lookin' after him—you know that."

"Yeah, I know," Jack agreed, then sighed and changed the subject. "You got money, Gus? You got food?"

"Yeah," Gus told him. "I thought I'd head over Kettle Creek way and join up with them boys for a while."

"Aww, Gus, no," Jack groaned. "Ya gotta stay outta Wyoming. Even here, or Montana ain't gonna be safe for ya anymore. Ya gotta disappear."

"No," Gus insisted. "I wanna stay around for when Malachi gets out. I gotta wait for him."

"Gus, ya ain't thinkin' straight," Jack threw back at him. "Morrison's gonna be comin' after ya. I'm surprised he hasn't already tracked ya down. You've been up against him before. Ya know what he's like. He won't quit until he's got ya. And he'll kill ya, Gus. He won't hesitate, and you know it."

"But why? What the hell's goin' on? The reward on me ain't that much. Why would he bother?"

"Cause the reward is just the beginnin'," Jack explained. "Governor Moonlight assigned Morrison ta get rid of the outlaw gangs in Wyoming, and he's payin' 'im good money ta do it. Elk Mountain was just the beginnin'. He ain't gonna quit with that. He'll take down the Kettle Creek Gang and the Turner Gang and all the rest of 'em, too. He's tenacious, Gus; that trap he set up ta get me and Nash was over a year in the makin', and then another six months of plannin' ta take down Elk Mountain. You, bein' the leader of Elk Mountain, he ain't gonna let you slip through the net. He'll be comin' after ya, Gus, and sooner or later, he's gonna get ya."

"Jeez, Kid," Gus's tone was on the rise again. "What am I gonna do? The West and outlawin' is all I know. I got nowhere's else."

"You could turn yourself in," Jack suggested, though he know that wasn't going to go over well.

"What?" Gus puffed. "To Morrison?"

"No, not to Morrison!" Jack sighed and thought about it for a moment. "I could go with ya to the sheriff here in Arvada. Sheriff Jacobs is a pretty good sort. Then I'll telegraph Taggard to come and take ya back. That way, Morrison won't be able ta get near ya."

"But I'd still end up goin' ta prison," Gus pointed out. "I ain't doin' that. If Lobo got eight years, then I'd end up gettin' ten ta twelve, and I ain't doin' it."

"That ain't necessarily true," Jack insisted. "You know Lobo did things before comin' ta Elk Mountain that me and Nash wouldn't a tolerated. The law finally caught up with 'im. That's why he got hit hard. They probably don't even expect 'im to survive. You'd likely get out sooner, and then you'd have a clean slate; you could start over."

"At what?" Gus hissed. "Like I said, outlawin's all I know. I ain't got no rich friends backin' me up. All I got is me."

"You don't know where it could lead," Jack tried to convince him to see reason. "Opportunities come along. Give it a chance. Give yourself a chance."

"No." Gus was adamant. "I ain't givin' myself up."

Jack sighed, and his shoulders slumped as he relented.

"Okay," he said, "but then ya gotta disappear. Ya can't wait on Malachi. Head to Mexico or up ta Canada, but ya can't stay here. You'll die if ya do."

"Fine," Gus conceded. "I'll disappear. I guess I still got some old friends who owe me. Maybe it's time I cashed in on those debts."

Jack nodded. "I've got some money up at the house, and I'll gather together some food for ya; you're gonna need all you can pack. I'll be right back. Just wait here and stay outta sight."

Penny gathered her skirts and trotted away from the door, then stood as causally as possible in the hopes of giving the illusion of having been there all along.

But Jack wasn't fooled. He gave her a stern look as he held out his hand to her.

"You should have at least gone to the front porch," he told her.

"If there had been a shoot-out, any one a them bullets coulda come through and hit ya."

She smiled and hugged his arm. "That wasn't going to happen. He was afraid of you. I saw it right off. He wasn't going to start shooting."

"Sometimes, scared people do stupid things."

"You would never have let it happen," she insisted.

Jack gave it up. He was never going to convince her that he was just as infallible as the next guy.

"Those are real good watch dogs we have there, Penny," Jack complained. "We get an outlaw hidin' in the barn, and not a peep out of 'em."

"I know," Penny sighed. "It's not Rufus's fault. He's getting old and deaf, and the other two don't start barking unless he does."

"Maybe it's about time we thought about gettin' another dog," Jack suggested as they headed up the steps and into the house.

"Oh no!" Penny was mortified. "That would break Rufus's heart. We can't get another dog to replace him until after he's gone. How often are we going to have outlaws showing up at our place, anyways?"

Jack snorted. "I can think of a couple of occasions already."

Fifteen minutes later, Jack returned to the barn with the supplies, but Gus was gone, disappearing into the wind and leaving no trace behind him.

***

Ten days later, Jack found himself again on the train heading to Laramie. He had taken to reading the paper or finding something else to do to occupy his mind on these trips, since staring out the window at the passing landscape only brought a cascade of sad memories. As it happened, on this trip, he had a lot of distractions to keep his mind off things, and then found himself wishing for some peace and quiet.

"Yes, at first I was scared," Penny told their friend. "But once I realized that Mathew knew the man and had the situation under control, then it wasn't so bad."

"You had the situation under control?" Josephine sent a skeptical look to Jack. "You and one of your ex-outlaw buddies were pointing guns at each other and threatening to shoot the barn apart, and you had things under control?"

"Damn it, Josey—you wanna speak up a bit, I don't think the people in the next car heard ya."

"Oh, come off it." She waved a dismissive hand at him. "Everybody knows who you are—get over yourself."

"There's such a thing as being discreet." Jack felt his temper rise. "And when we're in with Leon, you let me tell him about what happened. One wrong word and that guard could be all over it."

"Fine," Josey commented, now in an indignant snit. "I know when to keep my mouth shut."

Jack snorted.

"Will you two stop fighting?" Penny demanded. "And to think I was once jealous of you, certain that you were trying to move in and take my man."

Two sets of eyebrows shot up.

Penny smiled coyly. "I heard you tell that man in the barn that I was your 'gal'."

"Oh, well. I just meant—"

"He called you his 'gal'?" Josey exclaimed.

Jack felt ganged up on. "NO! I mean—I did, but . . ."

Penny smiled, then took pity on her friend, and she placed a reassuring hand on his knee.

"I'm just teasing you, Mathew," she assured him. "It was a stressful moment, and I'm certainly not going to hold you to it."

"Oh. Okay." But Jack wasn't sure if he was happy with this outcome or not.

"Thank goodness for that," Josey declared with emphasis.

Penny huffed. "What do you mean?"

"Oh no, sweetie." Josey patted Penny's knee. "I just meant that one wedding a year is more than enough."

"Oh, okay." Then Penny smiled with the knowledge that only a sibling could have. "Caroline starting to wear on your nerves?"

"Oh, you don't know the half of it," Josey complained. "Morning 'till night. All day long, all she talks about is this silly wedding. I'll be so glad when it's all over and done with. Then she and Steven can go play house on their own."

"I think the whole idea of gettin' married is that they'd no longer be playin' at it," Jack remarked, caustically. "I think by then, they're pretty serious."

"Oh, you know what I mean," Josey shot back at him. "I do like Caroline, but I am so ready to have my house to myself again."

Both Jack and Penelope smiled at Josephine's predicament. Young ladies in love can be so irritating sometimes.

***

Laramie, Wyoming

Leon was really looking forward to Jack's visit this time. He had received a letter from Jean letting him know about the Jefferies losing their baby, and that Jack would be delayed getting away from the ranch until Sam was able to return to work. Leon understood this, but he still held a grudge against Sam. Though he tried to be sympathetic for their loss, he was having a difficult time feeling sorry for him.

When the door opened to the visiting room, Leon's heart skipped a beat, and a genuine smile of pleasure took over his features. It had been so long since he'd seen either of them and his eyes sparkled with the surprise.

Officer Murrey was taken by surprise, too, and he tapped on the door leading into the prison proper.

"We're going to need two more chairs," he informed Officer Davis. "It seems we have a reunion going on in here."

Davis glanced at the visitors and snorted. "Right. Give me a minute."

Once the extra chairs were provided, Jack helped to get the ladies seated and sent Leon an exasperated look which caused the inmate to smile to himself. Obviously, Jack found it tiring to have the two of them underfoot. Instead of Josey being along to chaperone Penny, Jack was the one having to keep a constant eye on both of them.

"How are you doing, Jack?"

Jack rolled his eyes. "I'm fine, I guess. It's good ta see ya, Leon."

"Yeah."

Penny smiled at him. "I wanted to come out to visit you a lot sooner than this. But Mathew wouldn't let me. He kept saying there was too much going on. I suppose he thought I would just be in the way." She sent an accusing glance over at the person in question.

"He was right," Leon stood up for his nephew. "Things did get a little crazy there for a while, and you were better off away from it."

He smiled to lessen the reprimand. "But it's good to see you again," he grinned at the other lady present. "It's even good to see you, Josey"

"Oh well, that's a fine howdy-doo," she complained. "I come all this way just to receive a greeting like that? Why do I even bother?"

Leon sent her an impish smile. "You love me, and you know it."

Josey softened her stance; she couldn't resist this man when he turned on his charm. "Well of course I love you, you ninny," she admitted. "You two are my dearest friends. Just don't be taking me for granted, or I may not show up for your wedding day."

"My wedding day?" Leon was incredulous. "Since when am I getting married?"

"You know what I mean," Josey insisted. "Just don't assume I'm always going to be around to help you out, that's all I'm saying."

Leon and Jack exchanged humorous glances. To their collective memories, it was Josey who was always getting them into trouble, not helping them to get out of it.

"I swear," Penny interrupted, "the way you three are always at each other's throats, I'm surprised you're speaking to one another at all."

Jack laughed. "Aw, it's just in fun, Penny," he assured her. "When you've known someone since you were knee high to a hitchin' rail, you don't take insult too quickly."

"Well, I suppose," Penny rolled her eyes, still thinking they were all crazy. Then she smiled at Leon. "Did Mama mention to you the good news in her letter?"

"You mean the good news that the world has been saved from Sam's offspring?"

"LEON!" Jack couldn't believe his uncle had just said that.

"Sorry."

Jack scowled at him, not believing for one second that he was sorry.

"No!" Penny scolded him. "About Karma's foal."

"Oh." Leon smiled. "Yes, she did mention it, but she left the details for you to fill in."

Penny beamed. "She had a beautiful filly, Peter. A palomino. Her baby fluff is still kind of tawny, but once she sheds that, she'll sparkle like gold. She has a white star on her forehead, but it's hard to tell if she has any white socks yet, but again, once her baby fluff is gone, we'll know for sure. I was right there for the birth. I know you'll be pleased with her, Peter, she is such a nice little girl."

"I'm sure I will be pleased with her," Leon commented. "But what about your pa? Is he pleased with her? I thought he was hoping for a colt."

"Yes, he was a little disappointed about that," Penny admitted. "But overall, he's very happy with her, and will breed for the colt next year."

"How does he know he won't get another filly?"

"I don't know," Penny admitted and shrugged. "But he seems quite confident that we won't."

Leon looked a question to Jack, but Jack simply shrugged his shoulders. He had to agree with Penny on that; Cameron seemed pretty sure.

"Does she have a name?" Leon asked

"Daisy."

Leon laughed. "Yeah, that suits!" Then his expression turned melancholy. "How's the mother? How is Karma?"

"She's doing really well, Peter," Penny assured him. "She's so happy being a mother, she's bursting with pride. And Midnight is enjoying the babies too."

"Really?" Leon asked, glancing at his nephew.

Jack smiled. "Yeah. That old gelding really seems ta like bein' out with them young'uns. Go figure."

"Hmm. Imagine that."

"How are Lobo and Malachi doin'?" Jack asked, changing the subject. "Are they settlin' in okay?"

Leon's light-hearted demeanor dropped, and Jack almost regretted asking him.

"Well, you know Malachi, he just carries on being Malachi," Leon answered with a small smile. "He's doing okay, and I'm keeping an eye on him. I expect he'll be out of here in no time and looking for a job."

"Ha! Yeah."

"But Lobo," Leon shook his head. "He's not well, Jack. He was badly broken up by that horse, and even Doc Palin is worried he won't last the winter. His lung was damaged, and even now, he coughs all the time. If he were to get pneumonia . . ."

"Oh."

"Plus, he's so stubborn," Leon continued. "He fights against the rules, fights against the other inmates, fights against the guards. He's already been in the dark cell twice, and I don't know how many bruises he's sporting from the billy clubs. I don't know what the hell he's thinking."

"Maybe the same thing you were, Leon," Jack reminded him. "Seems ta me, you were doin' the same things."

"I wasn't that bad."

"Yeah, Leon, ya were."

"Oh."

Jack gave a frustrated sigh. "Well, if ya get the chance, say 'hi' to 'em for me. I'll come and see 'em as soon as they're allowed visitors."

Nash smiled. "I'll let them know. I don't think either of them has anyone else. The Elk Mountain Gang was all the family they had."

The uncle and the nephew locked eyes for a moment, each of them acknowledging their own good fortune in having one another, and a family as such now, to go home to.

"Speaking of which," Jack began and gave Leon a look that only Leon would understand. "I had another family member stop by the other day."

"Ahh," Leon nodded. Gus had shown up.

"He was still angry about a misunderstandin' between us concerning loyalties, but we talked about it, and he's fine now."

"Oh good. So, what's he up to these days?"

"Movin' around a lot," Jack told him. "I suggested he go visit a mutual friend of ours, you know, take care of some old business. But he weren't ready to do that."

"Oh. Too bad. There's not many options open for him anymore. Times are getting tough."

"Yeah, I pointed that out to 'im," Jack continued, "but you know how stubborn he can get."

Leon grinned. "Yup. You expect to see him again?"

"Probably not."

Leon nodded sadly. "No. Probably not."

He took a deep breath and glanced back at Murrey.

Murrey met his gaze.

Leon smiled at him, then returned his attention to Jack. "Things have taken a turn for the worse around here, too," he said, and without turning this time, he shifted his eyes toward the guard.

Jack waited. Obviously, it was something Leon wasn't willing to speak about, given the current situation.

"I know it's a long trip, but could you ask Steven to come by again?" Leon continued. "I need to speak with him."

Now Jack was worried. "Yeah, Leon, I can do that. Do ya want me to come back with him?"

"Yeah, if you can. That'd be good."

"Why are you two being so vague?" Josey piped in. "I can't even figure out what you're talking about."

Leon, Jack and Penny all sent her incredulous looks.

Even Penny could understand their reasons for covertness and wondered why in the world Josey was being so obtuse. Then Penny quickly picked up the conversation to get things flowing again and cover up the blunder.

"Is Mariam here today?"

"No, I don't believe she is, Penny," Leon answered her. "The infirmary has been quiet, lately, so she hasn't been coming over as often."

"That's too bad," Penny was disappointed. "I was hoping to see her."

"You could always drop by the orphanage," Leon suggested, then smiled. "I believe you know where it is."

Penny grinned. "Yes, all right," she said, accepting the slight teasing. "I might just do that." She glanced at Jack. "Would we have time?"

"Yeah, I suppose," Jack agreed. "You'll have to show me where it is though; I've never been there."

"No problem."

Murrey shifted his weight and Jack sighed.

"I guess it's time for us to be headin' out,' he announced.

"Already?" Josey complained. "We just got here!"

"Hour's up," Jack explained.

"Well, how would you know that, Jack?" she demanded. "You're not carrying a watch."

"I just know, Josey, all right?" Jack was starting to get frustrated all over again. "Just take my word for it."

"Fine," she retorted. "Geesh, no need to get testy."

The three visitors got to their feet, and then, for the first time, Penny realized that Peter was wearing shackles. She had wondered why he wasn't bringing his hands up onto the table, but it had not occurred to her that he didn't do it because he couldn't.

"Oh," she commented, not able to hide the tinge of shock in her voice.

Leon sent her a regretful smile. "The lot of a convict," he said, trying to make light of it.

"Yes, I suppose," Penny agreed. "Silly of me. I just didn't realize. I wanted to give you a hug goodbye." She glanced hopefully at Murrey. "May I give him a hug goodbye?"

Murrey actually sounded repentant. "No, Miss, I'm sorry," he informed her. "You need to stay on the other side of the table."

"Oh," she mumbled, her disappointment obvious. She looked into her friend's dark brown eyes, and her heart went out to him. "I miss you so much, Peter. May I come back to see you again?"

Leon smiled, wondering how he could have been so proud as to deny his friends the right to come and visit with him. There were so many other inmates here who had no one who cared enough to make the trip, and here, Leon had been pushing his friends away because of his own shame.

"I'd like that, Penny," he assured her. "I want to hear first-hand all about Daisy. And I understand that we actually do have a wedding coming up this summer, so I want to hear all about that, as well."

Penny smiled broadly when Leon mentioned Daisy, but then rolled her eyes at mention of her sister's coming nuptials. She, just like Josephine, would be happy when the whole thing was over and done with.

Josey rolled her eyes. "Oh brother," She voiced Penny's opinion completely. "Well, better you than me."

Then Murrey stepped forward, and taking Leon by the arm, encouraged him to his feet.

"I'll see ya, Leon," Jack said. "Steven and I will get back as soon as we can."

"Yeah, okay," Leon answered as he was being pressured toward the door. "Ladies. Thanks for coming. It was really good to see you."

"Bye Leon."

"Goodbye, Peter."

Then Leon was shuffled back into the prison proper, and the door leading to the outside world was shut upon him.

***

As the three friends drove back to Laramie in the rented buggy, Josey sat back and chatted, endlessly, about how much better Leon was looking these days, and isn't it a good thing that he was staying out of trouble now. She didn't notice that the couple up front were not responding to anything she said, and in fact, neither of them were really listening to her at all.

Both Jack and Penny were thinking back on their visit with Leon, and though neither of them said anything to the other, they both thought the same thing. What had Leon meant "Things were taking a turn for the worse"? That had not sounded good. Penny thought she would ask Mariam to keep an extra special eye on her friend over the next little while. Jack thought he would stop by Kenny's place before leaving town and ask the guard to keep an extra eye on his uncle over the next little while.

Something had changed, and neither of them liked the sound of it at all.

Josephine chatted on.

CHAPTER EIGHT
PLAN "B"

Laramie, Wyoming
Spring 1887

"What are your concerns, Mr. Nash?"

"I'm not really sure," Leon admitted, feeling ashamed of himself now, having dragged his friend and his lawyer back here on nothing more than just a feeling. "It's been a couple of weeks and nothing has happened, so maybe I was just overreacting."

"A couple of weeks since what?" Steven inquired.

Leon's face tightened as he tried to assemble his thoughts and explain the dark forebodings that had taken hold of him.

"Warden Mitchell has been backing off me all through this winter, mainly because of the pressure he had received from my lawyer, and my friends, letting him know that he was being watched. Thanks to you people, this winter has been a lot easier for me without the antagonism from the warden and the senior guard. A lot easier.

"Then you went to see Governor Moonlight. Well, we all know how that turned out." The other two gentlemen nodded agreement. "But what you don't know, is that the governor then sent a letter to our wonderful warden, informing him of the meeting, and that he practically threw you out of his office.

"The governor further emphasized that not only had he refused to grant me a pardon, but that he was supportive of Warden Mitchell's policies of prison management, and basically, gave Mr. Mitchell the go ahead to conduct matters here in any way he deemed appropriate."

This piece of information was met with silence.

Leon's anxiety was obvious, though he tried to cover it. He really had nothing to go on except a gut feeling. But he had learned to trust his gut feelings.

"So," Leon continued. "Mitchell told me that he's no longer going to be concerned about outside pressures; that if the governor of the territory is not going to give in to the 'rants and raves' of my supporters, then why should he?"

This statement was met with groans from the other men in the room.

Leon nodded, feeling more confident now that his concerns were being validated.

"I have to admit, I'm worried that Warden Mitchell will find a way to exact some kind of revenge upon me for the inconveniences we have subjected him to. God knows what he'll do if you take this case further."

"Are you saying you don't want us to take this to a formal hearing?" Steven asked him.

Leon sat back with a sigh. He looked at his partner, and Jack returned his gaze, sending Leon silent support for whichever course he wanted to take.

"I don't know," Leon admitted. "We already know that if we put pressure on the powers that be, it could have serious repercussions for me, being at their mercy as I am. On the other hand, if you back off and don't push, then I'll be in here for the rest of my life."

"Perhaps, Mr. Nash," Steven agreed. "However, if we are able to take this case to the Supreme Court and appeal your sentence, Warden Mitchell would have no control over that. Unfortunately, when it comes to a hearing with the Prison Board concerning the conditions here, you are the one taking the biggest risk. As you say, if Governor Moonlight has given Warden Mitchell free rein in his policies for running the prison, then us continuing to push for a formal hearing could result in a difficult time for you. Once the hearing is concluded, and if we are successful in forcing this issue, then it would definitely be to your benefit. But in the meantime, Warden Mitchell could do with you as he pleases, and we would have no recourse available to stop him."

Leon nodded. "That's pretty much what Warden Mitchell took a great deal of pleasure to inform me of."

"Aww jeez." Jack sat back, running a hand through his curls; it felt as though they were right back at the beginning again. That all their work and efforts had been for naught.

"What would you like us to do, Mr. Nash?" Steven asked.

Again, Leon sat back and thought about it. If his own hands had been free to run across his scalp, he would have done so. He sighed heavily.

"Do you think there is a chance that the Supreme Court will overturn my sentencing?"

"I don't know, Mr. Nash. Our petition hasn't been accepted yet."

"I really don't want to get hurt anymore," Leon admitted. "On the other hand, I sure don't want to spend the rest of my life in here, either."

Again, a blanket of silence settled over the room. The lawyer and the friend sat and waited for the convict to decide what risks he was willing to take, and what life he was willing to accept.

Leon weighed his options. "Well, the sensible thing to do would be to call it off. Lay low until a new governor came into power and then try again." He smiled and sent Jack a mischievous glint. "On the other hand, in the words of my overly protective partner, 'nobody has ever accused us of being too sensible.'"

Jack smiled and nodded. It didn't surprise him. Leon was never one to sit back and wait.

"All or nothing, gentlemen." Leon announced. "Consequences be damned. I have no intention of spending the rest of my life in this hell hole."

***

"Where are you, Jack? You look like you're miles away."

Jack turned his glazed eyes away from the landscape rolling past the window.

"Yeah. Sorry. I guess I ain't very good company right now. I've come ta hate this ride home from the prison. I'm always left with the feelin' that I should be doin' more, ya know?"

"Yes," Steven agreed, as he too looked at the scenery on the other side of the window. "Unfortunately, when dealing through the legal system, the wheels tend to move slowly." He turned a sharp gaze back to his companion. "But it's the only way to do it, Jack. You do realize that, don't you?"

"Well, yeah." Jack shrugged. He wasn't about to admit that he had been thinking about the good ole days when breaking a gang member out of jail was no big deal. "I'm worried about him, that's all. Things are so unpredictable in there, even with Kenny and Dr. Mariam watching over him. I can't help but think that maybe this visit will be the last time I'll see him alive. But I think that every visit, and I still keep goin' back. But now, with the warden gettin' pushy again, well, who knows what could happen."

"I know. But we're doing all we can. As soon as I get back to my office, I'll get to work on setting up a hearing. Aside from setting a date, I'll need to arrange for evidence to be presented to me, and confirm who is still willing to come forward to present their own testimonies. All of this will take time."

"I know, Steven." Jack smirked as another thought came to him. "Not ta mention ya got your weddin' comin' up."

Steven frowned. "Oh yeah."

Jack's face lit up with amusement. "Don't tell me you forgot you was gettin' married."

"No, no." Steven waved the accusation away with his own repentant smile. "No. There's just so much else going on right now. And since the ladies are doing all of the arranging for the big day, I haven't been thinking about it. Ha. But don't worry, I'll be there when I need to be. I am looking forward to it, when I have a moment to think about it at all."

"That's good. Ya wouldn't want Cameron comin' after ya with the shotgun."

Steven barked a laugh. "That's for sure." Then his smile softened. "No, I'd be a fool to walk away from Caroline. She's amazing."

"Yeah." Jack's thoughts turned inward again as he gazed out the window. "They both are."

***

Arvada, Colorado

Jack disembarked from the train in Arvada and made his way toward the livery to pick up Midnight and complete the last stage of his journey home. He had done this so many times over the last year and a half, he no longer thought about where he was going. His body was on automatic and his brain was everywhere but where it should have been.

Not surprisingly, he was brought up short when he walked right into a frilly brick wall.

"Oh! Miss Isabelle," Jack acknowledged her. "I do apologize."

"That's quite all right, Jack," Isabelle assured him with a sweet smile. "It's very nice to be bumped into by you—again."

"Ahh, yes ma'am," Jack responded with an embarrassed smile. "Still, it was rude, and I do apologize. I should be watchin' where I'm goin.'"

Isabelle slipped her arm through his and began to walk along with him.

"Your mind on other things, today?"

"Well, yeah," he admitted, "as a matter of fact, it is."

"Anything you would like to talk about?" She oozed concern. "I might be able to help."

"I don't really see how you could, Isabelle, but thanks for offerin'."

"How do you know?" she persisted. "Sometimes just talking about something can make it easier to deal with."

"Yes ma'am, that's true," Jack agreed, "but I'm worried about my partner is all, and I don't really see how you can help with that."

"Oh, HIM again," Isabelle pouted. "Don't you think it's time you let that go and got on with your life?"

Jack felt the hairs on the back of his neck bristle, but he told himself to stay calm and be polite. Isabelle wasn't the kind of person who could understand commitment, unless it was to her.

"No, Isabelle, it ain't," Jack told her. "And I don't intend ta let it go until we have him outta that place and back home where he belongs."

Isabelle stopped walking, and stepping in front of Jack, she placed her hand on his chest and looked up into his eyes.

"Jack, I'm sorry," she told him, "But you need to get on with your life. It's been over a year and nothing has come of all your efforts. You need to take advantage of what's being offered to you: get married and have a family of your own. I mean, let's face it; the Marshams aren't your real family, they're just a replacement. You need to find a woman who's mature and ready to settle down to a proper life." She sighed then and gave him a sad look. "Dear Penelope is so sweet, but pathetic, really, a young girl like her, trying hard to act like a woman. But it's obvious she doesn't have a clue how to treat a man."

Now Jack really bristled. His jaw clenched, but again, he reminded himself not to lose his temper. But he did take hold of Isabelle's hand that was on his chest, and pushed it away from him, perhaps clasping it a little tighter than what was comfortable for her.

"Let me tell you somethin', Isabelle, just so's we're clear. Penny is not a little girl; she is a young woman in her own right. She cares about me, and she cares about Napoleon, and she's in this for the long haul. The Marshams are the closest thing I've had to family for years, and they are not just a replacement. I am not givin' up on Leon, and any woman who claims ta care about me, but ain't willin' ta support me in this, ain't worth my time."

Isabelle puffed up to her full height and snatched her hand away from Jack's grasp.

"Fine," she snapped at him, feeling insulted. "Just you wait and see. No woman worth her salt is going to hang around and wait for you while you chase after a pipe dream. Your partner is never going to get out of prison, but by the time you realize that, any woman who might have wanted you will have given up and moved on to someone more worthy. You either grab hold of the opportunities while you can, or you're going to end up a sad and lonely old man."

"I guess that's just the chance I'm gonna have ta take," Jack answered, quiet but determined, "cause I'm not givin' up on my partner. Good day, Miss Isabelle."

Jack politely tipped his hat, then deftly stepped around the infuriated woman and continued his way to the livery stable.

Isabelle did not follow him.

***

Riding out to the Rocking M, Jack was still grinding his teeth and muttering obscenities concerning the audacity of some of the local female inhabitants of Arvada. The only good thing about the whole encounter is that now, hopefully, Isabelle had gotten the message, loud and clear, that Jack was not interested in her. Imagine saying that about Penny.

Just who did she think she was, insulting Penny that way? 'Silly little girl, pathetically pretending to be a woman.' How dare she say such things.

Penelope is a woman, and a beautiful woman at that. I know she cares about me and about Leon. She's given her support and loyalty unconditionally. Ya don't find a woman like that very often; one who's willin' ta put her own ambitions and desires on the back burner, ta stand up for a cause and stick to it.

Jack smiled as he thought about how determined Penny was to get to the bottom of things. It might not have been the smartest thing to do, but her convincing Mariam to get her into the prison, masquerading as a novice, really was a courageous thing to do. Maybe not smart, but certainly courageous.

Jack continued to smile, and his mood softened as he thought about his young friend and how much she had grown in the last two years. His smile deepened as he recalled the hug they had shared that day in the barn while he was still recovering from his injuries. She was no longer a little girl then, and now, she was all woman.

Jack came back to reality when Midnight stumbled, then picked himself up and stalwartly carried on.

It was then when Jack realized the old gelding had been trying to tell him something for the last mile, but Jack had been so deep into his own thoughts, he hadn't heard him.

Midnight was limping. It hadn't been bad at first, which is probably why Jack hadn't picked up on it through his own musings. But now, the limp was quite pronounced.

Jack pulled the horse to a stop and dismounted. He grabbed hold of the gelding's foreleg, down by the fetlock, and lifted the foot. Everything looked good in there; no stones pressed into the frog, or sticks rammed under the shoe. He put the foot down and ran his hands along the lower leg, then groaned. Sure enough, there was heat and swelling in that tendon—again.

Dammit.

Jack straightened with a sigh and gave Midnight a pat, then a rub on the neck.

"Yeah, that's all right, ole fella," he soothed the animal. "C'mon, let's get ya home."

Jack slowly walked on, leading the limping horse behind him until they finally headed down the lane toward the barnyard.

Karma spotted her friend coming, and raising her head, she sent out a welcoming whinny.

Midnight lifted his head, and pricking his ears, returned a nicker of his own. Then he dropped his head again and continued to limp after his human.

Jack got him into the horse barn and began to tend to the animal's needs. He got so deep into his own worries over his buddy that he didn't hear Cameron come in until the man was almost up to him. Midnight hadn't even responded to his presence.

"I see he's limping again," Cameron commented.

Jack jumped and felt the instant reflex to go for his gun, but he stopped himself before the muscles could respond. He straightened up with an embarrassed smile.

Cameron smiled back, knowing he had startled the younger man and recognizing the fact that he hadn't overreacted. The old ways and habits were slowly starting to fade away.

"Sorry," Cameron apologized. "I noticed you coming into the yard. How is he?"

Jack sighed, shaking his head. "I dunno. I don't understand why it ain't healin'."

"Hmm," Cameron commented. "Well, bring him outside. Let's look at him."

The two men and the horse went back outside, and Jack walked the animal up and down a few times while Cameron watched the gait and the way the horse favored the leg.

"Okay, Jack, hold him there a minute." Cameron came and ran his hands down the tender foreleg, gently applying pressure in certain spots and watching for the horse's reaction. He finally stood up and gave the gelding a pat on the neck.

"I don't know Jack, it really doesn't look good at this point."

"Yeah. It's that same leg, too. I don't know what's goin' on with 'im."

"It makes me wonder if Sam actually had anything to do with Midnight coming up lame, when you and Leon were arrested," Cameron mused. "Or if it was a simple coincidence, and the beginnings of something more chronic."

"Yeah. Or whatever Sam did ta make 'im lame never fully healed."

Cameron sighed. "I suppose we'll never know."

"I don't suppose so. Kinda water under the bridge now, anyway."

Cameron nodded. "How old is he? Do you have any idea?"

"Nothin' definite," Jack admitted. "He wasn't a young'un when I first got 'im, I know that much."

"How long ago was that?"

"Oh well," Jack rubbed his chin, thinking back to that day. "Gee, must a been at least ten years now. He came to me just by chance when me and Leon were still with Elk Mountain. He's the one I was ridin' when we first met you folks. Every time we had ta get rid of the horses, we always seemed ta wind up findin' each other again. Leon went through five horses to my one. I guess we was just meant ta be."

"Ha, yeah. Sometimes that happens," Cameron commented. "No wonder you're so fond of him. Like Leon with Karma."

"Yeah, I suppose."

"So," Cameron continued, "what do you figure his age was when you bought him? About ten?"

"Yeah, at least." Jack didn't think it necessary to mention that he hadn't actually bought the horse.

"Okay," Cameron reflected. "Into his twenties, probably. And a lot of rough riding and missed meals in there too, no doubt. Not to mention cold nights spent in the open. That frostbite he had, when we first met, might be what's causing this problem now."

"Yeah," Jack admitted. "I was afraid I was gonna lose 'im 'cause a that. He's been a good solid horse, ever since, though. I always tried to look after 'im."

"I don't doubt it," Cameron appeased his friend. "But still, that kind of life catches up with a fellow after a while."

"Yeah, tell me about it."

Cameron gave the black gelding a pat on the neck.

"In my honest opinion, I think it's time you thought about retiring him."

Jack's face fell. He couldn't imagine riding any other horse but ole Midnight. They had been together so long. Midnight was an old friend, whom Jack had come to rely on, and the solid gelding had gotten him out of more than one tight spot over the years. He didn't want to have to count on another horse to get him out of trouble when he really needed it.

"I'd give him a good home," Cameron continued, trying to give reassurance. "I could really use a wise, old gelding, like him."

"Yeah, but I need a ridin' horse, Cameron," Jack insisted, not willing to relinquish his buddy that quickly. "I can't really afford ta buy another horse, especially one of Midnight's qualities."

"Tell you what," Cameron offered. "I have about twelve two-year-olds that Sam will be breaking out this summer. Why don't you take a ride up to the holding corral in the north pasture and have a look at them? You pick out any one you want. Sam can break him for you, and we'll make an even trade."

"That don't seem fair ta me," Jack felt obliged to point out. "You givin' me a young, broke three-year-old, in exchange for a worn-out old gelding. You got some real fine horses up there; it just wouldn't seem right."

"You're right," Cameron agreed. "I'd be coming out ahead on the deal, that's for sure."

Jack frowned. "What do ya mean, ahead? You just said it was time ta retire 'im. How does that put you ahead?"

Cameron chuckled and nodded toward the two mares with their progeny. "I've been watching him out there with those foals. He's good with them, and they've both taken to him like he was made of molasses. Having a wise, old gelding like that, who has the patience to be with the babies, well, that's invaluable to me."

"It is?"

"Sure. There's only so much these babies can learn from their mothers, but if you can put a gelding like this in with the mix, well, he can teach them a whole lot more about horse etiquette than any wrangler I've ever met."

"And you think Midnight would be good for that?"

"Very much," Cameron emphasized, then smiled. "Good ole Uncle Midnight. He's got the wisdom and the patience to be able to teach those foals everything they need to know to be good horses. Especially when it comes to weaning time. Those babies take it hard when mom's not around anymore, but if they know Uncle Midnight, and he's still with them, well, things aren't so bad after all. Like I said, Jack, a gelding like him would be invaluable to me."

Jack gave his old horse a rub on the neck, still hesitant to give him up that easily.

"It's not like you would be saying 'goodbye' to him," Cameron pressed his case. "He'll be here for the rest of his days, and he'll be well looked after. You can see him anytime you like."

"Yeah," Jack mumbled, "but ridin' another horse, that just don't seem right."

"I know," Cameron concurred, "but this fella's not up to it

anymore. And I bet once you pick out a youngster that you like, you'll see the wisdom of it. Let Midnight retire and take life easy from now on. He's put in his years."

"Yeah, I suppose you're right," Jack had to admit. "And he does keep comin' up lame on that same leg, so . . ."

"Yes," Cameron agreed, sensing he'd won his case. "Let me put him back out in the field with the others. He's happy out there with them, you'll see. It's the right thing to do."

"I suppose."

Cameron took Midnight's lead shank and led the limping gelding over to the pasture gate. Instantly his head came up and his ears perked. He nickered to his friends in the field.

Karma raised her head from grazing and whinnied back. Then sweet little Daisy perked up her fine head and sent forth her own high-pitched baby whinny and, with tail flapping, came running over to greet her favorite uncle.

Cameron removed the halter, and Midnight limped out to meet Daisy halfway, then dropped his head down to graze. Karma slowly meandered over to join her friend, and before long, Spade and his mother made their way over as well. All were content then, and in good company. With tails swishing lazily in the afternoon sun, they carried on grazing until it was time to come in for supper.

Jack stood at the fence for a while and watched them, and though he knew it was the right thing to do for his horse, he still felt a definite heartache. Everything in his life seemed to be changing on him; old friends being taken away, while new friends were coming along to help ease the loneliness of their passing. But still, it was hard.

There had already been so many departures. First, Leon had been taken away from him. Then Hank was gone, then Charlie and Mukua. Elk Mountain was burned to the ground, and Lobo and Malachi were in prison along with Leon. And then there was Gus, alone and on the run. No telling what his fate was going to be.

Jack sighed and rested his chin on his forearms that were laid along the fence. Now ole Midnight was movin' on too.

Cameron gave his friend a pat on the shoulder.

"Come on, Jack," he said, "let's get ready for supper. Real nice beef steaks tonight."

***

Departures

Laramie, Wyoming

Leon was in the warehouse, keeping one eye on his two 'men', another eye on Boeman and Harris, and a third eye on Officers Carson and Thompson, all the while, trying to do his work without messing things up and drawing undue attention to himself. Life was complicated.

Boeman and Harris were respecting Leon's position so far. Boeman still had trouble swallowing, due to the bruised throat he had acquired during the fight and consequent prison riot, and the ex-outlaw leader knew they were just waiting for an opportunity to reestablish the pecking order. But they had learned their lesson and had no intention of coming at Leon straight on. They were willing to wait until they could get him alone, then gang up on him.

Leon was careful not to give them that opportunity.

Carson and Thompson were waiting for Leon to slip up on the rules, so they would have a reason to make up for lost time through the winter. The warden telling them to back off for a while had stuck in their craw. They could see that Leon was protective of the two new inmates, especially the smaller one, so maybe all they had to do was wait for an opportunity to use that protectiveness to their advantage.

Leon was careful not to give it to them.

Lobo knew Leon was watching out for him; he could feel his ex-boss's eyes upon him, even from a distance, and he resented it. Did Leon think that because he'd gotten injured that he was weak? That he couldn't take care of himself in here? He'd already had a couple of other inmates try to bring him down a peg or two, and they had ended up getting knocked down themselves. Even if Lobo ended up being punished by the guards for fighting, and had spent an hour doubled over and gasping for air because of his injured lung, well, that didn't mean he was weak and needed looking after. Leon was insulting him, and Lobo grew even more angry and bitter than he had been as a free man.

Malachi was oblivious to the role that Leon played in keeping him safe. He was aware of some of the inmates sending him dark glances, but when nothing ever came of them, he stopped being concerned about it. He went about his day-to-day duties with as much a carefree demeanor as an inmate, incarcerated at a territorial prison, could possibly have.

Whereas Leon respected Lobo's privacy, he stayed close to Malachi, sitting with him at mealtimes and always trying to get a workstation next to his. On the days when Leon was away, either in the laundry room or the infirmary, he had to hope that the message was clear enough to leave Malachi alone; that Leon's presence wasn't always going to be required. So far, this had been the case.

Spring drifted lazily into summer, and everybody was settling into their routines. Jack came for his regular visits and was as good as his word in taking time to visit with his other two friends, as soon as their curfew was up.

But where Malachi appreciated the visits and the chance to talk to someone he knew, Lobo soon made it clear that he wasn't interested in company, even going so far as to decline the invitation. So, Jack stopped asking after him, and Leon kept an even closer eye on him, in the hope of preventing him from sinking into a depression.

Penny and Josephine came for more visits as well, and Penny was always full of news about Daisy and, of course, the upcoming wedding.

During these visits, Jack and Leon usually didn't get many words in edgewise and would sit back and send the occasional smile to one another. Just watching Penny in her animated conversation was enough to lift Leon's spirits and help him to forget about his problems, at least for the hour that she was there.

Josey was Josey, so these visits were usually full of bantering and high-spirited fun between the ladies. Even the guard could not help but let the occasional chuckle escape at some of the verbal antics they got up to.

Work gangs were being assembled for projects outside the prison walls, and Leon wasn't the only one looking forward to a chance to get out amongst real human beings again. Aside from the usual broken fences and new barn roofs, it was apparently time to do repairs at the orphanage, so Leon ended up returning to that institution, even though it wasn't for as enjoyable an occasion as the previous time.

Still, he lucked out in that he, and a couple of the other trustees, got to paint the interior of the orphanage, so they did not have to work outside in the hot summer sun. The inmates had to wear the Oregon boot on their ankles but were still able to move around and do their jobs. The rifles were always present, of course, so even if anyone did contemplate dragging that 40 lb. block along with them in an escape attempt, they wouldn't have a chance of making it.

The children had been told to stay away from the convicts, but, yeah, good luck with that. Especially when they recognized their friend, Napoleon Nash. They were just as comfortable in his presence as they were with the Sisters, so the decree obviously couldn't include him. Some of the older boys even picked up paint brushes and felt it was an honor to assist their favorite outlaw in painting their walls.

Pearson and Davis were guarding the inside inmates, and though they were a little concerned at first with the children mingling with the convicts, everybody ended up working well together. They even seemed to be having a good time, so, yes it was bending the rules, but Carson wasn't around.

Lunch break found the various inmates outside on the porch, either sitting on the steps, or dangling their legs off the veranda and enjoying sandwiches and lemonade, and all the water they wanted. Not surprisingly, Leon found himself surrounded by various children of all ages, wanting to share their lunch break with him. Pearson stood close by, not interfering, but most definitely keeping an eye on things.

Sally, the little girl who had run up and hugged Leon during his classroom visit, now felt that she was privileged and moved in close to sit beside him. She smiled at him and gave him one of her cookies.

"Thank you, Sally," he commented, returning her smile.

She beamed with pleasure that he remembered her name.

"Are you going to come back to visit us again?" she asked, sweetly.

"I'm certainly going to try. We'll have to see what the Sisters say about that."

"I'm sure it will be fine with them."

Leon smiled at her confidence. "We'll see."

"Is the Kansas Kid going to come with you?" asked Todd.

His sister, Beth, sitting on the step below him, lit up with anticipation.

"I don't know," Leon admitted. "Some other things came up and I forgot to ask him. But I will."

This was met by smiles all around. Then Leon's attention was drawn away from his group of admirers to watch an exchange going on between Mariam and Kenny. They were speaking seriously about something, and Leon had the feeling it was about him. Sure enough, both people stopped talking and glanced in his direction. Leon frowned and sat there, looking at them looking at him.

Mariam smiled a farewell to the guard and made her way to the group sitting on the porch steps.

"Hello, Napoleon."

"Mariam."

"Officer Reece and I were just discussing the possibility of you coming for another social visit, once the repairs are completed on the orphanage."

"Oh." Leon smiled with relief. "Yes, ma'am, I'm willing, if the warden agrees."

"Good," Mariam answered. "From what Officer Reece says, I don't think that will be a problem." She smiled at the group gathered around them, and they all knew what was coming. "Now, children, let these men alone; they have work to do."

This proclamation was met with moans and groans of disappointment, but the youngsters all got to their feet and headed off to tend to their own chores.

The other inmates sitting around on the porch also moved off to return to their work.

Leon was about to join them when Mariam came forward and sat down on the steps beside him.

She placed her hand on one of his and gave it a gentle squeeze.

"I haven't seen you for a while, Napoleon. How are you?"

"I'm fine."

"I know you've had to deal with some sad news lately, along with everything else. Are you getting through that all right?"

"Yes." He moved his other hand to place on top of hers. "It was hard to hear about Elk Mountain at first. That was our home; the people there were our family. It was hard. Harder for Jack though, as he had to witness it."

"Yes," Mariam commiserated. "What must make it even more difficult is that the rest of the territory is rejoicing over an event that can only bring you pain. That's a very lonely place to be."

Leon smiled, then lifted her hand up and gave it a gentle kiss.

"Thank you," he said to her surprised expression. "Thank you for understanding something that most do not."

She nodded. "Officer Reece tells me that two of the men from your old hideout are now at the prison. Are they settling in all right?"

"One is. The other . . ." Leon shrugged. "I don't know."

"It's a long time until Christmas," she mused. "Is there anything either of them need right now?"

Leon laughed. "I think Malachi would kill for some chewing tobacco; he has a terrible habit there. I'm not sure if it's allowed, but . . ."

"I'll find out," she assured him. "If it is, I will be sure to get some to him."

"Thank you." Leon considered her question some more. "Ahh, it does start to get chilly here by mid-September, and Lobo is kind of sickly, so anything to keep him warm. Sweaters, socks, definitely a knitted hat, a blanket. Actually, both of them could use those things before the cold weather sets in. If it's too much, I can divvy up some of my winter things and pass them on. I can make do until Christmas."

"That's very generous of you," Mariam complimented him, "but we don't want you getting sick again either. I'll see what we can do; I'm sure we'll find something for them."

Leon nodded. "Thank you." The impish grin put in another appearance. "Some more cookies would be nice."

Mariam laughed out loud at the mischievous twinkle.

"I'll see what I can arrange."

"Yeah! Good."

The two people on the steps glanced up as Pearson approached them.

"C'mon, Nash," he said, "break has been over for half an hour. Time you got back to work."

"Ah, yes."

Leon stood up. He assisted Mariam to her feet, then gave her a quick kiss on the cheek in farewell.

"Goodbye for now, Napoleon," she returned. "I'll see you when you come for your visit."

"Goodbye."

He dragged his boot up the steps then went to carry on with his painting duties.

CHAPTER NINE
THE PECKING ORDER

It took three weeks to finish the jobs at the orphanage, and during that time, Leon still kept an eye on his two men. Being new to the prison, they had not been allowed to be part of the work gang but had stayed behind to carry on with regular duties. Still, they had managed to get outdoors in the yard whenever possible and were managing to stay out of trouble, even with Leon away most days.

Malachi was a happy man when he returned to his cell one evening, to find a packet of chewing tobacco sitting on his pillow, along with some warm clothing for the upcoming winter months. He began to wonder what all the fuss was about; as far as he was concerned, prison weren't too bad a place, after all.

Lobo, on the other hand, was not fitting in quite as easily as Malachi. He had a tan, but underneath it, his complexion held a gray tinge belying his poor health. He dropped weight and his cough got worse, even though they were into the warmest time of the year. His attitude was sour and mean, and he wasn't eating.

One evening, after working at the orphanage all day, Leon entered the prison community hall and surveyed the tables, looking for Lobo. He finally spotted him, off by himself and snarling at anybody who even thought about sitting down close to him. His plate of food sat in front of him on the table, untouched.

Leon felt irritation rise in him. He made his way to where Lobo sat, and, sending quick glances to the guard on the floor and the other guard on the raised lookout to ensure discretion, he suddenly gave the new convict a hard cuff across the back of his head.

Like the wolf for which he was nicknamed, Lobo sprang to his feet and, turning with a snarl, he prepared to attack his attacker. However, as soon as he saw that it was Nash, he stood down, just a fraction, and did not come at him. But the snarl remained, and the two men locked eyes, initiating the battle of wills.

Now Leon had the attention of both guards, but neither appeared concerned about breaking this up. Everyone knew a confrontation had been brewing between these two inmates, so the sooner it got resolved under controlled circumstances, the better.

The other inmates seated around the room watched this altercation with serious intent. Though none of them had what it took to challenge Nash outright, sitting back and watching someone else attempt it, could make for an entertaining dinner and a show.

Lobo's stance was menacing; his eyes were hard, his body tense and fists clenched. Every fiber of him wanted to get his hands around Nash's throat and choke the arrogant life out of him, and yet, he hesitated. Even without the Kansas Kid there to back him up, Lobo knew that Nash was a force to be reckoned with. He'd seen, with his own eyes, the leader of the Elk Mountain Gang, lightweight that he was, beat a man senseless for getting on the wrong side of him.

In just the course of a few seconds, Lobo had weighed his options and looked at the odds. He was not yet recovered from his injuries, and as much as he hated to admit it, he knew that his strength was far from where it should be. He also knew that Nash had been doing physical work outdoors for the past three weeks, and even through his summer tunic, Lobo could tell that Nash was skinny but fit and in a much better position to win a fight than Lobo was.

All this Lobo took in and processed in the space of those few seconds when the two adversaries challenged one another. Then Lobo backed down, though not gracefully. He remained tense, sending off aggressive waves, but he broke eye contact and sat back down at the table.

The atmosphere in the mess hall relaxed, but it was with disappointment, not relief, as the guards and inmates alike had to accept that there would be no fight tonight.

Leon collected his own plateful of supper, then returned and sat down beside his companion, and began to eat. He didn't look at Lobo, didn't send him any sign language or whispered orders; he just sat and quietly ate his supper.

Lobo got the message. He picked up his spoon, and though still tight-lipped with resentment, he began to eat. Leon didn't leave his side until Lobo had cleaned his plate.

Once the meal was finished, Leon got up, returned his plate to the counter, poured his cup of evening coffee, and returned to his cell.

Lobo sat and seethed, while everyone else avoided eye contact with him for fear of becoming the scapegoat. Lobo wasn't ready for things to be settled between him and Nash. Not yet. But after this incident, he always ate his supper.

***

During the following week, Lobo was in the warehouse doing the usual, when Officer Pearson approached him. Lobo glanced up, then, having learned some lessons the hard way, quickly dropped his gaze again.

"Convict, follow me."

Though the order itself was always comprised of the same words, it wasn't always spoken in the literal sense. Pearson had been warned never to turn his back on this inmate, so even though the order had been 'follow me', Pearson stepped to the side as Lobo came up to him, then taking the convict by the arm, proceeded to direct him in that manner to where they were going.

Where they were going was the infirmary.

Lobo walked into the ward looking even more suspicious than usual. Then he saw Leon, and suspicion turned to resentment.

The doctor glanced up with the arrival of the newcomers.

"Ah, there you are, young man," Palin acknowledged him. It seemed everyone was a 'young man' to the doctor. "Have a seat over here, I want to examine you."

Lobo looked rebellious when Pearson backed up the order with a slight shove in the direction Palin had indicated.

Leon walked over to stand by the doctor.

"Come on, Lobo," he said. "Just do it, will you?"

Lobo sneered but took note that Leon had just spoken and not been whacked for it, so he thought he would take the chance and see what happened.

"What are you doin' Nash?" he growled at him. "You ain't my boss anymore. Why don't ya just leave me alone?"

Leon's smile was tight.

Pearson and Palin kept out of the way, giving Leon the chance to exert control over his underling. As long as it didn't get out of hand.

"That's where you're wrong, Lobo," Leon informed him. "I may not have been running Elk Mountain, but I am your boss in here, and you'll do what I tell you." He allowed a quizzical expression to cross his face. "But I thought we already discussed this."

Lobo snorted but wisely decided to change the subject.

"Well, what's this all about then?" he asked, looking around the infirmary. "I don't need no exam."

"Your cough is getting worse," Leon pointed out. "I just asked Doc Palin here to have a listen and maybe he can give you something for it."

"I don't need nothin'." Lobo made a move toward the exit.

Pearson was suddenly in his face, blocking his way with a deftly handled billy club.

Lobo seethed, and he sent a glare back at Leon.

Leon's smile remained dangerous.

"Just accept it, will you, Lobo?" Leon's anger gave way to irritation at this man's stubbornness. "You're going to need all the help you can get to survive this coming winter. Believe me, I know."

"And what makes you think I want to survive it?" Lobo asked quietly, but with an edge that hit home. "I shoulda died out there, with Charlie and the Preacher, but instead I'm stuck in this cesspool with you and Cobb. Any man who would accept this over an honorable death, ain't worth the bounty money posted on 'im."

Leon's jaw tightened at the insult, and he made a move toward the other man, but Pearson stopped him.

"Nash! Back off."

The fire went out of Leon's eyes and he stood down, though his anger was still apparent.

Lobo's lip curled into a smile; apparently, Nash wasn't boss over everybody.

"Just do it, Lobo," Leon ordered him, then added in a menacing tone, "The guards aren't around all the time."

The smile left Lobo's face, and the two inmates locked into an optical struggle for dominance.

Again, it was Lobo who backed off. He snorted derisively, as though to say that it was no big deal, then he went over to the exam table and sat on it.

"It's about time," Palin mumbled. "It's not like I have all day to wait for little boys to stop playin' games. Take off your tunic."

"What?" Lobo growled at him.

"Your damn tunic!" Palin's growl was just as menacing. "Take it off. I need to listen to your chest."

Lobo sighed, then pulled his tunic off over his head.

Leon tried not to react to the signs of trauma to Lobo's right side. It was obvious that there had been extensive damage done when that horse's hoof had landed on him, causing crushing internal injuries.

Palin didn't react at all to the scarring. Either he was good at covering up what he thought or, compared to the injuries he'd had to deal with during the war, this was nothing spectacular. He put the earpieces of his stethoscope into his ears and placed the business end of it on Lobo's chest. He listened for about five seconds, then took one earpiece out and looked at the inmate.

"It would help me to hear what's goin' on in there if you'd breathe."

"Oh." Lobo almost looked embarrassed and then he took in a deep breath. He instantly started coughing.

Palin backed off until the spasm quieted. "Just breathe normally," he instructed. "There's nothin' to worry about, just relax."

"I ain't worried, and I am relaxed."

"Hmm."

Palin listened again, moving the instrument around to various places on Lobo's chest and occasionally taking two fingers and tapping around the lung area, then listening some more.

"Hmm. Okay, take a breath and hold it." Tap, tap, tap. "Hmm. Okay, release. All right, shift around here so I can listen to your back." Tap, tap, tap. "Take a breath, hold it." Tap, tap, tap. "Uh huh. Release. Hmm."

Lobo looked at Leon and rolled his eyes.

Leon smiled.

"Okay," Palin said, straightening up and pursing his lips. "You can put your tunic back on." He looked at Leon. "Yeah, you were right, Nash. There is certainly fluid in that lung." He looked at his patient. "When you cough, do you ever bring up any phlegm, or is it always that dry cough?"

"Naw, it's dry," Lobo informed him.

Palin nodded. "Yeah. That fluid's not goin' anywhere. The lung is damaged and probably isn't gonna get much better than it is now. We'll have to really keep an eye on things once the colder weather sets in. It would be very dangerous for you to get pneumonia with it like that." Palin looked at Pearson. "Can we get him some warm clothing, Mr. Pearson? Sweaters and a scarf for sure, to keep his chest and neck warm."

Pearson shrugged. "I suppose."

"I already spoke to Mariam about that," Leon said. "She has assured me that the Sisters will supply both Lobo and Malachi with warm clothing for the winter."

Lobo looked surprised. Why would anybody bother about him?

Palin just nodded as though he had expected as much.

"Good," he said, then moved over to his medicine cabinet. "I can give you something here to help ease that cough, make ya a little more comfortable anyway." He came back to the patient and handed him a bottle of fluid. "It'll make ya sleepy, so take a swallow only at night. Let Nash know when you're runnin' out and I'll get more to you. Okay?"

"Yeah, sure Doc," Lobo mumbled, "whatever you say."

Then, without even a glance at Leon, he got off the table, and Pearson escorted him back to the work floor.

Leon and Doc exchanged looks.

"He's one a your men?" Palin asked.

"Yeah."

"Has he always been that cantankerous?"

"Yeah."

"Fuck!"

"Yeah."

***

A few days after the visit with Dr. Palin, Leon was again escorted to the orphanage. It was much the same routine as the first trip had been, with two main differences. The first was that Leon now looked forward to his time with the children and the other, was that he was being transported in the open buckboard rather than the closed in oven of a prison coach. Even though he was still chained to the floor boards, it at least offered a bit of a breeze. Thank goodness for small blessings.

At this point, he had traveled back and forth between the prison and the orphanage so many times with the work gang, that the trip through town no longer held much interest for him. It was nice to occasionally spot a pretty girl or a fine horse, but other than that, it was just one more thing that he could no longer partake in, so why even bother looking.

Again, as with the previous visit, Kenny removed Leon's shackles once they were inside the building, but the boot remained in place. He then accompanied Leon into the classroom, leaving Pearson in the hallway to guard the door. Both men greeted the Sisters, and then Leon turned to face his audience.

"Good morning," he said, grinning his grin.

He was hit with a cascade of youthful voices.

"Good morning, Mr. Nash!"

"Wow," Leon responded. "You'd think I hadn't been here for months. I saw every one of you while I was painting this building."

"Yeah, but you were working then," William spoke up. "The Sisters and the guards wouldn't hardly let us talk to you."

"I suppose that's a good point," Leon conceded. "We had a job to do. Do you like what we did?"

"Yes!"

Leon grinned again, then settled back against the front desk.

Sister Cornelia, recalling the inmate's defensive reaction to the yard stick on his first visit, made sure to keep it away from him on this occasion.

"What shall we talk about today?" he asked the group.

"How come you had to wear that funny looking block on your foot when you worked here?" asked Todd. "Didn't that make it hard to move around?"

"Yes, it did," Leon admitted, "but with a bunch of us here, the guards had to be sure that we didn't decide to up and leave all at once. It was just a precaution, that's all. It does make it hard for us to move around while we are working, but it also makes it hard for us to run away."

"You could run away now," Melanie observed.

"We could help you," piped up Sally.

"Yeah."

"We could help."

"Ahh . . ." Leon didn't even bother to glance around at Kenny; he could already picture the look on that guard's face. "That's not a good idea."

"Why not?"

"Don't you want to go?"

Leon smiled. "It's not that I don't want to," he explained, "but I'd have nowhere to go. The main reason the Kid and I stayed free for so long is that the law didn't have any photographs of us, so not many people knew what we looked like. Now, there are a lot of pictures of me out there, and if I made a run for it, it wouldn't be long before every sheriff's office within a hundred miles would have a copy of my photo, along with permission to shoot on sight. Besides that, I don't have any money. I don't have a horse or food, or a change of clothes. I think I kinda stand out in these stripes, don't you?"

This was met with some embarrassed giggling and more verbal affirmations.

Leon nodded. "Then, on top of that, you see the rifle that friendly Officer Reece is carrying, and has actually lifted up to be in a more useful position at this point?" All the children glanced at Kenny, and some of the younger girls chewed their lips in concern. "Well, I happen to have it on good authority that Officer Reece is an excellent shot, so I don't think I would get very far." Now the classroom was silent. "Besides that, I gave my word. I promised Officer Reece that if I was permitted to come here and talk with you lot, then I would not try to escape."

This comment was met with mixed reviews. The younger children nodded acceptance of this statement, but a couple of the older, more skeptical boys, questioned the logic of it.

"Yeah, but you could break your word," Michael stated. "If the opportunity arose, wouldn't you go for it?"

"No."

"Why not?"

"Yeah, if ya had the chance."

"Yeah. What if the Kansas Kid came and broke ya out? Wouldn't you go then?"

"No."

Now all the children were confused.

"But why not?" asked Melanie.

Leon sighed and crossed his arms. He knew the answer, but how to explain it in a way that even the young ones would understand? He constantly marveled at the ability of children to come up with the difficult questions.

"Well, like I said," he began, "I gave my word. A person's word means a lot. If you give your word and break it, well, what else can you offer then that's of any value?"

Leon stopped talking in mid-thought, as the real meaning of what he had just spoken out loud, hit home with his own circumstances. How close had he come that night, oh so long ago, in the Cheyenne jailhouse, to breaking his word? And how many nights had he, since then, spent staring up at a ceiling he couldn't see, berating himself for the fact that he hadn't done it?

"Nash?" Kenny's voice cut through the inmate's silent reflections.

"What? Oh." Leon woke up and looked upon a room full of opened mouths and concerned expressions. "Sorry," he said with a fresh smile. "I was just reminded of something. Ah, where was I? Oh yes, why I wouldn't break out. Well, I gave my word, and a person's word is important. Also, if the Kansas Kid showed up to try and break me out, I wouldn't let him. There are repercussions for everything we do."

"What does that mean?" Sally asked.

"That means there's a price to pay for the choices we make. I believe we talked about that the last time I was here. Jack Kiefer received his pardon. If he came here to break me out of prison, then he would be breaking the law, and he'd be right back where we started. He's a free man now; he's no longer wanted. I would not be happy with him if he threw that away."

A knock came to the classroom door and Kenny opened it a crack to see what was up.

Leon glanced over just as Kenny stepped back to allow someone else to enter, and then the inmate's face lit up with childish delight. He was on his feet in an instant.

"Ha, ha. Jack!"

"Hey, Uncle Leon," Jack smiled at him as the whole classroom took a collective gasp. "Oh, Mariam. Hello."

"Hello Jack. Good of you to come," she greeted him. "Sister Cornelia, I'd like you to meet Jack Kiefer."

"Sister," Jack greeted her.

"Oh, hello, Mr. Kiefer," Sister Cornelia greeted him. "My, but we are getting some notable folks here today."

"Jack, what are you doing here?" Leon asked him. "I never got around to asking you about this."

"Yeah, I know. Kenny kinda took the initiative." At which point, the two friends shook hands, then simultaneously, each put their left hands on a respective shoulder.

Leon then pulled his nephew into a brief 'man hug', followed by a couple of slaps on the back.

"Besides," Jack added once they parted. "I was gettin' tired of you havin' all the fun."

"Ha, ha! You . . ." Leon gave him another pat on the back, then turned to their audience. "Everyone, this is my nephew, and my partner, Jack Kiefer."

Again, a room of open mouths and wide eyes met this announcement. Then all hell broke loose.

"The Kansas Kid!"

"Wow. Can we see your fast draw?"

"We got to meet both of you."

"Are you going to break Mr. Nash out of prison?"

"Where's your gun?"

"Why aren't you wearing your gun?"

"We want to see your fast draw."

"Whoa! Hang on," Jack responded, holding up his hands. "Geesh, Leon, what have you been feedin' these kids?"

Leon just smiled and shrugged. He still wasn't over being happy to see his friend.

"Why aren't you wearing your gun?" Todd asked again.

"Well, ahh, the guards thought it would be a good idea if I left that out in the hallway with Officer Pearson for now."

A collective; "Aww . . ."

"Can't we see your fast draw?"

"We'll see," Jack said. "Maybe later."

"Are you here to rescue Mr. Nash?"

"Yeah. Are you gonna break him out?"

"Ah, no," Jack admitted and sent Leon a quizzical look. "That weren't the plan."

"Why not?"

"I thought we just went over all that," Leon pointed out.

"But we want to hear it from him."

"Yeah. We want to hear if he agrees with what you said."

"Oh." Leon smiled at his partner and with a hand gesture, offered him the floor.

Jack sent him a cocked brow then accepted the inevitable.

"Ah, well, knowin' my uncle, I expect he's already explained it to ya." He rolled his eyes. "Goodness knows, he lectures me on it enough times. Honestly though, I think he actually likes it here, 'cause he sure gets mad at me for even hintin' that I might gather some old friends together for a big prison escape."

Leon snorted, but every childish face was wide eyed and open mouthed at the thought of a gang of outlaws storming the prison walls.

"There's a plan, eh, Leon?" Jack smiled as the thought took hold. "I could gather up the Carbon County fellas. I'm sure they've forgotten all about you and their leader . . . what was his name?"

"Doug Calhoun."

"Yeah, that's right. Anyway, I'm sure they've forgotten about you sickin' that posse on 'im, so's you could get clear."

Leon frowned. "Any stories he spread around about me deliberately crossing my tracks with his have been greatly exaggerated."

"Sure, Leon. Whatever you say."

Giggling bubbled up from the group.

Leon shrugged in a gesture of innocence.

"Honestly," he insisted. "Calhoun was dodging my every move. And that posse was closing in. Is it my fault Calhoun's tracks crossed over mine and the posse got confused?"

"So, you're sayin' that he's lyin' about you settin' 'im up?"

"He's an outlaw, Jack. You can't trust anything those fellas say."

Jack's brows shot up. "Really?"

The giggling escalated into quiet snickering.

"But," Todd spoke up, "you just said that you wouldn't break your word, and you're an outlaw. Why ain't it okay for you to lie?"

"Well . . . 'cause . . . I'm a more honorable outlaw than Calhoun was."

"Okay," Jack thought about this distinction. "You're sayin' then, that because we were a much better class of outlaw, that we're above lyin'."

Leon chewed his lip while he thought about this.

The children gazed upon them in baited anticipation.

Finally, Leon nodded. "Yes. That's what I'm saying."

"And you are tellin' the absolute truth by denyin' that you deliberately put Calhoun in the line of that posse."

"Yes. Well, to some degree . . . I mean, he was right there, but I didn't do . . . well, okay, maybe I did a little bit. Oh, all right! I set him up."

The room erupted into full-scale laughter.

"Yeah," Jack smirked at his uncle. "I don't think the Carbon County Gang would be too interested in helpin' us out."

"There's the Black Kettle Gang," Leon was all hopeful.

Jack scrunched up his face and shook his head. "Nah, Bill Weston's just as happy ta see you in prison. He and the Kettle boys were doin' real well until you took over Elk Mountain. You kept on beatin' 'im to the best pots."

"It's not my fault he didn't plan ahead well enough. Geesh. Well, what about the Cripple Creek Gang? We always got along okay with them."

"Yeah, but do you really want Harry Barton involved in your prison break?"

"Oh yeah." Leon frowned, then he shrugged. "That does it then. It's going to be all up to you, Jack."

Jack cocked a brow. "Oh yeah?" He glanced back at Kenny who was listening to this conversation with great interest. "Ahh, I think we kinda ruined the surprise aspect."

Leon followed Jack's gaze and locked eyes with the guard, then faced forward again.

"Yeah, I suppose so."

"Aww," William complained. "That don't mean you couldn't plan it for later. When nobody's expecting it."

"Yeah!" came the chorus from the assembly.

"Yeah, we'll help!" came another offer.

"We could get you some normal clothes. The livery man here has some."

"And I could steal some food from the kitchen . . .!"

"Calm down, children," Sister Cornelia broke up the rescue party. "Back to your seats."

Deflated shoulders and groans of disappointment took over from wild suggestions, as the more ambitious children shuffled back to their places.

"I think it's time to change the subject," Kenny's voice came from right behind Leon's elbow.

Leon's nerves jangled and he turned to meet those steel grey eyes boring into his. He twitched a smile then dropped his gaze.

"Yeah, ah. Time to move on."

"Awww!" came the general consensus from the room.

"No, he's right," Jack straightened up to settle the matter. "We was just teasin' anyway. The Territorial Prison is a formidable place. Even if we wanted ta break Leon out, it would be too dangerous. Ain't that right, Officer Reece?"

"No one's done it yet," Kenny said as he moved back to his post by the door.

"See?" Jack said to the class. "And even if we did break Leon out, we'd have nowhere ta go. We had our photos all over the newspapers when we went ta trial. Everybody knows what we look like now. There'd be no place left for us ta hide. So," Jack folded his arms and leaned against the desk, "that about sizes it up."

But then Leon nudged him for more.

"What about the other reason, Jack?"

Jack looked at him, innocently. "What other reason, Uncle?"

"You know what reason," Leon insisted. "It's probably the most important reason of all, the one you and I have discussed on numerous occasions. The one where I'd be really mad at you, if you even thought about throwing it all away."

"Ohh. You must mean the one about the pardon," Jack teased.

"Yeah." Leon nodded emphatically, then rolled his eyes at the assembly. He was a real showman when he wanted to be, and the children giggled appreciatively.

"Well, yeah. There is that," Jack agreed. He turned to the group with the manner of a child being told to repeat his lessons out loud, so he wouldn't forget them. "I was given the pardon, somethin' that Leon and I worked real hard for, and I was finally granted it." Jack stopped the play-acting and became more serious. "If I was ta break Mr. Nash outta prison, or even just try to, I would be breakin' the law, and so I would be throwin' away somethin' that is real important. Then what would all our efforts have been for? It'd be worth nothin'."

"So, you can't do anything?" Gillian asked.

"Oh, no," Jack denied that. "No. We're doin' everything we can, that's legal. We've got people on our side, out there. We have a good lawyer, and friends who have money that are willin' to support our cause." He stopped and met his uncle's eyes. "We're doin' everything we can, Leon. It's just gonna take some time ta get everything set up. Again."

"Yeah, Jack. I know."

There was a beat of silence as the classroom watched the silent communication pass between the two friends.

Then William spoke up. "Mr. Kiefer, sir?"

"Yes . . .?"

"That's William," Leon informed him.

"Yes, William?"

"We heard about what happened to the Elk Mountain Gang," he stated, hesitantly. "Someone said that you were there, sir. That you saw what happened."

The demeanors of both Leon and Jack sank into sadness, and instantly William felt contrite.

"Oh. Maybe I shouldn't have asked that."

"No, that's all right," Jack assured him. "Actually, Kenny . . . ah, Officer Reece, wanted me ta talk to you about that. Especially you older boys, who might be thinkin' that runnin' off to join an outlaw gang would be fun."

William and Michael exchanged glances while the rest of the group waited in strained anticipation.

"I didn't actually see what happened," Jack explained, "but I sure enough heard it. Ta be perfectly honest, I was hidin' under a seat in the passenger car, scared ta death that I was gonna get killed by a stray bullet, or a shard of glass, or a splinter of wood, or somethin' else, equally as humiliatin'.

"But the noise was deafening. Rifles firing, men yellin', some screamin'. And the horses! Nothing chills ya to the bone more than a horse screamin' in terror or in agony, simply 'cause it had the bad luck a bein' caught out in the middle of it all.

"A lot of people, and a lot of horses, died that day. Because I just happened to be on that train, I had ta go out and identify the bodies of men whom I have known for years. Men who were my friends. It was one of the worst days of my life, and I will never forget it."

Jack hesitated here, then looked at Leon, who was looking at the floor. The room was silent.

Jack took a deep breath and surveyed his enthralled audience.

"But as bad as that was, there was one thing that was worse. That was lookin' down at the dead body of someone I didn't even know."

Leon looked up at that, his brow creased.

"It was the body of a fifteen-year-old boy."

Leon groaned; he knew that sat heavy with his partner.

"He and his buddy thought it would be a great adventure to run away from home and join up with a real, authentic outlaw band," Jack explained. "They'd never done anything illegal in their lives, they both came from good families and had no reason to run off, other than that they thought it would be exciting. I'm never gonna forget the look on his friend's face, when I had ta tell 'im that his best childhood buddy had been killed, all 'cause they thought it would be an adventure."

The room was silent. William and Michael exchanged glances again, then looked away. That didn't sound like an adventure at all.

"So," Jack continued, "you don't wanna be runnin' off and doin' stupid stuff like that. It ain't worth it. You're gettin' a real good start on things here, a good life ahead of ya. Don't mess it up."

Mariam stepped forward, feeling that the children might have had enough reality for now.

"Perhaps it's time we called it a day," she suggested.

"Aww, no!"

"Not yet!"

"We haven't seen his fast draw!"

"Yeah, he said we could see his fast draw!"

Mariam sighed. Children could be so resilient, jumping from one extreme to the other at the snap of the fingers. She sent a questioning look to Jack. He smiled and looked back at Kenny.

"What do you think?" he asked the guard. "Can I show them the fast draw?"

Kenny was already one step ahead of him. With a smile, he held up Jack's belt with the six-shooter neatly tucked away in its holster.

Jack laughed. "Yeah, okay."

This affirmation was met with a loud chorus of excited exclamations, as Jack stepped forward to retrieve his gun from the guard.

"It's been unloaded," Kenny informed him.

"Ah, yeah," Jack nodded. "Probably a good idea." He then cracked open the chamber to show the children that the gun was indeed empty. "Ya don't wanna be handlin' a gun that's loaded unless you really mean business. I'm just gonna show ya my fast draw and we don't want any unfortunate accidents, do we?"

Worried expressions came back to him as the importance of what

Jack said sunk in.

Knowing he had gotten the message across, Jack returned to stand in front of the desk while he strapped his holster into place.

"Stand up, Leon," he said. "You're gonna be my opponent for today."

"Ho, ho!" Leon laughed amongst the giggles from the class. "Hardly fair. I don't even have a gun." He sent a mischievous grin to their audience. "What do you think? Should I ask Officer Reece if I could borrow his sidearm?"

Everyone sent expectant smiles toward the guard.

The look Kenny sent to the inmate did not need words to translate.

"Ah, no," Leon turned back to the children. "I don't think that's going to happen."

"It don't matter, Leon, you don't need a gun," Jack told him. "Just stand here and face me. Now hold your hands out in front of ya, spread 'em apart, palms facing each other like you're gonna clap them. Then when we're ready to, you try and clap your hands before I get the barrel of my gun between 'em."

"Sounds easy enough," Leon agreed. He raised his hands the way Jack had instructed and held his palms about six inches apart. He smiled cheekily at the class and moved his hands together until they were only an inch apart.

Jack cocked a brow at him, and Leon smiled again at their audience. In a flash, he snapped his palms together, then he jumped, startled to suddenly feel the barrel of Jack's gun nestled in between his two hands.

The room was filled with gasps of surprise.

"Wow! That was so fast!"

"Did you see that?"

"NO, I didn't see it!"

"Do it again, I didn't see it either!"

"Do it again!"

Leon looked a little put out. "That was hardly fair, Jack," he complained. "I wasn't ready."

"Leon, where does it say that, in a gunfight, I gotta wait 'til the other fella's ready?"

"Well . . ."

"Do it again!"

"Do it again!"

"Yeah, Jack," Leon agreed. "Do it again."

In the meantime, Kenny had opened the classroom door and beckoned to the other guard.

"Hey, Pearson, get in here; you gotta see this."

Officer Pearson came in and everyone waited to see the show again.

"All right, Leon," Jack nodded, "we can do it again. Just, ah, put your hands out like before."

Leon raised his hands, and, with another cheeky smile, he brought his palms together until again, there was only an inch between them.

Jack sighed and shook his head. Fine, if Leon was gonna be a bastard about it, so be it.

"Mariam," Jack asked, "could you say 'one, two, three, go'?"

"Certainly. One, two, three, go."

". . . Oh my—" Sister Cornelia allowed the comment to escape her, amongst gasps and oos from the children.

Even Mariam was impressed, although something told her, she really shouldn't be impressed by anything to do with guns and violence. Still, she couldn't help smiling.

Leon looked down at his hands to again feel the hard, cold metal of the gun barrel settled between his palms.

Pearson whistled, then he and Kenny exchanged glances. Kenny shook his head.

Leon looked into his nephew's laughing eyes.

"Aww, you ain't that fast," Leon teased him. "There's gotta be a trick to it."

"Yeah, right Leon," Jack gave his gun a couple of quick spins, then dropping it into his holster, he folded his arms and turned to face the sea of wide-eyed expressions laid out before him.

"Wow!"

"I still don't think I saw it!"

"Nobody can be that fast!"

Leon leaned back against the desk, smiling broadly. It was easy, pretending to be put out, but truth be known he couldn't have been more pleased. He knew Jack had been working hard, these past two years, to get his shooting arm back again, and now Leon could see that he had done it. Although he knew his partner was such a perfectionist in that area, he would probably insist that it still wasn't quite right. There's just no pleasing some people.

***

A short time later, the visitors had said their farewells to the children and stood in the hallway, getting Leon prepared for the trip back to the prison.

Pearson was busy cinching the belt around the inmate's waist and snapping his wrists into the cuffs, when he noticed Jack doing something that made him uneasy.

Kenny tensed as Jack nonchalantly cracked open his Colt-45 Peacemaker and began loading it with cartridges from his belt.

Kenny pointed at Jack's gun, shaking his head.

"Jack, don't do that here," he ordered. "After we've parted company, and you're on your way, then you can do whatever you want. But don't load your gun here."

Jack glanced up, and the look in Kenny's eye was not one of friendly advice, but of a guard who was responsible for the security of a prisoner; a guard who was in control and meant business. Jack then glanced at Pearson and noticed that he also, was tense and had repositioned his rifle to be ready, just in case.

Leon sent his partner a quiet, whimsical smile.

"Oh, yeah," Jack mumbled as he quickly tipped the cartridges into the palm of his hand, then slipped them into his pocket. "Sorry. Wasn't thinkin'." He dropped the gun into its holster, then he and Leon exchanged a look.

Mariam stepped out of the classroom and, closing the door behind her, she smiled at the group of gentlemen.

"Thank you again, for coming," she said. "That was quite an impressive show, Jack. The children are going to be talking about that for some time to come."

"Thank you, ma'am," Jack answered her. "I'm not as fast as I used to be, but it's gettin' better."

Leon snorted.

"Oh, sorry," he apologized as everyone looked at him. "Yeah, he's just as slow as molasses; never could aim straight, either. I have no idea how he got dubbed 'Fastest gun in the West'. Why, I bet that Sister Cornelia could outdraw him now, he's gotten so—"

"Leon!"

Leon smiled at Jack, but he did shut up.

"Napoleon, thank you as well for coming again," Mariam placed a hand on his arm. "I expect to be making a trip to the prison next week. Perhaps I will see you there."

"Yes, ma'am," Leon answered her. "I hope so."

"Yes. Good day to you all."

The group headed back outside.

The prison buckboard and Jack's rented horse were all there, waiting patiently for them, so Jack turned to say goodbye to his uncle.

This was suddenly, and unexpectedly, awkward. Jack hadn't thought about that; how it would feel to mount up on his horse and simply ride away, leaving his friend behind and in the custody of the guards. He found himself hesitant to leave.

"Leon . . ." The two men locked eyes, and Jack put a hand on his friend's shoulder. "It just don't feel right, leavin' ya like this."

Leon felt self-conscious and looked down at his shackled hands. He simply nodded and mouthed the word, "Yeah."

Jack glanced at the two guards who were standing a little way off but keeping a close watch on the pair.

"Jeez, Leon," Jack continued, quietly, "I gotta admit, despite all our high-falutin' talk to them young'uns, I feel like I just wanna slip ya a lock pick, then make a run for it, right here and now."

"Yeah, I know," Leon agreed, just as quietly. "Despite all our high-falutin' talk to those youngsters, I wish you could slip me a lock pick so's we could make a run for it." He smiled, sadly. "But ya know, I'm not under any illusions about our chances. Kenny's a good guy and all, but he wouldn't hesitate to shoot me in the back if I tried anything like that. Oh, he'd feel bad about it afterward but I'd still be dead. And then you would be in here for aiding in an attempted escape. Not to mention, this boot really would slow me down. And besides," his smile turned into an ironic grin, "I gave my word."

Jack glanced at the apparatus attached to Leon's ankle. "Yeah, I noticed that. What's it for?"

"To discourage me from doing exactly what we're talking about doing."

"Oh yeah, I guess. It looks heavy. Does it hurt?"

Leon shrugged. "When I have to wear it all day, like when I'm out of the prison on a work gang, my leg will ache all night. But when I'm only wearing it for a few hours, like today, it's not so bad. And Kenny usually takes it off once I'm secured in the wagon. I sure wouldn't want to wear it all the time, though."

"Geez. Well, I weren't serious about us runnin' off anyway. Just sayin' I'd like to."

Leon nodded. "I'm glad you came, Jack. It was fun."

"Yeah, it was."

"We'll have to do it again, sometime."

Kenny gave a discreet cough over by the wagon and Jack didn't miss the significance of it.

He glanced at Kenny, then put on a brave face to his uncle. "Yeah. Well, I best be goin'. I'll see ya in a few weeks. Don't think Penny will be with me for that visit, since we're gonna be real close to the weddin' by then, and I expect she'll be busy."

"Oh, that's right." Leon brightened. He had also recognized the signal from the guard, but he was reluctant to end the visit. "I expect to hear all about that."

"Oh, I expect you will," Jack agreed with a laugh. "Cameron's even gettin' me a new suit for the occasion. Tailor-made and all."

"I can understand that," Leon commented. "Doesn't want you embarrassing the family by showing up to a wedding in your trail duds."

"I got decent clothes," Jack protested. "Just . . . Cameron figures I'm gonna need somethin' more than just decent for the hearin', so we'll take care of both at the same time, I guess."

"Yeah. Well, that's good of him."

"It's too good, Uncle Leon," Jack insisted, feeling inadequate. "I have no idea how I'm gonna pay 'im back for everything he's doin'. He says it's him payin' us back, but . . . it just don't seem right, somehow."

"Well," Leon commented, thoughtfully, "you could always marry his other daughter."

"Leon!"

Leon gave a shackled shrug in his own defense. "Well, I'm just sayin' . . ."

"Yeah, I know what you were just sayin'. Why don't you let me decide what I wanna do about that, okay?"

"Fine," Leon mumbled. "No need to get all riled up.'

"Uh huh."

"Just looking out for you, Kid."

"Uh huh."

Leon sent him his impish smile, accompanied by a mischievous sparkle.

Jack couldn't help but laugh out loud. Then he put his hand on his uncle's shoulder and gave it a squeeze.

"I best be goin'," he stated, regretfully. "You watch out for yourself, okay? You've been doin' real good lately, so don't go gettin' yourself into trouble by watchin' out for Malachi and Lobo. They can look after themselves."

"Yeah, I suppose," Leon said. "Lobo has certainly made it clear he doesn't want help anyway."

"There ya go," Jack agreed. "I know you'll be keepin' an eye on 'em anyways, but just don't forget ta watch your own back."

"No, I won't."

There was a moment of silence between them, then Leon smiled and nodded.

"Come on, fellas," Kenny called over, realizing that subtlety wasn't going to work. "It's time we headed back."

Leon slumped. There was no way to ignore that summons.

"I'll be seeing you, Jack."

"Yeah."

Jack gave his friend another friendly pat on the shoulder, then turned and mounted his horse. He gave a quick nod to the guards, another look at Leon, then swung his horse around and loped away.

Leon stood still, watching him go and thinking again about how strange this was; Jack could come and go freely, without hindrance, while he himself was shackled and contained, and could not follow. All because of circumstance, all because someone in authority decided that this would be the way of it. Jack could mount his horse and ride away, and Leon could not follow.

Kenny approached the inmate. "Nash . . ."

"Yeah," Leon responded absently, while he continued to stare after his disappearing nephew.

"Come on, Nash," Kenny took hold of his arm. "Let's go."

Leon gave a regretful sigh, looked down at the ground, then up to meet Kenny's gaze. He sent one more glance after his departing friend, then allowed himself to be led back to the waiting buckboard

CHAPTER TEN
THE NEW HORSE

The Rocking M Ranch
Arvada, Colorado

Later that week, Jack and Penny saddled up Spike and the little bay pacer, Monty, and, packing themselves a picnic lunch, headed up to the north pasture to go scrutinize some horses.

Jack still felt uncomfortable about this whole arrangement, but Cameron refused to take no for an answer, and since Jack knew he would need a riding horse, he finally relented.

Penny found the excursion exciting and opportune. Exciting because she got to spend some time alone with her intended, and help him pick out his new mount, and opportune because it gave her an excuse to get away from the hustle and bustle of wedding preparations. The special day was still a little way off, but Jean wanted everything to be perfect. Everyone felt the strain.

"What do you think?" Penny asked, as they ate sandwiches while they rode. "Do you know what type of horse you want?"

Jack considered the question, then shrugged his shoulders. "I dunno. I guess I've been so worried about a young horse not knowin' how ta get me out of scrapes that it didn't occur ta me, until recently that I probably won't be gettin' into them types of scrapes no more. So, it don't really matter. Other than that, I suppose I'll know what I want when I see it."

"There's probably going to be some nice fillies in the group, too," Penny commented. "Papa doesn't keep them all as brood mares. Maybe you should try—"

"NO!"

Penny looked at him, startled.

Jack smiled to ease the sharpness of his retort. "Sorry," he said. "It's just, one diva in a partnership is enough. I'll be happy with another gelding."

Penny smiled. "Yes, okay. I know what you mean. Karma is a very fine horse, and she suits Peter well, but she does have 'personality'."

"That's for sure," Jack mumbled. "When I go for a ride, I wanna feel confident that I'm gonna reach my destination, not get bucked off into a ditch somewhere, 'cause my mare came inta season and decided ta become a little 'testy'!"

Penny laughed. "Yes, okay. We won't look at the fillies." Then she dropped her smile and became reflective. "Although, I sure am fond of Daisy. She did wiggle her way into my heart."

Jack snorted. "Yeah, like she really had to squirm hard to manage that. That filly had you wrapped around her little hoof the instant she landed in the straw."

"You're right," Penny agreed. "It was so exciting, watching her come into the world; I just knew she was going to be my horse. I'm glad she came out a filly—for purely selfish reasons, of course. If Papa had gotten his colt, well . . . I wouldn't have gotten my future riding horse."

This time, it was Jack's turn to laugh. "That kinda makes me wonder if you didn't have somethin' ta do with decidin' the gender of that foal, before it even hit the ground."

"Mathew! Don't be silly. You know that's impossible."

"I dunno, Penny," Jack teased her. "You can be pretty head-strong when it comes ta gettin' what you want."

"Well, I don't know about head-strong," Penny contradicted. "Determined, yes. Patient, yes. But head-strong?"

"Yes!" Jack smiled at her, and Penny sent him a mischievous smile back. "Ho, ho, Penny, darlin', you're flirtin' with me."

"Yes."

Their gazes locked for a moment, their expressions fluttering somewhere between serious and teasing. Then Jack looked away and pushed Spike onward, down the slope toward the line cabin and horse corrals.

Penny followed along behind, a subtle but pleased smile still lingering upon her lips.

***

Riding into the cleared yard of the cabin, Jack couldn't help but run a scrutinizing eye over the ten or so young horses milling around in the corral. At first glance, all of them seemed like fine animals, and Jack wondered if he was going to be able to pick one out of the group. Maybe he could just close his eyes and throw a lasso, taking whichever horse the loop fell over. That could work.

As the riders pulled up at the hitching rail and dismounted, Sam and Deke came up from the other side of the corral to greet them.

Deke was an old hand at wrangling horses and had been working this same spread for a lot of years. When the previous owners had up and sold the ranch, Deke ended up staying on and continuing to work for the new owners. The arrangement had worked out just fine for everyone concerned. He and Sam got on well enough, and the old hand didn't mind at all teaching the "youngster" everything he knew about wranglin' horses, and Sam was learning a lot.

"Howdy folks," Deke smiled his greeting, showing off a mouthful of missing teeth. "Hear tell, yer up here ta pick out a young horse fer yerself."

"Ah, yup. That's the plan." Jack shook hands with the old horseman. "Jack Kiefer."

"Yup, I know. Good ta meet ya, young fella." He tipped his head to Penny. "How do, Miss Marsham."

"Hello Deke," Penny smiled at him, then glanced at Sam. "Hello Sam, how is Maribelle doing?"

"She's doin' all right, considerin', Miss Penelope. Thank you for askin'."

"Well, c'mon, let's get this show on the road," Deke pestered. "How about you folks go stand by the empty corral there, and Sam and I will send them horses over to ya, one at a time. That way, ya can take a good look at 'em and see what ya think. You wantin' a colt or a filly?"

"Just send in the colts," Jack said as he offered his arm to Penny. They walked over to the second corral and waited for the show to begin.

It didn't take long before Sam and Deke had grabbed their lariats and squeezed through the fence of the first corral. Sam went to the adjoining gate and opened it for Deke to single out one of the colts and send it running through the opening and into the second corral. They'd give each horse about ten minutes to run around, showing off its gaits, before sending in the next horse, until all the colts found themselves running around the second corral wondering what in the world all the fuss was about.

At first, Jack didn't think he was going to be able to narrow down the possibilities very easily. He felt like a child who had been given full run of a candy store; there were so many choices, it was hard to decide. The first few that came trotting into the corral were fine-looking animals, but nothing stood out to make any of them more desirable than the others.

Then the fourth youngster came galloping in, and Jack perked up and took notice.

The colt was a bright chestnut with a star on his forehead, but no stockings. The first thing Jack noticed about him was his nice, easy, swinging gait. On top of that, making his transitions between the gaits: walk to trot, trot to gallop, then back down to walk again, were smooth and effortless. The colt had natural balance and could change his leads fluidly and without hesitation.

Jack liked the look of him.

A few more were sent through and nothing else caught his eye the way the chestnut had. That is, until horse number eight charged through the gate and started to show off his own attributes.

This fellow was a dark, mahogany bay with a thin white blaze running down his face and four white stockings. He had everything in his gaits that the chestnut did, but with a little bit of flash thrown in.

Jack took to him right away.

Still, he wanted to be sure. He and Leon had always tried to stay away from horses that had a lot of white on them, as they tended to stand out in the crowd and be noticed. A horse that was more nondescript, like the chestnut, was a wiser choice for an outlaw.

Jack had to keep reminding himself that he wasn't an outlaw anymore, and maybe it was time for something with a little bit more sparkle to it.

He watched the horses milling around together, taking note of their temperaments and their pecking order. The chestnut was proving to be quite dominant in his bearing; he laid his ears back and went after any of the other colts that got too close to him. The others were quick to get out of his way, having felt the sting of his teeth and the pounding of a well-placed hoof, on past occasions.

The bay was up there in the pecking order, but not right at the top. He was self-assured, but not aggressive, and only backed off from the chestnut and one other colt that hadn't interested Jack at all.

This was proving to be a difficult choice. Still, a horse that was too aggressive could be more trouble than it's worth, but did he really want one that was going to stand out in a crowd?

"Any of them catch your eye?" Penny asked him.

"Yeah, now that ya ask," Jack told her, and he pointed them out. "That chestnut over there, and the dark bay with the white legs."

Penny nodded. "Yes, I agree. Those were the two that caught my eye, as well. I also like that roan there, but I think he's a little too little for you."

"Yeah," Jack agreed with her. "I kinda like a horse to have a bit more height than that one. Course, they ain't full grown yet; he could catch up."

Penny shrugged. "Maybe, maybe not. If there are others you like, why take the chance?"

"Good point," Jack agreed. "Well, let's see what Sam and Deke have ta say. They've been workin' these horses, so I suppose they'll know 'em pretty good."

Penny nodded agreement, and Jack waved the two wranglers over for a conference.

"Anything ya like?" Deke asked.

"Yeah," Jack said and pointed out the two that had caught his eye.

Deke nodded approval. "You knows your horseflesh, all right. They both got good solid builds and strong legs. Nice comfortable gaits."

"Yeah, but you know their temperaments," Jack pointed out. "Which one do ya think would make the best ridin' horse?"

"Depends on what ya want," Deke commented, evasively. "Some folks like a bit a fire in their horses, others just want a good, steady mount. What ya lookin' fer?"

"Just a good, solid mount," Jack admitted. "I don't need fire."

Deke smiled and nodded. "I'd say the bay, then. They both got brains, but whereas the bay wants ta learn new things, the chestnut tends ta use his brain ta figure out how ta avoid learnin' new things. We'll break 'em both out right, and he'll make a fine ridin' horse, but he'll always have a bit of a stubborn streak to 'im. That bay will make ya a good, willin' horse. And we'll break 'im out right for ya, no need ta worry 'bout that."

"That's just fine," Jack agreed. "The bay it is."

"Good," Deke concurred. "Give us a month ta get 'im broke out, an' then I suppose Sam can bring 'im down to the ranch house fer ya. How does that sound?"

"Perfect," Jack said. "Caroline's weddin' will be done and out of the way by then, so it'll give him a chance to get used ta things without all the hubbub of a social gatherin' to confuse the issue."

"Sound thinkin'," Deke agreed. "Now that it's settled, you folks like some coffee before ya head back? It's a bit of a ride. Might as well take a break while ya can get it."

Both Jack and Penny smiled at the offer.

"That'd be mighty fine."

"Thank you."

***

Laramie, Colorado
Summer 1887

Leon sat on his bunk holding a large paper wrapped parcel that felt like it contained a manuscript rather than a letter. He was surprised that the guards had permitted it to come through.

With furrowed brow and a curious mind, he untied the string and allowed the contents to slide out onto his lap. Then he smiled with anticipation, even though a part of him knew that the words on the page might bring melancholy rather than joy.

> *Dear Peter,*
>
> *As promised, I am going to give you as detailed an account of our wedding day as is possible in the time allowed. Steven and I are heading out soo, on our honeymoon, for two weeks in San Francisco. Well, not all the two weeks will be spent there, some of the time will be spent getting there in the first place, then coming back again.*
>
> *Mathew commented that you both know some people*

in that city and even gave us the address of one: Frederick Redikopp, and told us to be sure to drop by and introduce ourselves. Mathew seemed to think that there was a joke in there somewhere, as he couldn't stop laughing. I thought this rather odd. He did, however, assure us that he would send Mr. Redikopp a telegram to inform him of our coming and to be sure to show us the sights!

Oh dear! I've jumped ahead of things here, haven't I? Josey and I spent the day before the wedding at the ranch, while Steven stayed in town because we all know that it is bad luck for the groom to see the bride before the wedding. I believe David Gibson and Mathew did a lot to keep Steven occupied throughout the evening and indeed, even seemed to manage to get themselves into some trouble of sorts at the local saloon. Not quite sure what that was all about. Nobody's saying.

Still, we ladies had quite the time together here at home, getting all the last-minute things ready for the big day. Of course, we had the ceremony here at the ranch and pretty much the whole town was invited (Don't be mad, Peter, but I even invited Sam and Maribelle. I still haven't quite forgiven him his transgressions, but after what they went through, Mama felt it would be a good gesture). Anyway—yes, we all had such good fun that evening, telling stories and finishing up the baking for the next day. It must have been well on to midnight before we blew out the lamps and headed for bed.

Mama even took me aside at one point during the evening to tell me a little bit more about what to expect on my wedding night. At first, I thought this was rather silly of her. Having grown up on a cattle ranch, I thought I had a good idea about what went on in the marital bed. But then, I came to realize that 'no', I didn't know! At first, I felt a little scared and skeptical. Steven has always been so kind and gentle with me, so of course, he wouldn't do THAT. That's disgusting. At which point, Mama laughed and assured me that I probably wouldn't find it disgusting once we got down to it.

Now, of course, that we've had our wedding night, I

must say . . . OH! No, I don't think I should say. I believe I have already said more than what is proper for a young woman to say to a man who is not her husband. But I must say that I never would have thought . . . OH. Never mind. You, being a man, of course you know all about this stuff, and indeed, I'm sure you must be laughing at my naivety.

But I've gotten ahead of myself again. It's just that I'm so happy! 'Caroline Granger', 'Mrs. Steven Granger'! Either way, it does have a nice ring to it, doesn't it? I can't believe that I am a married woman now. I thought I would feel different; that being married would somehow make me older or wiser, or just different. But other than being incredibly happy, I'm still the same old me.

It was such a lovely day. The weather could not have been nicer. Thank goodness it didn't rain! We had far too many guests to fit everyone into the house and everything was all laid out for an outdoor gathering, so we were fortunate there. The flowers and decorations that Josey and Penny had gathered and placed around at the tables were very appropriate and gave the air a wonderful scent of summertime freshness.

And I finally got to meet Steven's folks! They made the trip especially from back East, and they are such lovely people. No wonder Steven is such a fine man with parents like them. We all got along famously, and my only regret this that there isn't much time to get to know them better. Steven promised that we would visit them once we get settled. That will be lovely.

Mama gave me her wedding dress to wear and it was so beautiful! It was made from a lovely material that was so soft and silky to the touch, and it was embroidered with ribbons and lace, with yellow flower designs running through it all. I'm sure it must have had 100 little pearl buttons, too, that made it quite the chore to get into it. But once they were all fastened, it was a perfect fit. The veil I wore was also that lovely lace with the floral design. It was so pretty, and I was so excited when Mama pulled it out of her oak chest and presented it to me to wear on my day. I think Penny was jealous.

Of course, Papa gave me away, and he looked so different, but quite handsome, in his suit. He was pleased that I was happy but on occasion, when he didn't think I was looking at him, he looked a little sad too. But still, on the most part, I think he was happy, and I know he likes Steven very much.

OH! And Steven. Well, I always knew he was a handsome man, of course, but he looked absolutely gorgeous in his wedding attire. I must say that there's just something about getting a man all spiffied-up and into a suit that gets my heart a-pitter-pattering.

And Mathew—oh my! I knew he was handsome— well, of course, that's obvious. But seeing him dressed to the nines in that fine charcoal gray suit, just took my breath away, if I can say that about a man who was not my husband-to-be, while at my wedding. Still, he and Penny spent most of the day in each other's company when she wasn't performing her Maid-of-Honor duties, and I must say they made a very lovely couple. Maybe we'll get something going there yet.

Then, seeing Mathew all dressed up and looking so fine, made me think about what you would look like in a nice suit. Hmm. You would have been turning some heads as well, I'm sure. But then, of course, thinking along those lines, it made me sad that you could not be here to enjoy this day with us. I had so hoped that all this nonsense would have been cleared away and part of the past by now. I missed you being here very much, and I know Mathew did too.

Don't get me wrong, Mathew had a good time, and he and David seemed to be able to find something funny in just about everything that went on. Really, they were like a pair of little boys, continually laughing at some inside joke! But, just occasionally, when there would be a lull in their merriment, Mathew would take on a melancholy expression, and I knew he was thinking of you.

We all missed having you here, Peter, and I know that

Departures

Steven and I are taking time away for our honeymoon, but as soon as we get back, we will get busy with the preparations again. Steven has just about all the testimonies gathered up now for the hearing with the Prison Board and the main thing left to do is to get a date set up. Of course, the officials at the other end don't seem to be in any hurry to do this, so it's taking a lot of pushing and persistence to get them to sit up and take notice. Why does everything have to take so long!?

Anyway, sorry. I don't want to make you sad. This is supposed to be a happy letter, telling you all about our happy day! And it was a glorious day. Mama did so much to make everything come together and though she had help from most of the ladies here, she was still the one who organized it all. I will be forever thankful to her for that.

Mama actually did very well throughout the whole day, and I know she had a good time too, but the next morning, when Steven and I were leaving for our honeymoon, she had a hard time holding it together. I never really thought about how this was for her, watching me, a married woman now, leaving with my new husband to begin a new life. Once I realized it, I felt bad about leaving, almost like I was abandoning her. But then, being Mama, she saw my distress and quickly hugged me and let me know that all was well, and that she was very happy for me.

She must know that I love her dearly and that she will never be far from my thoughts. Denver is not that far off, so of course, we will be coming out for holidays and visits throughout the year. It's not like she's never going to see me again! Still, I suppose watching your children depart the family home must be difficult. But she still has Penny and little Eli to keep her busy, so I'm sure she'll be fine.

Anyway, back to the wedding day. Josephine is also quite the gal to have at a party. She was so full of high spirits the whole day, that it would have been impossible for anyone not to be affected by it. Of course, some of the ladies weren't quite sure how to take her, as she insisted on flirting shamelessly with all the men present, whether they be married or not! She even flirted with Steven. Can you imagine? But I've known her long enough now to know that she means nothing by it and that it's just her way.

The only thing that would have made the day more perfect, of course, would have been your presence. But I did as you suggested, and I held you in my thoughts and in my heart throughout the day, and so in a way, yes, you were here with me. I hope you thought to do the same at your end, and that you were able to feel some happiness and joy for me, on my wedding day.

OH—and my ring! Goodness gracious—how could I have forgotten about that? It's so beautiful. Of course, it wasn't until after the ceremony that I actually took the time to look at it, and then it simply took my breath away. It's a gold band (of course), but more than just that. Steven had it made especially for me, adorning the band with a lovely diamond and then including my birthstone— one on either side of the diamond. It's so lovely I can't wait to show it to you.

I love you so much, Peter, and aside from Steven, you are my dearest friend. Please stay safe and well, and I will come out for a visit again as soon as I am able.

With much love and warm wishes,
Caroline (Granger!!)

Leon sat back on his bunk and sighed. He took a sip of coffee and a nibble of cookie, and despite his efforts to feel differently, couldn't help but let a breath of sadness wash over him. He had remembered to keep Caroline in his thoughts on the day of her wedding, but even though doing so had helped her to feel his presence there, it hadn't helped him to feel the same way.

It had indeed made him melancholy and reminded him that, yet again, he was missing out on all the fun things in life. Still, he had sent her good wishes in his mind and tried to picture her all dolled up and looking every bit the blushing bride.

The eldest bird had left the nest. No turning back now. Josephine and Penny had gone on and on about the nice little house that Steven had bought in Denver, and how Caroline had gone on and on about getting it furnished and ready for the her and Steven to come home to.

Leon couldn't help but give a little chuckle about how much that must have cost the young lawyer. Still, Leon assumed the man could afford it.

God knows, Cameron was paying him well enough, and this case certainly wouldn't be the only one Steven had on his books.

Leon frowned as reflection entered his thoughts.

Odd, how some people fell into money naturally, while others scrambled and scraped their whole lives just to make ends meet.

Leon smirked. *Me and Jack. Well, I guess you could say we've had it both ways in our thirty-odd years of living.*

Though they had started life as dirt-poor, their transition into thievery and given them fifteen years of living the good life. Leon smiled as he munched another cookie. They'd had so much money, they had to become inventive to figure out ways of spending it all.

And Gabriella wondered why I wouldn't leave that life, at least not then.

Then "that" happened, and Gabriella was no longer part of the equation. He'd really started going after the big money then. He had been so hurt and angry, not only over Gabriella's betrayal, but at Wells Fargo too, for their hand in it. He'd really pushed things to the limit. Even his uncle, Mukua, had let him know that he was taking too many risks. Jack too. And Gus!

He snorted, then sighed as he thought about Gus.

He had no problem letting his feelings be known. As usual, Taggard had been right, too. I had gotten too cocky. It had gotten too dangerous.

Then they'd gone for the pardons.

Another huff.

And there we were, right back to being dirt poor again. Geesh, come around full circle. You know, if we'd been smart, we would have planned that better. Pulled a couple of big jobs, then gone for the pardons. At least then we would have had a stake. But nope, we jumped into that new venture with barely a dollar to our names. Oh, money came our way sometimes, but it never stayed for long, and we'd end up living hand to mouth. I never did learn how to save it.

What could one say about now? A person couldn't be any poorer than being in prison.

His thoughts drifted back to his last visit with his Shoshone family, and going on his spirit quest. How money had come into his vision and took on the form of his talisman. He had assumed that this vision was telling him that he would not be staying with the Shoshone, because money was not important to them, and in this assumption, he had been correct.

But now, he realized there was more to it than that. That money, or at least social standing, was something he was going to have to fight for. That it would be a constant ebb and flow throughout his lifetime, and he could never be sure of his standing. One thing he'd learned was to never take it for granted. When he was flush, he shouldn't get cocky about it, because the tide could turn on him again, at any moment. Maybe that's what his vision had meant, never take wealth for granted. It could be here one minute and gone the next.

He wished he still had his talisman though; his special coin. It had always brought him luck, until he'd come up against Morrison, that is. And now, with his coin, and his belt and hatband gone from his possession, he'd sure noticed how his luck had changed for the worse.

Then Leon started mumbling to himself and shaking his head at the way his life had turned out. And Jack's.

He was trapped. There wasn't much he could do about his circumstances. But Jack?

Leon shook his head with irritation.

How much longer is he going to wait? If he wants to reap any benefits from this life at all, he'd better get on with it.

There is no reason why Jack can't get married and still carry on the good fight to get me pardoned. Especially if he does marry Penny, because, goodness knows, she isn't about to give it up. Maybe seeing Steven and Caroline take this important step in their lives, will help Jack to see that he doesn't have to sacrifice one for the other; he could have both.

Leon took another sip of coffee and another nibble of cookie. Sigh Nothing like a wedding to make one reflective of their own lives, and the lives of their friends.

He knew he had to hang on as best he could for a little while longer. At least until after the hearing and the Supreme Court appeal, if they even get to the Supreme Court. But if nothing else, these two upcoming events gave him some purpose. He also felt an obligation to ensure that Malachi made it through his sentence without getting beat up or knifed.

Malachi had only gotten two years and it would likely be less than that; he was so amiable. Then he'll be out with his debt to the territory paid.

Leon could hold on for that long; he was sure of it.

Lobo was another matter. Not only did that inmate not want Leon's help, Leon hoped he'd be out of here himself by the time Lobo's sentence was completed.

Jeez, I hope so. I don't think I could last another eight years in here, just to watch over Lobo, let alone the eighteen-year sentence I still have coming if my parole is rejected. I don't think Jack could last another eight years of me being in here, either. Yeah, Jack has to get on with his life, sooner rather than later.

Leon nodded to himself. He decided right then and there, he'd hang on until Malachi got his release, or until all other legal avenues had been exhausted. After that, if he was still stuck in here, then he would do whatever he had to do to ensure that Jack Kiefer moved on with his life and started building something for himself, before it was too late.

CHAPTER ELEVEN
THE WINDS OF CHANGE

Laramie, Wyoming
Late Summer 1887

Leon stood in the yard. He leaned against the hand railing for the stairs which led up to the second floor of the warehouse. There were other inmates milling about, getting some fresh air before supper time, and there were the ever-present guards, ever presently watching. But Leon was alone. He stood staring through the far wall that was just one of the walls that enclosed him. He didn't see it; he wasn't seeing anything. He was lost in his own world.

He could feel the change in the air. Odd, how summer always went by so quickly, even in this God-forsaken place. Summer was one brief respite from the blowing snow and ice of winter. He could feel the wind now, disguising itself as a soft summer breeze, just waiting for the opportunity to turn mean, for the temperatures to drop and the leaves to change color.

Just waiting . . . waiting . . .

Malachi walked by, his jaws working on a plug of tobacco. His brown-stained teeth showed in a wide grin as he greeted his friend and protector.

Leon absently responded with a breath of a smile that disappeared as soon as the other man passed by. Malachi was heading over to walk the perimeter with Ames. It seemed that Malachi and Ames had struck up a friendship.

That could get interesting, what with Ames's predisposition for setting fires, and Ky's fascination with explosives.

Better keep an eye on those two.

Lobo wasn't in the yard, which didn't surprise Leon. Lobo didn't really socialize with anyone, lone wolf that he was. Even in Elk

Mountain, it had taken Lobo a couple of years before he really settled in as part of the gang. Leon's lips tightened in a show of irritation when he thought of his underling—oh, Lobo would hate being referred to as an "underling". A flash of a malicious smile loosened Leon's lips as he thought about how easy it was to get a rise out of that wolf.

What was the matter with that old reprobate, anyway? Leon's expression turned furtively reflective and his brow tightened. *What makes him think he's so different from the rest of us? Nobody likes being in here—well, except Malachi, maybe—so why can't he just accept his fate and stop acting like the whole world has done him a disservice? 'Any man who would accept this over an honorable death wasn't worth the money posted on him!'* Leon snorted. *And I thought Karma was a prima donna.*

He took a deep breath and let it out with a sigh. His thoughts returned to the visitors he'd had earlier that afternoon, and another smile played about his lips, only this time it was genuine and filled with affection.

Caroline had come by along with her husband of one month. Officially, it had been a visit with his lawyer, accompanied by his assistant, but, in reality, it had been a visit with his good friend, accompanied by her new husband . . .

***

Earlier that day
The Visit

"Oh, Peter, it's so good to see you. I had hoped to get out earlier, but as soon as we got back from San Francisco, there were so many things that had to be taken care of right away. Steven had many cases on the go that needed some immediate attention, since he'd been away from them for two weeks. And our new home needed some organizing if we ever intend to feel comfortable living there!"

"That's all right, Caroline. It's good to see you."

"San Francisco was fascinating! And your friend, Mr. Redikopp, was so kind and generous. He took us out to some of the finest restaurants I've ever been in—ones that I could never have imagined in my wildest dreams, they were so exquisite. And they had music with live orchestras, and even a singer who came out on the small stage to sing while we had dinner. I'd never heard anything so beautiful before. I would never have believed that a woman could sing like that, if I hadn't heard it with my own ears.

"And all the sights were so amazing. Though Mr. Redikopp wasn't able to spend every day with us, he did have one of his employees take us around town and to all the different attractions, so that by the time we'd return to our hotel room in the evenings, all I could do was sleep. Oh well, actually that's not entirely true . . ." Then she blushed sweetly and sent an embarrassed smile to her husband.

Leon's brows went up as his dimples peeked through, and he sent a humorous glance to Steven.

Steven was using all his practise as a lawyer in the courtroom to maintain a straight face, then the two men exchanged knowing smiles and the young lady prattled on.

"And did you see my ring? Isn't it beautiful?" She held out her left hand for her friend to see.

Leon leaned forward to admire the piece of jewelry and, he had to admit, it was an exquisite item. The instincts of the thief in him awakened as he assessed the value of the stones, and whether they would fetch more taken apart and sold separately, or kept intact and sold as a lovely piece of jewelry. He smiled and switched over to being just a friend, viewing it for what it was: a charming ring, given as a symbol of committed love.

"Yes, Caroline," was his quiet agreement, "it is beautiful."

"And he also gave me a lovely necklace and earrings as part of a matching set for the ring," she continued. "I should have thought to wear them today, so you could see them."

Leon smiled, his brain automatically calculating the value of such an exquisite collection of stones and gold.

"It's best you don't," he commented, with a smile. "Too many thieves around here for them to stay safe."

"I do wish you could have been at the ceremony," Caroline continued, without skipping a beat. "It was so lovely. Mr. Hendricks, the photographer in town, you know, he came out and took some photographs of the family. I will be sure to send you a copy just as soon as I can. Of course, it's nothing compared to how everything looked first-hand, but it'll be better than nothing. It will give you an idea anyway, of what a beautiful day it was. Why are you looking at me like that? What's so funny?"

"No, nothing's funny," Leon assured her. "I was just thinking about something you wrote to me in your letter."

"What was that?"

"That you didn't think you'd changed. That you thought you should feel different, now that you were married, but you didn't—that you were still just you. But you have changed, Caroline. Right before my eyes. You've blossomed into a beautiful young woman, and part of me is happy and excited to see you all grown up and starting out on this new adventure. But another part of me is sad. Sad to say 'goodbye' to the little girl who would rather be out bull-doggin' than wearing a dress and going to a social." He laughed. "The little girl who didn't mind defying a legal posse to protect us from their guns!"

Caroline sat quietly for a moment, scrutinizing her friend. Their eyes met and locked, and it seemed in that moment a lifetime of love and understanding passed between them.

Leon's eyes took on a sadness that he could feel right down into the pit of his soul.

Caroline sent him a soft smile, then, rules be damned, she got up from her chair, and walking around the table, she gave him a warm hug and kissed him on the top of his shaved head.

Leon hadn't expected this, and it took him by surprise, how good it felt to receive such a genuine hug from a young lady who knew him for who he was, and for what he was, yet still loved him dearly. He closed his eyes as he leaned into her arms, and she held him tight like that for a moment.

She whispered, "I love you. You'll always be my friend." She gave him another kiss and returned to her chair to sit back down beside her husband.

Leon grinned as he watched her go. Even though occupied with keeping his emotions under control, he was vaguely aware of Caroline's timing; waiting until an official visit, when there would be no guard to intervene . . .

***

Leon brought himself back to the present and made a quick survey of the yard.

He needed to pinpoint where Officer Thompson was, as he didn't feel like receiving a punch in the gut simply for having a smile on his face. There were so few pleasant memories from this place that the ones he did have, he tended to cherish, but that didn't mean he should let his shield down like that.

He released a quiet sigh of relief when he didn't spot Thompson anywhere around him. Officer Carson wasn't in the vicinity either, so maybe it was safe for him to dwell on the past for just a little while longer.

Officer Davis was in the watch tower, and Officer Murrey was casually walking around, swinging his billy club as both guards kept a general eye on the outdoor populace. Neither one of them made a habit of executing sneak attacks on the inmates, so Leon relaxed a little and allowed his eyes to close and to feel the soft breeze coax him back into his pleasant memories . . .

**

The Visit, con't.

Steven watched this whole exchange between his wife and his client, feeling a little bit of jealousy, but also feeling like he was an intruder on a private moment. He was accustomed to seeing his client taciturn and moody, or angry and hostile, or simply worried about his situation—and with good reason. But now that the moment had passed, he was smiling to himself at how the loving touch of a young woman could soften the toughest of hearts.

It reminded Steven of that day in the Cheyenne jailhouse, when Caroline had snuck into the cell to comfort her friend after his ordeal while on the stand. The defendant had still been shocky and vulnerable after those terrifying, repressed memories had re-surfaced and hit him so hard over the head. Then, there was Caroline, rushing forward to hold and hug him, totally oblivious of the disapproving stares of the male authority figures who were in attendance.

Though Steven had been in the background during that encounter, he can still remember smiling to himself at the pretty young woman's audacity and spirit. He admired her determination to be there for her friend, even though her presence in a jail cell was not considered "proper behavior" for a woman. Steven suspected that he might have fallen in love with her right then and there, it just took his brain a little bit longer than his heart to figure it out.

Steven abruptly came back from his own reminiscing and felt that perhaps it was time to move things along to the official content of the visit

"Mr. Nash," Steven got his client's attention, "part of our visit here today is because I wanted to bring you up to date on what we have accomplished so far, regarding your hearing. And since time is limited, we need to get on with it."

"Oh." Leon sat up straighter, completely focused now on his lawyer. "Of course, Mr. Granger, that's reasonable."

"Good. Officer Reece and Dr. Palin have agreed to send in testimonies, but neither wish to appear in person. I understand their reservations. Testimonials can be kept confidential, and the fewer people here who know about this beforehand, the better."

Leon nodded. "I understand that. When do you think we'll be able to get a date?"

"I doubt we will be heard before next spring."

Leon's face fell. "Oh," he mumbled. "That long? I had hoped before Christmas."

"I know." Steven looked sympathetic. "I'm afraid these wheels do not turn quickly. It is up to the judge to let us know when he can fit it in. Besides, it will probably take that long just to get everybody's testimonies organized."

"Yes, I suppose."

"Also," Steven continued, "I'm afraid your friend, Judge MacEnroe, passed away ten months ago."

"Oh." Leon's shoulders sagged with disappointment. "Yes, I am sorry to hear that." He glanced up suddenly, realizing he should clarify this comment. "I mean, not just for myself. Judge MacEnroe was an honorable person, and I am truly sorry to hear of his passing."

Steven nodded his understanding. "His assistant, Mr. Bailey, whom I believe you are also familiar with, has agreed to come forward to present Judge MacEnroe's testimony, if needs be. Post-mortem as it were."

"Ah," Leon nodded. He did recall Mr. Bailey, but he also recalled not being impressed with him.

"Dr. Soames will come forward if we need her, though she is reluctant," Steven continued. "She feels that her work in the prison is important, and if she makes too strong a stand against the system, she may be denied permission to continue with that work. Still, she admits to feeling concern about the way things are managed, so . . ."

"Yes." Leon became more engaged in the conversation now, feeling that they were finally getting into an area where he had some input. "I wouldn't want Doctor Mariam to feel that she is obligated to come forward. She's right. Her work here is very important; more important than just my situation alone. I would prefer it if she was not called forward to testify."

"I can understand you feeling that way, Mr. Nash," Steven said, "but we are uncomfortably close to not having enough eyewitnesses to the abuses here to make a hearing worthwhile. I believe that Penny's account of the unprovoked assault upon you by the senior guard will have a powerful effect but if we could also have Doctor Soames's accounts there to back it up and give details of other such incidences, that could just be what tips the scale.

"I had hoped that some of your fellow inmates would agree to give their own accounts of abuse, but none were forth-coming. I suspect they fear that word would get out that they assisted us and the reprimands could be harsh."

Leon nodded, a distant look taking over his features. Then a hint of a smile tugged at his lips.

"Yes. For a place that doesn't allow talking between the inmates, information still finds a way to make the rounds. I would have been surprised if any of them came forward."

"And it appears you were right," Steven said. "But I am still hopeful that Officer Reece will change his mind and come in person, rather than simply sending a copy of his records, but I realize he also has other issues to consider." Leon nodded agreement. "Still, with what Officer Reece and Doctor Palin are going to be submitting, well, as many different statements as I can get that all support the same accusations, the better our chances will be."

Leon pursed his lips and nodded again. "You're right, of course," he agreed, though reluctantly. "I just feel uncomfortable with these people taking chances on my account. Even sending copies of their records could still get Officer Reece and the Doc into trouble."

"They would not be doing it just on your account, Mr. Nash," Steven pointed out. "We are trying to formulate an argument against the Auburn Prison System itself. Showing through your case, specifically, and others generally, that the way the system is set up now allows physical, emotional, and psychological abuses to continue in the management of the inmates. And to show the negative long-term effects of those abuses upon the people who are unfortunate enough to be incarcerated within these walls.

"In cases such as these, risks must be taken to bring forth the truth and to force a change within the system itself. It could get dangerous. But those people who have shown a willingness to come forward, in whatever capacity, are already aware of this, since we will be challenging people in authority who do not wish to see the system changed."

Steven stopped and looked to his client for some indication of what he was thinking.

Leon's poker face was on, and he sat quietly, staring at nothing.

"We already discussed this, Mr. Nash, and you agreed to go ahead with it," Steven pointed out, forcing the convict to engage again. "Are you now having second thoughts?"

"No, no," Leon was quick to defend. "At least, not for myself. I understand and accept the risks for me. I just don't like to see others put at risk for trying to help me."

Steven sighed and sat back in his chair. He folded his arms and scrutinized his client again. Having defended Napoleon Nash during his trial, Steven had more insight into the man's character than Caroline did. He knew that Nash was protective of his friends, and that he tended to keep his cards close, and not letting too many people in past his defences This wasn't surprising, really, considering the life he had led since the death of his family, but still difficult to deal with under these circumstances.

Caroline was uncomfortable, sensing that these two men, whom she deeply cared for, were at odds with one another.

"As I have stated, Mr. Nash," Steven reiterated, "we are not doing this just for you. There is a far greater cause here than your situation alone. I realize you are accustomed to overseeing events; you are used to being in charge. You are a natural-born leader, even I can see that, and as such, you are willing to take on the responsibilities that come with leadership. You reap the benefits of success and you hold yourself accountable for the failures.

"But in this situation, you need to accept the fact that you are not the leader, you are not in control of these events, and you are not solely responsible for the outcome. Others are picking up that role and are willing to be answerable for their own choices. You have given the go-ahead for us to put forth your situation as our prime example, but beyond that, you have very little say over what is brought to light at the hearing. Nor can you influence who comes forward to testify.

"Others are making those choices for themselves. The outcome of this hearing, and the consequences, good or bad, that befall the other people involved here, are completely out of your hands. It is important that you understand this. That you accept the subordinate role in this situation and allow others to step up and take the lead. You are surrounded by friends here; friends who are willing to risk everything to help you and to see changes made in a system that is archaic to say the least. The question now is, are you still willing to accept your own risks by allowing them to do so? The last time we discussed this, you indicated that you were, and to be quite honest, it's a little late now to change your mind."

Leon sat silently, his mouth half open, and stared at the lawyer. He couldn't quite believe the reprimand he had just received, and that from a man who was at least ten years his junior. Leon smiled nervously, but for the life of him he couldn't come up with a response. Was he losing his edge? Was time spent behind bars muddling up his brain? Or could it simply be that, polite as the reprimand had been, the lawyer had managed to hit the nail on the head and force Leon to see the whole picture.

Once having realized this, Leon relaxed and nodded.

"Yes, you're right, Mr. Granger. Jack often accuses me of being too full of myself sometimes—and I guess he should know."

"Oh, Peter," Caroline assured him. "You're not that—arrogant."

He laughed. "Really?"

"Well . . ."

"Ah ha!" Then he dropped his teasing and nodded to the lawyer. "I have agreed to go ahead on this, and I will not back down. Of course, there is more at stake here than just my own personal future, and the people who want to see changes made should be able to step forward and testify. After all, if I'm willing to accept the risks, who am I to stand in the way of others doing the same?"

"My point, exactly," Steven agreed.

Leon glanced at his friend. "You made a fine choice for a husband, Caroline. I can already see that the two of you are going to do very well together."

Caroline beamed at her husband. "Yes," she agreed. "I think so too."

***

Once again, Leon came back from his musings and noticed a change in the dynamics of the prison yard. Nothing extreme, just that people were starting to make their way back indoors. Must be supper time. He pushed himself up from his leaning post and took one last look around. There was a soft breeze whispering around the yard, but there was a change in the feel of it.

Leon lifted his head and sniffed the air; yes, there was definitely a change.

A chill was coming.

***

Rocking M Ranch, Colorado
Autumn 1887

It was mid-morning on a bright, autumn Saturday, and Jack was in the barn saddling his new gelding.

Sam and Deke had done a fine job training the colt, and Deke had been right in his opinion that the young horse would make a willing partner. The more Jack became acquainted with the animal, the more pleased he was with his choice. All that was needed now, to make a great riding horse out of him, was more miles under his girth.

Riding a youngster again was fun.

He made a point of getting him out to different sections of the ranch, as well as going into town to get him used to all the different noises and contraptions that went along with being a horse in a human's world.

Today would be a little different though. Jack and Penny were going to get out for one more picnic ride before the weather became too chilly to make such an excursion enjoyable. Daisy was old enough to be left on her own for a while, since she wasn't completely dependent on mother's milk anymore. She also felt safe and happy in the company of her Uncle Midnight, so taking Karma out for a ride wasn't quite the issue that it once had been.

Jack finished tightening the girth when he heard the clop, clop of horse's hooves on the wooden floor of the aisle. He looked up to see Penny, wearing her very fetching riding habit, leading Karma into the barn for a quick brushing off and tacking up. There wasn't even a whinny of protest coming from the pasture, and Karma was unconcerned about her baby, so obviously, both were comfortable with the opportunity for some time apart.

"Where would you like to go this time, Penny?" Jack asked her. "The north pasture again?"

"No. We've been there so much lately." She tied Karma to the wall ring and picked up a brush. "Why don't we head over Pine Ridge way? Papa is thinking about buying a parcel of land up there and it would be nice to have a look at it. So many of our neighbors are still hurting after last winter. We were lucky."

"It was more than just luck," Jack commented, "but I ain't surprised your pa wants to help out where he can. Pine Ridge it is."

Penny made short work of getting Karma ready, and before many minutes had passed the two friends led their horses from the barn in preparation of heading out on their ride.

The two little dogs had been hanging around with the humans and then followed them outside to see if anything more was going on that they could be a part of. But once their humans had mounted up and were heading away, they knew they weren't going along, so they both settled in beside old Rufus, who was stretched out in the sun and hadn't moved a muscle all morning. He made a really nice pillow.

"Have you come up with a name for him yet?" Penny asked. "You've had him for a while now, don't you think it's time you stopped referring to him as 'the new horse'?"

"Yeah, I know," Jack sighed. "I'm not good at pickin' names. How about Midnight the second?"

"No," Penny responded with a bit of heat. "That's not fair to either one of them. Midnight is Midnight. You need to give this fellow his own name."

"Hmm, I suppose," came the mumbled response. "I guess I'm just waitin' for somethin' to come ta mind."

"Don't wait too long," Penny advised, "or his name is going to be 'Hey You'."

Jack grinned. "Yup."

"Oh, all right, I'll drop it." Penny gave in with a laugh. "Karma is fighting with me here. I think she's ready for a gallop. Shall we?"

"After you."

***

Two hours later, the friends casually sat their horses as they looked out over the aforementioned land parcel.

"What do you think?" Penny asked.

"I dunno," Jack admitted. "Just looks like land ta me. What would ya need it for?"

"We lost a lot of stock this past winter," Penny reminded him. "Land is money, and with this parcel, we'd have good grazing again to expand our cattle herd and try to build it back up. There are also good timber stands that will add to our lumber interests. Then, if we can improve the quality we already have with our horses, we just might be able to get the ranch up and running at a good profit again. The cattle used to bring in a good revenue, but now, maybe horses are the way to go. Our lumber is still doing well, but after last year's drought, we have to be careful how we harvest it."

"Yeah, I suppose. I guess I just don't know enough about business and buildin' up somethin' like this, ta really be able to give an opinion. All Leon and I ever did was live one day at a time, even when we had money."

"Well, yes. I can understand that," Penny commented while Karma stamped a back foot and swished at an annoying fly. "You probably didn't even think you had a future, so what was the point of planning for it?"

"Yeah."

"But you do have a future now," Penny pointed out. "It's not too late to start making plans."

"Yeah, I know," Jack agreed, then laughed. "I actually have a bank account. Can you believe that? The Kansas Kid has a bank account."

"Of course, you do," Penny said. "You have a job, you get paid, and you have a bank account. See, you're already planning for your future. You just didn't know it."

Jack stretched out his back, then leaned onto his saddle horn while the two horses grazed.

"Yeah, I suppose," he commented, though not sounding

convinced. "All I can see in my future right now is gettin' Leon his pardon. I can't focus on other plans 'til that gets taken care of."

"I know," Penny agreed with him. "That's important, and none of us are going to let that go." Jack nodded. "But that doesn't mean you can't still be laying the groundwork for your life after that. In fact, if you don't mind my saying, it seems to me that you are already doing this, whether you are aware of it or not."

Jack tensed, just a bit. He wasn't sure he liked the sound of that.

Penny realized she might have given the wrong impression and quickly backstepped. She reached over and put a consoling hand on her friend's arm.

"Oh, no, Mathew. I didn't mean to say that you were going to turn your back on Peter. None of us are planning on doing that. I just meant that you are settling into a new life now, a life that's offering you a future. Isn't that what you and Peter both want?"

Jack relaxed, then sighed. "I don't know. I suppose," he mumbled. "I just can't imagine movin' on into new ventures without Leon with me. We've always been partners—still are. It don't seem right ta be makin' plans for my future while he's still in there."

"But I'm not suggesting that you are," Penny defended herself. "Only that you are laying in the groundwork for when that future becomes available to you. For both of you." She sent him a coyish glance. "Hopefully that future will continue to be right here in Arvada. Everyone considers you a permanent resident of our town now, and whether you agree with me or not, I still believe that is a good thing."

Jack smiled at her. "Okay. I'll grant ya that much."

"Good." Penny considered the matter closed. "Now, how about we find a nice, comfortable spot and settle in for some lunch?"

"Sounds good to me."

It didn't take long for a spot under a tree to make itself available. Stripping the horses of their tack, they sent them out to graze close to the small stream that gurgled past their chosen site. Then they settled in for their own repast.

Short work was made of the sandwiches and lemonade, and then they sat back and relaxed for a while, enjoying the warmth that the fall sun was still willing to give them, before the afternoon turned the air chilly.

"So, do you think Karma is in foal again?" Penny asked, already sure of it herself.

Departures

"I expect so," Jack agreed with her unspoken opinion. "It's been over a month since we sent her and Daisy back to Pine Knot. There's been no sign of her comin' into season again, so, I expect she is."

"Yes, I think so, too." Penny smiled prettily. "Papa deserves to get his colt this time, and if Daisy is anything to go by, this new blood is really going to bring our breeding program up a few notches."

"Well, good," Jack nodded. "I know Leon is hopin' so too. I guess he's feelin' a little obligated to your pa, for all he has done and is still doin' for us."

"You don't owe him anything, Mathew," Penny informed him. "Actually, helping you and Peter now is his way of paying you back."

"I know that's what he says," Jack countered, "but we didn't really do nothin'. And besides, even what he feels we did do for 'im, he's more than paid us back for that. I mean, it was those idiots from back East who were willin' ta pay big money for some so-called history, who gave Cameron the break, not us."

"Well, it was because of you," Penny pointed out. "And even at that, you both did a lot to help us. That money you gave us seemed to be the catalyst that put all the rest of it in motion. If it wasn't for you and Peter, we would never have been able to sell that old ranch and buy this place, along with some good quality breeding stock. And since then, aside from this past winter, we've been growing by leaps and bounds." She smiled conspiratorially. "I do all the books for the ranch now. I know Papa is a very wealthy man, Mathew. Even after last year's devastation. Whether it was your conscious intent or not, it was you and Peter who gave this family the step up that we needed, and all we've had to do is help it to grow.

"So, don't you go feeling like you have to pay anything back, all right? Papa is just thrilled to be able to use Karma to get our new foundation sire, and that's enough."

"Yeah, all right." Jack smiled. "I suppose Karma will give him a colt one of these times."

Penny sent him a knowing smile. "I know she will."

Jack sent her a dubious frown, but before he could comment on her confidence, she shivered and changed the subject.

"I'm getting chilly. Let's say we head home, okay?"

"Yeah. It's gettin' on ta that time, anyway," Jack agreed. "I'll go collect the horses if you wanna start packin' up here."

Jack got to his feet and offered his hand to Penny, then he turned and headed to where the two horses were contentedly grazing. He was pondering Penny's apparent confidence concerning the gender of the new foal, when he was brought up short in his musings by the actions of the horses.

Simultaneously, both animals spooked on the spot, and with heads and tails up, they stared back toward Penny, wide-eyed and with flared nostrils blowing out their agitation.

Then Karma flattened her ears and, with a bellow of rage, she charged past Jack and ran at Penny in full attack mode.

Jack pivoted, pulling his six-shooter, just as he heard Penny's terrified scream. His brain spun. Penny stood with her back to him as Karma came at her at full speed and sent her sprawling into the dirt.

Jack froze. He couldn't believe what he was seeing.

Then the air was rent by the unmistakable roar of an enraged cougar. Penny's body had completely hidden the emaciated predator from Jack's view, and even now, all he saw was a blurred, tawny image before the big mare met the full force of the cat's leap. Amongst angry snarls and flailing legs, the cougar did a somersault over the horse's withers and landed on its back with an indignant grunt.

But it was on its feet again in an instant and screamed its anger at this foolish equine who had dared to interfere with its hunting. It charged at the horse, lashing out with claws ready to rip and shred the flesh from her bones, and teeth aching to sink into the neck and tear out her throat.

Karma jumped away from the lethal weapons. She nimbly hopped over the angry feline and in one swift movement, she stretched her head down and grabbed hold of the end of the cat's tail.

Penny ran into Jack's arms, her terrified gasps turning to sobs. They both shook with fear and adrenaline as they stood and watched in disbelief as Karma began her deadly dance.

With the end of the tail clamped tightly in her jaws, Karma started to spin on her hind quarters. Faster and faster she spun, swinging the cat in the air around with her. The cat was furious, screaming and snarling, and trying for all it was worth, to double itself over and get its front claws into the horse's face. But the centrifugal force was too much for the cat to fight against, and all its indignant rage was for naught.

Then Karma began to drop her head as she spun, slamming the cat into the ground. Spinning and slamming, spinning again and whacking the cat's head into a tree trunk, then spinning and slamming it into the ground again.

The cat screamed and fought, its legs flailing, until it encountered the tree trunk, at which point, there was a loud crack as the cat's skull exploded, and then the next whap into the ground broke its neck. After that, all Karma did was spin and pound a dead piece of meat.

Knowing she had accomplished her mission, Karma slowed her spin until she came to a complete stop. She released her grip on the tail, and the dead cat flopped onto the ground, a broken and bloody mass of tawny hair and useless claws. Karma reached down to sniff it; she pawed at it a couple of times to make sure, then snorted and shook her head. She looked at her two humans with pricked ears and eyes bright with pride. Then, with a toss of her dark chestnut mane, she trotted over to the young gelding who was trembling and sweating with fear, and in need of some reassurance.

Jack and Penny stood in each other's embrace and stared with open mouths at the dead cat, neither one of them quite believing what they had just witnessed. They were both still shaking with shock and were in no hurry to let go of one another.

Other than heart-pounding fear, Jack wasn't sure what he felt. Now that the attack was over, the realization of how close he had come to losing Penny filled him with terror that he was going to lose her; that his own stubbornness could have prevented a life of happiness with her, before it had even begun.

Now Penny was safe in his arms, pressing against him, and the feel of her breasts pushing against his chest sent electric impulses through his body. He could feel her heart beating wildly, and he held her tighter, not wanting to let her go. He was still shaking, and his breathing was heavy, but it wasn't just from shock now, it was with excitement and arousal.

"Oh, Mathew . . ." Her voice was just a shaking whisper as she clung onto him. "That cat was going to kill me. Did Karma really do that?"

Jack took her chin in his hand and tilted her face up until she was looking into his eyes. Her breath caught, and her heart was suddenly in her throat, as she saw the passion in those blue depths gazing down at her.

"Mathew . . ." It was a whisper on the wind.

"Penny," he breathed softly.

"Yes?"

"The name's 'Jack'."

Then he leaned down and kissed her fully on the mouth.

CHAPTER TWELVE
THE BETRAYAL

Passion rose in Penny, sensations she had never experienced before flooded her body. Not even that day, over two years ago, when she had brazenly stolen her first kiss from Jack, had she felt such arousal. She reached around him and pressed him into her embrace, feeling his body against hers and knowing that he wanted her.

She was filled with so many emotions that her whole core trembled. Her breath came in short gasps.

Is this it? Is this when I'm going to finally find out what it's all about?

She wanted him so badly, and her only concern was that, through her own inexperience, she might disappoint him.

She felt his right arm encircle her waist, pulling her in even closer to him, and then his left hand was behind her head and his kiss went deeper. She opened to him and suddenly felt her breath catch, not only with all the new sensations, but from the passions reaching up from her heart and grabbing hold of her throat from the inside, making it hard for her to breathe.

Then Jack groaned, and he pushed away from her. He trembled, and his breath came heavy, but slow. He shook his head and, caressing her cheek, he looked with regret into her eyes.

"We shouldn't do this." His voice was a wisp on the wind. "This ain't right. We should wait."

Penny felt a wave of disappointment wash over her. "No." Her voice trembled. "I don't want to wait."

"I don't want to hurt you," he said. "And it will hurt you. I don't want to frighten you."

"It's all right." She reached up to stroke his face. "Caroline told me about her wedding night; she told me what to expect. It's all right.

I'm not frightened."

He leaned into her, hugging her to him, and she could feel his breath tickling her ear.

"This ain't right," he repeated. "Your folks are trustin' me. We should wait until we're married."

Penny felt a thrill of excitement wash over her. Married! He'd actually said it. Now she wanted him more than ever.

"It is right," she whispered. "I want you." And she pressed her body against his, until she could feel his arousal.

He moaned with the intensity of her closeness. For an instant, flashes of the nightmare he'd had while convalescing at David's home, came back to him, but he knew that this was nothing like his dream. Even though Penny was responding to her desires, he knew she was still a maiden. But instead of being disappointed with her naivety, the knowledge that he would be furrowing into virgin soil caused his arousal to intensify rather than diminish.

He unbuckled his gunbelt and set it aside, then returned his attention to the young woman awaiting him. "I'm going to unbutton your blouse now. Is that okay?"

Penny giggled with nervous excitement. "Yes."

Jack smiled as his fingers made short work of the fastenings. He pushed the blouse off her shoulders and tossed it to the ground. Then, without asking permission this time, he tackled the undergarment, and it fell open. With his eyes on hers to see her reaction, he slipped his warm hand inside the material and gently cupped one of her breasts.

Penny caught her breath. She closed her eyes and moaned with the unexpected pleasure. Her nipples were alive with new sensations, so when Jack gently pinched one and began to roll it between his fingers, her eyes shot open, and she gasped for air.

Jack smiled. "Are you all right?"

She drew in a deep breath. "Oh yes. Oh my gosh . . ."

Jack took this as permission to proceed. He opened the garment, pushing it off her shoulders and letting it drift to the grass. And there he stood, gazing upon her breasts and thinking that they were the most beautiful breasts he had ever seen, and he'd seen quite a few.

"You're so beautiful, Penny."

She smiled, seeing the appreciation in his eyes as he gazed upon her nakedness. "Are they all right?" she asked him in nervous hopefulness. "Do you like them?"

Jack laughed. "Oh yes. I like them very much."

He came in to caress them again, then he slipped his hands around her waist and pulled her into a deep, sensuous kiss, feeling her breasts pressing enticingly upon his chest.

Penny allowed herself to be pulled in to him. Just as he loved the feeling of her breasts against him, she was intensely aware of his hard arousal pressing against her tummy.

Oh my, he's so big. I hope he fits.

He released her so he could pull off his own shirts. He didn't bother to unbutton them, but simply grabbed the material and pulled them over his head. Once discarded, he unbuckled his belt and his trousers then kicked off his boots.

She watched him do it, both her nervousness and excitement growing with this new adventure. She saw his erection peeking out through the opening, but she wasn't sure what to do with it.

He kissed her on the top of her head as he hugged her closer.

"Are you okay with this?"

"Yes. I just don't know . . ."

"That's okay. You ain't expected ta know." He breathed into her ear as he pushed his trousers down over his hips. "Feel your way."

Taking courage from his words, Penny allowed her curiosity to take hold. She pushed away from Jack and slid her trembling fingers upon his arousal.

Jack groaned with the excitement of her touch, and he encouraged her to go deeper.

"They're so hard," she whispered as her hand gently encased his sack. "Doesn't that hurt when you ride a horse?"

She heard a soft, husky chuckle. "They ain't hard all the time, darlin'. Only when they're awake."

"Oh."

Jack pulled her to him again and shifted so she could explore deeper. He groaned with pleasure from her presence.

"Does that feel good?" she asked.

"It sure does, darlin'. Oh, but no, you better stop doin' that."

"Oh. Did I do something wrong?"

"No. It just feels too good. If we ain't careful, I'll be done before we even get started."

Penny frowned. If it felt so good, why stop?

But she accepted his word and withdrew from the warm nest.

She felt him gently push her downward, and she went willingly. She lay back into the sweet-smelling grass, and he came down with her and kissed her again. She ran her fingers through his curls and then caressed his arm. He lifted from her and kissed her neck.

She giggled, cringing away from him. "That tickles."

"Do ya want me ta stop?"

She turned serious eyes upon him, and they locked gazes.

"No."

Jack kissed her again, then he sat up, and his deft fingers worked loose just enough buttons on her riding skirt for him to pull it off. He then turned his attention to her bloomers.

Penny's nerves jangled and she trembled with excitement. She groaned as her last shred of clothing was stripped from her.

She felt Jack's hand slide in between her thighs and then, to her surprise, his fingers, those strong, manly fingers, gently massaged her center.

Then she was hit with another surprise. She gasped and her body arched as Jack's talented caresses found her clitoris. She couldn't believe the sensations that surged through her—pain and pleasure all in one. The aching down below was unbearable, and her body squirmed with anticipation.

Now out of her control, her knees widened, and she opened for him.

Jack accepted the invitation. She felt his hard fingers slip inside her and begin to stroke. She was hardly aware of anything other than what he was doing to her, and the wild, exotic sensations his actions caused.

Just when she thought that it couldn't get any better than this, that the intensity couldn't grow beyond what it was, she was surprised again.

Still keeping his fingers caressing inside her, Jack came forward and began to kiss her tummy. Slowly, he kissed his way up to her breast and then his warm tongue encircled the nipple, titillating it into a hard erection. Sealing his lips around the pink flower, he sucked a mouthful of breast into his mouth and took a gentle hold on the nipple with his teeth.

Penny gasped as her body squirmed with longing. She didn't know if it was his mouth or his fingers still stoking her inside that fired her passion. Then he changed tactics, and those talented fingers found her hidden center again and began a focused assault upon it.

Penny writhed with the electrical impulse that surged her.

Oh, my goodness! Caroline never told me about this!

A soft scream escaped her lips as part of her wanted to escape the torment, but another part gasped with the pleasure. Her body started to buck, but he wouldn't let her go. He continued his assault upon her nipple and clit, using his weight to pin her to the ground.

All concern about hurting her was erased by his bent-up desire. She had opened the flood gates, and now he held her firmly, as she bucked and gasped, trying to get away from the torment, but not wanting him to stop.

The pressure inside her mounted as though she was going to explode at any moment. She felt like she'd wet herself.

Is that right? Is that supposed to happen?

Then, just when she thought she was about to reach the height of ecstasy, he released her. She groaned and collapsed into a panting puddle.

"Oh my gosh. Why did you stop?"

"Can't have ya reachin' too soon, darlin'. I ain't finished playin'."

Penny frowned through her panting. "What do you mean?"

But all he did was smile.

Returning his full attention to her breasts, his fingers squeezed and rolled her one nipple, as his mouth, along with that hard tongue, made an assault upon the other.

Her sexual desire already at a peak, Penny's eyes rolled back as she floated into heaven. Her lower body still pulsated from Jack's attention, but now both her breasts were alive and stealingss her breath away.

Nothing Caroline had told her of this moment came close to the reality of it. The throbbing down below intensified, as her hands clasped his, encouraging them to continue their assault upon her nipples.

But Jack knew that the time had come to take them both to the edge and beyond.

He again kissed his way down her tummy, pausing briefly at her belly button where the hard tip of his tongue dug in, causing her to cry out loud with the intense sensations.

But Jack didn't linger there; he was a man on a mission now. He carried on past her belly button and headed for the treasure. He felt the hairs on her nest of curls tickle his chin, and he smelled her sexuality inviting him to go further. He kissed her blonde tangle, and he felt her tremble and groan with desire. He wanted so much to dig into her with his tongue, but even in his fevered state, his instincts told him to not indulge in that intimate delicacy just yet.

She felt Jack lift up and position himself, his erection taking up space between her legs, and then his fingers probing, seeking out her wet invitation. She shifted her hips to make it easier for him to get on track. She was ready for him, there was no doubt about that, and once he was sure of his bearings, he gently pushed into her. She felt him enter and she gasped.

He forced himself to stop where he was. "Are you all right?"

She groaned. "Please . . .don't . . ."

Disappointment surged through him. Did he go too far? Was she still too young, after all?

She drew a deep breath, widening her legs for him.

"Don't . . . stop . . . now . . ."

Jack sighed with relief. Still only part way inside her, it would have been agony to pull out. Everything about her was drawing him in deeper. But he knew, despite his desire, and her willingness, he needed to take care. He went slowly, caressing her, not forcing his way in. As tortuous as it was for him to hold back, he advanced only a little bit at a time, and he watched her, looking for any sign that she was frightened, or that she wanted him to stop.

But that sign never came. Her back bowed just a bit, her eyes were closed and her mouth just partly open, with the occasional quiet gasp emitting from it. She let him come on, encouraging him to push inward, accepting the pain and drowning in the pleasure.

Then he hesitated again, as the reality of what he was doing broke through the drug of passion. This was it, the moment of truth. One more push and there'd be no going back. But instead of feeling guilt, he was overwhelmed with excitement and desire. Even as his logical mind told him this was wrong, his body thrust forward and he felt himself push through to the hilt.

Penny gasped and let out a groaning cry.

Jack hesitated, afraid that he had hurt her too much, but she smiled through her panting and pulled him in closer. She didn't want him to stop, not now—this was ecstasy, and she wanted more.

Finally, gently, Jack settled into her and marveled at how soft and warm she felt now that she completely encased him. He hugged her then, and started to kiss her, and she allowed this moment to engulf her.

"Are you okay?" His voice floated through her consciousness. "Does it feel good?"

"Ohh, it's wonderful," she whispered from her heavenly place. "I love the feeling of you inside me. When I first saw it, I thought it was too big to fit. But it's perfect."

Jack chuckled as he nestled into her neck. "Yeah, funny how that works."

He came down on her mouth then, kissing her hard as passion filled both their hearts. Then finally, he could wait no longer, and he began to thrust.

Penny gasped and rounded her back again. It felt so good and so natural, she couldn't understand why they had waited this long. Jack continued to pump faster and deeper, and she opened to him even more.

Then she felt the muscles deep inside start to tighten just as they had against his fingers, as though she were trying to push him out. But she didn't want him out and apparently, he didn't want out either, because that tightness only caused him to push harder.

They held on tightly to each other, their gasping breaths becoming vocal as their passions escalated. Penny tightened up on him, more and more, and she was amazed at what her body was doing, and that she even had muscles in there that could do that. Her body had taken over and she could feel it coming—something coming. She bucked and writhed, as Jack held on tight and his thrusting intensified. Then suddenly, she reached her peak and with a rush of ecstasy, her body convulsed, and she cried out with the joy of it.

Jack squeezed her as he continued to pump, then groaned with his own pleasure when he felt the rush of her ejaculation surround him and bring him to his own climax. He desperately clung to her, pressing his lips into hers as he felt his own orgasm coming to a head. He pounded into her, both of them moaning with each thrust, until he felt his release.

Penny lay back, exhausted.

Their breathing began to slow down, and Jack's thrusting became quieter, gentler, until he finally stopped completely. And there they lay together, holding one another in a mutual bath of sweat, listening to their hearts slowly returning to a normal rhythm.

Penny didn't want it to end. She felt as though she could lay there in the grass, encased in his arms for ever and ever. But gradually, she could feel herself losing him, and then he slid out. But he continued to hold her, and they lay there, caressing each other and whispering endearments, until they both started to feel the chill of late afternoon settling in, and they began to shiver.

Jack glanced up and surveyed the surrounding area. The two horses were contentedly grazing, and other than that, there was not another living soul around. He stood and offered a hand to his lady.

"I hate to say it, Penny, because it's going to be cold, but we better go to the creek down there and wash off. Otherwise, your folks are gonna know instantly what went on up here."

"Oh." A look of alarm flashed across her face, and taking his hand, she allowed him to pull her to her feet.

He stopped her and taking her naked body into his arms once more, he pressed her against himself and stroked her hair. He looked down into her eyes and smiled at her.

"Are you all right?"

She smiled right back up at him. "Yes. I'm better than all right. You're wonderful. I love you—I always have."

Jack smiled and pulled her into a deeper hug. "I know. I love you too. I'm sorry it took me so long to be able to say it, or even to allow myself to feel it. But I do, Penny. I do love you."

They held each other for a few more minutes, not wanting to let it go. Then they knew they had to and gingerly made their way down to the creek. The water was indeed cold, but they braved the elements and amidst laughing and playful protesting, they splashed each other down until they were thoroughly washed off.

Jack trotted over to their picnic area and making a point of not looking at the dead cat, he snatched up the picnic blanket and returned to Penny, so they could use it to dry themselves off.

Soon they were mounted up and heading for home, before darkness caught them still out on the trail.

***

Over supper, that evening, all the excited talk was about the close call with the cougar and what an amazing thing Karma had done to save her young mistress from certain death.

Cameron and Jean listened intently, feeling both fear over the safety of their daughter, and amazement over the actions of the mare. Any sign of self-consciousness or anxiety between the couple at the table was automatically accredited to the events of the day that involved a cat—and nothing more.

"Do you want to ride up there again tomorrow and see if you can salvage the pelt?" Cameron asked.

"Naw, no point," Jack said. "That cat was old and malnourished, which was probably why it risked makin' such an attack in the first place."

"Well," Cameron stated, "I guess that settles it. We can't have a memorable event like this take place, and not own the land where it happened."

"I'll certainly drink to that," Jack agreed and sent a quick smile to Penny.

***

The next morning, Penny came clomping down the stairs, all bright and happy, with a twinkle in her eye and a skip in her step. Her mother was in the kitchen getting breakfast going, and keeping Eli occupied, all at the same time.

"Penny!"

"Yes, Mama?"

"Could you please come in here and feed Eli his breakfast? He's being a little hellion this morning."

Penny's shoulders slumped, but she tried not to show her disappointment.

"Yes, Mama," she agreed, then quickly changed direction and headed into the kitchen rather than out to the barn where she knew Jack was feeding the livestock.

In the kitchen, Eli sat in his highchair, banging the spoon and flinging what was left of his oatmeal onto the floor and onto his mother, not to mention rubbing it into his hair.

"You little monster," Penny accused him.

Eli laughed at her. "Mo'ster," he agreed.

"Yes. Monster—you. You're old enough to be feeding yourself, you know."

He laughed again and threw another spoonful of oatmeal at his sister.

She snatched the spoon and bowl away from him and, grabbing a wet cloth, set about cleaning him up.

Jean smiled as she dished out another serving of breakfast for him.

"Try and get as much into him as you can, Penny," she said. "If he won't eat it, then he'll just have to stay hungry until lunch."

"Yes, Mama."

"That was some adventure you had yesterday," Jean commented. "Gives me the shivers just thinking about what a close call you had."

"Yes," Penny agreed. "It was very terrifying at first. But then watching Karma attack that cat—I didn't think a horse would do that."

"Nor did I. A mule will do something like that, but not usually a horse," Jean agreed. "I'd say that becoming a mother has awakened the protective instinct in her, and she certainly is fond of you."

"Yes, I suppose so,' Penny commented absently as she tried to spoon oatmeal into her squirming brother, "and poor Jack was absolutely terrified that cat was going to get me."

Jean stopped stirring the oatmeal and looked at her youngest daughter.

"Jack?" she asked. "Not Mathew anymore?"

"Oh! Umm," suddenly Penny was blushing. "No, well . . . we were talking about things on the ride, and he asked me to start calling him 'Jack' from now on." She shrugged self-consciously. "I don't really know why."

"Really," Jean's tone was dry. "You and 'Jack' both seemed awfully flustered when you got back here last night. Now your papa and I assumed it was because of the excitement with the cougar, but now . . . did something else happen?"

"No, of course not, Mama," Penny insisted, a little too quickly.

Jean smiled knowingly at her daughter. "Penny, is there something you want to tell me?"

"No, Mama." But someone was looking more and more guilty as the moments passed.

"Maybe I need to ask that question another way," Jean surmised. "Is there something you need to tell me?"

Penny stood quietly, looking down at her brother and trying to think of a way out of this without actually lying to her mother. Or at least, not lying any more than she already had.

Eli got impatient; it was one thing for him to refuse to eat, but quite another for his sister to stop feeding him.

"Penny?"

"How's breakfast coming along?" Cameron asked as he poked his head into the kitchen.

Both ladies jumped, and Penny nearly dropped the bowl she held.

"Oh, Cameron!" Jean admonished him. "You startled us."

"Sorry. Need any help?"

"Well, if you want to take the coffee pot out to the table, I'll dish out the oatmeal and we'll bring it in."

"Okay."

Cameron took the pot and disappeared.

Jean sent a stern look to her daughter. "We'll talk about this later, young lady."

"Yes, Mama." Penny bit her lower lip.

***

There wasn't much opportunity throughout the rest of that day for Jean to get the chance to speak with her daughter alone. But once her suspicions were aroused, she made a point of watching Jack and Penny together. To the casual observer, there were no obvious differences in how the two people interacted. Cameron was certainly oblivious. But Jean was not just a casual observer; she was a mother, and she knew her daughter very well.

The quiet smiles the two of them exchanged, a hand on his arm, a caressing of her hair, a gentle kiss on her cheek when he thought no one was looking. By the time evening rolled around, and Jean was knocking quietly on her daughter's bedroom door, there was no longer any doubt in her mind that the relationship had changed dramatically.

"Penny, may I come in?"

"Yes, Mama," came the resigned response.

Jean entered the room and softly closed the door behind her. Penny sat on the edge of her bed, with her hands folded in her lap, looking as guilty as a dog with a pork roast. Jean smiled at her daughter's discomfort and sat down on the bed beside her, putting an arm around her shoulders to give her a gentle hug.

"I take it that your relationship with Mathew has gone through some changes?"

Penny bit her lower lip again. "Yes, Mama."

"Are you happy about it?" Jean asked her. "Is it what you wanted?"

Penny brightened up. "Oh, yes Mama."

"He didn't force you, or pressure you in any way?"

"Oh, no," Penny was adamant. "Actually, it was more—"

"The other way around?" Jean finished for her daughter.

Penny looked guilty again. "Yes."

Jean smiled and then let go a deep sigh. "I suppose I shouldn't be surprised," she reflected. "You always were more outgoing than your sister. Once you decide you want something . . ." She frowned, not sure she wanted to ask the next question, but knowing she had to. "Is there any chance we might be in for a surprise in nine months' time?"

Penny gulped and hung her head.

"Oh dear." Jean sighed. "Well, there's nothing we can do about it now, but—"

"Then you're not mad?" Penny asked with hope starting to rise.

"Well, I'm not mad, but that doesn't mean I'm pleased about it either," Jean informed her. "The proper thing would have been for you to wait for your wedding night, just as your sister did. At least, I hope that's what your sister did."

"Did you and Papa wait until you were married?"

Jean sighed. She had hoped that neither of her daughters would ever think to ask her that.

"No. No, we didn't," she admitted.

"Were you sorry you didn't wait?" Penny asked. "Did it ruin your wedding night?"

Jean smiled in fond remembrance. "No, it didn't. Actually, I have to admit, it took away the stress of all, so we were able to really enjoy our first time together as a married couple." Then she turned serious. "But that doesn't mean that this can carry on. You took an awful chance, but it's done now and there's nothing we can do about it. I just hope you're going to get away with it, this one time. But no more. Do you understand?"

"Yes, Mama," Penny agreed. "Even Jack has said much the same thing. We have to wait."

"Good." Jean was relieved, and then she sighed. "I don't like keeping secrets from your father, but in this case, I think we will all be better off if he doesn't know. Oh, your father would skin Jack alive. But no more. And I'll say as much to Jack too, if need be."

Penny smiled. "Jack?" she asked.

"Considering the direction things are going, I suppose it's time I got used to calling him that, don't you think?"

Penny's smile was filled with relief that she hadn't been chastised more severely, but in hindsight, she should have known that her mother would understand.

"Thank you, Mama."

The mother and daughter hugged, and Jean gave her daughter a kiss on the forehead.

"Now, will you come down and join us for evening tea?"

Penny nodded. "Yes."

***

A couple of evenings later, Jack was in the barn getting the horses settled for the night. It was about half an hour before the gloaming would set in, and though there was a bit of a chill in the air, it was still pleasant enough for Jean and Cameron to sit on the front porch with their cups of tea.

Jack was trying to build up the nerve to go and speak with them. Penny was occupied inside, giving her brother a bath prior to bed; it was the opportune moment.

Now or never. No guts, no glory. The early bird gets the worm— no, that's not right. That one doesn't really apply.

Damn, I can't believe how nervous I am. I feel like I'm gonna throw up. Oh, that wouldn't be good. He rubbed his hands against his trousers. *Even my palms are sweating. This is ridiculous.*

Finally, he stepped out of the barn and looked toward the house. *There they are, sitting casually on the porch, drinking their tea. I should just go over and say my piece; now or never. . .* his legs wouldn't move. He rubbed his palms on the seat of his pants again. He heard Jean laugh.

Oh, they're laughing about me now, isn't that just great. Oh brother. Well, it's gonna be dark soon. If I'm gonna do this, I better get over there and get it done.

***

"There he is now, Cameron," Jean said. "I'm sure this is it."

"What makes you think he is going to ask now, after all this time?"

Jean shrugged. "Oh, just put it down to a mother's intuition."

"Uh huh," was Cameron's opinion of that. "Well, he certainly looks nervous enough. Oh, he seems to have lost the ability to walk straight—he's going in circles now."

"Poor man," Jean commiserated. "We should put him out of his misery."

"I have a gun in the house," Cameron suggested.

Jean laughed. "Don't you dare. Well, if he doesn't get over here soon under his own steam, I'll call him over. Otherwise, Penny will be done with Eli and the opportunity will be lost. We'll have to go through this all over again."

"Heaven forbid," Cameron mumbled under his breath. Then, "Oh, here he comes."

"Evenin' folks," Jack came up the steps as he rubbed his palms on the seat of his pants, yet again.

"Good evening, Jack."

"Evening Jack. The horses all settled in?"

"Ahh, yup."

Silence.

"Something on your mind, Jack?"

"Ah, yup. Ahh, yessir."

Silence.

"Yes?"

"Well, I was hopin' that . . . ahhmm . . . I mean, I've known Penny for a long time now, and well . . . I know I'm a lot older than she is, and I don't really have much ta offer her, other than just me . . . but I was thinkin' . . ."

Oh brother, Cameron thought, *this is worse than Steven. Come on Jack, out with it.*

"Ahm," Jack was stumbling. "Well, I was hopin' that you would let me see your daughter."

"You see her all the time, Jack," Cameron pointed out. "You hardly need my permission to do that."

Jack stood with his mouth open for a moment, looking at Cameron. Oh, he was making a mess of this, and he knew it.

"No. I mean—I would like your permission to court her," Jack finally got out.

"Oh. To court her," Cameron repeated. "Well, that is a surprise. We certainly didn't see this coming."

"Cameron," Jean quietly reprimanded him.

"Oh," Jack mumbled. "Well, I know I don't have much education, I mean, not like Steven, or David, and I don't really know yet what I'm gonna do to provide for her, I mean, I ain't really given that much thought yet, what with Leon still in prison and all. I mean, I'm sure Penny could do much better than an old worn-out saddle tramp like me . . ."

"Are you trying to talk your way into this family, or out of it?" Cameron asked him.

"Well . . . into it. I hope."

Silence.

"Oh, for heaven's sakes." Jean broke under the strain. "Of course, you have our permission, Jack." She came down the steps to give him a hug, and a kiss on the cheek. "And we're pleased to give it."

Jack went weak in the knees with relief, and then he grinned like a fool as he returned Jean's hug.

"Jeez, you had me worried there for a minute."

"Only a minute?" Cameron asked as he also approached Jack, then shook his hand and gave him a slap on the back. "I must be losing my touch. Of course, you have our permission, Jack. We were beginning to wonder what was taking you so long to ask."

"Oh. Well . . ."

"C'mon. This calls for something stronger than tea," Cameron announced. "Let's go inside and have a drink. It's getting dark out here, anyway."

***

The small group made their way indoors. Cameron went to the cabinet and took out the bottle of brandy that was only poured for those "special occasions", then he took down four shot glasses, so everyone could have a celebratory toast.

"Where's Penny?" the father asked, looking around.

Penny poked her head out from the kitchen. "I'm here," she announced quietly, her whole body anxiously asking the question and awaiting the answer.

"Yes," Jack told her with a huge grin.

"Yes?" She bounced into the room and threw her arms around Jack's neck. "Oh, I'm so happy!"

Jack laughed and returned her hug. "So am I—and relieved. I don't think I was that nervous at my trial."

Then Penny jumped around to her parents, hugging them each in turn.

"Oh, Papa, thank you. Mama—thank you. I'm so happy."

"Good," said Cameron as he handed out the glasses. "You're supposed to be." He raised his glass in a toast. "To my daughter; Penelope, sweetheart, you've grown into a fine young woman, and I couldn't be prouder of you. I know this is just the first step toward a more serious commitment, but it is a first step that I am very pleased to condone. May it be a joyful journey."

Everyone raised their glasses.

"Thank you, Cameron."

"Thank you, Papa."

Glasses tapped, and everyone took a drink.

Penny grimaced.

CHAPTER THIRTEEN
MOVIN' FORWARD

Laramie, Wyoming

Leon's dimples took over his face with the smile he beamed as Jack sat down at the table opposite him.

"You did it, didn't you?"

"Did what?" Jack asked him.

"Don't give me 'did what'," Leon threw back at him. He sent a furtive glance back at Officer Pearson then leaned forward and continued in a whisper, "Ya did Penny, didn't you."

"Jeez, Leon. Do ya have ta put it like that?" Jack griped. He should have known he wouldn't be able to hide it. His uncle could read him like one of them dang books he was always delving into. "But, yeah, we . . . got together."

"Yeah, ha, ha!" Leon was so happy, he almost bounced out of his chair. "That's great. It's about time. Was it good?"

"Well, yeah." Jack squirmed. "Course it was good. We . . . well, you know . . . we . . . yeah, a course it was good."

"Aww, that's great, Jack." Leon couldn't stop grinning. "And Penny's happy? You didn't hurt her, did you? You didn't scare her off?"

Jack sent his uncle an incredulous look.

"Of course, I didn't scare her off. I was real gentle—well most of the time. But she liked it. I didn't do nothin' she didn't want." His expression softened with remembrance, but then he frowned at his uncle. "What is this? You've never been overly interested in my romancin' before."

"Yeah, but this is different," Leon defended himself. "I mean, this is the real thing, right? You're not just stringing her along, right?"

"Of course, it's the real thing," Jack threw back at him, all indignant. "What kinda guy do ya think I am?"

"Well," Leon shrugged, "a guy."

Jack glared at him. "You're a fine one ta talk. How many broken hearts have you left on your back trail?"

"Not nearly as many as you, Casanova."

Jack frowned. "Casa, what?"

"Ah, never mind. And you definitely have an advantage these days. It's not like I'm getting any in here," Leon frowned with disappointment, then mumbled, "At least, not the kind I want."

Jack paled slightly and looked uncomfortable. "Oh. I never thought . . ."

"Naw, don't worry about it," Leon told him. "One fella tried when I first got here, but he didn't get very far." He smiled as a wicked gleam sparked his eyes. "And it probably took him a good month before he was capable of trying it with anyone else. No—those fellas leave me alone now."

"Yeah, that's good," Jack said, and meant it. "It just never occurred to me that stuff like that would go on in here, but I suppose . . . it does make sense . . ."

"Oh yeah." Leon nodded and cocked a brow. "Doesn't mean I have to take it, though. No; the only excitement I can look forward to is getting second-hand details from you."

"Yeah, well, you're not gonna be gettin' much of that anymore, neither," Jack informed him. "Penny and me are officially courtin' now, so I'm done visitin' the brothels."

"Really?" Leon cocked an incredulous brow. "So . . . you're staying celibate now, or are you and Penny going to . . .?"

"No! We're not gonna," Jack insisted. "That one time, well, it just happened. I respect Penny, so no, we're gonna wait 'till we get married."

"Ohhh . . . I see." Leon was skeptical. "You're planning on getting married soon then?"

"Just as soon as we get you outta here."

Leon's brows went up. "Ahh, jeez, Jack. I mean, I really appreciate you wanting to wait for me, but that could be a while yet, you know. You really think you can hold out that long?"

"I'm just gonna hav'ta," Jack insisted. "Penny and me discussed it, and neither one of us wants ta get married until you can be there too. And I promised Cameron that since Penny and me are now officially courtin', I would stay away from the brothels. That was the agreement."

Leon continued with his skepticism. "Is that a promise you can keep?"

"Yeah, Leon, it is!" Jack defended himself and the virtue of his lady. "It's just like the promise we made to the governor ta stop robbin' and such. It was tough at times, but we did it, didn't we? I'm just gonna hafta be strong."

"Uh huh. You've said this before and look how long that lasted."

"Yeah, well . . ." Jack looked abashed. "I'll just have ta try harder." Then he grinned. "Look at it this way; it'll give me even more incentive ta get you outta here sooner."

Leon grinned. "Yeah, there is that." Then he sat back and scrutinized his nephew. "Do Jean and Cameron know about your little 'indiscretion'?"

"Jean does," Jack admitted. "Cameron don't. And we're all gonna try ta keep it that way."

"Hmm, that's wise. Still, how do you feel about that?"

"I dunno." Jack contemplated the question. "I thought I would feel guilty about it, you know, goin' behind his back like that, after everything he's done for us, and all. But, I don't. Now I feel guilty about not feelin' guilty. You know what I mean?"

"Knowing you, yeah, I know what you mean."

"What does that mean?"

"Well . . . just that you feel obligated to Cameron. We both do. And fathers are pretty protective of their daughters." Leon allowed a whisper of a sardonic smile to touch his lips. "Even I'm aware of that."

"Yeah."

"And you know that what you did was going against him," Leon continued, "so, you think you should be feeling guilty about it. On the other hand, you and Penny are adults, and your intentions are honorable; you're not just using her, then throwing her aside. You're planning on marrying her. So, as adults, there's no reason for you to feel guilty. You kind of put yourself into a no-win situation there, my friend."

"Yeah, I know," Jack agreed. "All the more reason why we can't let it happen again."

"Hmm. Yeah well, good luck with that one."

"Yeah."

"So, how's Karma doing?" Leon asked, sensing it was time to change the subject. "Is she in foal again?"

Jack brightened up and grinned. "Yeah, we're pretty sure she is, and at this point, I'm tendin' to agree with Cameron that she's gonna have a colt this time."

Leon creased his brow. "Everybody keeps saying that, but I don't get it. How could you know?"

"Well, Penny explained it to me and showed me the breeding records ta back it up," Jack said. "Accordin' to that, the first two times ya breed a stallion to the same mare, it's likely you'll get a colt one time and a filly the next. But it's gotta be two years in a row. After that, it's anybody's guess."

Leon's expression became skeptical, and by the time Jack was finished with his explanation, Leon was looking at him as though the world had gone mad. Even Officer Pearson gave a cynical snort at the conclusion of this statement, and Jack felt himself at a bit of a disadvantage.

"I know it sounds like just a fluke," Jack conceded.

"Uh huh," Leon agreed, along with a disbelieving nod from Pearson.

"But it's all right there in the breedin' records," Jack insisted. "Over the years that Cameron has been breedin' horses, this is the pattern that has emerged, so I would have ta agree; Karma is likely gonna give Cameron a colt this time."

Leon shrugged. "Okay, Jack. I guess time will tell."

"Yeah, that's what I said." Then Jack smiled and moved the conversation along. "There's somethin' else Karma did that completely amazed me—I didn't think horses would do such a thing."

"Oh yeah?" Leon's face beamed with pride in his mare, even though he had no idea what she had done.

As Jack proceeded to inform them of Karma's encounter with the cougar, both inmate and guard listened with amazed intensity, neither one quite believing what they were hearing.

"That's incredible," Pearson commented. "I've never heard of a horse doing that."

Both ex-outlaws glanced back at the guard, and he shrugged his shoulders in his own defense.

"Well, it is incredible," he insisted.

Leon looked back at his nephew and smiled. "He's right. That is incredible." He sat back, and his expression turned reflective. "I mean, I always knew she was intelligent and loyal, but I never would have thought that a horse would do something like that." A hint of sadness drifted across his face. "She and Penny must have a really close bond."

"Yeah, Leon, they do," Jack agreed. "But Penny will be takin' over Daisy for her ridin' horse. Even she knows that Karma is yours. She don't wanna move in on that. Jean thinks it's more because Karma has become a mother and is in foal again, so her protective instincts are high, right now. She recognized the cougar as a threat and acted accordingly. Thank goodness she did too, 'cause I wouldn't have been able to stop it."

"Wow, that's amazing," Leon reflected, then grinned. "I always knew she was a good horse."

"Yeah, Leon, she's a good horse," Jack conceded the point. He became serious again. It was obvious to one who knew him so well, that there was something else on his mind, but that he was reluctant to bring up.

"What is it, Jack?"

"What? Oh . . . well, I was just thinkin'. . ."

"What?" Leon hated it when Jack had something to say but was having a hard time getting it out. All it did was add to the suspense.

"Well, I was just thinkin' . . ."

"Yes," like a teacher to a shy student.

"Well, I know it's the second-year anniversary of you bein' in here, and I was just . . ."

Leon smiled, ironically. "And you were just wondering how I was handling it."

"Yeah," Jack admitted. "You took it hard last year, so . . ."

"Yeah, I know." Leon shrugged his shoulders and looked away. "I don't really think about it anymore. You know—whatever."

"What do ya mean, 'whatever'?" Jack asked. "I mean, I'm relieved that you're not depressed like you were last year, but now you make it sound like it don't matter; like ya don't care no more. You're not givin' up on us, are ya, Leon?"

"No, no," Leon insisted. "I guess I'm just more accepting of things being the way they are now. I look at Lobo and see how he's fighting everything and everybody, every step of the way, and looking at it from this end, I can see the futility of it. Then you said that I was just as bad, worse, even, when I first got here." He took a deep breath and shook his head. "It's just not worth it. It's like hitting your head against a brick wall."

"Yeah."

Leon chuckled. "Then I look at Malachi, and there he is, walking around with that same old grin on his face all the time. I'm thinking he's got it over all of us. He's just coasting through his sentence, Jack; he's going to make it. He's going to get out of here and be none the worse for it."

"Yeah, well, don't forget that a lot of that is because you're protectin' 'im," Jack pointed out. "If you weren't in here with him, I doubt he would be so easy goin' about it all."

"Good point," Leon agreed. "I just wish that Lobo would let me do the same for him, but you know Lobo."

"Oh yeah," Jack nodded. "How's he doin' with that cough?"

"Better. Doc Palin gave him a tonic to help ease it, and I make sure he takes it. But I'm still worried about him. If he gets sick this winter, it could easily be the end of him."

"Do ya want me to ask Jean ta knit him a sweater and stuff?" Jack asked. "I know she wouldn't mind doin' it."

"Yeah," Leon agreed. "Mariam has already brought over some winter things for them, but the more the better, I suppose. I don't really need any more clothes. Some of Jean's home baking always goes over well, though. Ahh, more candles—oh, and writing paper. What they give me here hardly lasts a week."

"Okay, I'll tell her," Jack assured him. "I should be able to get in here a couple a more times, but here we go again, full steam into winter."

"The winters are hard, all right," Leon agreed. "Not having many visitors is the worst of it, now that I have enough clothes to ward off the cold. But then, getting letters from everyone makes up for it a little bit. It's always kinda nice, coming back to my cell to find parcels and letters sitting there, waiting for me."

"I can imagine. And you know the girls will keep on writin'," Jack assured him. "David's busy, now that he's a family man, but he does ask after ya. I know he'll write if he can."

"Yeah, I know. I expect Caroline is going to have other things on her mind too, now that she's married. Life goes on."

Pearson shifted and gave a little cough. The partners didn't even bother to acknowledge the signal; they both knew what it meant.

"Okay, Leon," Jack said. "I'll try to get in again next month. Steven might come with me then too and bring ya up to date on what's goin' on."

"Sounds good."

"I'll see ya." Jack stood up to take his leave. "Take care of yourself."

"Yup," Leon agreed, then smiled. "And you take care of that young lady of yours."

Jack grinned. "Yeah, I will. See ya later."

***

Laramie, Wyoming
Winter 1887

Winter hit hard and early that year.

One day, Leon was standing in the yard, smelling the cold freshness coming in on the late autumn breeze that blustered around him. Then, the next day, the prison was covered in a thick blanket of snow that didn't look like it was going anywhere, anytime soon. Everyone settled into the regular winter routine and prepared to wait out the cold months as best they could with what they had.

As usual, Leon kept a close eye on his two charges, making sure they stayed warm, and eating and drinking enough to keep healthy. Lobo's cough didn't seem to be getting any worse from the colder temperatures, and Leon began to relax and hope that the wolf was going to make it through his first winter all right. Malachi continued to be Malachi, and so long as he had a steady supply of chewing tobacco, he was content enough.

There were the usual tensions around the work area, as it was impossible to avoid the antagonistic individuals in that confined space. There were always those silent little challenges making their way around the assembly, and the pecking order was continually challenged.

Very few of the lower-end inmates bothered Leon; they all knew where he stood, and by the same token, they didn't bother Malachi much either, knowing he was under Leon's protection. They all kept a wary eye on Lobo though, just waiting for him to show some sign of weakness, but the ready snarl and hard stare from him kept most at bay.

Boeman, Harris, and Mackenzie were still circling the pack, though to a lesser degree than before the altercation that had ignited the riot. They were still hoping to get Leon off by himself, but now that winter had set in and everyone was confined to the indoors, that scenario became less likely. There were too many guards and other inmates around to single any one out from the pack for any length of time.

The fire bug, Ames, proved to be a thinking young man. He figured it out, along with everyone else, that Malachi was being protected, so he soon buddied up with that inmate. His intentions were not totally self-involved, as he did like Malachi well enough and was glad for the friendship. But he was also hopeful that by sticking close to Malachi, the span of Leon's protection would fall upon him as well. He had no illusions concerning his place in the natural scheme of things.

The winds continued to blow outside the prison walls, and nobody wanted the work detail of heading outdoors to clear away the front gate or the road leading into the yard. It was too cold.

Then Christmas itself turned out to be disappointing.

On the 23rd of December, a blizzard hit Colorado and Wyoming, and it kept everybody locked down and indoors for close to a week. Those guards who lived in town, and were on duty when the blizzard hit, ended up having to share sleeping accommodations with those guards who were permanent residents. Encroachment on established territory and over-crowding in the guards' dormitory made for resentments and short tempers.

Doc Palin was among the employees who could not get home for his customary few drinks after another wretched day, and this made him sour. He, at least, had privacy, bunking in the cell that was usually occupied by Mariam, but with no whiskey to warm his soul, his down time was a misery.

To make matters worse, the Sisters of Charity could not get to the prison for the holiday, so even that greatly anticipated pleasure was deprived the inmates. There were many assurances being put about that they would come bearing gifts, just as soon as the weather permitted, but it still made the actual day bleak and depressing. Even Dr. Mariam was not able to get in to conduct services, and everybody was snarky.

The fireplaces at the end of the aisles were all lit and burning, but that wasn't enough to take the chill off the prison. Leon spent the day in his cell, lying on his cot and all bundled up in numerous layers of warm clothing, being thankful that he had them. He drank coffee and was trying to read *A Christmas Carol*—again. But for the most part, he ended up simply staring at the same page and thinking about what a lousy Christmas this had turned out to be. He didn't even have any cookies.

On top of that, the guards naturally took their frustrations out on the inmates. Most of them had families at home celebrating the holiday as best they could, so for those stuck at work, knowing they were missing out on a warm family gathering, their current situation was taken personally.

The attitude of the prisoners was far from sympathetic. It was more along the lines of: *Now you know what it's like to be stuck in this hell hole, day after day, night after night. Get over it.*

The next day, in the warehouse, everybody was still in foul moods, inmates and guards alike, so it didn't take much to light the spark and set off the explosion. The only question after the fact was whether it had all been part of an elaborate plan, or simply certain individuals taking advantage of an unexpected opportunity.

***

Leon was working alongside Malachi, trying to attach some particularly coarse straw to the handle of a broom, when a loud crash from the other side of the large work floor caused everyone to jump and look over.

Leon couldn't see what was going on at first, but he had seen the beginnings of enough fights by now to know the signs of an altercation. Within seconds, the dynamics on the floor changed, and the inmates began to cluster around a section of the room where the two combatants were obviously getting into it.

The rule of silence was broken as the onlookers began rooting for their favorite fighter. Yells of encouragement burst from the audience, while certain curses and grunts emanated from the two combatants. It was proving to be a serious altercation, and the arrival of the guards swinging their billy clubs, only escalated the violence, rather than breaking it up.

Departures

Leon put his work tools down and was about to head over to the fight when he felt Malachi grab his sleeve. He looked around to meet those stark, blue eyes, which on this occasion, were expressing both fear and worry.

Malachi shook his head. "No," he said, not too worried about rules at this point. "Don't be gettin' involved. That there be trouble."

"It's all right, I'll be careful," Leon assured his friend. "But I'm the medical assistant, remember? The Doc isn't here yet, so that means I'm the one on hand. Don't worry, Ky, I'll only get close if I'm needed."

Still, Malachi didn't let go of Leon's sleeve.

"I still don't like it," he insisted. "It don't feel right."

"What? Are you turning into the Kid now?" Leon teased him. "Relax, it'll be fine."

Leon moved off, and Malachi stayed where he was, his back up against the worktable. He looked around him with an anxious expression. He felt vulnerable as he brought his focus around again to watch Leon's disappearing back. Malachi enjoyed a good fist fight as much as the next outlaw—so long as he wasn't in it—but the fights in the prison were often brutal, resulting in a lot of bloodletting, and that was too much for him. Now, here was the best friend he had in this place heading straight for it, and Malachi couldn't help the knot of dread that took over his stomach.

Leon came up behind the wall of inmates but was very careful to keep his distance. Everyone was fully focused on the center ring and none were too concerned about where the surging sea of humanity took them. Lack of caution could easily cause a person to get trampled.

The fight was still in full swing, as Leon could hear the two men shouting at each other, not to mention the crash of work tables overturning and metal utensils clattering to the floor. The guards were still trying to make their way in through the mass to break it up, but one of the challenges of a good fight was to keep it going. The only way to keep it going was to keep the guards from getting to it and breaking it up.

Then Leon felt a tingle of dread shoot up his spine, and anger tightened his jaw. The first coherent words he heard from the peanut gallery had just verified his worst fears.

"C'mon, Lobo—let 'im have it."

"Jeez, Harris, you're usually faster than that."

Oh crap, Lobo's involved; what a surprise. When is that idiot going to learn that he's not up to a fight?

His leader instincts taking over, Leon tried to push his way through the human ring, to get to his friend, but he wasn't having any more luck with this than the guards were. Frustrations mounted, and Leon felt his anger rising.

Suddenly, there was a loud, collective *Whoaaa!* from the crowd, then everybody turned on their heels to make a fast getaway before any of them could get singled out for punishment.

Leon fought to stay on his feet; the rush of the pack threatened to sweep him along with it, but he dug in and continued to push his way through, toward the epicenter.

The guards didn't pay much attention to Leon. They were more concerned with getting the larger group of inmates broken apart and heading back to their workstations before everybody ended up in a lockdown situation. Tempers were high due to the enforced bad-weather confinement, and more than one inmate received bruises from the billy clubs before the troublemakers were settled into compliance again.

Meanwhile, Leon ignored the sounds of battle coming from behind him as he zeroed in on the prone figure of a man lying on the floor. He groaned in disappointment as he recognized Lobo, who was clutching his torso and gasping for air. Leon ran to him and was down by his side in an instant.

Leon leaned over his friend. It wasn't good.

Lobo's hands were covered in blood, and he grabbed at his sweater, trying to pull it away from the wound in his left side.

Leon grabbed his hands and held on.

Lobo struggled to breathe and talk at the same time.

A very gurgled "Nash," made its way past his lips, but then that was followed by a frightening rush of foamy blood and air bubbles.

Leon felt fear clutch at him, and he pulled Lobo's sweater and tunic up and away from the gaping wound in the man's side. Harris had slid a knife in between Lobo's ribs, puncturing his left lung. He had then pulled the knife out, leaving his victim there to drown in his own blood.

Bubbles popped their way out of the wound as air leaked from the injury. Leon pressed both his hands over the open gash, trying to seal it off, trying to save his friend from suffocating.

"Just hang on, Lobo," Leon encouraged him. "They'll have gone for the Doc. He'll be here any minute. You'll be all right."

"No," came the harsh, gurgled response.

"No, it's all right, Lobo. Just . . ."

Lobo began to fight. He tried to roll away and pushed Leon's hands off the gaping wound.

Air bubbled forth again.

"No! Lobo, what are you doing?" Leon grabbed his friend and rolled him onto his back as he tried to re-establish his pressure hold over the wound.

Lobo was having none of it.

The wolf showed his teeth in a bloody snarl and lashed out at his former boss.

Leon was knocked back and off balance, while more precious air surged from the damaged lung.

Lobo lifted an arm to block more assistance. "No—" It was more like a strangled gurgle than a word. "Let'm die . . ."

"What?" Leon couldn't believe what he was hearing. "No! Come on now. You're talking nonsense. Don't you dare give up on me. Doc Palin will be here any minute—"

"NO!"

Lobo tried to sit up, pushing Leon away from him again, fighting him with what little strength he had left. Then he fell back, gasping and harsh coughing hit him. He rolled onto his side and vomited frothy blood.

Leon held onto him, feeling desperate, trying to get him to accept help. *Where is Palin? Why isn't he here yet?*

Lobo lay back again, relaxing, and just for the briefest of moments, Leon thought his friend had given up struggling and was going to accept help. But one look into Lobo's glazed-over eyes crushed that hope. Another rush of foaming blood gushed from Lobo's mouth and then Leon heard the now too familiar sound of a gurgling death rattle in the throat, and his friend went limp and was quiet.

Leon was shaking and gasping for air. He was in shock.

He couldn't understand how Lobo could do that. He'd just let go. He hadn't even tried to fight for his life. In fact, it had been just the opposite; he'd fought to die.

Leon's bloody hands grabbed Lobo's, and he held on tight. He fought to keep his emotions down since even dry tears would not have been appreciated by the hardened criminal who now lay crumpled on the cold floor.

Leon continued to gasp in lungfuls of air, then, swallowing down the tightness in his throat, he sat back on his heels and stared down at the dead man as though he still couldn't believe it.

Then Palin was there, squatting down on the other side of the victim, and Leon raised his sorrow-filled eyes to meet the doctor's. Palin reached over and put a hand on Leon's shoulder, then looked down at the body lying between them.

"Nasty wound," he commented quietly, "and considerin' he was already weak in that area, it's not surprisin' he didn't make it."

"It's not that," Leon murmured, disbelief still mingling with his sorrow. "He fought me, Doc. He didn't even want me to help him. He just . . ."

Palin nodded his understanding. He gave Leon's shoulder a squeeze.

"Yup," he said, "some of 'em do that. Decide they'd rather be dead than be here. He kinda indicated that right from the start, though, didn't he?"

Leon dropped his eyes and nodded. "Yeah, he did."

Palin patted Leon's shoulder a couple of times, and sending his assistant a reassuring smile, he pushed himself up.

Then, from across the work floor there came the clatter and yelling of another fight breaking out. Leon groaned. What was with these people, today? He showed no inclination of getting up to investigate, figuring that since Palin was already here, he could deal with any medical issues that arose.

But that decision got turned around on him, when he heard Malachi's voice raised in a yell, followed by the crashing of a work bench being pushed over. The inmates began their whooping again and another fight was on.

Leon sighed, but stood up and turned to go investigate. Then he felt Palin grab his shirt sleeve.

"No, Nash. Stay outta this one," the doctor suggested. "This is too much of a coincidence. You're bein' set up. Stay out of it."

Leon shrugged. "It's one of my men," he stated bluntly, as though that should have been obvious. He then turned and headed toward the sounds of the altercation.

He began the journey to the other side of the floor at a reluctant walk, but as fear rose in him that Malachi was going to end up the same way as Lobo, the walk became a run, then the run became a charge. He slammed into the back wall of men and started to force his way through, using elbows and knees to jab and punch anybody who didn't move aside fast enough.

A quick scan of the assembly before him showed Officers Murrey, Davis and Thompson doing their best to get this second insurrection shut down, but with Pearson and Reece busy dealing with the most unruly rebels from the first fight, they were having a hard time. Leon pushed through and found himself front row, center, of the second fight and his anger rose another notch at the audacity of the assault.

Mackenzie was standing behind Malachi and holding the smaller man in an arm lock, rendering him harmless, while Harris came at him with a broom handle.

Leon had to hand it to Malachi, because, despite being ganged up on, he was holding his own. Smaller than Leon, and of a gentler nature, he was still wiry and tough, and could move fast when he had to. Despite MacKenzie trying to hold him still, Malachi still found a way to twist and turn and duck every time Harris took a swing at him. The blood running from his nose indicated that he hadn't been successful every time, but poor Mackenzie was the recipient of the blows, more often than not, and he was getting pissed.

Yelling out in anger, Leon ducked his head and charged, aiming for Mackenzie. He hit him with a full body check from the side, sending himself, MacKenzie and Malachi all sprawling to the floor in a tangle of arms, legs, and prolific curses.

Harris was getting mad now. He charged the prone group, and swinging the broom handle like a sledgehammer, he came after Leon with malicious intent.

If it hadn't been such a violent attack, it would have been funny. Malachi had rolled under a worktable to get out of the way, while Leon was on his back, watching Harris and keeping his eyes on that club of wood. He twisted and turned and rolled back and forth, using his legs to knock over chairs or move tables—anything to keep out of striking range of that broom handle.

Harris roared with frustrated anger, looking very much like a man attempting to club to death a rat that was refusing to stay still.

The three guards on the floor tried their best to get through the jeering, jostling, spectators, but the inmates took great pleasure in blocking every move they made.

Carson was on the run from the warden's office, where he had been discussing scheduling, when he'd gotten word of trouble in the warehouse. Pearson and Reece had deposited their troublemakers into their cells and were also on the run back toward the scene of the crime. Palin was doing his best to stay out of the way, confident that his services would come in handy later.

Meanwhile, Mackenzie scrambled to his feet and was doing his best to stay out of swinging range of Harris, when, quite unexpectedly, a hand nipped out from under a table and Mackenzie had his leg snatched right out from under him. He went down hard, taking a table and a whole box full of working tools with him. Then Malachi was out from his hiding place and, sitting on Mac's chest, started punching him for all he was worth.

Unfortunately, Mackenzie was a much larger, heavier man than Malachi, and though the Elk Mountain member got in numerous effective punches, it wasn't long before Mac got fed up with it. Twisting his torso over, he dislodged the smaller man and sent him skidding. Then Mac was up and, grabbing Malachi by the front of his shirt, hauled him to his feet and began punching him in the face.

Malachi started yelling and brought his arms up over his head to ward off the attack, but aside from that, there wasn't much else he could do to escape the assault.

Leon saw red, and he briefly wondered if the ineffective attempts from the guards to break this up was deliberate. Then he heard Malachi yell and his blood boiled. He knocked over another chair to block Harris's attack, and then was on his feet and charging before the other man had a chance to recover. Leon hit Harris full on with a shoulder block, and both men were sent sprawling into the sidelines, taking four or five of the spectators down with them.

Everybody scrambled out of their way and the two adversaries were on their feet again. But Harris decided he'd had enough. He had been up against Nash before, and now that the odds were no longer in his favor, he dropped the broom handle, and turning tail, pushed his way through the crowd and out of the fight.

Leon grabbed the discarded club and made a run for Mackenzie.

Swinging the weapon low, he rammed it, full force, into the back of that inmate's knees, collapsing his legs out from under him.

Mackenzie gasped with painful surprise and let go of Malachi. His legs buckled and he started to go down, just as Leon again swung the club and cold-cocked him behind the ear, dropping him to the floor and out of the fight.

Leon looked up to meet Malachi's eyes just in time to see those blue orbs suddenly widen with surprise, and then Leon felt someone grabbing his tunic from behind. Thinking it was Harris coming back for more—or maybe even the oddly absent Boeman—Leon swung around and brought the club down onto the top of Officer Thompson's shoulder. There was a loud crack as Thompson's collar bone snapped and the guard went down to his knees with a shocked yell of pain.

There was an instance of silence, as every inmate still on the floor stopped what they were doing. Then, as if in collective agreement, every one of them turned tail and headed at full speed back to their cells, the memory of their last all-out riot still too fresh in their minds for any of them to be wanting a repeat.

Leon stepped back in surprise and dropped the wooden handle to the floor with a loud clatter. He knew he was in trouble now even before the first billy club landed its blow. Then the guards were onto him, whacking and batting him as he went down. He curled himself into a ball, bringing his arms over his head, trying to protect himself. But the blows and kicks kept coming until he thought his brain was going to explode.

He could hear Malachi yelling, and to that man's credit he was doing his best to get between Leon and the guards, trying to shield him from the blows. He hated the fact that his "boss" was being beaten simply for trying to protect him. Then, fortunately for the time being, Carson, Reece, and Pearson arrived on the scene and quickly restored order to the chaos.

"Murrey, Davis—back off 'im!" Carson yelled. "God dammit. Pearson, get that other one over to the infirmary and take Thompson with you."

"Yessir," Pearson responded. Stepping around the detritus of the fight, he grabbed the still unconscious Mackenzie by the arm, and hoisting him up, started to drag him in the direction of the infirmary

Thompson was standing and holding his useless left arm, but he swayed and looked as though he might just pass out at any moment.

Fortunately, Dr. Palin was still in the vicinity, so he came over to lend the guard a hand. Turning, he glanced down at Leon, then looked to Kenny. That guard simply shook his head and rolled his eyes; he wasn't in charge here. It wasn't up to him what happened next.

Carson was still swearing. "Jesus Christ. Can't I even go for a meeting with the damn warden without all hell breaking loose down here? And what a surprise—here's Nash right in the middle of it."

Carson stepped forward and glared down at the prone man, who was still rolled in a ball and not moving. Malachi sat on the floor between Leon and the guards, a protective arm thrown back over his friend's shoulder. He was scared to death, looking up at all these men who were armed, and bigger than him, but he was still reluctant to surrender his friend to their mercy.

"Davis!"

"Yessir."

"Get this one to the infirmary as well. I'll decide on their punishments later," Carson ordered, with a gesture toward Malachi. "Tell Pearson to stay over there to guard them, then you get back here pronto. Understand?"

"Yessir."

Davis took hold of Malachi's arm and began to haul him to his feet.

"No," Malachi protested. "No, I wanna—"

"Are you talking back to a guard, convict?" Carson yelled at him.

Malachi cringed and, shutting his mouth, he instantly looked away. There was nothing else for it, even he knew that. With one despairing look down at his friend, he allowed himself to be led away.

Carson then nudged his boot under Leon's torso and rolled him onto his back. Leon groaned and opened his eyes; just about every inch of him ached with pain. Fortunately, he was bruised but not bloody, battered but not broken. He lay there doing his best to find a way to breathe that didn't hurt.

Squatting down beside him, Carson grabbed Leon by the front of his tunic and pulled him up into a sitting position.

Leon gasped, then tried his best to support himself, while not looking the senior guard in the eye.

"I swear, Nash, you must be startin' to like me," Carson said to him, "because you just gave me exactly what I wanted for Christmas." He smiled and gave the inmate a couple of slaps across the face, just to make sure he was listening. Leon jumped, and his eyes opened wider. "I told you what I would do to you if you ever assaulted one of my guards again—and what do you do? You go and assault the same guard. Yep, you must really be startin' to like me."

Leon groaned, while Carson stood and looked at Reece and Murrey.

"Wait here with him until Davis gets back," he ordered, "then get Nash over to the hoist. I'll meet you there."

"Yessir."

Carson turned on his heel and walked away.

CHAPTER FOURTEEN
TWO STEPS BACK

Kenny closed his eyes, letting out a dejected sigh. This was not going to be pleasant. He shook his head and looked at the inmate, who still sat upon the floor, trying not to fall over.

"Aww, Nash, why'd ya do it?" Kenny asked him. "You assault a guard, practically under Carson's nose, and there's not a damn thing I can do to help you. What the hell were you thinkin'?"

"He's one of my men," Leon mumbled.

"Who? Cobb?" Kenny confirmed. "I know that, Nash, but both him and Lobinskie, being assaulted at the same time? You must have realized it was a setup, and yet you walked right into it."

"He's one of my men."

Kenny stood silently for a moment, then sadly nodded in understanding. He looked at Murrey and Davis, who had just returned, and sent them a simple gesture to carry on with their duties. The two guards each grabbed one of Leon's arms, hauled him to his feet and dragged him off to receive his punishment.

A few minutes later, Leon found himself in a room that he'd never been in before, and it didn't take him long to know that he didn't like it much. It wasn't a big room, quite small actually, and, as usual, there were no windows, or heat. The floor and walls were of cold concrete and the shadows made by the two oil lamps hanging on the far wall gave the chamber a sinister, otherworldly chill.

About a foot down from the ceiling, there was a wooden beam that stretched across the length of the room. On that beam, there was attached a pulley system with a rope running through it, with one end running straight down to the floor and the other end angling across to slide through a ring attached to the far wall. The only furniture in the room was a bench and a bucket filled with water.

Leon felt dread clutch the pit of his stomach. He began to think that even the dark cell might be preferable to what was going to happen in here. His teeth started to chatter, but whether it was from fear or the cold in this dank, ominous room, he didn't know.

Davis went over to the bench and picked up a leather strip. He returned to the inmate, and pulling Leon's arms behind his back, snugly tied his hands together.

And there they stood, waiting, with Davis standing beside Leon, holding onto his left arm, while Murrey stood in front, so that Leon had no choice but to simply stand there, his eyes looking down. The knot in his stomach became a fist, twisting his innards.

Then he heard voices coming toward them. It was Carson and Kenny. Kenny was speaking quietly, trying to sound reasonable, but it didn't appear that he was having much impact.

"Nash didn't intend to assault Thompson, you know that. It was a set up to get Nash into trouble."

"Well, it worked," Carson agreed, "cause he sure as hell is in trouble."

"You're letting Boeman play you," Kenny continued. "He's the bastard who should be in here for punishment."

"Boeman wasn't anywhere near either of those fights."

"Yeah, what a surprise," was Kenny's sardonic response. "You know damn well that anything Harris does is because Boeman told him to do it. Harris doesn't have enough brain cells to think up any of this stuff. He's brutal, but he's a lackey, and you know it as well as I do."

"Yeah, I know it," Carson responded as the two men entered the room. "But if Nash hadn't been involved in the fight, and holding a weapon, then he wouldn't have hit Thompson. End of discussion."

"Nash was only protecting one of his men." Kenny didn't agree that the discussion was ended. "Cobb was getting ganged up on."

"The guards were on their way to break it up," Carson pointed out. "The worst Cobb would have got is a busted nose or some cracked ribs."

"Or dead," Kenny pointed out.

"Lobinskie was already at death's door," Carson was starting to get angry. "Hardly a surprise; nobody expected him to last the winter anyways."

"All I'm saying is—"

But Carson turned on his subordinate, finally having had enough of this discussion.

"I told Nash what I would do to him if he assaulted one of my guards again, and now he has. How much respect would I warrant if I didn't do what I said I'd do?" Kenny was getting ready to answer when Carson cut him off. "NO! Don't bother. You're too soft, Reece. If you want respect from these convicts, ya gotta let them know who's in charge. You can't expect these outlaws to change who they are. I knew it would just be a matter of time before Nash pulled something like this again, because that's who he is; it's his nature. The only way to get men like him to submit is to crush them, and sooner or later he will submit, because I'm not gonna give him a choice. That's it. End of discussion."

Leon took an involuntary step back as Carson barreled down on him, but all he did was back into Davis. Then, Carson had him by the arm and was hauling him backward, to the dangling rope.

"You two," Carson ordered his guards, "get over there—get ready to haul."

Leon was nauseous with fear. He didn't know what was coming, but he knew he wouldn't like it, not with the way Carson was so eagerly looking forward to it. Carson had said he'd hang Nash if he assaulted a guard again. Hang him, but not kill him.

How do you hang someone without killing them? Oh crap. His heart pounded a stampede in his ears. *What the hell is Carson going to do?*

Leon looked to Kenny while he felt Carson tie the loose end of the rope to his bound hands.

Kenny met his eyes with a tight jaw and a slow burn rising.

But Kenny was just as helpless as Leon in trying to stop this. There was nothing he could do about it. But that didn't mean there wasn't something he could do to prevent it from happening again, and Kenny was just about mad enough now to be willing to take the chance.

"All right," Carson ordered, "start hauling."

Davis and Murrey both had a hold on the other end of the rope, and they started to pull down on it so that Leon's hands were pulled up toward the beam.

Leon's breath came in gasps now, as realization of what they were doing to him, really and truly came home. He locked onto Kenny, hoping that having him to focus on would help him to block out the pain. But it didn't.

Leon felt his arms being pulled up behind him, and then they reached the limit that they could comfortably go, but Murrey and Davis continued to pull. Leon's shoulders took the strain and he began to lean forward as he was slowly being hoisted up off his feet. Every muscle in his body tightened. He closed his eyes, and his mouth opened as he felt the strangling fear start in his lungs, force its way up his throat and then burst out in a scream of agony. His shoulders were on fire.

"Stop—!" came out as a strangled cry.

Carson sneered, and grabbing Nash's chin, shook it until the inmate, his breath coming in short, ragged gasps, forced his eyes open and looked into the guard's sadistic face.

"Don't worry, Nash. I'm not gonna cripple ya," Carson jeered at him. "We're just gonna make it feel like we are—for the next five hours."

"No . . ." ripped from Leon's throat in a jagged protest.

Reece felt sick. He couldn't stop it but that didn't mean he had to stand there and watch. He turned on his heel and walked out, still hearing Leon gasping in torment, until he turned a corner and re-entered the prison proper.

Pearson spotted him and came over to ask him something, but one look at his boss's expression caused him to do an about face and head off in another direction.

Reece was beyond fuming; his jaw was tight, and his gray eyes had turned to hard steel. This was the final straw; he'd had enough, and if he knew his wife as well as he hoped he did, then she would not only understand the actions he was about to take, she would be right in there cheering him on.

***

Leon heard buzzing in his head as the concrete room began to spin, then to fade out into a black velvet backdrop with amazing colors shooting and swirling across his field of vision. The buzzing was chased away by the blood in his ears as it pounded out a drum beat from a long-ago ceremony. A vision of Nat-soo-gant, his grandfather, came to him. The old medicine man danced and swirled, his feet and his medicine rattle beating out a tattoo in time with the drumming in

Leon's head.

The image and the drumming began to fade and the buzzing in his ears became louder and louder as the searing pain in his shoulders began to diminish. Then the strangest of sensations started in the pit of his stomach and made its way up, toward his head, like a huge wave of nothingness.

He felt an overwhelming sense of relief, because he knew he was just on the verge of passing out.

Yes. Sweet blackness. Take me away, take me to the spirit world, where I can disappear into a vision. Where I won't feel the pain anymore, where I won't feel anything anymore.

Then Tchaikovsky's violin concerto started dancing across the tapestry of his mind, and the swirling colors waltzed in sync with the melody, ebbing and flowing, bursting bright and then fading. He could see his grandfather again, off in the distance, waltzing to the violin. Then everything faded as the music and the colors mixed in together, then spiraled away from him, both being sucked into the nothing that became total blessed blackness.

Then Leon was coughing, sputtering—fighting to breath, and the searing pain stabbed at his brain again. He was floating inside a gray well of concrete and he was cold and in agony; he wanted to die. He spit water out of his mouth, and it dripped down his chin as he forced his eyes open. Davis stood in front of him, holding a tin cup that he'd just used to splash water into the inmate's face.

"Wake up, Convict 312!" he ordered. "How are you supposed to benefit from the punishment if you keep passing out?"

Leon groaned as Davis sat back down to continue his watch. The inmate lost count how many times he passed out and how many times Davis hit him with the water. He tried to hold on to his music, but reality pushed through and turned the music into pain. He tried to focus on new words to decipher, but they all ended up translating into pain. He tried to think of Karma and their wild, joyous gallops, but all the wind brought to him was pain. Pain filled his world, his universe, his reality. Pain was all he had. It was all he could ever remember having and it was all that he could foresee in his future.

He passed out again, and with what little Shoshone he had, he pleaded with Huittsuu-a, his mother, and with his grandfather, the wise and powerful Nat-soo-gant. Pleaded with them to help him, to relieve him from this pain and take him to where they now resided.

Mukua floated into view, shaking his head. The spirit world was not ready for him, at least not yet. His pleas fell upon deaf ears as he was forced back into consciousness again.

But it wasn't with water; this time, he was being jostled. His head draped over a shoulder and somebody was holding and lifting him up, taking the strain off his shoulders.

Leon's whole awareness was filled with Kenny's scent, and in his mother's tongue, he babbled his thanks to the spirits. He was vaguely aware of Davis snorting with humor over something, but he didn't care. Relief washed over him as Kenny's soothing tone drifted through his consciousness and put his mind at ease.

***

Four hours into the punishment, the weather had finally cleared enough for Carson to decide it was time to head home. He'd been stuck at the prison for nearly three days and felt the need for a beer and a decent meal before grabbing some sack time in his own bed.

Kenny had been there just as long, but he had something else to attend to before heading home to his wife and children. As soon as he was sure Carson was well and truly gone, he headed back to the dungeon.

Collecting Pearson along the way, the two men entered the room and didn't hesitate going about their business. Kenny went straight to Leon and, getting himself underneath the convict, he brought his shoulder up so that Leon's head draped over it, then wrapping his arms around the inmate's waist, lifted him up to bring slack into the rope.

Leon groaned, then under his breath, began mumbling incoherently.

Recognizing it as heathen speech, Davis snorted with distain, but a quick glare from Kenny shut him up.

"Take it easy, Nash," Kenny assured the semi-conscious man. "I've got ya." He looked to Pearson, who stood by the ring embedded in the wall. "Okay, Pearson, untie him and then get over here and help me lower him down."

Davis had come to his feet upon the arrival of his superior, and now he frowned, concerned about how this change of events was going to affect him. "Ahh, Mr. Carson said to give him five hours. It's only been four."

"Mr. Carson has gone home for the day so that makes me senior guard," Kenny pointed out. "I say he's had enough. Do you have a problem with that?"

"Umm, no sir, Mr. Reece."

"Good. You're relieved of duty for the day, Mr. Davis. Go home."

"OH—yessir! Thank you, sir," and Davis made a hasty retreat, before his superior could change his mind.

Pearson untied the rope from the ring and came over to assist his boss. He placed his hands against Leon's back to steady him, and Reece slowly bent his knees, taking all three of them carefully to the floor. They managed to get Leon laid out flat on his stomach without jarring him too much and then did a quick check over.

Leon's wrists were raw and bleeding from the leather bindings that still dug into his skin. Kenny tried to untie the knots, but the leather was wet with blood and would not give in to the tugging. Kenny cursed under his breath, his jaw tightening in anger again at the brutality.

"Do you have your knife with you?" he asked Pearson.

"Yeah." Pearson reached inside his jacket and pulled out a small flat blade that he kept hidden in a sheath under his right arm.

The guard wasn't supposed to carry a knife inside the prison proper in case an inmate overpowered him and got hold of it, but it had come in handy on more than one occasion and Kenny chose to overlook the infraction. Right now, he was glad he did.

Pearson slid the knife between the binding and Leon's skin, but it was a tight fit and the skin was so swollen, it was not an easy task. Kenny used his fingers to push the skin down so Pearson could get the point through without cutting into the flesh. It took some persistence and a couple of close nicks, but they finally managed it, and Pearson started to saw away at the leather.

This part didn't take long, and Leon groaned in pain as his hands came free and dropped to the floor by his side. He tried to move, tried to get himself rolled over so he could sit up, but any attempt to move his arms only resulted in shooting, nauseating pain assaulting his senses.

Kenny placed a hand on his shoulder. "No, Nash, stay still. The muscles and tendons in your shoulders are going to be badly damaged, so don't even try to move."

Leon wanted to answer, but all that came out was a strangled moan. He lay there and focused on breathing through the crushing pain in his chest.

"Go to the infirmary and get the stretcher," Reece ordered the guard. "There's no way we can walk him over there without pulling on his arms, so we'll have to carry him."

"Yeah, okay." Pearson was on his feet and gone before he had finished confirming the order.

Kenny sat back in a more comfortable position, keeping his hand on Leon's shoulder. He sighed again, and a subtle, ironic smile flitted across his lips.

"I don't know, Nash, we seem to find ourselves in this position a little too often."

Another soft moan from the convict. His lungs felt as though they were on fire.

***

Half an hour later, Leon was stretched out on his back, in a bed in the infirmary.

Malachi hovered. He had been over earlier to get treated for his minor injuries from the fight but had pestered and cajoled Doc so much over the welfare of his friend, that Palin had allowed him to hang around. Now, he had even less intention of leaving, and Doc and Kenny both agreed he could stay and sit with Nash for now, if that's what he wanted to do.

"How are Mackenzie and Thompson doing?" Kenny asked Palin while the doctor was preparing a dose of morphine for his patient.

"They'll survive," Palin grumbled. "Thompson can go home soon if someone will drive him, then he'll need six weeks off while that bone heals. Mackenzie can go back to his cell tomorrow. With that concussion, I want to keep an eye on him over night."

"Yes, all right," Kenny agreed. "What about Nash?"

Palin sighed and glanced at the newest arrival. "Jeez, that Carson's a fuckin' asshole. Have I said that before?"

Kenny smiled. "Yeah Doc, ya have."

"Well, it bears repeatin'! Anyway, we'll have to wait and see. I'll clean up his wrists, but it's gonna take a while for his muscles to heal. I'm sure they've been badly torn up. He can probably go back to his cell in a couple of days, but he won't be doing any work for a least a month."

"Oh no," Kenny groaned. "He's going to drive everybody crazy."

"Oh yeah," Palin agreed. "He won't be able to do much writing either, but he'll be able to read, so maybe Dr. Mariam can come up with something to keep him occupied for a while."

"I sure hope so," Kenny was emphatic. "Nash with nothing to do is like a bear coming out of hibernation. Maybe we can pawn him off on the orphanage for a while."

"There's a thought."

"Hmm. Well, Doc, I'm heading for home. I'll see you tomorrow."

"I'll be here," came the caustic response.

The two men went their separate ways, and Palin came over to Leon to administer the drug.

"How are you doin', Nash?" the doctor asked him, just to get his attention.

Leon sent him a weak smile, and looked at him through slitted eyes. "Ky's been singing me lullabies."

Palin's brows went up and he glanced at the other inmate.

Malachi looked down at the floor, feeling embarrassed.

"Just some ole songs we'd git ta singin' in the bunkhouse," he mumbled in his own defense. "Ain't what I'd call 'lullabies'."

"That's fine," Palin assured him. "Keep 'em comin'."

Malachi grinned.

"Here, help me get him sitting up," Palin said. "But don't touch his arms. Get a hand under his shoulder, like this, then we'll push him up together."

"Yeah, okay Doc."

Once Leon was sitting up, Palin sat on the bed and supported him there with his shoulder, then put the cup to the patient's mouth.

"Okay Nash, you know the drill."

"Is it morphine?"

"Yeah."

"Oh, good."

Once Leon had the draft down his throat, Palin went to his supply cabinet and took out disinfectant, padding, gauze, tape and scissors. Everything he'd need to get those wrists cleaned up. With the help of his new assistant, they got the job done.

***

Kenny Reece, all bundled up in his coat, hat and scarf, retrieved his horse from the stable and made his way toward town for some well-deserved time off. It was a clear night, the stars bright and sharp in the cold, dark sky, but it wasn't as late in the evening as Kenny would have thought. One of the things about working three or four days straight, without a real break, is that you tended to lose track of time.

Quite a few people were still out and about that evening, taking advantage of the break in the weather to do some socializing, or just get out for some fresh air. He nodded greetings to more than one acquaintance as he trotted his horse down the snow-packed roadway, heading toward the main street of town.

He got into a battle of wills with his horse as they passed by the street leading to their home, and he could understand the animal wanting to get back to his own stall and a good feeding. But Kenny had an errand to run before going home, and it wasn't one he felt could wait.

He continued down the road, past the mercantile, the sheriff's office, and the café, then turned at the hitching rail by the telegraph office. Much to Kenny's relief, the light was still burning inside, so he dismounted and entered the warm interior to take care of business.

George looked up from behind his counter and his coffee, frowning at the blast of cold air that accompanied the patron. But seeing who it was, he then smiled a greeting. "Hey there Kenny. How's life behind bars?"

Kenny rolled his eyes. "Oh brother. I don't even want to go into it."

George smiled. "Okay. What can I do for ya? There's nothin' here for ya to pick up."

"No, I know," Kenny answered. "I want to send two telegrams, both with the same message."

"Okay," George got his paper and pencil ready. "Where are they going?"

"One is to Mr. Steven Granger, Denver Colorado. The other is to Mr. Jack Kiefer. Arvada, Colorado. Both to say: 'Count me in.', and then, you know, K. Reece.

"That's it?" George sounded disappointed.

"Yup. They'll both know what it means."

"Okay, Kenny. I'll get these sent off right away."

"Thanks. Good night."

"Night."

Kenny exited the office. He re-mounted his horse, and much to the animal's relief, pointed his head toward home.

CHAPTER FIFTEEN
REASSESTMENT

Laramie, Wyoming
January 1888

Leon was in his cell, sitting on his cot playing solitaire, eating cookies and drinking coffee. It was evening. The weather had finally cleared up enough for life to become mobile again. Most of the inmates and guards were in better spirits, now that the Christmas festivities had finally taken place, and everyone had received timely gifts.

But Leon himself struggled to stay optimistic. He was hurting inside and out—again. He was in constant pain; his chest and shoulders ached and complained with the slightest of movements. The simple act of reaching for his coffee cup or flipping over a card might cause him to suck his teeth and silently curse his situation. He even found it hard to breathe.

Doc Palin came to his cell at night and rubbed liniment into his patient's muscles, so at least he could sleep, but he would still wake up periodically, feeling as though he was suffocating. Were his muscles ever going to recover from their ordeal? Palin said yes, given time. Everything seemed to take time.

Movement by his cell door caught his eye, and he glanced over to see that old black and white tom cat staring at him. Leon returned the stare. The feline flattened its ears and hissed. Leon symbolically flattened his ears and hissed back. Startled, the cat jumped, then took off down the corridor to tend to other matters. Leon made a habit of closing his cell door whenever he wasn't in it, for fear of returning to find cat urine on his blankets. One more enemy to add to his list.

Ten minutes after that, more movement caught his eye and he

glanced up to meet Boeman's icy stare. This time Leon's hackles really rose, and the two inmates glared at each other for what seemed an eternity. Then Boeman's lip curled in what, apparently, was supposed to be a smile, and he turned and walked off down the aisle toward his own cell.

Leon was left sitting on his cot, sending a stream of silent curses after the man. There was a reckoning coming with that one, but Leon was in no condition for a retaliatory attack yet, and he knew it. It was going to have to wait.

Half an hour after this, Leon noticed movement again, and he sighed with irritation. Couldn't these people leave him alone? He looked up, sending daggers to the intruder, then instantly regretted his mood and softened the points.

Malachi stood in the doorway, holding two cups of hot coffee and wearing a hopeful smile.

Leon smiled back.

Malachi's grinned deepened, and he came into the cell. Sitting down on the cot, he offered Leon one of the cups.

Leon slowly lifted his hand to accept it, and his whole countenance tightened with the pain the movement cause.

Malachi's smile dropped, and he looked concerned. "You handlin' this?" It was no more than a whisper so the guards wouldn't hear.

Leon shrugged then grimaced. He smiled to cover it up and accepted the cup.

"I'll be all right." He picked up the tin of cookies that Jean had sent him. "You want a cookie?"

Malachi's face lit up like a child given a puppy, and he helped himself to a couple of them to have with his own coffee.

Leon placed the tin back onto the cot between them, indicating that Malachi could help himself whenever he wanted, and they settled in to play double solitaire.

The two friends spent the rest of the evening in this pastime and were quite content to do so. Twenty minutes before evening lockdown, Officer Murray came by the cell and let them know it was time to break it up.

Malachi grabbed one more cookie, sent Leon a cheeky grin, then headed down the aisle toward his own cell.

Leon carried on with his solitary game, until the buzzer sounded for all the inmates to present themselves for the night-time roll call.

Damn. Carson's still here.

The senior guard was systematically working his way down the row of cells, checking off names as he went.

Leon tried hard to disappear where he stood, but he knew he wasn't having much luck. As a second option, he made sure he kept his eyes lowered and did nothing to antagonize the guard. He hated to admit that he felt fear of this man; there weren't many men whom Napoleon Nash was afraid of, but Carson had certainly become one of them.

"So, Convict 312, how ya feelin' tonight?" Carson just had to ask.

"Fine, sir," came the quiet response.

"Uh huh," Carson smirked, ticked Leon's name off the list, then closed and locked his cell door before carrying on down the aisle.

Leon sighed with relief as the door shut him in. Though he still couldn't shake the feeling of being caught in a trap, there were times when the closed and locked cell door gave him a sense of security, and this was one of them. He lay on his cot, staring up into space and feeling down in the dumps. He started to raise his right arm to place under his head, then quickly thought better of it, as the pain shot through his chest, and he had to fight to get a breath of air.

When is this hell going to be over?

Never, was the answer that came back to him.

***

Arvada, Colorado, Winter 1888

When Jack first received Kenny's telegram, he'd been pleased that the guard had changed his mind about coming forward in person. Then, after considering it for a few moments, he began to wonder what had happened to bring about the change of heart. Once this thought occurred to him, it wouldn't let him go, and the first chance he got, he was back in town and sending a telegram.

What happened?

And the simple response.

He's fine. Discuss later. Lobinskie's dead. Sorry. Knife fight.

Now Jack was really nervous. Apparently, Lobo had gotten himself into a fight and, knowing Leon, he got himself into trouble trying to help. Winters were always difficult, especially when they had been on the run, but now, Jack hated them because the snow and cold temperatures kept him isolated from his uncle. All it took was a telegram like this one to get him antsy and frustrated at the forced inactivity.

Jack blew on his hands and rubbed them together as he made his way to where his gelding was tied up and waiting for him. He had decided to call him *"Gov"*. Short for governor, of course, thinking that, maybe, giving the young horse that name might bring them some luck.

Jack looked up to see Isabelle heading his way, but as soon as she saw him, her nose went up in the air and she instantly turned on her heels and headed off in the opposite direction. Jack smiled to himself. You can't please everyone.

Word had gotten around that Jack and Penelope were now courting, and, for the most part, the news had been greeted with playful teasing. The majority of the comments had to do with how long it had taken Jack to get around to making it official. Isabelle, on the other hand, had become surlier than ever, and commented to her friends that it would never last.

Jack shrugged his shoulders at Isabelle's attitude, and mounting his horse, he headed out to the Rocking M to help Sam with the evening chores. After supper, he was going to retire to his room and sit down to write a letter to his uncle and find out from him just what it was he thought he was playing at.

***

Leon:
What the hell are you playing at? You know who, has had a change of heart about you know what, and now Kenny says that Lobo got himself killed in a knife fight. Why is it,

I find it hard to believe that you were not involved in all this
in some way? What happened? Are you all right?
   Jack

***

Laramie, Wyoming
Winter 1888

Leon sat on his cot that Saturday evening and gave a snort of amusement upon reading the letter from his nephew. He had several letters scattered about his cot from different people, some wishing him a Merry Christmas, and others just keeping in touch. There were even some from the orphans that were full of kind words and humorous stories about their Christmas celebration.

They were also adamant that Mr. Nash come to visit again, as soon as the weather permits, and of course, bring Mr. Kiefer along too. Leon had to admit that hearing from those youngsters did lift his spirits.

But for the most part, his mood was melancholy and had been since the ordeal with Lobo. He couldn't shake it this time, that feeling of hopelessness. The feeling that nothing was going to improve, nothing was going to change. That he was never going to get out of here.

Still, Jack's letter, so abrupt and to the point, could not help but bring a smile to his face, and he settled in, then and there, to respond to it. He did not, however, plan on going into any detail, especially regarding the punishment, as he knew that would only serve to frustrate and worry his partner even more. He kept things ambiguous and hoped it would suffice until spring.

   Jack;
   I am sorry to say that we did lose Lobo here around
Christmas time. He and one of the other inmates got into a
fight and he was stabbed with one of the work knives. I
tried to help him, but Lobo, being true to form, would not
let me, and he chose to die instead. I still can't decide if
that was an act of great bravery or great cowardice. I
suppose, all I can say is that right from the start, he made

it clear he'd rather be dead than be in here, so when the opportunity presented itself, he simply took it. So, maybe it wasn't brave nor cowardly; it just was.

Malachi got himself into an altercation as well on that same day. Both the Doc and Kenny think that it was a set up to get me into trouble, it being of general knowledge that I had taken both Lobo and Ky under my protection. And of course, it worked, because I did go to assist Ky and ended up taking much of the blame.

All us inmates, who were involved with the fight, were sent for the usual punishments, but all is fine now. I'm okay and so is Ky, so there really isn't anything for you to worry about, 'cause let's face it, you've got enough to worry about with that hearing coming up, so go give 'em hell, okay!

Looking forward to seeing you in the spring, and hopefully there will be some good news.

Have you named that damn horse of yours yet?

Leon

Leon sat back and re-read the letter, and was satisfied that it would do. Just enough of what was normal chaos around this place, so as not to set off any alarm bells, but still letting him know that some things had indeed happened.

He set that letter aside and picked up another one that was awaiting his attention and saw it was from Jean. He smiled. If anyone could lift his spirits, it was her, and since he knew how busy she was at home, any letters from her were all that much more appreciated.

Dearest Peter:

I think all of us got hit hard with the winter storm that came through just in time for Christmas. I hope the bad weather did not totally ruin what small enjoyments you get from that season, as I'm sure you all look forward to them a great deal.

The holidays here were affected by the storm, and Christmas Day was quiet. No one was going anywhere, so of course, we did not see Steven and Caroline, nor even David and Tricia, as everyone was dug in and waiting it out.

We did make the best of it though, and dinner was pleasant enough with just the five of us here. Eli is getting so big! He's running everywhere now and talking constantly, and he is so fond of Jack. They have planned this spring to go for a ride up to the north range to look at the calves and new foals. Of course, Eli is determined that he is going to ride Midnight all by himself and be a real cowboy, just like the hired hands.

We did have one sad event take place here, near the beginning of this month. Our old hound dog, Rufus died. Of course, it wasn't a shock to anyone, as he has been slowing down quite a bit over the past year or so. I suppose this winter was just too much for him. I don't believe he suffered really. Jack found him curled up on a nice, cozy nest of straw in the barn, with the two little dogs staying close until we came out to find him.

Of course, Penny was very upset, as she is so fond of all the dogs, and it took some time for a smile to come back to her face after that. Pebbles and Peanut did a lot to lift her spirits and whenever she was outside, they hovered around her and jumped into her lap any time the opportunity presented itself. It so amazes me how animals seem to know when someone they care about is distressed. But, of course, they were also upset over losing their buddy, so I suppose it was a mutual mourning ritual.

I'm sure we will have no trouble finding ourselves another good dog come spring. There are usually one or two neighbors who are quite happy to find homes for new puppies that whelped out during the winter, so we will probably have our pick.

Also, Sam and Maribelle are expecting again! Sam is so thrilled, and everyone is keeping their fingers crossed that everything will go better for them this time. Thank goodness Sam's mother is living with them now. She has been no end of support for the young couple and is insisting that Maribelle stay off her feet and take it easy, especially through the winter months. David is keeping a close eye on the mother-to-be and is also encouraging her to stay quiet.

Little Daisy is doing well and actually, she's not so little anymore! She's almost caught up to her mother in height and only needs time to lose her gangly legs and baby build before she's going to be quite the looker! She and Penny have a marvelous relationship and indeed, it's very humorous to see Penny in the field with both Daisy and Karma following her around like a pair of large dogs wanting attention. I think that once Daisy is broke out, she and Penny are going to make a real pair.

That is all for now. I hope you are staying warm and continue to eat enough. And please, stay out of trouble! The hearing is set for the middle of March and everyone is hopeful of a positive outcome, so be patient and have faith.

With much love, Jean

Leon sat back and considered Jean's simple advice.

Yeah, be patient and have faith. That's what everyone keeps saying, but nobody says faith in what. Faith in the system? Yeah, that's a joke. Faith in God? Is there such a thing?

Many of the people I care about and respect seem to think so. Ata-i believed it without a doubt, and Ata-i was the wisest man I knew. And what about those times when I have entered the spirit world? When I can feel the presence and hear the voices of those who have passed, I must be somewhere. And if there is a spirit world, then it stands to reason that something is in charge of it. But then, what is it? And who's right? Everyone seems to have their own ideas.

He sighed, then frowned. *Or maybe it's just all hallucinations, and we've been tricked into believing in something that doesn't exist. Let's face it, if it was truth, then wouldn't everyone believe in the same thing? Maybe just faith in friends. Well, that's tangible. That's something I can see and hold onto; I know my friends are real. So yeah, faith in my friends. Yeah.*

***

Wyoming Territory

Gus Shaffer was fed up with trying to convince Harry Barton to be careful of any job coming their way that seemed too good to be true—because it probably was. Gus had gone up and wintered with the Cripple Creek boys, but he had no intention of staying there permanent. Since having been leader of his own gang, trying to take orders, especially from such an inferior as Barton, didn't set well with him.

Besides that, he wasn't an idiot, and he knew that the Kid had been right. There was no place in Wyoming that was safe for him. Actually, there was no place in Wyoming that was safe for any outlaw, now that Marshal Morrison was on the hunt. Knowing this, he had still made his way back into Wyoming territory after leaving the Rocking M, mainly because he had nowhere else to go.

He did it smart, though; he stayed out of the larger towns and only went into the smaller ones when he needed supplies, buying when he could, and stealing when he had to. Fortunately, he knew all the back trails that "law-abidin" folks had no clue about; the ones that only outlaws and old Indians had any idea were there and where they led to. He made it.

Cripple Creek had been happy to take him in. Everyone had heard about what happened with Elk Mountain and were sympathetic to the ex-leader's plight. On top of that, George Carmon, the only other member of that ill-fated gang to get away, had also run to Cripple Creek, looking for a haven to call home. He had been colorful in his description of the events that had destroyed The Elk, and everyone had listened in awed silence.

Unfortunately, they were all in denial when it came to their own situation.

"Why would lawmen like that bother coming after the likes of us?" Douglas asked during yet another pointless chat around the bunkhouse stove. "We're just small-time bandits. We ain't worth the money it would cost 'em ta come this far out."

"I gotta agree," George Carmon added. "Elk Mountain's been the most successful outlaw band in the history of the territory. Especially when Nash had been runnin' things. So it ain't surprisin' Morrison would put some effort inta takin' 'em out."

The room went silent for a moment at the mention of the great outlaw leader who now languished in prison.

Young Mr. Hanson was the first to speak up. "Too bad about Nash," he mumbled as he stared into his coffee cup. "I woulda liked to a met 'im. I hear he's real smart."

Gus snarled at the implication that the gang had gone down-hill since he had taken over. Even though he knew this himself, he didn't appreciate others insinuating it.

"Not smart enough ta stay outta prison," Gus snarled, but then he brightened and looked around at the fellas sitting at the table. "But that's what I've been sayin'. Once Morrison decides he's comin' after ya', he don't quit. And it don't matter that you fellas ain't worth much. The governor is payin' him extra ta clear out the gangs. You fellas have gotta disappear. Maybe head south."

Snorts and hoots of laughter made the rounds.

"You're jumpin' at shadows, Shaffer," Carmon accused him. "I guess I can't blame ya after what happened to the Elk. But I think you're just runnin' scared. Nobody's gonna bother with the likes of us."

"Ain't you fellas listenin' ta me?" Gus couldn't help the edge in his voice. "It don't matter what you're worth as outlaws, you're worth more as corpses. Morrison ain't gonna stop. I'm tellin' ya this fer your own good."

For a moment, Gus thought he had made some headway as worried expressions made the rounds.

Then Douglas laughed. "Naw! If that were the case then none of us would be safe anywheres."

"Dammit!" Gus rattled the coffee cups as his fist hit the table. "That's exactly what I'm sayin'! You fellas gotta get outta here. The sooner the better."

Strained silence again made the rounds.

"Nobody's goin' anywhere till spring," Carmon pointed out. "And if what you're sayin' is true, and we ain't safe anywheres, then we might as well stay put and carry on as usual. I still think you're just spooked. Morrison was only out ta get The Elk Mountain Gang, and he did. He got his glory by gettin' Nash and Kiefer ta trial. Takin' out Elk Mountain was added gravy. He's not gonna be bothered with the likes of us."

And so it went.

Gus spent all that winter trying to tell those boys about what was gonna be waiting for them come spring, and how they'd better be careful. He'd even sat with Harry Barton up in the leader's cabin, over a bottle of old corn whiskey, trying to convince him of the danger they were in. But it was to no avail. Nobody believed him, or maybe, they just didn't want to.

When spring finally appeared after a long, cold winter, Gus bundled up his meagre belongings and prepared to depart.

Wet slush mixed with mud covered the yard as Gus led his horse out of the barn. Most of the fellas had pulled on boots and warm coats to come see him off.

"You're a fool, Shaffer," Harry Barton said for the umpteenth time. "This ain't no time to be hittin' the trail. I know you're insistin' on goin', but why don't you give it another couple a weeks? Maybe even a month. We could still get more snow comin' down before the true thaw takes hold. Ya don't wanna be caught out in the open for that."

Gus simply shook his head as he made last minute preparations to his saddle and gear.

"What I don't wanna be caught in is another ambush. And that's what's comin', boys. Mark my words."

"Stop with the doom and gloom," Carmon snarked. "This is a good place here. Not as lucrative as Elk Mountain, but we did well enough last season. Besides, if Morrison really is out to get ya, where are ya gonna go? He's just gonna follow ya."

"I'm gonna head west, maybe north." Gus shrugged. "I ain't never seen the ocean. Hell, even Morrison ain't gonna follow me that far."

He was met with blank stares as the men stamped cold feet and tugged their coats in more snuggly. Apparently, to most of them, seeing the ocean was about as likely as finding the pot of gold.

"That's fine for you," Carmon said as he spit to the side. "But what about Cobb? I thought you guys was partners, but now you're plannin' on just runnin' away and desertin' 'im. That ain't very loyal."

But Gus just smiled and shook his head. "Don't you worry yourself about Malachi Cobb. We got our arrangements. You boys should be worryin' about yourselves." He then added, as he mounted his horse. "I'll be seein' you fellas—That is if ya don't hang around too long."

"We all think you're a fool," Barton told him. "But if you're bound and determined ta go, then travel safe."

"You, too." Gus reached down and shook hands with the boss. "I hope the best for all of ya."

Then Gus nudged his horse and they splashed their way across the yard toward the main trail out.

"Yeah, have a good trip," Carmon called after him, then laughed. "We'll be thinkin' about ya while we're drinkin' whiskey in the nice, warm bunkhouse."

Gus simply sent them a quick wave back then rode away to the accompaniment of their hoots and laughter.

He never saw any one of them fellas again.

***

Two weeks later, as Gus was approaching the Wyoming/Idaho border, he took the chance of stopping in a small spit-in-the-dirt town to replenish his supplies. He was feeling the need for a hot meal and a warm bed, as well.

He put his horse up in the livery, then checked himself into the hotel. The clerk gave him a barely concealed look of disgust and suggested that perhaps the gentleman would like a tub, soap and hot water sent up. On the house, of course.

Much to the clerk's relief, Gus accepted. He was hungry, but he also knew the effects that two weeks on the trail would have on the olfactory senses of the other café patrons. He didn't want to call attention to himself, and that last little heist he'd pulled had netted him fifty dollars, so he was well-heeled for the time being. Might as well take advantage.

He had to admit, that bath felt real good. He hadn't realized how stiff and sore his muscles had become, or how cold his feet were, until he got the chance to soak them in some hot water for a time. Now he was feeling like a civilized man again instead of some scruffy drifter. He'd even spent fifty cents to have his clothes laundered and patched up, and he was quite content to stay soaking in that tub until the clerk returned his attire to his room.

Yessir, by the time Gus had soaked, shaved, and re-donned his newly laundered clothing, he was looking and feeling like a new man. He headed to the café, secure in the knowledge that no one was going to be looking at him twice. He settled at a small table in the corner and ordered the first square meal he'd had since leaving Cripple Creek.

Venison steak with all the fixin's, two portions of apple pie, and all the strong coffee he could drink went down real well. He was just settling into his final cup of coffee before heading over to the saloon for a real drink, when he noticed an old newspaper setting on the table next to him.

He should have known by then, that no good news comes from a newspaper and that simply picking one up to casually browse through always brought trouble. It didn't take long, either. Right on the front page, in big, bold, letters that even Malachi wouldn't have missed, despite the fact he couldn't read, was a headline that sent a shiver down Gus's spine and caused him to seriously consider changing his plans.

MORRISON PUTS AN END TO CRIPPLE CREEK! ANOTHER OUTLAW GANG BITES THE DUST!

Gus's jaw tightened as he settled in to read the story that, by the date on the paper, was already a week old.

Sure enough, those idiots had ignored Gus's warnings and had jumped at the first hint of a nice, fat, payroll delivery coming through their territory by stagecoach. What a surprise that the coach had been minus a payroll, but full to the brim with lawmen and rifles. Not to mention, the whole posse of badges that had come charging out from cover as soon as the shooting started, trapping the outlaws in a deadly crossfire.

Gus cursed under his breath while reading the grisly details, causing two ladies at another table to send him disapproving glances from over their teacups. Gus practically snarled at them, then realized he'd better behave himself if he didn't want to attract attention. He went back to reading the paper—quietly.

Just like with Elk Mountain, the assault on Cripple Creek had been two-fold. The first attack hitting the outlaws in an ambush, using the hefty payroll as bait, then the second attack infiltrating the hide-out and eliminating the few gang members who had stayed behind to guard it. Most of the outlaws had been killed outright. Three had been wounded and taken prisoner, but one was not expected to pull through. The other two would soon be joining Napoleon Nash and Malachi Cobb at the territorial prison.

Amongst the dead was the leader, Harry Barton, and ex-Elk

Mountain member, George Carmon, making Gus Shaffer the only outlaw to come up against Tom Morrison—twice—and manage to escape capture and stay alive. Gus read further, and the more he read, the less he liked it—especially when it started to get personal...

> *'. . . when asked about Gus Shaffer, the marshal noticeably bristled, then assured this reporter that he wasn't done with Shaffer yet.*
>
> *"I have no intentions of allowing Shaffer to escape justice," Marshal Morrison stated. "He might like to think I'm going to just let him go—that I have bigger fish to fry, but he is sadly mistaken in this assumption. Gus Shaffer was the leader of the Elk Mountain Gang, and I fully intend to bring him down. He can run, but there's no place he can go where I won't find him. He's running out of places to hide, and sooner or later, I'm gonna get him, and that's a promise!"'*

Now it was Gus Shaffer's turn to bristle. This was getting to be too much. Was he supposed to spend the rest of his life looking over his shoulder, waiting for the bullet in the back that Morrison promised him? No man could live like that, and no outlaw worth his reward would put up with it.

Gus snarled to himself and crunched the paper in his hands.

The two ladies at the other table tisked, then stood up and hastened their way out the door. Apparently, no place was suitable for the more cultured citizens of this small town.

Gus watched them leave without really seeing them. He had other things on his mind. Finally, he got up, paid his bill and headed to the saloon for a whiskey or two. He needed to think, and there was no place better for that then elbow up to a bar with a shot of whiskey for company, and nobody to bother him.

By the time he headed back to his hotel room for the night, come hell or high water, he knew what he had to do. And knowing that, he slept well.

***

The first week of February found Leon feeling better and getting back into his regular routine. Though still sore, he could handle the light duties of Doctor's Assistant for his usual one day a week in the infirmary. There were a few patients taking up bed space, keeping them busy, but Doc Palin made sure that Leon did not over-exert himself. Mariam was in attendance as well, along with a legitimate novice this time, who truly was considering a life in the service of the church. As was Mariam's tendency, the young novice got her baptism by fire while tending to the ill and injured at the prison.

Two of the patients who were in the ward at that time were there due to a persistent run of a flu virus, and Mariam, along with her helper, were kept busy tending to their needs. It was generally hoped that the two young men would recover fully from their illness and be back to their regular duties before the month was out. It had been a bad winter for this virus, but so far, no one had developed pneumonia, and the medical staff hoped to keep it that way.

The third patient was Boeman, and he was not sick, he was battered and broken. A mild concussion, a broken arm, and two broken ribs, to be precise. Nobody knew for sure what happened; he claimed he slipped on the icy steps outside—again. Since nobody witnessed it, there was no one to say otherwise. It should be noted though, that every time Leon walked past the bed where that sleeping patient lay, a small, self-satisfied smile twitched at the corner of his mouth, and the pecking order had been re-established once again.

The novice, Julia by name, was taking to the tasks at hand like a natural, and Mariam had high hopes for her. The gruffness of some of the patients didn't seem to deter her and her gentle care of those who were sick did wonders for the patients' state of mind.

Leon smiled at her whenever they were in proximity of one another, and even though she had no problem looking the other inmates in the eye, with him, she tended to be shy and always looked away. The first opportunity Leon had to speak to Mariam in private, he asked her why this would be, since the young woman didn't seem to be shy around anyone else.

Mariam smiled and placed a reassuring hand on his arm.

"You intimidate her," she informed him, gently.

"What?" Leon was incredulous. "What did I do?"

"No, Napoleon, you didn't 'do' anything. She grew up with her brothers all reading about Napoleon Nash, the Kansas Kid, and the Elk Mountain Gang, so she is well aware of who you are."

"Oh." Leon looked embarrassed.

"You must be used to that by now," Mariam stated. "You must know that amongst the younger people you are quite a notorious, but dashing figure."

Leon nodded. "Yes, ma'am, I suppose I do. I guess it's just that I don't feel the part. It's understandable with the orphans; they're looking for a role model, and I can see how the lives we led could appear to be exciting. But Julia is a young woman and should know better."

Mariam smiled. "Maybe, maybe not," she surmised, most unhelpfully. "Just give her some time to get to know you, and she'll get over it."

"Hmm, yeah," Leon mumbled. "Give her time to see that there's nothing about me that's worth admiring."

"That's not what I meant, and you know it," Mariam scolded him. "My, but you're down on yourself these days. What's the matter?"

Leon shrugged and looked down. "I dunno."

"You're still missing your friend, aren't you?" she observed. "You've lost so many friends these past few years. It's easy for us to forget about that in our day-to-day routines. And you don't say anything; you just keep it all bottled up inside. No wonder you're feeling down."

Leon smiled. "Now who am I going to talk to in here about stuff like that?"

"Oh, come on now, Napoleon, really!" Mariam was incensed. "You can always talk to me. And you write home often enough and have people there you can talk to." She sighed and looked at him even deeper. "But you know that, don't you? What is it? What is it that you don't want to talk about?"

"It's just . . . I feel like . . ." Then his mouth hardened into a tight line and he didn't want to say anything more. She would only tell him he was being foolish.

"What? Please tell me. I won't pass judgment on you."

Leon looked at her. There she was doing it again. That woman thing of reading a man's mind.

He sighed and took in a deep breath. "Just sometimes, not all the time, mind you, but sometimes, I think that maybe Lobo had the right idea, that's all."

"That's all?" Mariam responded with raised eyebrows.

"Napoleon, please tell me you're not seriously contemplating that."

Leon smiled at her. "No, Mariam, I'm not. Like I said; sometimes I wonder, that's all."

She nodded and patted his arm. "All right. But promise me, you'll come talk to one of us if you ever start to feel serious about this. Okay? Just because your friend chose death over a hard life, doesn't mean it was right."

Leon flashed his dimples and nodded. "I know. And I will come talk to you if I start considering it. I promise."

"Good."

"NASH!"

Kenny Reece had been off for a few days in exchange for the enforced overtime he'd had to put in at Christmas. He returned to work feeling rested and optimistic, until he found out that Boeman was back in the infirmary, all broken up. Slipped on the stairs? Again? Wasn't that interesting.

Leon jerked his head around at the angry beckoning. When he saw that guard coming at him with his billy club out, and intentions of use written all over it, he panicked. He felt Mariam grab hold of his shirt sleeve, but he pulled away from her and, spinning, he tried to make a run for it. But, of course, there was nowhere to run to.

Kenny was on him in an instant. Giving him a push, he shoved the inmate into the nearest wall, spun him around, then had that billy club lengthways across his throat.

"What the hell are you playing at, Nash?"

"What?" Leon croaked. He had to struggle to get the words out, but angry as Kenny was, he still only used enough pressure to hold Nash against the wall and not choke him. "What'd I do?"

"What did you do?" Kenny repeated, and he pulled Leon away from the wall and used the billy club to point over to the unconscious Boeman. "You retaliated, didn't ya! You just had to get back at him for Lobinskie, didn't ya?"

"But it was Harris who did—"

Kenny pushed him back into the wall again and leaned into him, staring him in the eye.

Leon dropped his gaze. He knew better than to fight against a guard—even Kenny, or maybe, especially Kenny.

Kenny was livid. "Don't play me for a fool," he yelled. "Harris is Boeman's puppet. You know that just as sure as I do. You went after him, didn't ya? You waited until you had him alone and then you hit him. And don't you even think about lying to me. You did it, didn't ya?"

"All right!" Leon's resentment flared. "All right, I did it!"

"Oh, Napoleon . . ."

Leon tried to ignore the disappointment in Mariam's tone.

"I thought you were smarter than that, Nash," Kenny was still seething. "We are this close to a hearing and you pull stuff like this? How do you expect us to get any kind of justice at all if you keep insisting on dealing out your own brand of revenge?"

"Justice?" The anger and resentment that Leon hadn't even realized he was repressing, flared out. "What justice? Boeman, Harris and Mackenzie conspired to gang up on my men. They killed Lobo! And all they got was a slap on the wrist and a stint in the dark cell. I accidently strike a guard and I got hung from the ceiling like a slab of meat! How's that justice?"

"It wasn't," Kenny admitted. "It wasn't justice. That's what this hearing is all about. I thought you understood that. You keep on telling Jack that he needs to start doing things the legal way now. That he can't go back to the way you did when you were outlaws. But then you turn around and do exactly that yourself. Is Carson right, Nash? Is the only way to get you to see reason is to break you? Do you want me to join forces with Carson to crush you into the ground?"

"No." Real fear whispered in his tone. "God, no."

"Then you are going to have to start thinking," Kenny told him. "You are going to have to stop this bullshit. Because right now, Nash, you are still acting like the outlaw that you were, which makes me think that maybe you still are that outlaw. That you are never going to change. That you are never going to be safe to release back into society. That you are always going to be dangerous and unpredictable!"

Kenny was startled out of his anger by Leon's reaction to those words. The inmate flinched, as though he'd be struck, and the blood drained from his face.

"That's what Judge Lacey said," Leon whispered.

"What?"

"The judge at my trial. Just before he sentenced me to life in this hell hole, he said that I was a dangerous man with no real intentions of reformation."

A beat of silence weighed heavy in the infirmary.

Kenny's anger eased. "Well, you're doing a good job of proving him right."

"I'm never going to get out of here," Leon mumbled.

Kenny released a stressed sigh. He ran a hand through his short hair and turned around to suddenly be brought up short by the numerous pairs of eyes that had been focused on the argument.

"Oh crap," he mumbled. "Ma'am, I apologize. I didn't realize you had your novice with you today. I'm sorry, Miss. I don't usually lose my temper like that."

Julia smiled at him, accepting his apology, but she still hovered close to Mariam.

Kenny sighed again and glanced back at the inmate.

"Carry on with your duties, Nash," he said. "We'll talk later, when I'm not quite so angry with you."

Leon nodded, looking dejected.

Kenny walked toward the far exit and nodded at Palin.

"Doc. See ya later."

"Ken."

The guard exited, and the whole room breathed a collective sigh of relief.

Palin smiled at his assistant.

"Well, Nash. I bet you're wishin' I still had that bottle of whiskey around here somewhere, ain't ya?"

***

By the time Leon's next shift in the laundry room came around, Kenny still had not made a point of coming around to talk with him. In fact, it seemed to the inmate that the guard was doing everything he could to avoid speaking to him. Leon was anxious about the whole situation. He'd been walking around with a guilty knot in his gut ever since Kenny had come to visit him in the infirmary, and it was getting worse as time went on.

Finally, Leon decided it was up to him to clear the air and get things settled. Sometime around mid-morning, Kenny strode into the laundry room, casually tossing a balled-up pair of socks into the air and catching them, then repeating. Nash glanced up from folding dish towels, and Kenny stopped tossing the socks and sent a speculative look to the inmate.

"Funny thing," he commented, "but there's something about a pair of socks falling from above and hitting me on the top of the head that makes me think someone in the laundry room wants to have a word."

Leon couldn't help his impish smile. "Yessir, Mr. Reece," he admitted, then shrugged his shoulders. "Sorry."

"Well, at least it was socks and not the iron."

Another twitch of a smile. "Yessir."

"What's on your mind, Nash?"

Leon looked uncomfortable. He wasn't used to backtracking on his choices. He was still too accustomed to being the boss, and being the boss meant that you were always right, even when you were wrong.

"Ahem," was the feeble beginning, "I just wanted to apologize."

"Oh, yes? For what?" Kenny was not going to make this easy on him.

Leon slumped in defeat, rolling his eyes. "For . . . going after Boeman."

Silence. Obviously, Kenny was waiting for something more.

Leon shuffled. "I just, umm . . ." This was proving to be harder than he thought. He took a deep breath and decided to go for broke. "It's always been that way for me. Ever since the orphanage, I was taking responsibility for others. Then it was Jack, but gradually that grew to include the Elk Mountain gang.

"Even when Cortez was running things, the pressure was on me to get the safe open. They were counting on me, you see. If I failed, it wasn't just me who went hungry, it was everyone. And the better I got at what I did, the more Cortez and the gang counted on me to do the job right.

"When Cortez disappeared, it came as the natural next step for me to take over and continue to run things. By then, I was responsible for not only seeing the plan through, but for coming up with the plans in the first place.

"I had to—don't you see? I had to be on top of everything and everybody. Our very survival depended upon it. Then, there's always somebody who wants to take over, so I had to be tough. I couldn't let any of them think they could contradict me or defy my orders, so if any of them tried it, I had to retaliate instantly. It was just . . . that's the way it was.

"You saw what Lobo was like, and he wasn't really an exception. Most of the men I had to control were hard, and some were downright mean and wouldn't hesitate to slit my throat if they thought they could get away with it. On top of that, many of them were older than me. New fellas coming into the gang would think I was some little pup who'd simply lucked into the position. They saw me as easy game. I had to be brutal sometimes; I had to be ruthless just to keep them in line.

"I don't think I could have done it without Jack backing me up. But that's the way it was, the way it's always been. Jack and me, we looked after each other, but I was still the leader; I was still responsible.

"When you've been doing something a certain way all your life, it's kind of hard to stop. Somebody goes against me or mine, it's second nature now to set it straight."

Kenny nodded as he took all this in.

"Yeah," he finally acknowledged this testimonial. "You've had a hard life, Nash. I know that. Nobody's denying it. You had to be tough to survive, I know. I see it all the time in here, with the people who come and go from this place. But you have a couple of things going for you that those others didn't have, and I suppose because of that, I expect more from you."

Leon smirked. "What have I got? What makes me so special?"

"Jeez Nash. Don't you know?"

Leon shrugged and shook his head.

"Well, for one thing, you have friends. Friends who are staying true to the cause and who are willing to do whatever it takes to help you. That, in itself, should be enough to make you realize that this isn't just all about you. You have an obligation to hold up your end in this, and to not do stupid things that are only going to create more problems and make your friends' jobs all that much more difficult."

Leon stood silently, disappearing inside his own head. He had just been reprimanding himself for this very thing, and now, here was Kenny putting it into words.

"Then, for another thing . . . Nash?" Kenny got the inmate's attention focused back onto him. "You're smart. You've got to be the smartest man I've ever known. Too smart for your own good, it seems. So smart that you end up doing stupid things because you think you're still in control. You think you're still running the show."

Leon snorted. "How could I be running the show from in here?"

"Exactly. But you're so used to being in charge that you still insist on acting as though you are, even though, as you say, how could you be from in here? And yet, you're constantly thinking, you're constantly trying to get your own way. You know what the rules are and you're always trying to find a way around them and not get caught."

Leon subconsciously wiped the palms of his hands against his trousers. They felt sweaty.

"Yeah, I suppose," he conceded. "Everybody keeps telling me to let go, to take a subordinate role in these events, and I keep on agreeing to do that but I'm beginning to think I don't know how." He hesitated, wondering how much of himself he should reveal, then, shrugging his shoulders, he continued: "I can never get my mind to shut down."

"What?" This odd confession took Kenny by surprise. "What do you mean?"

"This brilliant mind that everyone keeps saying is so wonderful," Leon explained. "It won't turn off. Oh, I've learned certain techniques to quiet it down at night, so that, usually, I find a way to get to sleep. Dr. Mariam has helped me out with that. But still, some nights, I don't get to sleep at all. You all comment on how hard I am to handle when I have nothing to do, but I don't mean to be. My mind won't settle, and sometimes, it just about drives me crazy."

Kenny looked perplexed; this was a new one on him. "Have you spoken to Dr. Palin about this?"

"Yeah, a bit," Leon admitted. "He'll give me a low-dose sleeping draft for when it's bad, but he says the more I use that, the less effective it will be, so it's better if I can find another way. But the point is, I'm always thinking about solving puzzles because I have no choice. My mind won't shut down. I suppose that's where my problems lie; it's becoming second nature to me now, to just start scheming. I guess, maybe what I need to do is change the direction my mind wants to go in."

Kenny smiled. "See. I told ya you were smart. Now that you've thought about it, you've been able to see for yourself where your problems lie and, maybe, you can start doing something about them."

"Yeah? How?"

"Turn the other cheek," Kenny suggested. "If Boeman or Harris antagonize you, let them. Like you said, force your mind off into another direction. Instead of thinking about how to get back at someone, think about clever ways to avoid them. There's more at stake here now, than just your pride, Nash. A lot more a stake."

"Yeah."

"I've noticed that you don't feel the need to go after Mr. Carson, yet he has done you more damage than anybody else. Why is that? Is it just because he's a guard, or do you accept him as the boss, and you don't want to go against him—or is it something else?"

"Ahh, well . . ." Leon thought about this for a moment. "You remember that day you found me laid out in here, all bruised up, with a cracked rib?"

"Yup," Kenny nodded. "I've often wondered what that was all about."

"Yeah. Well, that was Mr. Carson letting me know what would happen if I even thought about going after him. And I, for one, believed him."

"Ah!" Kenny nodded again in understanding. "Hold that thought, Nash. And maybe try and extend it to Boeman and Harris."

Leon snorted.

"Yeah, I know," Kenny continued, "but if you convince yourself that retaliating against those two would bring about the same repercussions as going after Mr. Carson, then maybe you can convince yourself to leave them alone."

"Yeah." Leon was skeptical.

"It might surprise you to know that Cobb is doing all right on his own," Kenny informed him. "He's made friends in here, and even those who are not his friends, recognize him as a 'non-combatant' and are willing to leave him in peace. Did it ever occur to you that it was you making sure that everyone knew that Cobb and Lobinskie were under your protection that caused them to be singled out that day?"

"You're saying it's my fault Lobo was killed?"

"No," Kenny assured him, quietly. "Lobinskie did that to himself. He made it clear, right from the start, what his intentions were. Unfortunately, once an inmate decides that he'd rather be dead than in here, there's not much we can do to prevent him from killing himself. Even if we tie him to his cot and lock him in his cell, if he maintains that attitude, sooner or later, he'll find a way.

"The point I'm trying to make is that if you had left it alone, let them find their own footing, well, Cobb, at least, would probably have been all right. I can understand you wanting to help them settle in at first. I expected you to. I even encouraged you to. Let them know what to do to avoid fights and punishments. But once they had that figured out, perhaps if you had backed off and let them set their own guidelines, it might have been easier all around.

"It's only because Boeman knew he could get to you through Cobb that he was singled out. And you played right into it. You're smart enough to know better, Nash, but you walked right into the trap anyway."

Leon became defensive. "I couldn't just stand by and let Ky get beat up. Especially after what had just happened to Lobo."

"But he wouldn't have been getting beat up if you hadn't taken on the role as his protector!" Kenny felt frustrated. He knew Leon was trying to wrap his mind around this concept, but it was so foreign to his usual mind-set, he had a hard time with it. "If you had just let things be, allowed Cobb to find his own footing in here, then Boeman wouldn't have had a weapon to use against you. Do you understand what I'm saying?"

Leon stood with creased brow, looking perplexed. He was taking in Kenny's words, and being as quick as he was on the intellectual level, it didn't take long for the epiphany to hit him right between the eyes. He groaned with the realization of what a fool he had been.

"I keep falling back onto my old habits, don't I?" he mumbled. "I don't even realize I'm doing it, but I keep making the same mistakes."

"Yeah," Kenny smiled, "but I'm told that the first step in correcting bad habits is to recognize what they are in the first place. You just have to let go of this need in you to be in control. I know it's hard, it's not what you're used to, but you really do need to step back. To be honest, I think Mr. Cobb is capable of getting through his sentence on his own. You're correct in that he is not particularly bright, but he is likeable. He is a most unusual outlaw."

Leon laughed out loud. "He is that!"

"So, you see, you don't need to be in control of everything," Kenny continued. "You can relax." He smiled, "For your first lesson in humility, maybe you should try making friends with that old tom cat."

Leon's smiled dropped. He didn't like the sound of that at all.

Kenny continued to grin as he tossed the pair of socks over to the inmate, then turned to go.

"Carry on, Mr. Nash. You're doing a fine job here

CHAPTER SIXTEEN
THE HEARING

Cheyenne, Wyoming
March 1888

It could not have been a chillier or damper day if they'd put in a request for it. At least it wasn't snowing. Jack and Penny sat in the foyer of the Cheyenne courthouse, trying to warm up while waiting for the council room to become available.

Steven and Caroline were already there, somewhere. Steven was probably getting some last-minute things arranged for the hearing that was scheduled to start in half an hour.

Jack was nervous, which was not surprising considering how much was riding on what was being presented, and what the outcome could mean for Leon in particular, and the whole Auburn Prison System in general.

Penny was concerned that she wasn't going to come across as plausible and repeatedly went over her own testimony in her head.

Kenny was around somewhere and had the reports from Doctors Palin and Mariam to back up much of what others were going to be stating, first-hand.

But that was about all they had. Everyone was concerned that it might not be enough.

Then the waiting was over when Steven, with Caroline acting as his assistant, arrived to announce that the meeting room was open for them.

Penny and Jack stood up together. Penny brushed Jack's shoulders and straightened his tie. He gave her a nervous smile.

"Wish me luck, darlin'," he mumbled to her.

She smiled. "Luck, darlin'."

His smile broadened, and he gave her a hug. "Same to you."

The couple followed Steven, since he seemed to be the only one who knew how protocol worked within the government buildings. Even though Jack had been here before, he still felt out of place, and Penny was struggling with her effort to not be intimidated. Finally, Steven turned to a large set of double cherry wood doors, which he opened outward, then ushered everybody through.

None of the officials were present yet, so the group had a chance to get settled into chairs lined up at a long table which had been set up for their use. There was also a line of chairs set along the opposite side of the table so the officials, once they arrived and got seated, would be facing the presenters. Everyone quietly took their seats and got settled, while Caroline, who had brought notes for her husband, now opened the satchel and started to get the paperwork organized.

They were a subdued group. The atmosphere in the room was not only one of nervousness over the importance of their mission, but, as in most government proceedings, the air of power—and intimidation, lingered over everyone.

Penny smiled as she noticed Kenny Reece bringing up the rear of the group as they all headed in. She still appreciated what a fine-looking "older" man he was, and now, especially when he was wearing a suit instead of his guard's uniform, she thought him to be especially handsome.

Jack smiled at seeing him, if only for the fact that he had shown up, and the two men shook hands in greeting.

"Kenny, thank goodness," Jack exclaimed quietly, the room itself encouraging soft tones. "I was afraid you'd gotten lost or decided not to come after all—or somethin'."

"No, no," Kenny assured him as he sat down. "I was just getting the other testimonials to the board members, so they would have a chance to look over those statements before we got under way."

"Ah," Jack nodded. "Do you think we have enough?"

"I certainly hope so," Kenny said with a sigh, then started to get his own notes in order. "I'd hate to think that I've put so much on the line just to have it amount to nothing but trouble."

"Yeah."

The far door opened, and four official gentlemen made their way into the chamber and got themselves settled at the table. There was some subtle coughing and rustling of papers and then it appeared the meeting was ready to proceed. A rather large man with the rather large white whiskers who had taken the seat in the middle of the table, now called the assembly to order.

"Mr. Granger," the whiskers said, "is everyone here who wishes to be a part of this hearing?"

Steven stood up. "Yes sir, Mr. Ludlow. Everyone is present."

"Fine," Mr. Ludlow rumbled. "I will introduce the other members of the board and then we shall proceed. On my right is the medical director, Dr. Simons. On my left is the director of mental health, Dr. Dalton. To my far left is Mr. Lancaster, my secretary. Now, if each speaker would identify themselves at the time they present their statements, that would be fine. So, Mr. Granger, if you would please state the reason for this hearing."

"Yes sir," Steven responded. "We are here to present an argument concerning the procedures of the Auburn Prison System and to question its legitimacy and effectiveness in the treatment and long-term rehabilitation of persons incarcerated in the U.S. Penitentiary at Laramie City."

"Fine, Mr. Granger," Ludlow acknowledged the statement. "As I'm sure you appreciate, this is a highly unusual situation. Prison reform is not generally discussed with non-board members. However, Mr. Granger, you were so adamant in your repeated requests for a meeting we decided to break with protocol and give you this opportunity. Mr. Lancaster will take notes on what is said here, but, I give no guarantee that any of it will leave this room."

"Yes sir," Steven agreed. "We understand, and we thank you for this opportunity."

"Fine. Please present your case."

"Yes sir. We would like to present for consideration to the board the supposition that the Auburn System of dealing with inmates is archaic. The way the system is set up not only allows for, but encourages abuses both physical and psychological, to be inflicted upon the inmates in the guise of 'punishment'. I am also presenting to the board the supposition that the wardens in charge of the prisons nation-wide are allowed too much freedom in how they interpret the guidelines that have been laid down in the management of those prisons. Stricter overviews of how these institutions are run need to be put in place.

"We have come here today prepared to present eyewitness accounts of unwarranted punishments being inflicted upon inmates by the guards. We intend to argue that many of these punishments could be more accurately described as torture inflicted out of personal vendettas, rather than any legitimate desire to discourage certain behavior, or to ensure the safety of prison personnel.

"I will now call upon our first speaker, Miss Penelope Marsham, to give her eyewitness account of an unwarranted assault inflicted upon one of the inmates."

Steven nodded to Penny and sat down, leaving the floor open for her.

Penny swallowed nervously, but Jack gave her hand an encouraging squeeze, and she stood up to present her accounting.

"Good afternoon," she began quietly. "Ahhmm, my name is Penelope Marsham and—"

"Please speak up, Miss Marsham," Mr. Ludlow requested. "We can't hear you."

"Oh! Sorry." Penny blushed and Jack gave her hand another squeeze under the table. "My name is Penelope Marsham," she repeated with more volume, "and I've been a friend of Peter's for many years now—"

"Excuse me," Mr. Ludlow interrupted her again. "Who is 'Peter', and how does he relate to this case?"

"Oh! No, I mean Mr. Nash. Mr. Napoleon Nash," Penny stammered. "I'm sorry."

"Fine, Miss Marsham. Please continue."

"Yes, of course," Penny agreed. "I was in the prison infirmary and saw—"

"Excuse me," Ludlow interrupted yet again. "You were in the prison infirmary? How is it that a young lady such as yourself was inside the prison infirmary?"

"I was there assisting Dr. Mariam Soames with the care of some of the inmates," Penny explained. "I was considering taking on a life of service to the church, and Dr. Soames was kind enough to allow me to help her in her duties. In this manner, I could get some experience and see if it was the life I truly wanted."

"And was it?" Ludlow asked her.

Penny dropped her gaze for a moment. "No, I don't think so."

"All right, Miss Marsham, carry on. What did you see in the

prison infirmary?"

"Well, they beat him for no reason!"

Ludlow sighed. "You'll have to be more precise than that, Miss Marsham. Who beat whom?"

"Oh, yes, of course," Penny mumbled. "I do seem to be making a mess of this."

"That's all right, Miss Marsham. Just relax and take your time. And please, try to be precise in your statement."

"Yes, I will." She took a deep breath, and feeling Jack's supportive presence beside her, she continued. "I saw the senior guard, Mr. Carson, beat up on Mr. Nash for no reason. Mr. Nash had only been doing his job as the doctor's assistant, and the guard was accusing him of breaking rules that warranted punishment. But the punishment was brutal and underserved. It seemed to be more of a personal vendetta rather than a—"

"Just state the facts, as you saw them, Miss Marsham," Ludlow reminded her. "Your personal feelings in the matter are not relevant at this point. How do you know the punishment was undeserved? If the guard stated that Mr. Nash had broken certain rules, then it seems to me that the guard was within his rights to administer punishment."

Penny took another deep breath; she knew she had to get her emotions under control. She had to start making sense here, or none of what she said would be of any use.

"I was with Dr. Soames in the infirmary, helping with some of the duties there when one of the guards came in to say that Dr. Palin was needed on the work floor. Apparently, there had been a fight amongst the inmates and one of the men had been stabbed. Dr. Palin grabbed some essentials and we all went to the work area to tend to the emergency. When we got there, there was a man on the floor with one of the work knives in his side. Mr. Nash was kneeling beside him, putting pressure on the wound, trying to stop the bleeding. The atmosphere was very stressful; apparently one of the other guards had tried to pull the knife out and Mr. Nash had stopped him from doing so—"

Again, Mr. Ludlow stopped her. "Did you see this, Miss Marsham? You have just stated that when you arrived in the work area, Mr. Nash was beside the injured man and tending to him. Now you say that he had to stop another guard from pulling out the knife. Did you actually see the guard do this?"

"Oh. No," Penny admitted. "That happened before we arrived. All I saw was Mr. Nash trying to tend to the injured man. And Mr. Reece was there, supporting what Napoleon was doing. Then, of course, Dr. Palin and Dr. Soames moved in and took over. We carried the injured man back in the infirmary."

"Fine, Miss Marsham. Carry on. But please, try to stick with what you personally witnessed—not what you think happened, but what you know for yourself did happen."

"Yes, sir. We got the injured man into the infirmary and Dr. Palin, Dr. Soames, and Mr. Nash went about treating him. When he was finally resting quietly, Mr. Nash went to sit over by the counter, and Dr. Palin spoke with him there. I don't know what they were saying, but it seemed friendly enough. I saw Mr. Nash smile.

"Then Dr. Palin left to do paperwork or something, and Mr. Reece also left the infirmary. It was then that Mr. Carson and one of the other guards entered and approached Napoleon. Everybody became nervous; you could feel it in the air, that something bad was about to happen.

"The two guards positioned themselves so Mr. Nash was trapped, and then they started talking to him. But it wasn't friendly; it was threatening. They accused him of breaking rules while on the work floor, and the fact that he was only doing his duty as the medical assistant didn't seem to matter to them. They were determined to find fault with his behavior.

"Dr. Mariam tried to reason with them, but they shut her out. Dr. Palin returned and tried to stop the harassment as well, but Officer Carson pushed him down. Then they started to . . ."

Penny stopped talking, sudden emotion at the recollection of the beating caught her throat and threatened to strangle off her words. She felt Jack's foot gently touch hers under the table and her determination to be heard took over.

"They beat him! He had done nothing! He had been totally submissive to them, and they beat him with those awful clubs. Even after he went down and rolled in a ball, trying to protect himself, they carried on kicking him."

Penny's other hand went to her mouth as she fought to hold back the sob which threatened to burst forth. She so hated that about herself, this tendency to start crying when things got difficult or upsetting. She had to gain more self-control. She fought against the emotions and finally took a deep breath and looked to Mr. Ludlow.

"I had to stop them," she stated, matter-of-factly. "I couldn't just stand there and watch that beating carry on."

"You had to stop them, Miss Marsham?" Ludlow asked. "How did you manage that?"

"I got in between them," she stated. "I told them to stop hurting him."

There were some smiles passed amongst the board members as they tried to picture this slip of a young woman standing up to two prison guards.

"And did they stop?" Ludlow asked.

"Yes, they did," Penny puffed up with pride. "Then Dr. Palin was back on his feet, and he told them to get out. They had overstepped their authority and the warden was going to hear about it. Officer Carson said something else to Napoleon at that time, but I don't know what it was. Then they left."

"All right, Miss Marsham, thank you. You may sit down. Now, I have Dr. Palin's statement here which pretty much supports what Miss Marsham has described, but he was not on the floor himself at the time of the apparent assault upon the guard, Officer Thompson, I believe. Mr. Granger, do you have an eyewitness to this assault?"

"Yes, sir, I do," Steven announced, then nodded to Kenny.

Kenny stood up.

"Good afternoon, gentlemen," he greeted the board. "My name is Kenneth Reece, and I've been a guard at the U.S. Penitentiary at Laramie City for twenty years. I've seen a lot of things go on there that I feel, at this point, should not be allowed to continue. But I will focus on this particular incident, as it does demonstrate the typical attitude of some of the guards toward the inmates.

"I was on the work floor when the inmate, Mr. Ames, was stabbed in a fight between himself and another, unidentified, inmate. The knife entered Mr. Ames here," and Kenny indicated on his own ribcage where the knife wound had been. "Mr. Ames was laying on the floor, obviously in a great deal of pain. Officer Thompson, one of the junior guards, approached the inmate and grabbed hold of the knife handle with the apparent intent of pulling the weapon out.

"Mr. Nash, who is the medical assistant to Dr. Palin, recognized this act as being detrimental to the welfare of the injured man, and came forward to stop the action.

"He told the guard first to not pull the knife out, but when officer Thompson ignored him, Mr. Nash physically pushed him away, then stepped in to apply pressure to the wound until Dr. Palin and Dr. Soames arrived to take over.

"Officer Thompson took exception to this treatment from an inmate and began to beat Mr. Nash across the shoulders with his club.

"At this point, I intervened. As the official medical assistant, Mr. Nash was well within his rights to do whatever was necessary to ensure the proper treatment of an injured man. It is generally accepted that the usual rules for an inmate's conduct are suspended when an injured man's life is at stake, and that was indeed, the case here. Although it is a punishable offence for an inmate to push a guard, under these circumstances, a temporary loss of privileges would have sufficed. Dr. Palin later commented that Mr. Nash's actions on the work floor saved Mr. Ames's life.

"It is also generally accepted that when the medical assistant is in the infirmary tending to his duties there, he is not subject to the rules that he would be when out on the work floor, tending to his regular duties. Officer Carson was not within his rights to accuse the inmate of breaking any rules and was certainly not within his rights to delve out punishment in that manner.

"If there had been some dispute over the legitimacy of Mr. Nash's actions that day, then Officer Carson should have taken that up with Warden Mitchell. At that point, if it had been deemed appropriate, proper punishment would have been ordered and executed in a controlled fashion. Done as it was, it can only be called an act of unprovoked abuse against a man who was only doing his duty.

"Since this incident, I'm sorry to say, there has been another situation take place that became the deciding factor for me to attend this hearing. A fight broke out that involved several inmates, including Mr. Nash. This fight did result in the death of one inmate. The death was not caused by Mr. Nash, again, he tried to do what he could to save the man, but he was unable to. Mr. Nash's other actions during this incident did warrant some form of punishment, but not to the extent it was given.

"Indeed, it is my opinion that what Officer Carson inflicted upon Mr. Nash that day could only be called torture and went far beyond what would have been considered appropriate punishment for the misdeeds perpetrated."

At this point in Kenny's testimony, Jack sat up with interest. Leon had said nothing about torture in his last letter. In fact, there had only been a casual mention of "the usual punishment" for fighting. What had happened that Leon felt he could not tell his best friend and partner about?

"This is a dangerous accusation to make, Officer Reece," Mr. Ludlow cautioned him. "Are you sure you wish to continue with this testimony?"

"Yes sir," Kenny was adamant. "I believe that it is important for this incident to be brought to light so that the members of this board will have a clear understanding of what is happening in our prisons."

"All right, Officer Reece. You still hold the floor."

Kenny nodded. He paused to collect his thoughts, then began his narrative.

"As stated, during this fight, the inmate, Morrice Lobinskie, was killed. This man ran with the Elk Mountain Gang, so Nash took it to heart. Then a second member of his old gang was attacked.

"Nash's emotions were running high by then, and even though he was aware that it was a set-up, he nonetheless, went to the defense of his other friend. The four-way battle that ensued was fierce. Nash's blood was up, and he was fighting for his life and the life of his friend.

"Now, again, it was Officer Thompson who decided he was going to simply step in and break up the fight. Mr. Thompson, without identifying himself first as a guard, put a hand on Nash's back, and that inmate, still in a fight lust, swung on the guard and struck him on the top of the shoulder, breaking his collar bone."

Jack groaned, shaking his head. So much for his uncle staying out of trouble.

"As soon as Nash realized what he had done, he became passive and backed off the guard. Unfortunately, the other guards in attendance did not back off and they beat Nash to the floor and ultimately had to be ordered off him by the senior guard, Officer Carson.

"At this point, I was concerned for the safety of Mr. Nash. As already exhibited to the members of the board by Miss Marsham, Officer Carson can be overly aggressive when dealing with Mr. Nash. Nash is an extremely intelligent and charismatic individual, and unfortunately, Officer Carson tends to resent those qualities in an inmate and will do everything he can to break him. All in the guise of legitimate punishment.

"In this instance, I'm sorry to say, Officer Carson went too far. I am agreeable to the argument that Mr. Nash was deserving of some form of punishment for fighting, and for striking a guard, albeit, accidentally. But Officer Carson overstepped his authority in this case, and as mentioned before, it was what transpired next that convinced me to step forward and bring to light some of the abuses that have been taking place at the prison."

Kenny hesitated again and glanced regretfully at Jack and Penny. He knew, since he always read over Nash's mail, coming and going, that Nash had not told Jack of this incident, at least not in detail. None of Nash's friends knew anything about this event, and Kenny realized it was going to be hard for them to hear about it now.

He took another deep breath and continued. "What happened to Mr. Nash at the hands of Officer Carson at this point, can only be described as torture. I'm sure you gentlemen are aware of what it means to subject an individual to 'strappado'."

The men on the committee all paled and looked uncomfortable. Mr. Ludlow nodded. Steven groaned. Jack and Penny exchanged a questioning look, neither of them recognizing the term. It was Steven's reaction that set Jack's nerves on edge.

"Nash was forced to endure four hours of it," Kenny informed them. "He was never dropped any distance, which would surely have dislocated his shoulders, but he was left to hang in agony for the duration. In fact, Officer Carson had ordered it to last five hours, which could have resulted in Mr. Nash's death but, fortunately, I was able to take over and bring him down after four."

"He survived four hours of strappado?" Dr. Simons asked, speaking out of turn in his consternation. "Drs. Palin and Soames did make reference to this in their testimonies, but neither were an eye-witness to it. I was sure they were mistaken, since I was part of the committee that had it abolished."

"I'm sorry to say that they were not mistaken, Dr. Simons, and that our prison, at least, is still set up for it," Kenny observed dryly. "Even if it is not generally used, the option is there if the senior guard or the warden choose to utilize it."

A heavy silence fell upon the room as the board members considered this unfortunate situation.

Jack's concern turned into a knot of dread that hit his stomach and stayed there. He didn't know what strappado was, but by the context of the conversation, he already knew he didn't like it.

"This incident with Mr. Nash, though extreme, is an example of many such abuses that have been allowed to continue at the prison," Kenny carried on. "The Auburn System was put in place with all the best of intentions. But even with the open-ended guidelines on punishments put aside, the psychological benefits that were initially intended by the system's structure have proven to be unsubstantiated."

Dr. Dalton, the director of mental health for the prisons, allowed a nervous cough to come fourth and quickly tried to turn it into a simple clearing of his throat.

Kenny noted it but ignored it and simply carried on with his testimony.

"In the twenty years I have worked within the structure of this system, I have seen the mental stability of long-term inmates deteriorate rather than improve with the enforced social isolation. Aggression and frustration build up over time, resulting in tensions between the inmates and resentments toward the guards.

"On the other side of the same coin, depression often takes hold of certain individuals, and suicides are not uncommon within our walls. Indeed, there have even been instances of former inmates who have served their time and been released, only to find they can no longer function within our society. They often return to criminal behavior, or, in some cases, end up taking their own lives after the fact.

"It is my opinion, based on years of experience at the prison, that changes are called for. There need to be stricter guidelines put in place when it comes to administering punishments, and that these guidelines be enforced, not only by the warden, but by a committee such as this, to ensure its integrity. The ruling that prisoners are not allowed to talk to one another, though sound in its original concept, the reality of it, and its consequences, need to be examined more closely. Personally, again, based on my experience, I have found the effects of this ruling to be detrimental to a person's sanity rather than helpful to them in gaining insights into their previous criminal behavior.

"I highly recommend to the board members that a group of officials be sent to the Laramie prison to carry out an inspection of the institution and of the people who are in charge of its operation. I also recommend that the current system of running the prison needs to be re-examined and re-structured to lift it out of the archaic bog that it is currently wallowing in. The fact that most of our inmates are released back into society in a worse state of mind than they were in when they entered the institution, is a loud and clear warning that the current system is not working.

"On that recommendation, I now conclude my testimony. I thank you, gentlemen, for your time."

Kenny sat down.

The room remained ominously silent until Mr. Ludlow roused himself from his trance and took control of the meeting.

"Ah, yes! Thank you, Mr. Reece. Your comments are enlightening to say the least. Shall we continue?"

"Yes, ah . . ." Steven recovered his composure and nodded to Jack.

Jack stood up and acknowledged the three officials.

"Good afternoon. My name is Jackson Kiefer, and I've known Napoleon Nash all my life. He's my uncle, my business partner, and by best friend. I suppose that makes me the best person to talk about how prison life has changed 'im."

Jack hesitated a moment to collect his thoughts. He'd had all of this sorted out, with notes on what to say and when to say it, but now that he was here and facing these people, his mind had set the brakes and was fighting against him. He brought his hand up to cover a nervous cough, then absently scratched his chin to get focused and thinking clearly again.

"Leon's a proud man," he continued, "and, I suppose, like most of us he can be stubborn when he feels that he's in the right. He's also real intelligent. Some might even say, himself included, that he's a genius. More than anything else he's a natural leader.

"But over these few years that he's been in that prison, he's changed from the outgoing, confident man I've always known, to being sullen, indecisive, and afraid for his own safety.

"I used ta think that being on the run was dangerous, but it ain't nothin' compared ta what my uncle is now faced with every day. I see 'im sinkin' further and further into depression with each visit. I'm livin' in fear of what's gonna happen to 'im in there. Not that I think he is gonna do anything to himself, but that one of the guards, or even one of the other inmates, is gonna kill 'im.

"That shouldn't be. If he is in the custody of the Auburn Prison System, then that same system should support the inmates and make sure they're safe from the brutality that Leon has already been subjected to.

"Leon had already learned not ta trust people. I suppose, two young teenagers tryin' ta make their way on their own, presented easy marks for people out ta make a buck, and every time we got burned, well, that was just one more reason not ta trust the next fella we come across. So, trust, friendship, loyalty, well, Leon just don't hand them things out easily. But when he does, he means it. Yessir, ifn you ever earned Leon's respect, he would stand by ya to the bitter end."

At this point in Jack's narrative, Kenny became reflective. Not only did Jack's reasoning for Nash's behavior reflect what Nash himself had confided, but the significance of that confidence was not lost on the guard. For some reason, Nash trusted him, and now realizing what a rarity that was, Kenny was even more determined to see that changes were made.

Jack continued. "I don't know what 'strappado' means, but from the reactions of you folks, I get the feelin' it ain't somethin' nice. Lettin' men like Warden Mitchell and Officer Carson do as they want is simply leavin' the door open for abuse as far as I'm concerned.

"As I said, Leon has always been kinda skeptical about most folks' intentions and now, it seems, he's lost all hope. Is that what prison is supposed ta do to a man? Strip 'im of everything that makes 'im a person? Of takin' away the very skills he needs ta make a life outside them walls?

"That ain't right. Not at all. I'm real angry right now, angry that right from Governor Moonlight, all the way down through the warden and the senior guard, this kinda treatment is allowed to continue. And I wanna know just what you folks, who are supposed ta care about the treatment of the inmates, are gonna do about it."

Jack released a deep sigh and glanced down at his notes, hoping he had gotten everything out that he'd wanted to. He looked up to the board members and gave a nod.

"I suppose that's all I have ta say about that," he concluded. "Thank you for your attention, and I hope I have been able ta get ya to see things a little different."

Jack sat down, and they all waited while the board members finished jotting down notes and making quiet comments between themselves.

"Thank you, Mr. Kiefer," Ludlow acknowledged. "We will certainly take your comments into consideration. "Mr. Granger, are there any more testimonials you wish to present at this time?"

Steven stood up to face the board. "No sir, Mr. Ludlow. This concludes our presentation."

"Fine. I suggest we take a short break and return here at 3:00 p.m. At this time, Mr. Granger, you may present your closing statements."

***

Ten minutes later found the group sitting around a large table in the visitors' lounge. A stove was in the corner offering both warmth and coffee to help ease the time awaiting appointments. Unfortunately, the mood was strained. Everyone had been aware that Kenny's testimony was going to have some disturbing content, but no one had realized how disturbing.

For Steven, who was already aware of strappado, the knowledge that this form of punishment had been inflicted upon his friend and client was enough to sicken him into stunned silence.

Once the group settled in the lounge, Steven took the time to describe the form of punishment to those who were not aware of its meaning.

Penny was sullen. She sat staring into space and holding onto Jack's hand with both of hers, allowing her coffee to sit untouched and cooling. One part of her tried to imagine such a thing, while another part of her only wanted to block it out.

Jack was angry. Not just at this one revelation, but at so many different things. Not only at those people to whom he had already referred during his testimony, but he was angry at himself for his inability to get his uncle out of there. And, he was angry at Leon. Why had his uncle not told him about this? Why had he kept it hidden? The usual punishment for fighting! What the hell was that all about?

"Try not to be too angry with him, Jack," Kenny's voice broke through his silent raging. "I'm sure Nash didn't tell you because he knew it would upset you, and there was nothing you could have done about it anyway."

Jack shot a glance at Kenny. Had his thoughts been that easy to read?

"I suppose," he mumbled, and took a drink of cold coffee through the hard line of his jaw.

"Officer Reece's testimony was disturbing," Steven pronounced, "but also, very effective. Thanks to the testimonials from both of you, along with Dr. Palin's medical reports, and Dr. Soames's testimonial backing them up, I believe we've been successful in getting their attention."

Jack snorted, his optimism at a low ebb.

"I know, Jack," Steven commiserated. "I know it sounds callous, and I certainly don't mean it that way. But this incident may have just given us the ammunition we need to get some action happening here."

Jack rolled his eyes. He was in no mood to be placated.

Penny continued to hold his hand, trying to be supportive. She looked at her sister, but neither of them seemed much in the mood for chatting.

Steven took a deep breath. The motivation level in this group was dipping down into nil.

"Do try to stay positive," Steven said. "We have presented a very solid case here. But keep in mind, no matter what the board decides, changes will not happen immediately. What I'm hoping for here is to simply get the wheels in motion, make the board members aware of what is happening so they can begin an investigation."

Jack sighed. "I guess that does make sense, but it sure ain't encouraging. Mitchell could make Leon's life a living hell before an investigation can get in there."

"I know," Seven agreed. "But we were all aware of the dangers here, Mr. Nash included. Believe me, Jack, it's the only way to get any improvements at all in that prison."

Jack simply nodded. He felt Penny squeeze his hand and he smiled at her as he returned the gesture.

Thank goodness for friends.

***

Three o'clock found the meeting once again in session.

Steven snapped open his briefcase and took out the notes for his closing statement. He then set the case onto the floor and stood up to address the board members.

"Mr. Ludlow, Dr. Simons, Dr. Dalton, I am now prepared to present my summary and closing statements to the board."

"Thank you, Mr. Granger," Ludlow responded. "You may proceed."

Steven glanced at his paperwork to get his bearings, then focused his attention on the board members.

"In the case of the Auburn Prison System itself, I can only reiterate what Mr. Reece has already petitioned; that people of some authority need to re-examine how the Wyoming Penitentiary in Laramie City is being managed. They need to instigate stricter adherence to the guidelines controlling the manner of punishments used, and the level of severity allowed, not only by law, but by decency.

"We also put to the board that the Auburn Prison System needs to be re-examined. That the dictate of total silence amongst the prisoners has a severe detrimental rather than beneficial effect upon long-term inmates and should be abolished. Also, we put to the board, that under controlled conditions, physical contact should be allowed between inmates and their friends and family. We are social creatures, gentlemen! Being deprived of those very basic needs cannot help but create issues for those individuals who are subject to the current system.

"As I'm sure we are all aware, Wyoming is quickly moving toward statehood. Governor Moonlight has shown his commitment to bringing our territory up to the challenge of attaining that goal by hiring Marshal Morrison to clean up the outlaw bands that are still wreaking havoc amongst the citizenry. The governor has also done a lot to update many longstanding, but now archaic rules and laws, and to also assist companies and small businesses to grow and develop, thereby strengthening our territory's financial base.

"Now, with Marshal Morrison running for mayor, we can expect Rawlins to move forward and support the changes deemed necessary for this move toward statehood.

"But I believe how we treat our less fortunate citizens, the elderly, the ill, the poverty stricken, and our prisoners, is equally as important. What a feather in the cap of Wyoming as a new state, to be able to show, by example, how to be compassionate and how to encourage the population to prosper and grow. And to be able to show a long list of released inmates of our prison system, returning to life outside those walls as completely reformed and socially adjusted citizens, rather than suicidal misfits, who are no longer capable of settling in and contributing to society.

"With that, I conclude my statement. I can only hope that we have been successful in stating our case with eloquence and conviction. Thank you for your time and consideration."

Steven sat down, and the assembly awaited the next step.

After a few moments of conferring, Mr. Ludlow turned to address the group.

"Ladies and gentlemen, this has indeed been a most enlightening afternoon. This hearing will now be adjourned for the day, as it is getting late. Tomorrow morning, I shall present the testimonials of this hearing to Governor Moonlight, along with the other statements from Doctors Palin and Soames, and the late Judge MacEnro's representative, Mr. Barkley. We will also give Governor Moonlight our recommendations at that time, so he will have all the information we do, and can then make an informed decision. This hearing will re-convene at 1:00 tomorrow afternoon. At such time, I will inform you of this board's decision concerning these matters. This hearing is now adjourned."

***

"What do ya mean, he's runnin' for mayor?" Jack was incensed. "When did that happen?"

"About a month ago," Steven admitted. "I'm sorry, I guess I never even thought to mention it. He's been a U.S. Marshal for a several years now, so him taking the next step in his career did not seem unusual."

The group sat around a large table at one of the local restaurants, trying to relax and unwind from the stresses of the day. However, Steven's casual announcement that Morrison was moving up the political ladder was not helping Jack's digestion.

Sheriff Taggard Murphy had joined them to offer support and further testimony if it had been required. But mainly he was there because he was just as involved in Leon's situation as anyone else, and he wanted to hear the decision first hand.

When Jack turned a sharp, accusing glare at him, he almost

regretted coming.

"Did you know about this, Taggard?" he demanded.

Taggard sighed, knowing he was in for another argument with the overly taxed ex-outlaw.

"Yeah Jack, I did know about it. And no, I didn't tell ya. And before ya start yellin' at me and demandin' 'why', it was for the very same reason I didn't tell ya about the raid on Elk Mountain. It only woulda made ya mad at a time when we needed ya to be focused, and there's nothin' you could do about it anyway. Besides that, Morrison being elected as mayor won't have any effect on our endeavors now. He may not even win, he's so busy gettin' after the rest of the Wyoming gangs. It is springtime, and that does seem to be his favorite season to go hunting."

"What about Gus?" Jack asked. "Morrison was determined ta track 'im down, but I ain't heard nothin'." Then Jack sent Taggard a suspicious glare. "Or is that one more thing you decided not ta mention?"

"No. I'd a told ya if Morrison had found Shaffer. The last I heard about Gus Shaffer he was holed up with the Cripple Creek boys, at least for the winter."

Penny rolled her eyes, and Jack groaned.

"I told that idiot to stay away from the other bands," Jack growled. "Morrison was gonna be after them, and he should head north or south—anywhere but stayin' here."

"What do ya mean, you 'told him'?" Taggard's tone turned hard. "When did you talk to Gus Shaffer?"

"Oh! Well . . . umm," Jack and Penny exchanged guilty looks. "Gus came to the ranch shortly after Malachi and Lobo were sent ta prison. He thought I'd had somethin' to do with settin' up that ambush, and he wanted ta talk about it."

Penny glanced down at her plate as she recalled the incident. "I must admit, he frightened me. After Jack talked him into putting his gun away and letting me go, I realized he was just scared, but at first, I had no idea how that was going to go."

Taggard was on a slow burn as he turned his attention from Penny to Jack. "What was that!"

Jack sent Penny a quick glance and she bit her lip, realizing that she may have over-stepped by mentioning the encounter.

Jack waved it away as inevitable, then focused on calming the waters. "He was just scared. I had it under control; nobody was gonna get hurt. Gus backed off fast enough, and we was able to talk it out."

"Uh huh," was Taggard's skeptical response. "And you just let him walk away? At the very least, you shoulda let Sheriff Jacobs know he was in the area. Like I said before, you gotta decide which side of the fence you're on."

Jack looked sheepish but stuck to his guns.

"He's a friend, Taggard. I'm not gonna turn on a friend. I tried to convince 'im to turn himself in ta Jacobs, then I could send you a telegram to come get him, keepin' Morrison out of it altogether. But he weren't havin' any of it.

"So, then I told him his best bet was ta get outta the country, or at the very least, this part of it. I told him if he stayed in this area, Morrison would track 'im down and probably kill 'im. I hoped he'd taken that advice and disappeared. If he's up with the Cripple Creek boys, he don't stand a chance. Morrison's gonna get 'im for sure."

"You can't know that, Jack," Taggard responded, after a moment of heavy silence. "Maybe Shaffer has already left those boys and has taken your advice. Maybe he's already out of the country."

"I doubt it," Jack responded. "He said he wanted to wait for Malachi, and I'm willin' ta bet that's exactly what he's doin'. That bastard, Morrison, is gonna get 'im, and it irks me that he should benefit from the things he's done. Next thing ya know, he's gonna be in the senate, and then—oh no! What if he becomes governor? Ah jeez. We gotta get Leon outta there before that happens, or he's never gonna see the light a day again."

This premonition was met with some skeptical smiles.

"I highly doubt that would happen, Jack," Steven assured him. "Marshal Morrison certainly has aspirations, but even if the governorship was one of them, it would take him years to reach that level."

"All he needs is twenty," Jack mumbled.

"Well, let's not yell 'till we're hit," Taggard suggested. "I, for one, think we have a pretty strong case here; we oughta get some good results coming out of it."

"I agree," Steven added. "If this doesn't get some action, then nothing will."

"Yeah, I suppose." Jack then perked up and addressed the group. "In any case, I wanna thank all of ya for comin' forward like this and tryin' ta help. Especially you, Kenny, you've got more on the line here than any of us."

"I couldn't sit back and watch those abuses any longer," Kenny answered. "I only hope it makes a difference. Changes can sometimes be slow to happen, but we have to start somewhere."

Jack nodded, then tried to convince himself to eat something.

***

By 8:00 the supper had wound down, and everybody went their separate ways. It was a wet and chilly night, so no one felt like spending time out on the town. Besides, they were all tired after their stressful day. Hotel rooms seemed to be next on the agenda for the ladies, and though the men headed to the saloon for a relaxing beer, they were not too far from calling it a night.

The next morning dawned chilly and gray again, but at least it had stopped raining. They all met for breakfast, but though the coffee tasted real good, appetites were still at a low ebb.

"How are your youngsters doin', Kenny?" Jack asked, just for the conversation.

Kenny smiled. "They're fine. The boys still want you to come by and show them your fast draw, and Eve already has the wedding plans finalized."

Everyone glanced over at this comment.

Penny's brows went up. "Who's Eve, and what wedding plans?"

Jack smiled and gave Penny a kiss on her hand. "Evelyn is Kenny's youngest, who thinks that she's in love with me. Apparently, she has decided that I'm gonna marry her."

"Really?" was Penny's response.

Kenny nodded. "She's quite adamant."

"I'm afraid she's going to have to get in line," Penny commented. "This man is already taken."

"Oh, I dunno, Penny," Jack speculated. "Just 'cause we're courtin', well that don't mean a man can't still be checkin' out his other options. Evelyn's a real pretty little—"

"Don't you dare," Penny teased him and punched his arm. "Besides, I'm sure she's much too young for you."

"Ho, ho—there's the pot callin' the kettle black. I seem ta recall you havin' a lot 'a arguments supportin' May-December matches."

"That's different!"

"I'll say," Kenny laughed. "You have nothing to worry about, Miss Marsham; my Evelyn is not yet ten years old. Still, if she had another six years on her, you might have been in for some competition there."

Penny smiled. "I'm sure she's a real sweetheart. I'd love to meet her sometime."

Kenny nodded. "We'll see what we can arrange. She might be a little jealous of you though, so watch out."

"Nothin' like bein' surrounded by admirers ta make a man feel special," Jack observed, with a grin.

***

It seemed to take forever for 1:00 to finally roll around, and by 12:30 everyone's nerves were on edge again. They all gathered anxiously in the hallway until the doors to their chamber opened, and the group made their way inside. Once seated, they waited nervously for the board members to arrive and get settled, then amidst subtle coughing and needless paper shuffling, the meeting got underway.

"Ladies and gentlemen," Mr. Ludlow acknowledged them all. "I'm glad to see you could all make it back. Let's get started, shall we?

"In the matter of the Auburn Prison System and the effectiveness of its rehabilitation of the criminal element, we would have to question the very reasons for incarceration in the first place. Do we send our criminals to prison to be rehabilitated, or to be punished? I'm afraid this is a question that has been debated endlessly by far more informed individuals than those of us gathered here today.

"As it stands now, the Auburn system has been very effective in controlling the criminal element, and we see no reason to make changes to that system as a whole.

"However, in the more specific case of the Penitentiary at Laramie City, there would appear to be evidence of some misuse of power by those in authority. The best system in the world cannot be expected to work successfully if the people within it do not adhere to the guidelines laid down by it. Therefore, it has been agreed that an inspection of the prison and its contingent of employees, including the warden, will be undertaken and that any misuse of authority will be rectified.

"This concludes our hearing ladies and gentlemen. I want to thank you for your patience and your obvious commitment to these issues. Good day."

The members of the board did not waste any time gathering up their pointless paperwork and making a hasty retreat out the back door.

The members of the assembly sat in disappointed silence, nobody moving while the reality of the words gradually soaked in. Eventually, big sighs could be heard, and people began to shift in their chairs and make eye contact with one another.

"Well, that could have gone better," Steven understated. "If the board members feel that incarceration is for punishment and not rehabilitation, then they may not take this situation seriously."

"But Mr. Ludlow did say they'd look into it," Penny pointed out. "I mean, if they send someone there to really see what is going on, won't that make a difference?"

"Yeah, for a while," Jack mumbled. "But they won't be at the prison forever, and once they're gone, Mitchell will just go right back to how he was doin' things in the first place."

Caroline shuffled her husband's unneeded paperwork and stuffed them back into his brief case just to give herself something to do. "We may have just made Leon's life worse, not better," she commented.

"We all knew the risks," Steven said as he pulled the brief case closer to himself and rearranged his notes. "Even Mr. Nash understood that there could be consequences to this hearing. Once Warden Mitchell is aware that he is being watched, he could very well back off for now. If an investigation into the prison does indeed take place, they could find enough evidence to have Mitchell removed from his position."

Jack harrumphed. "Yeah, maybe. But how long will that take?"

Steven snapped his briefcase closed and stood up. "What did you expect? That the board would send someone to the prison this instant and all Mr. Nash's problems would be over? It doesn't work that way, Jack."

"Yeah, I know." Jack's tone was sardonic, as he pushed himself away from the table. "A man will grow old and gray waitin' for the legal system ta get the job done."

Both Steven and Kenny sent Jack hard looks.

"Oh relax," the ex-outlaw assured them. "I ain't gonna do nothin'. I guess I've been law-abidin' too long ta go back to the old ways now. That don't mean I can't reminisce though, do it?"

Steven smiled and gave Jack a pat on the shoulder.

"No, I guess it doesn't."

"As long as that's all you do," Kenny added then sent Penny a pointed look. "And that goes for you, too, young lady. You're developing quite a reputation for being unpredictable."

Penny smiled at the compliment.

"Thank you. But no, my undercover days are done. Caroline and I will just have to keep those letters going to the governor's office."

Caroline laughed as she and her sister linked arms.

"We certainly will! We have not yet begun to fight!"

Steven rolled his eyes as the gentlemen followed the two ladies out of the room.

"Mr. Mitchell has no idea of the wrath headed his way."

***

Laramie, Wyoming

"How did it go?" Leon asked.

"Better than it could have gone, but still not all we had hoped for," Steven answered.

Leon frowned and looked at Jack. "Is there going to be an investigation or not?"

Before Jack could answer, Steven took the floor again.

"Mr. Ludlow did agree to send someone here to investigate the allegations. The members of the board were shocked to hear about the punishment you received last Christmas."

"They weren't the only ones who were shocked," Jack grumbled. "Why didn't ya tell me what they'd done? 'Usual punishment', my ass."

Leon's brows flicked up at Jack's language.

He sighed. "What would have been the point? There was nothing you could do. Besides, Kenny knew all about it, and if anyone was going to present it rationally to the board, it would be him."

"Yeah, well, ya still coulda told me."

Leon gave up the discussion as a lost cause and turned back to Steven.

"So, are they going to look into it?"

"Yes," Steven said, "But the main problem is how the Prison Board of Commissioners define the role of the prisons. Though there are those who feel the prison system should be focused on reforming the behavior of criminals, so they can be released back into society as functioning, law-abiding citizens, there are still many who feel that prison is for punishment."

Leon groaned. "So, all the abuses going on here are considered acceptable?"

"Not entirely," Steven assured him. "There are two doctors on the board, one of medical science and the other for mental health. Both gentlemen have now been alerted to what is going on here and I expect they'll be interested in the extent to which their recommendations are being abused."

Leon sat back in his chair and nodded. "Does Mitchell know he is about to have company?"

"Not yet. Mr. Ludlow wants to get a plan of action organized before sending anyone here. But it will happen, Mr. Nash. The fight is just beginning."

Leon laughed. "That's almost what I'm afraid of." He sent Jack a ironic smile. "Here we go, partner. It'll be interesting to see how Mr. Mitchell feels about being investigated."

Jack's lip twitched as the worry that was constantly with him tightened a notch. "Yeah."

"We do have some good news though," Steven said. "I received word this morning that the Supreme Court has accepted our petition. We have two months to prepare."

Jack cocked a brow at him. "They accepted it?"

"Yes. And I'm surprised at how quickly they'll hear our case. Often it can take a year or more after acceptance before the appeal. So, we lucked out there. It also means that having it close to the end of their season, we won't have to wait for months to get their decision. It just means that I have to scramble now to get our case organized.

"Apparently, the court feels, as I do, that this case could have significant ramifications on how deals made with the governors' office concerning undercover work and possible pardons should be handled."

Leon smirked. "But not on my case is particular?"

"It is your case that is in question, Mr. Nash. The decision the Wyoming Supreme Court comes to concerning yourself will affect how this type of arrangement will be handled from now on. I believe that when Governor Warren granted Mr. Kiefer his pardon, he made a big mistake by doing so."

"What?" Jack sat up straighter. "What do ya mean? You don't think I shoulda got it?"

"No, no, Jack, that's not what I meant. Governor Warren, in granting you a pardon, basically admitted that there had been an arrangement between you. Therefore, it stands to reason that the arrangement also included Mr. Nash."

"Oh. Yeah, okay." Jack relaxed again. "That do make sense."

Leon still didn't look convinced. "So that's all you've got to go on? Jack got a pardon, therefore, I should have as well?"

Steven sighed, feeling ganged up on. "No, Mr. Nash, that is not what I'm saying. If we need to, we can use Miss Jansen's admission of coercing you into committing fraud. That may help us to some degree."

"I told you: I don't want Josie being pulled into this. I won't have my friends going to prison just to help me."

"I realize that, Mr. Nash. She will be granted immunity in exchange for her testimony, and no one outside the appeal need know of her involvement. However, we may not even need it. We have two new witnesses coming forward who were prevented from testifying at your trial and, I believe, the information they will present could sway the court in your favor."

Leon frowned. "What witnesses?"

"I can't tell you. Not yet. They're risking their careers by coming forward so the longer I can keep them anonymous, the better. Please, be patient."

Jack and Leon shared a glance and a sigh that was not lost on Steven.

"I know," he assured them. "But there is enough for you to deal with right now. Once the Board of Commissioners gets in touch with Warden Mitchell, things could get ugly here. You need to remain focused on this situation. Let me worry about the supreme court. I will inform you of the particulars when I can."

Leon remained silent for a moment. He still didn't like being left out of the loop, even though he had agreed to it. But Mr. Granger had a point. Leon had enough to deal with as it was.

"All right, Mr. Granger. I'll watch my back in here, and I will trust you to watch my back out there."

"Good.

***

Warden Mitchell sat at his desk and re-read the letter he had received from Governor Moonlight.

The governor was not a happy man.

> *Mason:*
>
> *Well, this is a fine pickle you've gotten us into—and just in time for the elections, too!*
>
> *I know I said you could have free rein when it came to handling your prisoners and your prison, but strappado, Mason? I thought you had more common sense that that. What's wrong with a good old fashion lashing? It worked wonders during the war, and I don't see any reason why it shouldn't work now.*
>
> *I've even got that blow-hard of a Texas rancher on my case—still! I'm almost tempted to send you a copy of the letter he wrote to me about this most recent incident. It's pages long, GODDAMMIT. He's even threatening to bring the Texas governor in on this case and really start being a thorn in my side. What is it with Texans: they think they run the whole bloody country.*
>
> *Now my hands are tied with that dang-blasted hearing, and all those self-righteous officials looking at me and wagging their heads. I have no choice but to bow to their decree and send in a committee to look at how you are running things over there.*
>
> *Just show them around, Mason, no need to go into details. They'll take a look, talk to a couple of the guards and maybe an inmate or two, just make sure they don't talk to that Nash bastard! It's him and his cohorts who*

are responsible for this, you know. Never would have thought that an outlaw could have so much power from inside a prison, GODDAMMIT.

One of your senior guards, Ken Reece, was at the hearing as well, along with some written testimonials from your prison doctor, so I'd be keeping an eye on those two, if I were you. Might even be better if you found a way to get rid of them altogether. Going on about unwarranted abuses, etc.! Damn, Mr. Reece even had the audacity to suggest that the whole Auburn Prison system needed to be examined and adjusted to fit 'modern times'. Seems to be working fine as far as I'm concerned.

Anyway, sorry for the inconvenience, Mason. But like I said, my hands are tied. With us heading towards statehood, the last thing we need is to be accused of torturing our prisoners. Just watch your back and be careful. And lay off the hard-core stuff for now, okay? Once the committee gets their snoot full and leave, then you can do whatever you want, so long as it gets the job done and I don't hear about it!

T. Moonlight.

Mitchell ground his teeth and scrunched the letter up into a seething ball.

That backstabbing bastard! he snarled. *First, he says I have free rein to run the prison anyway I deem fit, and now, after a little bit of pressure from the bleeding hearts, he's running to his corner to hide. Close to statehood, my ass. What a fucking hypocrite.*

And that Reece and Palin, what a surprise they're involved in all this. I'll have to do something about those two. But what? It can't be too obvious, right after the hearing. It would look awfully suspicious if two of the main opponents suddenly got fired from their jobs. No, that wouldn't do at all. It would just make me appear even more guilty of wrong-doing, and I'm not guilty of anything other than running a prison the way it needs to be run.

These do-gooders have no idea what it's like trying to keep order in this place. Thank goodness for people like Carson, and now Thompson, too; they know how to do things around here. You can't mess around with these convicts. They're hard, vicious people, who only respect hard and vicious treatment. They'd run amok if people like Reece were running the show.

Oh well. What's done is done. I'll just do what the governor suggests and play the toady to those officials when they arrive. It sure would be nice to have a heads-up as to when they were coming. That would give me a chance to make sure Nash and Reece, and Palin, are out of the way. Damn! All I need is Nash to start mouthing off. That convict is more trouble than he's worth.

Hmm, what to do, what to do. This conundrum is going to take some thinking.

***

Leon was in the dark cell. He lived in the dark cell. Time had no meaning inside the pitch blackness and it seemed he would never got out of the dark cell. He was cold and damp, and he hugged his knees to his chest, shivering against the darkness.

Then he heard it, that soft imploring whisper that sent a chill down his spine.

Napai'aishe, my babi, why did you abandon me?

Even though Jenny had been only an infant when she died, and had no voice of her own, he knew it was her. He knew it was his *nammi*, his sister.

Napai'aishe, where did you go? I screamed for you. I cried for you, but you ran away. You left me. You left me . . .

He tried to shut her out, knowing that it was a dream, knowing that she was long in her grave and had no power over him. But she still came to haunt him when his resistance was low. Like now.

Then the darkness began to fade back to a steel gray, and he wasn't in the dark cell anymore, he was in the concrete room full of ropes, and hoists, and pain. He felt a scream strangle his throat and he tried to back out of the room. He needed to get out. But he backed into someone, and spinning around, he came face to face with Carson, and the guard was laughing at him.

What's the matter, Nash? Don't you wanna play anymore?

NO. Please! I'm sorry. I didn't mean to. Please don't hurt me. Please.

Carson just laughed and grabbed his arm. Leon fought against him, tossing and turning, trying to pull away, but Carson had him in a vice, and Leon couldn't get loose. Then the guard was standing over by the far wall and continuing to laugh at him. Leon pleaded for mercy, but the guard wasn't listening; he didn't care.

Leon's wrists were tied with ropes and his arms were pulled out to the side. He fought and pleaded, as he struggled to get away, but the ropes tightened and continued to pull as he felt his muscles tearing. He screamed, just as much in terror as in pain as the ropes pulled at him, and he could feel his tendons stretching beyond endurance, until they finally snapped. His skin tore apart, and he felt the joints dislocating as his arms were ripped from his body.

He screamed and screamed . . .

"Nash! Wake up, goddammit. You're gonna get the whole prison in an uproar. Wake up!"

Leon was startled into consciousness. It was dark, except for the low lantern light in the aisle way. It was nighttime. Leon lay on his cot, gasping for air as the blood pounded in his ears, and his shoulders throbbed with pain. It was a warm night, but he was bathed in a cold sweat. He shivered, and his teeth chattered with fear.

"Dammit, Nash," he heard Officer Davis complaining from the aisle, "if you're gonna go mad, do it in silence, will ya?"

Then the lantern and the footsteps moved on.

Leon lay gasping in the semi-darkness, fear still holding him in its grip. He grabbed his blanket, and wrapping it around himself, he pushed into the corner of the wall and hugged his knees. He continued to shiver for some time while the numbness in his extremities slowly dissipated. His breathing continued to be ragged, as he rubbed his eyes and held his head, trying to calm himself down.

I'm going mad, I can feel it; that loss of control. I don't even know who I am anymore. Everything I thought I was is being challenged. Everything I've always thought to be the truth seems wrong. I have nothing left to hold onto, nothing to believe in, nothing to hope for.

He held his head in his hands and would have wept, if he could remember how.

He sat like this for a long time, holding himself, protecting himself within a ball of his own making. Finally, he fell back to sleep, still pushed into the corner of his cell with his back to the wall.

***

Arvada, Colorado

Jack Kiefer trotted his young horse down the lane toward the Rocking M. It was a warm spring day, and everything was coming up green and fresh; new life was everywhere.

He smiled as he glanced into the pasture on the right side of the lane and looked at the ever-increasing herd that inhabited it.

When he and Leon had first come to the ranch, this pasture had been set aside just for Karma and Midnight. Now those two still occupied the green space, but Daisy and Spade, along with his dam, Molly, as well as Monty and Spike, were also part of the group. Gov would be joining them, as soon as Jack wasn't in need of him anymore that day.

Jack's grin increased as he looked at the two brood mares, both large and uncomfortable with their current pregnancies. They were keeping one another company under the larger of the willow trees, standing beside each other, nose to tail, and each swishing flies away from the other's face. It was a lazy scene, and Gov looked at them, longing to join in on the group grazing.

Jack gave him a pat on the neck.

"Patience, young man," he spoke softly. "You'll soon be out there with them."

They jogged into the yard, with Gov dancing a bit as the two dogs and one large puppy came bouncing and barking out to greet them.

Jack maneuvered his horse around the canines and headed him over to the first barn where he would untack the animal and then get him settled in the pasture for the rest of the afternoon.

Once that was done, he strolled toward the house, and then noticed Jean sitting on the porch steps, playing with Eli. That is until the youngster noticed his Uncle Mathew and came at a run to greet him.

"Hey there, Mr. E!" Jack greeted him. "How are ya doin' today?"

"Good!" Eli insisted, as he grabbed Jack's hand and pulled him toward the porch, as though that wasn't where his uncle was headed in the first place. "C'mon—we're playin' a game called x's and o's."

"Really? Well, that sounds interesting," came the non-committal response. Jack could see that Jean was a little melancholy and his focus was on her, rather than on the three-year-old boy trying to get his attention. "Jean, is something wrong?"

Jean looked up. "Oh, Jack. I'm sorry. I didn't notice you."

"Uh huh." Jack sat down beside her on the step.

Eli sensed that things were moving toward an "adult" talk, and he settled in to play his game on his own.

Jack touched Jean's arm. "What's wrong?"

"Oh well," a wistful expression saddened her eyes as she watched her son playing. "David was by earlier. It seems that Maribelle has lost her baby again."

"Oh," Jack mumbled.

He put his arm around her shoulders and pulled her into a hug as a tear rolled down Jean's cheek.

"This is silly," she complained, as she impatiently brushed the moisture away.

"No, it ain't," Jack assured her. "You, more'n most of us, know what that loss means. You know what Sam and Maribelle are goin' through."

"Yes, I suppose." She absently reached out and brushed a lock of white blond hair from her son's eyes. Eli giggled at her, then went back to his serious play. "It just reminds me how precious our children are. And I thank God every day for the ones I have."

Jack tightened his hug and the two friends sat in silence for a few moments.

Jack felt out of place, comforting his friend about something that was more of a woman's issue. But he did feel badly for Sam and Maribelle. He knew how much they wanted a family and how hopeful they had been with this second attempt.

Though he had never lost a child himself, he had lost siblings and seen, first hand, the grief that parents go through. And occasionally, memories of his baby sister sprang up and caused his heart to ache. He, just like Leon, had known too much loss that way.

"They can try again, can't they?" Jack asked. "They're still young."

"No," Jean shook her head. "Maribelle had a very hard time of it—worse than the last one. David nearly lost her. He doesn't think she'll be able to get pregnant again and shouldn't even try. It's for the best, I suppose, since she probably wouldn't survive a third episode. Still, it's very sad. They wanted a family so badly."

"Yeah."

Then Jack got hit with an idea that came to him completely out of the blue. He tensed, as one often does when they know they've come face to face with an epiphany.

"What?" Jean asked.

"Well—I just had a thought."

"Don't keep me in suspense, Jack. What is it?"

"I've been to the orphanage in Laramie a couple a times now," he explained, "and you know, there are a lot 'a kids there who would love ta have parents of their own. Maybe it's not the right time ta mention it ta Sam—kinda early, I suppose—but . . . maybe. Give 'em time ta get over this disappointment, and maybe they'd be open to it."

"Adopting?"

"Yeah. I mean, why not? Sam and Maribelle really want a family, and them kids really want parents. Why not?"

Jean brightened as the possibility of it took hold of her. "That's a wonderful idea, Jack. What would they have to do to arrange it?"

"I dunno," Jack admitted. "The next time I'm out there, I'll ask Mariam about it. Maybe Sam and Maribelle could come with me later in the summer and meet with the Sisters and the kids. See if any of 'em fit."

Jean smiled and patted Jack's knee.

"This is very thoughtful of you," she said. "Oh, I do hope they will consider it. This could be exactly what they need. You're offering them some hope here. Once you've had a chance to speak with Dr. Mariam about it, then perhaps David can suggest it to them. It's a wonderful idea."

Jack smiled.

CHAPTER SEVENTEEN
THIS CHANGES THINGS

Laramie, Wyoming
April 1888

Spring brought the promise of warmer days as well as a return of visitors. It wasn't long before pressure from the orphanage prompted visits to that institution as well.

Leon did his best to be upbeat during this current visit and what with his profound natural ability to pull the wool over a person's eyes, he fooled just about everyone. He was not fooling Jack, however, and nor was he fooling young Sally, who seemed to already have a natural affinity for the infamous convict.

Most of the chatter during this visit had revolved around the previous Christmas, and how everyone had to buckle down and accept the confinements that the bad weather had dictated. They also got going about the gifts they had received and how they all still managed to have a nice supper, and did Mr. Nash have a good Christmas too?

Leon simply smiled and made some non-committal comments, and Jack rolled his eyes and wished his uncle would pull himself out of the slump he was in.

Finally, the conversation did move on to a subject that tweaked Leon's attention and brought up his interest level an honest notch or two.

One of the older boys, Michael, took advantage of a lull in the conversation and spoke up with some news of his own.

"Me and Henry are going to be leaving next month," he informed the visitors, "so, we probably won't be here the next time you come for a visit."

"Oh?" Leon sat up straighter. "Have you been offered something?"

"Yeah," Michael stated. "Mr. Harker, who owns the Two Blazes ranch, just north of town. He needs a couple of wranglers to help with the livestock, and he figures me and Henry will do just fine."

"Yeah!" Henry piped up. "I know it'll be hard work, but I love being around the horses, and we're gonna have a place to live and get paid to boot. It'll be great."

Leon and Jack exchanged knowing smiles. It'll be hard work, all right.

"Well now, that's real good," Jack complimented them. "Get out there and be your own men—start buildin' somethin' for yourselves."

"Yes," Leon agreed. "Nothing like ranch work to keep you out of trouble. Right, Jack?"

Jack snorted at him. "Yeah. You fellas will be kept busy, that's for sure."

"Have you ever done any ranch work?" Michael asked the two ex-outlaws.

"Ohh, yeah! Lots of ranch work," Leon admitted. "There are quite a few cattle drives in our pasts, aren't there, Jack."

"Yup," Jack nodded. "Good, honest work, though."

"Why didn't you stay with it?" Henry asked.

"Because we weren't good, honest people," Leon sniped.

Jack sent him a reproving look.

Over by the door, Kenny knitted his brow, taking note of Nash's cynicism during an occasion which usually brightened the inmate's mood.

Their audience sat quietly and stared back at them, not quite sure how they were supposed to take that comment. Was he joking or was he . . .?

"What's the matter, Mr. Nash?" Sally asked from the second row. "You don't seem very happy today."

Jack sent him a "now see what you've done" look, and Leon did have enough sense to feel guilty.

"No, you're right, Sally, I'm not feeling very happy today," Leon admitted. He had made a promise to himself that he was never going to lie to these children, and he sure wasn't about to start now. "I'm sorry. It's not your fault, and I shouldn't be taking it out on you lot. I lost a friend just after Christmas, and I suppose I'm not quite over it yet."

"Oh," Melanie responded. "That's too bad."

"Yeah," Charlie agreed, with some true feeling. "It's not nice to lose a friend."

Then Sally, being the intuitive soul that she was, once again ran up to the front of the room and took her friend's hand in both of hers and looked up at him with her big brown eyes.

"We're sorry that you feel bad, Mr. Nash. Can't we make you feel better?"

Leon smiled down at her, no longer surprised or uncomfortable with this child's display of uninhibited affection. He didn't answer her for a moment, he just looked into her eyes and stroked her soft hair.

"No, I don't think you can, sweetheart," he finally told her. "But I appreciate you wanting to try."

He put his hands under her arms and lifted her up to sit beside him on the front desk.

Kenny was unsure about this move and came in a little closer, but Mariam caught his eye and gave a subtle shake of her head.

"It'll be all right," she whispered. "Let's just see how this plays out."

Kenny relaxed a little but continued to keep a close watch.

As soon as Sally was settled in, she leaned into Leon and hugged his arm, but then her brow creased as she noticed his wrists. The act of hugging him had pulled the cuff of his tunic sleeve up just a bit, but far enough that the angry and still red welts left by the tight, blood-soaked leather bindings were exposed for all to see.

Leon was about to pull his sleeve over the welts, but Sally was too fast for him. She reached down and softly caressed the partially-healed injury, then leaned into him again, hugging his arm even tighter. She couldn't possibly know how deep her friend's pain went, nor the full reasons for it, but she knew he was hurting. In her own childish and innocent way, she did manage to help him feel a little bit better.

"How did you get those?" asked the older William. Sometimes boys had no tact.

"Ahh, well." Leon found himself in a dilemma again; how was he going to tell the truth without being vindictive? "I got into a fight and accidently hit a guard. That's a big no-no in prison, and I got punished for it."

"You hit a guard?"

"Eww."

Even the children knew what an extreme breech of protocol that was, relating it to being right up there with striking one of the Sisters. The alarmed eyes in the room shifted to Kenny, then back to Leon, the silent question hanging in the air.

"No, no!" Leon was quick to assure them. "It wasn't Officer Reece."

There was a collective sigh of relief at this assurance. Officer Reece had become just as much a part of these gatherings as Nash and the Kansas Kid. Nobody would have liked strife within the group.

Leon grinned. Pulling his arm out of Sally's embrace, and despite the pain the movement still caused, he draped it around her shoulders and hugged her to him. Sally was quite content to stay right there.

**

Fifteen minutes later found the group in the hallway with Pearson, once again, getting Leon ready for the ride back to the prison.

Jack decided that this was as good a time as any to discuss an important matter with Mariam.

"Ah, ma'am, what is the procedure if a couple wanted to adopt one of the orphans here?"

Both Leon and Mariam raised their eyebrows.

"Were you and Penny planning on marrying sooner than intended and then adopting?" Mariam asked him.

"Oh—no! It ain't for myself. Although, I'd never thought a that. That's not a bad idea." Jack stored the concept away for future use. "But no, I ain't askin' for myself."

"Oh, all right," Mariam smiled. "It's quite simple. The couple in question must come here for an interview first, to make sure they would be suitable. And, of course, if they are financially able to support a child. Then we would go from there. I always try to get a feel for a couple who wish to adopt so I can make suggestions as to which child would best fit into their family. I take it you know this couple?"

"Yes, ma'am," Jack assured her. "I've known 'em for about three and a half years now. They've tried ta start a family of their own, but unfortunately, both attempts ended sadly, and our doctor has recommended that they don't try again."

"Oh dear, that is sad," Mariam said. "But I'm sure if you recommend them, we should be able to fix them up with one of our children. The only unfortunate thing about this is that we can't find homes for them all. But we do what we can."

"I know," Jack conceded. "I'll see if I can bring 'em out with me ta meet you. Maybe next month."

"That would be fine," Mariam agreed. "What are their names?"

"Sam and Maribelle Jefferies."

Leon snorted.

Three of the other four adults present sent him questioning looks. Jack's look, however, was not questioning; it was irritated.

"Goddammit Leon, will you get over it!"

"Well, I—"

"No! I've had enough of this from you. Why can't you just let it go? Even Caroline can't understand why you're still holdin' a grudge. Sam did nothin' more'n what you and I have done on occasion. And he had good reason for doin' it. Or is your ego so badly bruised by the fact that he put one over on us, and you didn't see it comin', that you are never gonna be able ta forgive 'im?"

Leon was hurt. He stepped back, as though Jack had hit him, and he stood staring at his now shackled hands, not saying a word. This was the second time Jack had stepped up to the plate and chewed him out for selfish behavior. It made him feel, more and more, as though he were losing his grip on reality; losing touch with that part of himself that made him who he was.

Was he so far out of the scheme of things now, so stagnated in his own life, that his nephew had moved ahead of him to take over the leadership role? Had he been right in his earlier assumption that Jack Kiefer no longer needed his uncle to watch out for him?

Well, why should he? How can I watch out for him while stuck in this place? Jack has learned how to do that for himself. He had to, or he wouldn't have survived; he wouldn't have been able to move ahead.

The tables had been turned. Somewhere, somehow, when Leon hadn't been looking, Jack had surged ahead and taken over the lead.

Leon felt lost.

"C'mon, Leon. Goddammit, don't look like that," Jack said

quietly, feeling guilty again for having raised his voice to his uncle, who was obviously going through a difficult time. "I didn't mean—"

"No, Jack, you're right," Leon assured him. "You're not the first person lately, to tell me that I take things too personally; that I have to learn how to let go." He smiled at the senior guard. "Isn't that right, Officer Reece?"

Kenny simply smiled and nodded.

"I'm sorry, Mariam," Leon continued. "Sam and Maribelle would make fine parents. Any one of those youngsters would be lucky to become part of their family."

"Thank you," she said, placing a hand on his arm. "I'll certainly keep that in mind."

"Well, Mr. Pearson," Kenny spoke up. "I think it's time we got heading back. Is the wagon ready to go?"

"Yessir."

"All right. Dr. Soames, again, thank you for your hospitality. Jack, are we going to see you tonight for supper?"

"Yeah, Kenny, I'll be there," Jack assured him. "Obviously, there's more to discuss here than I thought."

Kenny nodded, then took Leon by the arm. "Come on, Nash. Let's go."

"Leon . . ." Jack tried to get his partner's attention; to apologize again and to say goodbye.

But Leon did not look up. He placidly allowed himself to be led away, down the hall and out the front door.

Jack's shoulders slumped.

"Goddammit," he mumbled, then groaned. "Oh, I'm sorry, ma'am. It seems I've been blaspheming all over the place here. I apologize."

"That's all right, Jack," she assured him. "I understand your distress. Come and sit with me for a few moments. I'll get one of the novices to bring us some tea. We need to have a talk."

Jack nodded but, inwardly, he groaned. Suddenly, he felt like that child at Blessed Heart again, who was about to receive a lecture on bad manners and undesirable behavior. But, much to his surprise, fifteen minutes later found him seated comfortably in an armchair, with a nice warm cup of tea and honey soothing his nerves and relaxing his stress.

"I know Napoleon is making things difficult for you these days,"

Mariam began, "but please try to be patient with him."

"I am tryin'," Jack insisted, "but he's not givin' me much ta work with. It's like he's given up on everything and everybody. I don't know. He's been in slumps before, and we were always able ta pull him out of 'em, but not this time. It's like he won't even meet us halfway."

"Yes, I know. I truly thought that spending time with the children would brighten his spirits; it always has in the past. But obviously, not this time. The incident last winter . . ." she shook her head, regretfully. "I don't know, Jack. He may not ever fully recover from that ordeal. And if we can't even get him to go to services . . ."

"Yeah. I don't know what ta do."

"Just carry on doing what you've been doing," she advised him. "No one has done more for him than you. I'm still amazed at the loyalty and support you've shown him." Jack snorted. "No, Jack, I mean it. Many people claim to be friends to the end, but you and Napoleon truly are."

"Yeah, well, I wish he'd remember that."

"He will. You just keep on doing what you've been doing, and we'll trust and pray that he will find his way out of this dark place he is in right now. He's a strong man. He'll come back to you."

***

The wagon ride to the prison was tense and, for the first half, silent. Kenny sat across the buckboard from the inmate and watched him intently. The inmate was more than aware of the scrutiny and had to make a conscious effort to not let himself squirm.

Leon was feeling antagonistic.

Why was Jack going to have dinner with Kenny and his family— again?

If Leon had been willing to take a closer look at the emotions he felt, he would realize that the primary one was petty jealousy. His best friend was moving on, building new friendships, forging new loyalties, and leaving Leon behind to rot in prison.

The fact that this was what Leon had been telling Jack he should do was irrelevant. Leon, telling him to do it, and Jack deciding for himself to do it, were two very different things. Now, here was Kenny sitting there, staring at him. Boring into him with those gray eyes, trying to break him. Trying to make him crack.

Leon was determined that he wasn't going to crack, that he wasn't going to give in, but as the ride continued, his resolve weakened. If it had been Carson playing the dominance game, Leon could have withstood it until hell froze over. He would never have given that guard the satisfaction of seeing him squirm under the assault.

But with Kenny, it was different. Maybe it was because Leon cared about what this guard thought of him, that caused him to finally unravel. His tense and hostile stance crumbled and, about halfway back to the prison, it completely fell apart. Only then did Kenny avert his eyes; only then did he release the inmate from the scrutiny.

Then Leon really began to squirm.

He shifted uncomfortably in his seat. He released several heavy sighs, coughed nervously, and tried to look everywhere but at the guard.

Kenny sat quietly, waiting.

Dammit. Leon's anger rose again, then guilt, followed by contrition. Next came admittance, next, apologetic, and then, downright shameful of his behavior. Shoulders slumped, another heavy sigh.

Kenny waited.

Finally, "All right!" came the abrupt surrender.

Pearson flinched up in the driver's seat. He had been unaware of the silent battle for supremacy that had been taking place behind him.

Kenny calmly turned his gray eyes back to the inmate. "Something on your mind, Nash?"

Leon seethed, his jaw tightening. He was back to being angry again, but it was too late to retreat.

"I'm sorry, all right?" Leon threw at him. "Isn't that what you want to hear? Want me to apologize for behaving like an ass—again. I always seem to end up apologizing to you, and I don't even know what I'm doing wrong half the time."

Kenny cocked a brow.

Leon slumped.

"Well, no . . . okay. You're right, that's not entirely true. I usually know when I'm behaving like an ass. But what's it to you? Why should I have to apologize to you for my behavior? You don't hear me apologizing to Officer Pearson here, or to Thompson, or—heaven forbid, to Carson. Like I would ever apologize to that bastard—oh, and now I suppose I'm expected to apologize for calling Carson a bastard. Hell, I broke Thompson's collar bone and I never apologized to him. Don't intend to either, dammit! He had it coming even if I didn't do it intentionally. Not that it mattered, though, did it? I still got hung out to dry.

"Hell, maybe I should start planning to attack the guards. If I'm going to get punished for it anyway, I might as well have the pleasure of anticipating the assault in the first place. Wouldn't that make life in the prison interesting? Oh look, Nash is on the rampage—again! Oh well, how many times can we hang him from the ceiling? Might as well just do it the one time and get it over with; just leave him there until he suffocates. One less uppity inmate to worry about.

"Oh hell, what's the point? I keep on trying to do the right thing; trying to get by without getting into trouble, and it just doesn't seem to work out. Why should I even bother? I don't know. I suppose it's better than sitting around, doing nothing."

Leon stopped talking. His eyes peered out upon the active main street through Laramie City without really taking note. Then his gaze returned to the man sitting across from him.

"There's just nowhere in that entire prison where I feel safe, ya know? Carson has come at me in the infirmary and the laundry room. Jeez, the laundry room wasn't even for something I had done, right or wrong, but for something he just suspected me of thinking of doing! How fair is that? How am I supposed to win with those odds? Of course, I guess that's the point, isn't it? I'm not supposed to win, am I? The convicts lose every time, all the time.

"Well, no, I guess that's not entirely true either. Dr. Mariam does what she can, and Doc Palin is a good guy; we actually have fun together, sometimes. And you've always treated me fairly. Yeah, you only beat me up with the club when I deserve it. Well, no—you're right. That's not true. You're a decent enough fella. What the hell are you doing working in a prison? You should be a mayor or something, not a bloody prison guard!"

Both Kenny's brows arched and one corner of his mouth twitched to a smile.

Leon didn't notice.

"Oh, but I sure would be in dire straits if you weren't a prison guard. Ohh, I don't even want to go there. I've never even thought about that before—that's scary. Not planning on going anywhere, are you, Kenny? Oh—ooops, sorry, didn't mean to call you Kenny. I meant Mr. Reece. I mean, I guess it's just because Jack calls you Kenny, and I suppose I do too when we're talking about you. But I know I shouldn't call you that to your face. And it's not like we're saying anything bad about you when we're talking about you. It's all good.

"Now I suppose you and Jack are going to be talking about me tonight, aren't you? What's up with Nash? Why is Nash being such an ass these days? What can we do to get him out of his slump? I know what you can do. You can get me the hell out of here, that's what you can do! I'd feel a whole lot better then—I can pretty much guarantee it. But I suppose Jack knows this. I know he's doing the best he can, but he's fighting an uphill battle, that's for sure."

Leon gazed down at the chain that ran from his shackled hands down to the bolt in the floor of the wagon.

He sighed.

"I don't know what else to do. I guess that's why I'm so down these days. I can't see any more options open to us. I guess I'm just feeling like I'm going to be stuck in here forever. I mean, that's my sentence, isn't it? Twenty years to life. Even if the hearing does change how things are done, I'm still going to be stuck here. Forever. I doubt the Supreme Court is going to change that. There's no end to it, and I just don't . . ."

Leon paused for breath, giving his thoughts time to settle.

Kenny sat quietly, knowing more was still to come.

Leon gave a big sigh, then started up again.

"Jeez, Kenny, I just don't know who I am anymore. Oh, there I go calling you Kenny again. Still, if you haven't hit me for it yet, then I guess it's okay with you for right now. Can't be doing that in front of anybody else, though, can I? Well, I guess I did it in front of Officer Pearson here, but he doesn't really count."

Pearson's back tightened just a smidge. He didn't care for being disregarded so easily.

Leon didn't notice and simply smirked as he carried on with his observation. "Do it in front of anybody else, and you'll be after me with that billy club, won't you? I mean, why not? Everybody else hits me with the bloody thing; I guess I shouldn't be surprised that you do it too. Just like in the infirmary. Well, no, I suppose I had that one coming, and you didn't actually hit me, did you."

Another heavy sigh.

"Even Jack's mad at me," Leon mumbled, feeling sorry for himself. "I can't believe he's sided with that little upstart of a backstabber, over me!" He paused, looking down at the floor of the buckboard, deep in thought. "But maybe he's right. Maybe my ego was so bruised that I can't accept the fact that some 'youngster' outwitted me. I mean, isn't that just the icing on the cake?"

Another stretch of silence. The buckboard continued to bounce and rattle its way back toward the prison.

"I have been thinking about what you said to me," Leon finally continued. "About how I'm still behaving like an outlaw and that, maybe, I'm just not ready to be released yet. You know, that really hit home. Because, if you think that then how is the parole board going to think any differently?" He became contemplative, then continued quietly, almost as though he was talking to himself. "I feel like I'm losing my grip here, Kenny. I don't know what to do. I used to like myself, but now I don't even know who I am.

"I look back at the person I used to be, and I don't even like that person now either. I mean, you're right. I've been making choices all my life just to satisfy the immediate need, without giving any serious thought to the long-term consequences. Now, here I am still doing the same thing."

Another heavy sigh, another long-term silence.

Leon gave a subtle nod to himself.

"I'm beginning to think that you and that judge are right," he continued, "that I am beyond redemption, beyond reformation. I am who I am, and I just get lost trying to be anything different. And what's the point of even trying? I'm never going to get out of here. I'm going to be stuck in here for the rest of my life." Then he perked up and smiled. "Of course, nobody says that the rest of my life has to be for much longer."

Kenny cocked an eyebrow with that comment.

Leon didn't notice; he was off on his own train of thought.

"I mean, that's kind of my choice, isn't it? Nobody can force me to carry on if I decide that I don't want to, can they? Still, I don't suppose I'm ready to go down that road just yet. 'As long as you have life, you have hope.' That's what a friend of mine said to me an eternity ago. 'As long as you have life . . .'" Leon stared into nothing for a moment, then smiled and raised his eyes to meet Kenny's gaze.

"When is the presidential election?"

"Umm." Kenny was taken by surprise with a question that was so out of context. "Ahh, early in the new year, I think."

Leon nodded. "Early in the new year," he repeated. "Well, I suppose I could wait around until then."

Rather abruptly, the wagon gave a slight lurch and Leon glanced up to find that they had come to a halt inside the prison yard.

Pearson climbed down from the driver's seat, and Kenny stood up in preparation for unloading the prisoner.

"Well, Nash," he commented, "glad we could have this little talk."

"Yeah."

***

The officials could not have arrived at the prison on a more opportune day.

When the secretary had knocked on the office door to inform the warden of his important guests, Mitchell sighed in disbelieving relief at the lucky coincidence. Officer Reece and Napoleon Nash had left for the orphanage only an hour previously, and they would be gone from the prison until mid-afternoon. This was plenty of time for these nosey intruders to be shown around and placated, then sent on their official way. The only one the warden had to keep an eye on now was Dr. Palin, and that shouldn't be too difficult.

"Gentlemen, gentlemen," Mitchell greeted the three officials. "Please, do come in. Have a seat."

The three men from the Board of Commissioners entered the office and settled into the chairs that had been provided.

"Warden Mitchell," Mr. Ludlow greeted him, "may I introduce Dr. Simons and Dr. Dalton. I do believe you know why we are here."

"Yes, yes, gentlemen," Mitchell assured them. "Such nonsense, really. I'm sure that once I show you around, you will see how efficiently this prison is run. All these accusations of unwarranted punishments—completely ridiculous and unfounded." He sighed and shook his head to emphasize how silly it all was. "But we must keep the governor happy, I suppose. All part of playing politics."

"Warden Mitchell, this is hardly a game," Simons pointed out, already not caring much for the warden. "I expect you to take these accusations seriously."

"Of course, Dr. Simons," Mitchell assured him as he sobered and became contrite. "It's very serious. May I offer you gentlemen some brandy? I really do have a very nice—"

"That won't be necessary, Warden," Ludlow interjected. "I think it best we get on with the inspection."·

"Oh." Mitchell was disappointed. "Yes, of course."

***

The four gentlemen walking across the prison yard toward the warehouse where they encountered Carson.

"Gentlemen," Mitchell began, "this is our senior guard, Officer Carson. He oversees the prison, making sure it runs smoothly, and that the inmates all behave themselves. Mr. Carson, these gentlemen are from the prison board. They're here to make sure everything is proper and that the inmates are all treated fairly. Perhaps you could assist me in showing them around."

"Yessir, Warden," Carson agreed, though his expression portrayed the opposite. "This is the work floor."

"Yes, Officer Carson. We can see that," commented Dr. Simons. "We are also aware of what happens on the work floor. I believe we are more interested in the accusations of unwarranted punishments inflicted upon the inmates by certain guards. Yourself in particular."

"I assure you gentlemen, any punishments that have been handed down to the inmates have been warranted," Carson sleazed. "Some of these convicts can get aggressive and need to be handled in a like manner, or they don't get the message. If they behave themselves, then they have nothing to worry about."

"Hmm." Simons was not convinced. "Perhaps if we could have a word with the inmate in question. Mr. Nash, wasn't it?"

"I'm afraid that won't be possible today, Dr. Simons," Mitchell informed him, again silently thanking the fates for this excellent timing.

"Why not? Is he being punished for something?"

"No, no." Mitchell laughed at the obvious snipe. "No, no. Mr. Nash and Officer Reece are at the orphanage today, speaking with the children."

All three of the officials perked up. This was interesting.

"They are at the orphanage?" asked Dr. Dalton. "Is this a common occurrence?"

"Well, yes," Mitchell informed them. "Two or three times a year, Officers Reece and Pearson escort Mr. Nash to the orphanage where he spends the afternoon speaking with the children. They all seem to enjoy it, and the Sisters have stated that the children find it beneficial to hear, firsthand, about the perils of choosing the criminal path."

There was a moment of stunned silence.

"Odd," Dr. Dalton finally commented. "Officer Reece said nothing of this at the hearing."

"Really?" Mitchell fringed surprise. "I don't understand why not. Unless he was trying to paint as bleak a picture as he could of life here at the prison. Just to try and win his case, such as it is."

"Yes," Dr. Simons mumbled. "Interesting."

"Hmm. Well, shall we return to the main building?" Mitchell suggested. "I'll show you the assembly hall. We have a library there and conduct services every Sunday for those who wish to attend. It also is used as the dining hall. The inmates enjoy three squares a day, and I haven't heard any complaints about the food yet."

"I believe we would rather look at your medical facility first, Warden," Simons countered. "Perhaps have a word with your prison doctor. I believe he lodged some complaints, himself."

"If you insist," Mitchell agreed. "Of course, I must warn you that the prisons don't attract the top of the line, when it comes to doctors. It's hardly a prestigious position, so the medical men whom we do get here are usually on the outer rim of their profession, if you get my meaning. You might want to take Dr. Palin's opinions with a grain of salt."

"We'll be the judge of that, Warden Mitchell," Simons assured him. "Just lead the way."

***

In the prison proper, the four men entered the infirmary to find the doctor nowhere in sight. The ward itself was clean and orderly, and the three officials were impressed with how well maintained it was. There were no patients present, which wasn't unusual for the time of year; other than for the occasional injury, serious illnesses generally waited until the winter months. The visitors occupied themselves by looking around and being impressed by the apparently well-run facility.

Then a loud crash came from the adjoining office, followed instantly by a string of obscenities that would make an old army sergeant blush.

Then the doctor made his appearance accompanied by a torrent of swear words, until he came face to face with the surprised expressions of the officials. "Oh. Now, just who the fuck are you, and what are you doing in the middle of my infirmary?"

"Dr. Palin," Mitchell tried to sound discreet, "these gentlemen are from the prison board. They are here to follow up on the accusations of abuse presented to the board by Officer Reece—and yourself, if I'm not mistaken."

"Oh." Palin had the grace to look contrite. "Shit!" He coughed to cover his embarrassment. "I apologize for my language. I didn't realize there was anyone else here."

"Yes, of course, Doctor," Simons responded. "Umm, I understand you had some complaints about the senior guard and his management of the prisoners."

"Oh. Carson—that fucking prick!" Palin cringed, then sighed with resignation. "I'm sorry, gentlemen—old habits. And that Carson pisses me off. Anyway, yes, that guard is a sadist; he should be fired, as far as I'm concerned."

"Oh, really now, Doctor," Mitchell placated him. "That's a tad extreme, don't you think? Officer Carson is simply doing his job by keeping the inmates in line."

"Doing his job?" Palin snarked. "He had no right comin' in here and beatin' up on my assistant—and you damn well know it."

"Excuse me, Dr. Palin," Dr. Dalton intervened, "are you referring to the incident that happened last year, involving Mr. Nash?"

"You bet your ass, that's what I'm referrin' too," Palin said. "Nash was just doin' his job, and he saved that young fella's life out there on the floor—he did nothin' wrong. That bastard, Carson, with his little lackey, Thompson, came into my infirmary and beat the crap out of 'im. That's just one incident involving Nash, and he isn't the only one who's been terrorized by that asshole." Palin pointed an accusing finger at Mitchell. "You know as well as I do that Carson beat John Two Feathers to death four years ago. Fell down the steps, my ass!"

"That could never be proven, Dr. Palin," Mitchell reminded him, barely keeping his temper in check. "You know that."

"Yeah. Nothin' can ever be proven, can it, Mitchell?" Palin threw back at him. "And stuff that can't be covered up, you find a way to justify."

"Perhaps that is because the punishments handed out are justified," Mitchell responded. "Being a doctor, I can understand why you might not agree with that assessment."

"You call strappado justified?"

"The inmate struck a guard. You know that is a serious offence."

"By accident!" Palin snarled. "And Bowman was behind all that anyway. You know it as well as I do."

"It makes no difference who started it, Dr. Palin, Nash stepped way out of line, just like he always does. It was time to put a stop to it. Being the warden here, the severity of punishments is left to my discretion, and Officer Carson has been well within his rights in dealing with both these transgressions."

"He had no right comin' into my infirmary and—"

"Gentlemen, gentlemen, please!" Mr. Ludlow interjected. "Obviously, there is a difference of opinion here. I believe we have heard enough, Warden Mitchell. If we could return to your office now to discuss this. Dr. Palin, thank you for your time."

"Hmm," Palin grumbled. "Fine. Good day to you too."

***

Back in Mitchell's office, silence weighed heavy over the four men, until Mr. Ludlow coughed discreetly and broke the stalemate.

"Well, Warden Mitchell, there are certainly discrepancies that need to be considered. We will recommend to Governor Moonlight that we send a man in here to take a closer look at the situation. Perhaps next time, Mr. Nash will be available to answer some questions."

"Of course, Dr. Simons. Whatever you think necessary."

The officials took their leave, and Warden Mitchell sat at his desk and fumed. He was seething. Damn that Palin and his big mouth. Mitchell almost had those busybodies satisfied with the way he ran the prison, then Palin just had to throw a wrench into the whole thing. Damn him. Something was going to have to be done about this.

CHAPTER EIGHTEEN
THE CONVERSATION

Kenny had initially invited Jack for dinner again because his two boys would not stop pestering their father to get the ex-outlaw there to display his fast draw. It wasn't fair—they bemoaned—that those orphaned children were privileged enough to not only see it, but to meet both Nash and Kiefer, when the sons of the almost senior guard were being deprived of this honor.

If they couldn't meet Napoleon Nash, then at least the Kansas Kid could come out for a second visit and display his talents. After all, he had promised that he would. Kenny had finally relented, especially when little Evelyn, whom he could never resist, beseeched her father with those soft gray eyes and asked, very politely, if Mr. Kiefer could please come to dinner again.

Kenny had sighed helplessly at his wife, who smiled and set about planning dinner for a guest. Now, of course, Kenny was glad of Jack's planned visit, since, as the ex-outlaw had observed himself; there was a lot that needed discussing.

It was later that evening, after the long anticipated fast draw display, and a very fine supper were completed, when Jack and Kenny retired to the back porch for brandy and a cigar. It was a pleasant evening; still light and warm enough to be comfortable for them to continue their discussion outdoors until twilight chilled the air.

Evelyn had managed to settle into Jack's lap, and much to her father's amusement, snuggled in to eventually fall asleep listening to her hero's heartbeat, and his voice rumbling soothingly in her ears.

"Shall I take her off your hands, Jack?" Sarah offered when she came in search of her youngest. "I don't want her to be a bother."

"Naw, that's okay," Jack said. "She ain't no bother. Besides, she's so comfortable it would be a shame to wake her up just ta put her ta bed."

The parents exchanged quiet looks, then the mother returned indoors to pass the evening with her own endeavors.

"How was he today after we parted company?" Jack asked with some trepidation.

Kenny sighed wearily and rolled his eyes. "Oh brother," he complained. "I was beginning to question my stance on abolishing the 'no talking' rule. Has he always been like that? I mean, it took him a while to break down and start talking, but once he did, he wouldn't shut up."

"Yeah," Jack assured the guard. "Like I told ya before, it's when he won't talk that ya gotta worry. If he's talkin', then maybe he'll pull himself outta this."

"He didn't want to at first," Kenny admitted. "I really had to challenge him, and he got angry; he resented it."

"Hmm," Jack took a sip of brandy. "If I try pokin' at 'im when he don't wanna talk, he just turns nasty, then digs in even deeper. I'm kinda surprised he opened up to you like that."

"I have an advantage over him that you don't have."

"Oh?"

"I'm not his friend," Kenny pointed out. "I don't have to worry about the aftermath. I can push him far harder than you ever would, and he knows he's at a disadvantage with me because I won't let him get away with insolence. Sometimes, it takes a person who's not as close to him as you are to get him off balance enough for the barriers to break down."

"Yeah, I suppose," Jack admitted with a slight twinge of resentment. "I gotta disagreed on one a your points though. You are his friend, Kenny. One of the few friends he has in that place. He respects you, and Leon don't give his respect easy."

Kenny nodded. "I remember you commenting on that at the hearing. And, I suppose I already know you're right about it. He's usually very respectful toward me, far more than to any of the other guards. Especially now."

"What do ya mean? Why now?"

"He's angry, Jack," Kenny explained. "He's angry and bitter over what happened this past winter. It's like what I told Thompson, way back when he first hired on. I told him that if he treated Nash fairly, then they'd get along fine. That Nash was smart enough to know when he deserved punishment, and to know what was fair and what wasn't. Mr. Thompson didn't listen. I'm afraid he'd already been too much influenced by Carson. So, anyway, of course Nash knew that what they did to him was unjust, and he is so very angry. He's been keeping it bottled up for the most part, although he did blow up at me just before the hearing about the injustice of it."

"You're kiddin'!"

"Oh, I'd pushed him," Kenny admitted. "I was angry with him at the time, and I shoved him into a corner in more ways than one."

"Why were you angry with him?" Jack asked, feeling protective of his uncle. "What did he do?"

"He went after Boeman in retaliation for Lobinskie," Kenny explained. "Hit him hard too, really hard. Laid him up for a good couple of months or more. I was so pissed off at Nash at that point. The hearing was just around the corner and we were all working toward it, and I thought working together. Then he went and reverted to type and did something that was so condemning to our cause, I was about ready to strangle him. I know you're not going to like this, Jack, but I've felt for some time, and now more than ever, that Nash isn't ready to be released from prison yet."

Kenny was right about one thing; Jack did not like the sound of that. He tensed and was instantly defensive.

"What?" he demanded. "How can you say that? I thought you were on our side here. How can you think that being in that place is helping him?"

Evelyn stirred, disturbed by the sudden antagonism in her pillow. Jack stroked her hair and gave her a gentle hug to calm her back to sleep, and in so doing, calmed himself down as well.

Kenny watched and waited until both his daughter and his guest had settled again.

"I didn't say that place was helping him, not the way it's being run now. That's why I was at the hearing, to try and bring some reform into the prison system, and to have stricter guidelines on the uses and severity of punishments. I am supportive of the up-coming case with the Supreme Court. I hope it reduces Nash's sentence, or perhaps makes him eligible for parole at some point. But I do not support an instant release for Napoleon Nash."

"Well . . . but, why not?"

"Because up until quite recently, Nash had never given me any indication that he had changed his perspective. If he had been released at the time of the hearing, I am confident that he would have, well reverted to type, just as he did with Boeman. And, just as with Boeman, he would have felt justified in doing so. I mean, Jack, his whole trial was based on him justifying why he became a conman, an outlaw. He used the Civil War, and the tragedies that befell both of you during that time, as the reasons for his later conduct. By holding on to that self-righteousness, he simply helps himself to justify those feelings of entitlement and, therefore, will never truly accept responsibility for his actions."

"Yeah, but those things happened, Ken. It's not like he made them up to use as an excuse. They really happened."

"I know," Kenny acknowledged. "But they didn't just happen to you. I lost everything I had known and had accepted as my life, because of that war. So many people lost their livelihoods, lost their families, lost their homes. You and Nash were not the only ones. And you certainly weren't the only ones to end up in an orphanage. Too many children lost families; too many children witnessed terrible things. But how many of them rose up to become the territory's two most wanted outlaws?"

"Well then, you must think that I got off easy," Jack commented, quietly. "That I didn't deserve the pardon. That I should have been hanged just like DeFord and the judge wanted."

"No." Kenny shook his head. "No, I don't believe you deserved that, Jack. I don't know if you deserved the pardon or not; that's not for me to say. I do know that you've done better with it than Nash would have. I don't know why. Maybe your temperament is more grounded, more solid. I know you had problems with your temper before, but you seem to have learned how to control it, and you've learned patience too, that much is obvious. You also accepted responsibility for your behavior, and you apologized for it, right there in court, in front of the whole assembly. That couldn't have been easy to do, but you did it. Those are huge steps forward, Jack. Steps that Nash has yet to take."

"But he's the one who kept us on track for the pardons," Jack insisted. "He's the one who kept us true—"

"And he's the one who repeatedly lost his temper during his trial. He's the one who was found in contempt. He's the one who was convicted of running a scam."

"Yeah, but—"

"I know, Jack!" Kenny interrupted him. "I know all the excuses you're going to come back at me with. Miss Jansen blackmailed you. You were just as much a part of it as Nash was. He was being loyal to his friends. I know."

Now Evelyn became fully awake, the sounds of her father's harder tones invading her peaceful dreams. She stretched and moaned irritably, while rubbing her eyes.

Fortunately, Sarah had also been disturbed by the raised voices on the porch and came out to investigate.

"Oh dear," she commented, when she saw her squirming daughter. "Come along, sweetheart, let's get you to bed."

Jack helped to lift the child up to her mother, and both men looked contrite.

"Sorry ma'am . . . ah, Sarah," Jack apologized. "I suppose we were gettin' a little heated there."

Sarah smiled as she hoisted her groggy daughter onto her shoulder, but when she turned away from Jack, she sent a reproving look to her husband.

"Sorry," he obediently responded.

"Fine," Sarah accepted the apologies. "I have more coffee on. Would you gentlemen like some?"

"That's a good idea," Kenny accepted. "I can get it, if you like."

"No, no," Sarah gave Evelyn a small shift. "You sound like you're in the middle of an important debate here. Just let me get Eve to bed and I'll bring it."

The ladies left, and Jack and Kenny looked across at one another, knowing that the interruption was probably fortuitous in that it gave both men the time to calm down.

"Anyway," Kenny continued, "I suppose the point I'm trying to make here, is that you have grown beyond the outlaw you used to be, and Nash has not. You could argue that he has been stuck in prison so hasn't had the chance to move on, but I don't think I agree with that. Most of the problems Nash has experienced since his incarceration have been brought on by his own attitude and decisions. Until recently, he still saw himself as being in charge, as being above the rest of us, and that the rules simply didn't apply to him."

Kenny paused again, considering how he was going to explain his next point.

"I have been pressing him hard with the intention of getting a reaction from him. I've said things to him that hurt, and, I know, scared him, as well."

"Scared him?"

"Oh yes," Kenny nodded. "I knew it was dangerous to press him that hard. But I had to make him stop and re-examine who he is and what his motivations are, or he is never going to make parole. The danger with that, of course, is pushing him too hard and driving him right over the edge."

"What do you mean?" Jack asked, not feeling comfortable with this. "You mean his sanity?"

"No, not that." Kenny reflected where he was trying to go with this. "Perhaps his confidence. His sense of self. I had to make him stop and realize that he was simply repeating the same behavior that sent him to prison in the first place. If he doesn't come to realize this, and start trying to change that behavior, then if he does get released, he'll just go right back to being Napoleon Nash: outlaw. Napoleon Nash: conman. And feel that he is justified in doing so."

Jack's brain spun. He took a deep breath, then let it out, slowly.

"Jeez, Ken, how do you think up all this stuff? How do you even recognize it?"

Kenny sat back with a smile. "Well, I've been a guard for a lot of years now, and I've seen plenty of inmates come and go. And I've seen a lot of them come back. All a person needs to do is pay attention, and the patterns start to show themselves. Once Nash is released, the last thing I want to see is him coming right back in again."

"Ohh," Jack sighed. "I never even thought a that. I've been so focused on gettin' him out in the first place; it never occurred ta me that he might end up doin' stuff that would get him sent right back again. Oh brother!"

Sarah arrived with the coffee and some hard fruit cake left over from Christmas.

"How is it going?" she asked as she placed the tray on the table between them. "Making any progress?"

"I dunno," Jack admitted. "I feel like we're goin' backwards."

"Oh no," Kenny smiled as he picked up his coffee, "you're getting the gist of it."

Jack sat back with a sigh and took a sip from his own cup. He was appreciative of the hot beverage right now, and thanked Sarah for suggesting it.

She smiled and retreated, leaving the men to continue with the obviously intense conversation.

"So," Jack began again, "is he beginnin' to see what it is he's doin' to himself?"

"Our conversation coming back from the orphanage today would suggest so, yes, But, he's at a very vulnerable stage right now. He's scared. He's had the carpet pulled out from under him and he's questioning everything. He's hurting, inside and out: emotionally and physically. The hearing fell short of accomplishing what he wanted, and he now has very little hope for the appeal with the Supreme Court.

"As I said, and as you've noticed yourself, he's angry and bitter over the strappado incident at Christmas. He feels betrayed, and I guess we can't fault him for that. But I'm concerned he's not going to get over it this time. With everything else that has happened, perhaps I came down on him too hard." Kenny stopped and shook his head, realizing that he was second-guessing himself. "But no, I had to challenge him. It's like, to be able to save his life, to force him to re-assess himself, I had to push him right to the edge of the abyss and hope that he has the strength to step back from it."

Jack felt a tingling of fear grip his heart as the full meaning of Kenny's words sank in.

The two men sat in silence for a few moments, sipping their coffee, as the evening started to close in upon them.

"I know you've thought about it," Kenny said quietly. "You're afraid for him and of what he might do."

"Yeah." Jack swallowed as the old fear tightened his throat. He shook his head as he hid the thought away. "But that's just me, thinkin' about the worse that could happen. I don't think Leon would actually . . . I mean, I can't imagine him givin' up that way. It just ain't him. Even when we were kids, even when it seemed hopeless, he was the one who kept me goin'."

"Or is it that you simply don't want to see it?" Kenny suggested. "That the thought of it brings so much pain that you force it away and convince yourself that it simply couldn't happen?"

"No," Jack shook his head, "that's not Leon—he won't give up. I've gotta hold on to the belief that he'll step back, you'll see."

Kenny made no comment. He knew Jack would have a hard time hearing this and probably would not be willing to accept it. Maybe that was a good thing. If Jack refused to accept the possibility, then maybe he simply would not allow Leon to accept it either.

Kenny had been around this block too many times, and he recognized the signs, but he still allowed himself the privilege of hoping. Nash did have friends, inside the prison and out, and perhaps, if they all stuck together and kept at it, they would be able to keep the inmate going.

But Kenny's one real fear was that Nash would end up getting hurt again; that he'd get pushed down that one extra notch. Down to that final rung where the next step would be just as simple as letting go into oblivion.

CHAPTER NINETEEN
SHAFFER'S CHOICE

Carbon County, Wyoming
April 1888

Gus Shaffer smiled to himself. It was a humorless smile; hard and cold, to match the look in his eye. This is what he had planned, and it was satisfying to see everything fall into place just as he hoped it would. He had turned his horse's head back into Wyoming after reading the newspaper article. He didn't want to have to look over his shoulder. He didn't want to spend his days wondering when the bullet would come out of the dark and send him packing.

Once back into home territory, he began his quest by deliberately mapping out Morrison's movements, following every choice the lawman made, begrudging every life the man took. Gus sat by the campfire at night thinking about what that marshal had done over the past four years, and he'd grind his teeth and curse the very ground the lawman walked upon.

First it had been Kiefer and Nash. Even Gus knew how close the Kid had come to dying at the hands of that bastard, and then what happened to Nash was even worse. Gus hadn't always seen eye to eye with that young, arrogant, little . . . but that didn't mean Gus would have wished life in prison on him, either.

Next, Hank had been taken out at the snap of the fingers—no warning, nothing. Just BANG and he was dead before he left the saddle.

Then, that ambush. Yeah, in hindsight, Gus berated himself for not seeing it coming; that train had been too good to be true, and too good to pass up. So, Charlie, and Mukua, and now Lobo, had been added to the lengthening list of the deceased. Not to mention all those other fellas who hadn't been with the gang quite so long. Add to them, now the Cripple Creek boys. The list was getting too damn long to ignore.

Then there's Malachi, his own partner, still stuck in that damn prison. He'd been there coming up on a year now and definitely hating every minute of it. Gus ground his teeth and strangled his coffee cup just thinking about it all.

He knew Morrison was on his trail. It hadn't been hard, really. All Gus had to do was predict the lawman's direction of travel, then simply put himself in harm's way. Leave a cold campfire, hidden, but not too hidden, file a notch into one of the shoes on his horse, use money he had snatched from the previous town to buy supplies in the next town. Yup, Gus knew how to cover his tracks when he wanted to, so it stood to reason that he would know how to lay a track when this became his objective.

Morrison had gotten cocky and followed that track like an old hound dog on the scent.

Gus sat back against his saddle to have a smoke and didn't care that his campfire was shining out like a beacon in the night. Let that bastard come. Hell or high water, death or triumph, Gus Shaffer was going to put an end to it, one way or another.

The following morning, Gus turned his horse's nose toward a labyrinth of trails and gullies. He knew it well, since the gang had used it on numerous occasions to lose a posse or some persistent bounty hunter. It was the perfect place for what Gus had in mind and all he had to do was make sure the posse following him didn't get lost.

Sure enough, within an hour of entering this confusing maze, the seasoned outlaw had to turn back and leave fresh signs for the posse to latch onto. Left to their own devices, they would have become hopelessly turned around long before the sun had reached its zenith. Gus snorted and shook his head. No wonder they all stayed thieving for so long. If this was the best the opposing side had to offer, it stood to reason that they relied on ambushing their quarry to be successful.

Finally, Gus arrived at the spot that he had been aiming for. The trail was narrow, room for only one horse at a time to come along it. Rock faces rose on either side, which would make for good cover. Gus was planning a little ambush of his own, and he didn't care how many of those posse men he ended up killing, so long as Morrison was one of them.

Gus got busy covering his tracks. He knew the posse was no more than half an hour behind him. That would give him just enough time to confuse the issue. The ground was hard here, almost like rock, and Gus turned back on his own trail, his horse's hooves leaving only an occasional scuffing, indicating that a horse had come this way, but leaving the direction of travel ambiguous.

The posse would assume the outlaw had kept on going straight ahead. The only way it wouldn't work is if they had an Apache with them. He chuckled to himself as he recalled making a similar comment some years back, to his then boss. Nash had insisted that a Shoshone would be far more of a menace than some dried-up old Apache.

At the time, Gus wondered at the comment. What difference did it make? An injun was an injun. But now, he knew better. So, for old time's sake, he changed it, "as long as they didn't have a Shoshone with them." Moot point anyways; considering how easily this group had gotten lost, Gus highly doubted the possibility of any kind of Indian in their ranks.

Gus continued to backtrack for about a hundred yards, until he found that little side trail that would take him off the main path and up into the rocks. Once there, he would be able to settle into a hiding place, with a full view of the trail below him.

He turned his horse onto the narrow track, then dismounting, he grabbed some loose foliage and quickly but thoroughly brushed away the tracks that would give away his movements. That done, he remounted and booted his horse into a lope, up the hill and into the rocky landscape that offered a natural cover for anyone who knew where to find it.

Once he found the spot he was looking for, he dismounted, and leading his horse into a small gulley where it would be well hidden from sight, he tied the animal to some scrub brush. He pulled his rifle from the scabbard, then, digging into his saddlebags, he pulled out two boxes of cartridges, one for the rifle and one for the six-shooter. Then he made his way up the side of the gulley and over to the edge of the embankment.

There he found a nice little dip in the ground tucked in behind two large boulders for cover with just enough space between them for his rifle to set, and his view of the trail below him unobstructed. He sat down, leaning against the boulders and loaded the rifle, then his six-shooter. He placed both boxes of cartridges on the ground, close enough for him to quickly re-load either weapon if needs be.

He gave a little snort at that thought. He doubted that he would be re-loading.

With all the preparations taken care of, Gus took a deep breath, held it for a few seconds, then released it. He did one more quick check to be sure his horse was out of sight, then settled in to await his pursuers.

He was surprised at how calm he felt; he had expected to be dealing with cold sweats and a knotted gut by now, but he was unexpectedly relaxed.

Maybe that was normal when you'd already made up your mind that you weren't going to survive the encounter anyway. Maybe it was the hope that you were going to get out alive that brought on the nervousness. If you already accepted that it was a one-way trip, well then, what was there to be nervous about?

Gus smiled and nodded his head. Yeah, that made sense.

He tensed and stared down along the trail below him. He heard something. A hoof striking rock, maybe? A horse snorting? He wasn't sure what but something. He pulled the rifle up and rested the barrel between the two boulders, watching and waiting for the first of the riders to come around the bend and into his sights.

He listened and waited. *What's takin' 'em so long? They should be coming around that bend by now—jeez, they didn't get lost again, did they?* Then he caught his breath and got ready; he'd definitely heard it this time, the jingling of a bit, the snorting of a horse. They were coming. He sat up straighter, and aiming his rifle toward the bend, he settled into the stock and squinted along the barrel, waiting for the first rider to come into view.

He knew he couldn't start shooting right away. He had to wait until the whole posse was on that stretch of trail and compromised in their position. He'd wait until they were all there, then he'd single out that bastard, Morrison, and blow him to kingdom come. After that, he'd just keep shooting until he ran out of bullets or was dead. He didn't care which.

Gus watched and waited. Then—there it was, a horse moving into sight. But then . . . what? There was nobody on it. It was just a lone horse, plodding along the trail with its reins wrapped around the saddle horn.

Gus watched and waited. Then there it was, a horse moving into sight.

What the hell?

The outlaw heard a noise behind him, and lifting the rifle, he swung around to face the new threat, but he wasn't quite fast enough.

He got only the briefest glimpse of a man and the loud report and flash of a rifle firing on him. At the same time, by instinct alone, his own rifle went off in self-defense. A burning, like lightening, seared across his ribcage and he knew he'd been hit. He cocked the rifle, preparing for round two, but then the gun smoke cleared, and the lawman was sprawled on the ground and not moving.

In the next instant, he heard another rifle shot coming from down below, and he felt rock splinters dance up and attack the side of his face. He flinched away, then swung around again and prepared to return fire. But the scene below him was pandemonium. There was nothing for him to focus on for a useful attack. Riderless horses galloped in circles. They weren't panicked yet, but nervous and hopeful of a way out, and their movement caused enough confusion and dust to complicate matters.

Gus was still trying to find a target when another rifle shot sounded, and the bullet hit the rockface close enough to make the outlaw duck. He knew he had to get out of there. He didn't mind dying; his life, as he knew it, was over anyway. But he'd be damned if he died and didn't take Morrison with him. He might not have been able to save his gang, but he sure as hell was going to avenge them.

He grabbed the boxes of cartridges, and bending low, he made a run for his horse, snatching up the groaning deputy's fallen rifle as he went. Once he was away from the edge, he was out of the line of fire so he was able to tuck the boxes into the saddle bags, secure one of the rifles in the scabbard, then swing aboard his nervous horse without interference. He kicked the animal into a gallop and headed full speed down the other side of the ridge and out onto the flat country, heading for the cover of a stand of pines.

He knew that posse would follow him, and this was a good thing. He'd draw them out in the open, out where he could see them coming. Then he could take his time, find his target and end this game before it became a losing one.

Gus galloped on, sending up a trail of dust off the hard ground that could be seen for miles around. A quick check over his shoulder and he could see a larger billow of dust rising into the air and following his own track. They were coming after him for sure, so he turned eyes forward and pushed his horse onwards, until he came to that stand of trees and had to rein the animal back, so he could maneuver in amongst the underbrush.

Once inside the cover, Gus turned the horse to the left and pushed him onward as quickly as he dared in this tangled footing. His horse responded gallantly, keeping the forward impulsion going, but still turning on a dime when asked to and not hesitating to jump over branches and dead fall whenever such things were in their way.

Finally, Gus was satisfied with his position, and pulling the horse to a halt, he dismounted and tied the animal to the branch of a tree. He then grabbed the second rifle from the scabbard and got himself leaning up against another tree that was big enough for cover, but still give him an excellent view of the open ground before him.

If the posse followed his trail, they would have to gallop right past his hiding place, and that was exactly what he wanted. It didn't take long, either. Within seconds of him setting up, he began to make out individual horses and riders in the dust cloud. The pounding of the hooves and the snorting of heavily run horses filled the air and announced their arrival. The fugitive lifted the rifle and made ready.

Gus saw Morrison right away. He wasn't a hard man to spot, considering that the only other person in the group who was bigger than him was Mike Schumacher, and Gus wasn't interested in Mike. The outlaw cocked the hammer, got the Marshal in his sights and pulled the trigger. But just as he did that, another deputy moved forward and inadvertently took the bullet for his boss. He jerked slightly, then fell from his horse which panicked and, without any guidance from above, bucked and veered away.

Fortunately, the first horses coming up behind had the presence of mind to jump over the fallen rider so he could avoid being trampled. He stayed down though; he knew he was a sitting duck where he was, and the closer he stayed to the ground, the less likely he was of getting another bullet heading his way.

Gus cursed his bad luck. He quickly cocked the rifle again and took another shot before the posse had time to react. He was too quick though, and his aim was off. Morrison's horse was hit and went down in a dust-raising skid, while Morrison himself was thrown clear, only to scramble back to use the downed animal as cover.

The remainder of the posse members pulled their horses around, and in an instant, every rifle was aimed at the trees. A barrage of bullets exploded into the foliage, zinging and pinging through the leaves and branches.

Gus's horse panicked, and pulling back from its tethering, began to buck and plunge in its effort to break free and run away from the deadly assault. But Gus had tied him securely, and the horse was not able to pull away. Fortunately, none of the bullets found a target and everyone continued to breathe.

Gus ducked in behind the big tree trunk. He could have sworn he felt the tree shudder as the missiles thunked against it and became embedded in the wood. When he turned back around, rifle at the ready, he cursed again as he noticed four of the deputies had broken away from the group, and splitting into pairs, were maneuvering around to out-flank the outlaw and pin him down.

Gus fired bullet after bullet toward the pair to his left, hitting one of the lawmen in the arm and then taking down his horse. The animal snorted, angry at being knocked off its feet. The rider kicked clear, and the horse got its legs under itself again and scrambled up. With head and tail held high, and reins flying out behind, the gelding galloped off a few hundred yards before stopping and turning to see what was going to happen next.

In the meantime, the de-horsed deputy lay low, clutching his broken arm and looking for any kind of dip in the ground to roll into for cover. He needn't have worried though, because Gus wasn't paying him any attention. He fired more shots after the second horseman, hoping to bring him down before he reached the cover of the trees. No such luck. Horse and rider disappeared into the foliage and would soon be making their way back to where the outlaw was positioned.

Gus then swung the rifle to his right, just on the outside chance that the other two were still in the open for easy targets. The outlaw cursed again. They were gone from sight. Gus knew he had better move, and move fast, or he was going to be trapped. But just as he pushed away from the tree, he heard the rifle shot and then he got punched so hard in the left shoulder that he was sent sprawling face first into the greenery.

He swore a blue steak, knowing he had been hit again, but a lot worse this time. His collar bone was broken, and the pain was so bad, his whole left arm was numb and on fire all at the same time. He forced himself to his feet and, leaning awkwardly against the tree again, he swung the rifle up and, supporting it along a branch, fired shot after shot toward Morrison and the two wounded deputies who had all taken refuge behind the marshal's dead horse.

The rifle emptied, and Gus nearly dropped it, feeling like he was going to faint, but knowing he had to get to his horse before they had him boxed in.

"Give it up, Shaffer!" he heard Morrison yelling at him. "You got nowhere else to go. You haven't killed anyone yet. Be smart. Give it up before ya do somethin' you could be hanged for!"

Gus snarled at having to listen to that bastard's voice. The idiot still hadn't figured out that Gus had no intention of getting out of this alive. He only had one goal, and he was not inclined to give up on that just yet.

He made another attempt to get to his jittery horse, and this time, he did it. Adrenaline was all that got the second rifle back into the scabbard and himself up into the saddle. He almost ended up back on the ground again, as shots came at him from deeper inside the woods. The deputies had made it around to flank him, and they had cut off any retreat he might have been able to make in that direction. He was beyond cursing now. With his left arm useless, he swung his horse's head toward the open landscape and booted him forward.

The pent-up animal lunged ahead and, digging in with its hind quarters, burst clear of the foliage and headed at a full gallop straight toward the three men hiding behind the dead horse.

Now it was the three lawmen who were yelling and cursing and scrambling to meet this unexpected assault. By the time they got over the surprise and had their rifles ready to shoot, the horse was upon them. The three men instinctively ducked as the large animal rose up and, tucking its legs, leaped over the human obstacle. The horse landed with a grunt, then spraying the grounded men with dirt from its powering hind feet, took off at a gallop again, to head off across open country.

By this time, the three mounted deputies had come charging out from the copse of pines and were firing their rifles after the escaping outlaw. Fortunately for Gus, none of the wildly flying bullets hit their mark. Gus galloped on, his horse's hind feet leaving little puffs of dust behind him as they went.

The three horsemen reined in by their boss, but by this time,

Morrison was fuming, and with an angry gesture, he yelled them on.

"Go get 'im! I want that son of a bitch's head on a spike! Go run 'im down!"

They didn't need any more encouragement than that, and with big Mike leading the way, the three men took off at a gallop after the disappearing speck.

"Dammit," Morrison cursed again in his frustration. "Who would have thought that some two-bit, dirt outlaw like Shaffer would be givin' us so much trouble? Damn him to hell!"

Alex and Karl, who were sitting in the dirt, made no comment.

***

Half an hour later, there was still no sign of the depleted posse's return. Morrison had done his best to tend to the injuries of his deputies, and fortunately none of the men were wounded badly, just enough to hurt. At this point, the sun was high and getting hot out there in the open, and the flies buzzing around the dead horse were beginning to irritate. To a man, all three decided it would be more comfortable to move into the shade of the trees. Picking up what supplies they could from the dead animal, they headed for cover.

It was close and muggy inside the woods, but it was still cooler than sitting out in the open sun, and everyone settled in to await the return of their compatriots, hopefully with a prisoner or a corpse in tow. Twenty minutes more of waiting and Morrison spotted a dust trail rising into the air and hoped that it was the deputies returning. But as the source of the dust got closer, the marshal grunted in disappointment. It was only the two loose horses deciding that their best chances for survival lay with returning to the men who fed them, even if they did on occasion get shot at.

Still, Morrison surmised with a sigh, they were going to need those horses, so it was a good thing they decided to return. Leaving his rifle with the injured men, he walked back out toward the returning equines to catch them and bring them over, into the shade.

Morrison approached the horses slowly, not wanting to scare them off again, and though they blew and tensed at his arrival, they allowed the human to snatch up their trailing reins and be taken back into servitude once again.

Then, both horses spooked and jumped away from him, trying to break loose, and Morrison grabbed onto the reins even tighter. Next, he heard Alex and Karl shouting at him, then gunfire from their six-shooters, that caused the lawman to look around at what all the fuss was about.

He barely had time to see a third horse barreling down on him at a full gallop, and the angry, snarling expression on the face of the wounded outlaw, before the horse ploughed into him and sent him sprawling. The two riderless horses jumped away and got themselves out of there—again, while Gus hauled on his horse's mouth to slow it down and turn it back around.

He sent his horse back toward Morrison. Ignoring the bullets coming at him from the two wounded deputies, he charged the fallen man. Morrison scrambled to his feet and pulled his revolver. Gus dropped the reins and pulled his own revolver. His horse stayed true to its line and continued straight at the marshal. Both adversaries took their shots at the same time—point blank, and neither one missed their mark.

Morrison took the bullet in the lung and went down again, coughing blood.

Gus took his to the right upper chest, ploughing through his shoulder and lodging itself against the inside of his shoulder blade. He dropped his revolver and grabbed onto the saddle horn as best he could, desperate to stay on his horse. Said horse, now free from the guidance of its rider, joined up with the two loose animals and all three took off at a gallop across the open landscape.

The two deputies ran toward their boss, shooting their revolvers as they came. With their injuries, neither was able to wield a rifle, so they did the best they could with what they had.

At the same time, the small posse that had trailed the outlaw in a full circle, came bursting from the trees and went charging after the escaping fugitive.

Gus hung on for all he was worth. He had no control over where his horse went, but a full gallop anywhere was better than the alternative. He couldn't hear the revolvers shooting at him, but logic told him they were, and he hoped to goodness that they wouldn't find their mark. He did hear rifle fire join in on the assault, then again, felt himself getting punched in the back. He fell forward against his horse's neck, but still managed to hold on, despite the pain and the struggle now, to breathe.

The rifle fire continued behind him, and it wasn't fading away. One of the loose horses beside him stumbled and collapsed in a jumble of kicking legs and flying dirt. Gus carried on, knowing that the horses had smelled water and were heading for the river that he knew was out there, just waiting for them.

The small posse stayed on the outlaw's trail, determined to ride him down, but after the first mile or so, they stopped firing at him. It was just a waste of bullets anyway, since they knew the man had been hit several times. All they really had to do now, was stay with him and simply wait until he collapsed from blood loss.

Gus knew he was getting weaker. Those last two hits were serious, and he was losing blood at a dangerous rate. But he was determined not to stop, not to give in to those bastards. He knew where he was going, he knew this country like the back of his horse's neck. He didn't even have to think about it.

His horse stayed true to its course and the landscape began to change to more rolling hills and greenery. Soon he was hidden from sight and into the blessed coolness of the trees. He could practically smell the water on the breeze. The horses needed no encouragement to stay at a steady gait towards it. The loose horse trotted on ahead, eager for a drink and knowing they were getting close.

After what seemed an eternity, and with his body getting weaker and his brain becoming fuzzier by the minute, Gus finally made it to the river's edge. Oh, it was so nice here, so cool and refreshing. The gentle breeze rustled the leaves, and the peaceful river glided by, lapping up against the rocky banks. The outlaw felt weak and dry with thirst, and the river invited him in.

He wasn't feeling pain anymore, just a quiet serenity; an acceptance of what was to come. He leaned forward against the horse's neck, and with some effort, managed to bring his right leg over the cantle of the saddle, then slide to the ground. His legs couldn't support him, and he ended up on his knees. Before he knew it, he was face first, flat out on the rocky flood plain of the riverbank.

His horse nervously stepped away from him, then went to join his companion for a much-needed drink from the river. Gus stayed where he was for the moment, trying to convince himself to move. Then, both horses, their mouths still full of water, shot their heads up, and with pricked ears, looked back the way they had come. Gus knew the posse was catching up with him and would probably be there at any moment. That knowledge itself gave him incentive to move, since there was no way he was going to give them the satisfaction of taking his body in for the reward.

Through a haze in his brain and a buzzing in his ears, he dragged himself up to his hands and knees and pulled his resisting body to the river's edge. He didn't hesitate and continued into the water. It felt cool and comforting, and then the current took him, and he relaxed in the embrace of the river, as he drifted away.

***

Laramie, Wyoming
April 1888

"I suppose you've heard the news," Jack commented to his uncle.

Leon nodded. "Yeah. Kenny left the article in my cell the other day. The mood around here hasn't been too jovial, I can tell you. Carson's constantly glaring at me, like what happened to Morrison was my fault."

"Yeah. Well, any excuse I suppose."

"Yeah."

"How's Malachi takin' the news about Gus?"

Leon creased his brow and shrugged. "I don't know. I thought he'd be more cut up than he is. I mean, he's looking sad and going through all the motions, but it's like it's just an act. And you know Malachi never could hide what he was feeling. Kind of makes me wonder if he knows something we don't."

"What? Ya mean like maybe Gus ain't dead?"

Leon shrugged again. "They never did find his body."

"Yeah, I know, but from the amount of blood that was on the horse and along the riverbank, Mike figures he got shot up pretty bad. It just don't seem too likely."

"Hmm," Leon didn't sound convinced. "How's Morrison? Still breathing?"

"Yeah, he is. But they weren't able to get the bullet out—too risky, you know."

"Yeah."

"Eventually, he may cough it up on his own, but in the meantime, he's sure not gonna be ridin' out after any more outlaws. Gus accomplished that much anyway. He took that bastard out of commission, and that was no mean feat."

"Yeah," Leon agreed, then smiled. "Good ole Gus. Showed us all up, didn't he? In the end, he was the one who got the job done."

Jack nodded, and they sat for a moment in quiet remembrance of a lost friend.

"I rode up to the spot," Jack admitted. "The area by the river where Mike said they lost 'im. You know it, Leon, that spot where the river runs wide and there's that bit of a flood plain that gives easy access to the water at this time of year. We'd often stop ta let the horses drink there on the way back from a job."

"Oh yeah," Leon nodded. "Yeah, that's a nice spot."

"So, I just went there ta pay my respects, you know," Jack continued. "I felt like I needed to, and ta thank 'im for doin' what we hadn't been able to. I guess I was there for about half an hour, just takin' in the peacefulness of the place, and then I heard that high pitched screech from up above. I looked up and saw five eagles, way up there, you know, just casually circlin' the area.

"One of 'em let out that screech again, and I felt a shiver go through me. It was like, well, almost like a tribute, ya know? Hank, then Charlie and Mukua, then Lobo and now finally, Gus. Then one of 'em broke away from the group and flew off in another direction. I kinda thought that was odd at the time. But now, after what you say about Malachi's reaction, it does kinda make me wonder."

Leon smiled at him. "Gee, are you starting to get all sentimental on me here, nephew? Starting to believe in signs?"

Jack laughed. "Naw. I never did go for that sorta stuff. It always seemed to me ta be an awful lot a pressure ta put on a bird. I figure he just got hungry and went off huntin'. But still," he shrugged, "it was weird."

"Hmm, coincidence," stated the forever cynic. "Still, nice to see the eagles like that, circling over the old hideout. Kind of a nice send-off for the boys."

"Yeah."

"How's Mike doing?" Leon asked. "I wonder about him sometimes. Running with Morrison is going to get him killed one of these days."

"Naw, he's fine," Jack assured him. "He wasn't one of the deputies who got injured."

"That's a surprise," Leon commented, "considering how big he is you'd think he'd make an easy target."

"Yeah, but Gus weren't after anyone other than Morrison. The three deputies who were wounded, were just accidental, you know. Alex Strode got hit, but he's gonna be all right. Broken arm, but he'll survive."

"Oh, that's good," Leon seemed relieved. Aside from the fight at the Marsham's ranch on the day of their arrest, Morrison's deputies had always treated Nash well enough, and he would hate to hear that Gus had killed one of them. "Although, if Gus is still alive, he better remain 'dead' or the law is really going to be after him with a vengeance. They'll up his reward, and then every lawman and bounty hunter will be trying to collect on it."

"Uh huh. And we both know how much fun that is," Jack agreed. "If Gus is still alive, I'm hopin' he'll do what I told 'im ta do in the first place, he needs ta get outta the territory and stay out."

"He's not going to do that, at least, not permanently," Leon predicted. "Malachi is getting out of here soon. If anybody deserves an early release, it's him. I'll bet you my lucky coin that Gus is going to hang around and wait for him."

"You still got your lucky coin, Leon?"

"Well, no," Leon conceded, "but that's beside the point. It's the thought that counts."

"Uh huh."

Leon smiled, then conveniently changed the subject.

"So . . . any news from home?"

"Oh. Yeah—jeez, how could I forget about that?" Jack brightened with good news. "Yeah, Karma had her foal. Penny wrote ya a letter all about it. I left it with the guard out front there, and hopefully you'll get it this afternoon."

Leon grinned. "Good! I'll look forward to reading about it."

"Yeah. I'll leave it for Penny to fill ya in. All's good though, everybody's fine."

Leon held onto his grin. "Good. How's everyone else doing? Jean and Cameron all right, and the girls?"

"Yeah, everyone's fine," Jack assured him. "Cameron and Jean send their regards. Even Eli says 'hello'."

Leon laughed. "That's good. I guess he's getting big now, isn't he?"

"Yeah, he's growin' all right," Jack confirmed. "He's gonna be out there ridin' drag before too much longer."

Leon laughed again. "Better him than me."

It was a relief to see his friend smiling again. Leon had been down for so long this last time, Jack wondered if they were going to be able to bring him out of it. But Leon was nothing if not resilient, and he seemed to be making his way back to the surface. Perhaps the warmer spring weather had something to do with it. He still wasn't his normal, high-energy self, but at least he wasn't wallowing in despair anymore.

Jack had been concerned the news about Gus would bring his friend down again, but it didn't seem to have done that. Of course, if Leon was thinking that Gus was still alive somewhere, somehow, then he wouldn't be mourning his loss just yet. Jack hoped his partner was right. He did have a point; the outlaw's body had not been found, and Jack knew from their own experiences that stranger things have happened. Still, he wasn't holding out too much hope.

Malachi was the one who would be taking it the hardest, and it might just be that he couldn't accept the death of his friend and partner, at least not yet. It was a hard thing to accept, the loss of a partner. Jack had faced that possibility more than once, and it never got any easier. It had only been sheer luck that he'd never had to accept that event as fact, at least, not yet.

Jack sighed to himself. Time would tell.

"Anything else happening?" Leon interrupted Jack's musings. "What about Sam and Maribelle? Have they gone to see Mariam yet?"

Jack's jaw dropped in surprise, and he found himself speechless for a moment. He hadn't even intended to mention Sam to Leon for fear of what his uncle's reaction would be. Then, to have Leon bring it up himself, caught him flat-footed.

"Ah, yeah . . ." Jack stammered. "Yeah, they're over talkin' with Dr. Mariam now. They seemed to be gettin' along real well when I left 'em to it. I have a feelin' it's all gonna work out fine."

"Good." Leon nodded. "It'll be a lucky break for one of those youngsters, and I suppose, Sam and Maribelle will do all right as parents. I'm hardly the one to be judgmental about that."

"Yeah. Well—that's just the way things worked out, Leon, for both of us."

"Yeah, I suppose."

"I'll keep ya up to date on what happens. Oh, but then, you see

Mariam more often than I do. She'll probably let ya know."

Leon nodded. He shifted, clinking the chains that secured his hands to the belt.

Jack sensed his partner's mood starting to dip again.

"Ya goin' ta services again, Leon?"

"Naw."

"What about them new words," Jack asked, hopefully. "I ain't got any from ya lately. Are ya still doin' that?"

"Naw."

Jack sighed. This was going to be harder than he thought.

"Why not? I thought you were enjoyin' that."

"Well, yeah, I was. I guess, I just got bored with it."

"Oh."

"Doc Palin's keeping me busy, though."

"Oh." Jack perked up. This sounded promising.

"He's been giving me some of the higher end medical books to read now, and they're quite challenging." Leon showed some enthusiasm for his topic. "Looking at strange diseases and conditions of the brain and all that. I never would have thought the human body was so fragile and could have so many things go wrong with it. It kind of gives you a different slant on things, you know?"

Jack grinned. "Yeah. That's good. Nothing like another point of view."

Leon nodded with raised eyebrows in full agreement.

Officer Pearson shifted his position a bit, and Leon glanced back at him, wondering if their time was up. Pearson sent him a subtle negative so Leon turned his attention back to his friend.

"How are Jean and Cameron? They doing all right?"

"Yeah, they're fine."

"And Eli? He's okay?"

"Yeah, they're all fine, Leon. Why do ya keep askin'?"

Leon shrugged. "Ahh . . . I've just been having weird dreams lately. People I care about being pulled apart by ropes or trampled by horses. I even had a train run me down the other night. It was weird. It was like, no matter where I ran or how many twists and turns I made, the tracks followed me, and of course, the train was following the tracks, until I finally got pulled down, under the engine."

Jack grimaced. "All those trains we robbed, comin' back ta haunt ya."

"Hmm. And doing a good job of it, too. Ole Mr. Davis is getting fed up with me screaming in the night. Kind of gets the other inmates upset, you know. Can't have that."

Jack turned serious. "Jeez, Leon, you havin' nightmares like that on a regular basis?"

Leon shrugged and looked at the empty space just above Jack's left shoulder. "Yeah, well. Comes with the territory, I suppose. Don't worry about it, Jack. I shouldn't have mentioned it. The doc is going to give me something to help me sleep, so, all's good."

"Yeah," Jack sounded dubious. "Still, I—"

"No, Jack! Listen, I told you, don't worry about it. Geesh. Now you're going to turn into a mother hen, aren't you? I shouldn't have said anything."

The two men sat quietly for a few moments.

Leon was definitely in a mood again. What a bronco ride: up and down. Jack never knew who he was going to get when he came for his visits, or even who he was going to get within the same visit. Case in point, Leon was grinning at him now, the old sparkle back in his eyes.

"You and Penny staying honest?" he asked, mischievously. "It's been a while since—"

"Yeah, Leon, we have," Jack cut him off. "It's important, we have to."

"Okay," Leon conceded. "That's good, I guess."

"Well, yeah," Jack looked embarrassed. "That first time, well it just happened—but it shouldn't have. I should have been more in control and I'm gonna make sure it don't happen again. I didn't feel guilty about it right away, but as time went on and it really sank in what we had done, then yeah, I started ta feel bad. After all that Cameron and Jean have done for us, and that's how I thank 'em? That weren't right.

"I dunno, Leon, I think you and me are just so used ta takin' whatever we want, without givin' any thought to the consequences, or how our actions might end up hurtin' other people, that we just don't think beyond the act itself. But then, I did start ta think about how Cameron would feel if he found out about that. He would have felt betrayed. And he would be right—it was a betrayal. He was trustin' me and I blew it.

"Then, I started thinkin' about what happened between you and Gabriella, and how all it took was the two a you, that one night, and .

. . I got real worried then, Leon, I gotta admit. I was walkin' on eggshells for a good couple a months there, just waitin' for Cameron to come after me with the shotgun. Thank goodness nothin' happened—but I sure ain't gonna put either one of us through that again."

"Yeah," Leon commented sadly, his expression and mood dropping into the deepest depths again.

"Aww, Leon, I'm sorry." Jack was truly contrite. "I didn't mean ta bring that up and throw it in your face. It's just my situation brought it to mind, is all.'

"Yeah, I know Jack. It's all right," Leon tried to brighten himself up. "What happened, happened. Nothing we can do about it now."

"I know. But still." Jack sighed. "Gabi don't blame you, ya know."

"Doesn't she?"

"You know she don't," Jack insisted. "There's a lot more to it than that."

"Yeah, Jack, I know. You're right," Leon conceded, "and you're right about you and Penny, too. Best to play it safe." Leon grinned, his dimples putting in an honest appearance. "And you are right about another thing. She is awfully young. She might come to her senses and realize that she doesn't want you, after all."

Jack sent him a look, but it was backed up with relief. If Leon was teasing him about that, then he was trying to pull himself up and into better spirits.

"Thanks for your support there, Leon," Jack threw back at him. "Always knew I could count on ya ta back me up."

"Uh huh."

Then Jack couldn't help it, and he broke out laughing.

***

When Leon got back to his cell, there was a thick parcel sitting on his pillow waiting for him. He smiled in anticipation, looking forward to hearing news about his favorite girl, and of course, to hear things from Penny's joyous descriptions was always a treat. It was too nice a day to sit inside, so Leon tore open the paper wrapping, snatched up the bulky letter and made his way outside and into the yard.

He paused for a moment when he reached the bottom steps, and took a quick look around, taking note of who was there and who wasn't. Ames and Malachi were walking the perimeter and minding their own business. Mackenzie was by the fence, but there was no sign of Boeman or Harris, so that was a good thing. Ohh, Thompson. Ever since Nash had broken that guard's collar bone, he'd been looking for any excuse to make the inmate's life miserable. Well, since when was that new? Leon would just have to keep an eye on him.

He looked around to the bench that was in the little alcove under the steps of the warehouse and was relieved to see it unoccupied. He went over and sat down. He got comfortable and leaned into the corner, while bringing one knee up to support his arm as he read the letter.

Yeah, news from home was always a welcome treat, and news about Karma only made it better.

Dear Napoleon:

Nash felt a slight twinge of disappointment at this address. Ever since the hearing, both Penny and Caroline had started calling him by his legal name, and though he didn't really mind, it seemed like it was one more thing that had disappeared from his life. One more innocence lost.

He released a silent sigh then settled in to continue reading.

I know that Jack is going to be taking this letter to you, so I'm sure he has already told you that Karma's second foal is on the ground. He promised me that he wouldn't say any more than that, though, so I am going to carry on here with the assumption that he kept his word.

Karma had an easy go of it, this time. Probably because she had already been through it once before and knew what was going on. It was almost as though she was looking forward to her new foal, and couldn't wait to push him out into the world so she could meet him

And yes, Papa was right! She did have a colt this time. And what a big, beautiful boy he is. He's almost an exact copy of his mama. He's that same dark, liver chestnut, which I know is not that common a color, because I sure don't see it very often, and he has her same lovely white socks on his back feet. The only real difference is that he has a full, but not too wide, blaze on his face, whereas Karma has the star and snip.

He really is gorgeous and with all the quality that Daisy had promised, and OH, you should see Papa! He's so thrilled to finally get his colt. He hasn't stopped grinning from that day to this. I can't wait for you to see him, Napoleon, as I'm sure you'll be impressed. With him, and with Daisy too, of course.

She is getting to be quite the handful and is really giving Sam a learning experience in getting her to mind her manners. It's not that she's mean, or stubborn, and certainly not stupid. But she has a very ironic sense of humor and tries to put one over on Sam whenever the opportunity presents itself.

Not to brag, or anything (well, maybe a little bit), but she is very different with me and will do anything I ask her, so long as I ask her in a way that she understands. That is so often the challenge, isn't it? With animals, it's not that they're stupid or that they don't want to please you, it's just that it's up to us to learn how to ask them, and that's where things can get difficult.

Perhaps if Sam asked her differently, he might get a better response, but I have no idea what 'different' is. I'll have to do some research on that. But then Daisy and I do have a special bond, much like you and Karma do. Karma will let others handle her and ride her, and I know she does like me, but she will always be your horse.

Jack tells me that Sam and Maribelle are thinking of adopting one of the children at the orphanage, and I think this is a wonderful idea. They were both so heartbroken over not being able to have children of their own, and once Jack mentioned it, it seemed like such an obvious solution to their predicament. Jack even hinted that once we get married, as well as having our own (God willing), perhaps we could adopt a child. I suppose he figures that since he grew up in an orphanage, and knows what it's like to not have family, well, it would be giving something back, wouldn't it? I'm all for it. Why not?

Speaking of children, Eli is really becoming quite his own man now. He has somewhere gotten the idea that he runs things around here and is becoming more and more obstinate in demanding his own way. He is also very verbal. I have no idea where he gets that from. Since he has learned how to talk, he doesn't shut up. Of course, Jack comments that it reminds him of someone else he knows, and I suppose it doesn't take much of an imagination to guess whom he is referring to!

Actually, Eli and Nathan Gibson get along very well, and I expect they will grow up to be close friends. I mean, they are close in age, after all, and Mama has already given Tricia many of the clothes that Eli has grown out of. It's quite funny to see little Nathan trying so hard to keep up with Eli, and wearing the same cute little outfits that Eli was wearing himself, only a few months ago. A real reminder as to how quickly they grow.

But then, look at how quickly Daisy is growing! It seems like only yesterday that she was a cute little cream puff, no bigger than our new colt, and now she is almost as tall as her mama. I wish you could see them, ~~Peter~~ Napoleon; they both carry Karma's stamp on them, which of course, means that they are very impressive.

I do hope you can come home soon. It seems like it's taking forever to get anywhere—oh, I mean for you to have to be in that horrid place for so long, not that it's a long time to wait for my wedding! Of course, it is a long time to wait— but that's not what I meant—oh, you know what I mean. We all just miss you so much, and we want you to come home.

I better close off now. Mama sends her best and tells you to stay safe. I'm hoping Jack will be agreeable to me and Josey coming out for another visit soon. It would be so nice to see you again. Take care of yourself.

With much love,
Penny

Leon sighed and leaned back against the wall. It was always bittersweet, getting letters from friends. He looked forward to them and would be devastated if they stopped coming, but it still made him feel homesick, like life was passing him by.

He looked around at his surroundings and wondered just how much longer he would be having to call this place 'home'.

Oh damn. Thompson's looking at me. That guard took the broken collarbone incident far too personally. And now, adding to that, what happened to Morrison. . .

A knot of apprehension squeezed Leon's heart.

The inmate casually got to his feet and headed back indoors. The warm afternoon had suddenly turned chilly.

CHAPTER TWENTY
THE SUPREME COURT

Cheyenne, Wyoming
Spring 1888

Jack wished he could loosen his tie as he and Penny sat in the gallery of the court room. It wasn't so much that he was hot, but rather that he was anxious. He was used to these impressive halls and chambers where high, legal decisions were made, but this legal decision was even more important than the hearing considering the impact it was going to have upon Leon's future.

"Relax," Penny tried to loosen his grip on her fingers. "You've done all you can. It's up to Steven now."

Jack heaved a sigh. He noticeably relaxed then smiled at his lady. "Yeah, you're right. At least I don't have ta get up in front of them judges and give my accountin'. That's all on Steven this time."

"It is." Penny slipped her hand from Jack's loosened grip, gave her fingers a shake then returned them to Jack's softer hold. "Steven is very nervous, but he's doing a good job of covering it up."

Jack's attention went to Steven who was standing at the podium facing the long table where the two court justices and one chief justice were already seated.

The dark polished wood and lush carpeting encouraged hushed tones so the rustling of paper from all those preparing for the appeal was the prominent sound in the room.

Behind him, Jack could barely hear Josey in conversation with Caroline and was thankful she had finally learned how to keep her voice down. The public were allowed to watch these proceedings as long as they remained respectful.

Jack jumped when a hand clapped his shoulder, and a deep voice greeted him.

"Hey, Jack. I guess I shouldn't be surprised to see you here."

A couple of frowns from the floor turned their way.

"Jeez, Frank. Keep it down, will ya?"

Frank glanced at the legal assembly where some members were still sending him sour looks.

"Oh, right." Frank's volume dropped. "We ain't back at head office now, are we?" He nodded a greeting to Penny. "Miss Marsham."

Penny smiled and nodded back then she pretended to take interest in the proceedings on the floor as her grip tightened on her escort's hand.

***

Steven took a deep breath as he steadied his nerves. There is a first time for everything. Steven had never presented an appeal to the Supreme Court before, but he knew once he got started his nerves would settle. At least, this is what he told himself.

He had everyone's depositions in front of him, and each of the court justices also had copies, so he knew he was prepared. He knew he could not make a pretense of sorting his notes for much longer. It was time to get this session started.

He straightened up, gave his papers a tap on the podium to level them, then faced the music.

"May I proceed?"

Chief Justice Maginnis nodded.

"Mr. Chief Justice, and may it please the court. My name is Steven Granger and I represent the plaintiff in this case, Mr. Napoleon Nash. I reserve ten minutes for rebuttal.

"This is a wrongful interment appeal. I will present three essential points that have already been presented to Your Honors for review. These points are fundamental in how the government views its obligation in honoring promises made to criminals in exchange for information or actions.

"It is not uncommon for arrangements of this nature to be made and even if the contract is not in writing, there are usually witnesses present and both parties are expected to honor the agreement.

"My second point is more specific to my client's situation. In the case of Mr. Nash, and his partner, Mr. Kiefer, this contract was not honored. After the arrests of Mr. Nash and Mr. Kiefer in the spring of 1885, then governor, Mr. Francis Warren, did not intervene and both men remained in custody until their trials. Then again, when Mr. Nash went to trial in August of 1885, the Governor's Office remained silent about the agreement even to the point of suppressing testimony from witnesses concerning the legitimacy of it.

"You now have copies of the depositions from both these witnesses including their reasons for not coming forward during the trials.

"My third point involves the case of Mr. Kiefer. By the time he went to trial in October of 1885, the governors' office changed its stance and honored the agreement by presenting Mr. Kiefer with his pardon."

"October?" Justice Corn interrupted. "Why did it take so long for Mr. Kiefer to go to trial? Surely the two cases were connected."

"Yes, Your Honor," Steven said. "Mr. Kiefer was seriously wounded during their arrest through no actions of his own. It wasn't even certain he would survive and even then, it was some months before he was capable of standing trial."

"Thank you. Please continue."

Steven nodded and found his place again. "I suggest to the court that since Mr. Kiefer was given a pardon then there was an arrangement already in place, and Mr. Nash should also have received one."

"You are surmising that Mr. Nash was part of the arrangement." Justice Blair pointed out. "How do you know this?"

Steven took a moment to pull up two of his depositions. He flipped through the top one until he found the required statement.

"This testimony is from Mr. John Higgins who was the secretary for Governor Hoyt when the agreement between Mr. Hoyt, Mr. Kiefer, and Mr. Nash was brokered in May of 1880."

Jack frowned. Higgins? The name sounded vaguely familiar, but he couldn't, for the life of him, picture the man.

"Excuse me again," Justice Corn interrupted. "You keep referring to 'the contract' or 'the agreement'. What exactly was this arrangement that the Governors' Office supposedly made with your client?"

"Governor Hoyt offered both Mr. Nash and Mr. Kiefer pardons

in exchange for one to two years of working undercover for him. Each successive governor agreed to and took advantage of this arrangement for five years until the time of my client's arrest."

"We are aware of Marshal Morrison's campaign against the Wyoming outlaws," Justice Blair stated. "Why would he have targeted Nash and Kiefer, knowing that they were under contract to the governor?"

"He did not know," Steven stated. "Governor Warren instructed Marshal Morrison to rid the territory of its outlaw gangs. Since the Elk Mountain Gang was strongest, the marshal went after them first. The governor did not mention any concessions to be made to Mr. Nash or Mr. Kiefer. It was agreed that if the knowledge were to leak out, then Nash and Kiefer's effectiveness at covert operations would become moot. It had to be kept hidden, which is why there was no written contract."

The justices were silent as they considered this information.

Justice Corn spoke up first. "And you now have witnesses to this agreement?"

"Yes, Your Honor," Steven confirmed.

"Please, continue."

Steven nodded. "Mr. Higgins states that 'Though I was not present in the Governor's office when the deal was struck, I was often in a position to overhear conversations pertaining to it. There is no doubt in my mind that Nash and Kiefer were under a verbal contract with the Wyoming Territorial Governor's Office.' Also," Steven opened the second deposition, "Mr. Frank Carlyle—"

"Excuse me, Mr. Granger," Justice Blair interrupted. "Before you continue, why did Mr. Higgins not come forward during Mr. Nash's trial?"

"Mr. Higgins had signed a non-disclosure agreement when he accepted the position of secretary to the Governor's Office. He not only feared losing his job if he came forward, but also the possibility of going to prison."

"That is understandable," Justice Blair agreed. "However, when it comes to legal proceedings, Mr. Higgins could have utilized his First Amendment Rights. He may have lost his job, but he would not have gone to prison."

"That is true, Your Honor, and Mr. Higgins greatly regrets his reluctance to come forward earlier. He was not fully aware of his rights at that time."

"Thank you, Mr. Granger. Please continue."

"Mr. Frank Carlyle has been employed as a detective with Wells Fargo for the last twenty-five years. He has shown himself to be a resilient agent who is above reproach. He has been successful on many undercover assignments and has been entrusted with delicate and confidential duties.

"In his deposition, Mr. Carlyle states: 'On the morning in question, I was called into Governor Hoyt's office and was surprised to find the outlaws, Nash and Kiefer, along with a sheriff, Taggard Murphy, in attendance. I was then made aware of the agreement between these three men and the governor. That if Nash and Kiefer stayed legal and accepted the occasional undercover assignments, then after a couple of years they would have earned their pardons. Sheriff Murphy was apparently their sponsor, and Governor Hoyt requested that I also maintain contact with Nash and Kiefer to ensure that they stuck to their side of the deal. I was also expected to work with them on some of the more, shall we say, delicate assignments.

'At first, I was skeptical. Nash had proven himself to be a cocky son-of-a-bitch, and I doubted that he would be able to stick to the conditions of the agreement. However, after working with Nash and Kiefer for five years, I had come to change my opinion. Both were serious about starting new lives and earning the pardons that had been promised.'

"Again," Steven continued, "Mr. Carlyle states that the contract was for one to two years, at which point a decision would be made concerning the promised pardons. He also refers to the fact that he worked with them for five years, up until the time of their arrests. At which point, the Governor's Office did nothing to intervene."

"And why did Mr. Carlyle not come forward as a witness at their trials?" Justice Corn asked. "Had he also signed a non-disclosure agreement?"

"No, Your Honor. Mr. Carlyle was conveniently sent out of the country before news of Nash and Kiefer's arrests could reach him. By the time he returned to the States, Mr. Nash was already incarcerated at the U.S. Penitentiary at Laramie City. He offered to testify at Mr. Kiefer's trial, but the deal made with the Governor's Office became a moot point."

"Yes," Chief Justice Maginnis said. "I recall that trial taking some interesting twists. And yet, Mr. Kiefer did receive a pardon. Why was that, Mr. Granger?"

"Public pressure, You Honor. Knowledge of the arrangement between these parties was spreading and rumors of an untrustworthy government were becoming rampant. Governor Warren decided that the best course of action was to present Mr. Kiefer the pardon in order to appease the citizenry and maintain his good name."

"Hmm." Chief Justice Maginnis sat back and drummed his fingers upon the desk top. "Why did you wait so long to petition for an appeal to be heard at this court? You had your witnesses. Why the delay?"

"Sheriff Taggard Murphy had testified at both the Nash and Kiefer trials, stating his first-hand knowledge of the agreement. However, doubt was cast over his statements when it was learned that Sheriff Murphy had previously been an outlaw himself and had run with the Elk Mountain Gang. It was also noted that he and Napoleon Nash had been friends for many years.

"Also, Mr. Higgins had yet to come forward and, considering his position, his testimony is vital to our appeal."

Chief Justice Maginnis looked down his nose at the attorney. "Considering you also had Mr. Carlyle's first-hand account of the arrangement, I have the distinct feeling that you are leaving something out."

"Umm, well. Yes, Your Honor."

Magennis's brows arched when Steven did not continue. "Well, Councilor?"

"If I may be blunt."

"Please do."

"Judge John Lacey presided over both the Nash and Kiefer trials, Your Honors. It is his ruling on the Napoleon Nash case that we are appealing here. Up until recently, Judge Lacey also held the position of Chief Justice of this Supreme Court. I felt it was unlikely that Chief Justice Lacey would override his own ruling in this case."

There was some minor shuffling and paper rustling from the justices.

Chief Justice Maginnis frowned as he leaned forward.

"This court is impartial, Councilor. If Judge Lacey had still been sitting as Chief Justice at this time, he would have relinquished his seat and another judge would have taken over for this case. With your new witnesses and their testimony, the appeal would have been decided irrespective of who the presiding judge was at the original trial."

"Of course, Your Honor. My apologies." Steven conceded the point, but still held to the opinion that he had best served his client by waiting. "Thank you, Your Honor. My time is now expired."

Steven gathered his papers and retired to his seat.

***

"Mr. Chief Justice, and may it please the court. My name is Hugo Doleman. I am honored to represent the Governor's Office involving the 1885 case of The Territory of Wyoming versus Napoleon Nash.

"In response to Mr. Granger's statement that the arrangement between Mr. Nash and the governor's office was to extend no longer than two years, former Governor Hoyt states," and Mr. Doleman referenced his notes, "'No mention of a time limit was discussed at the time of the agreement . . .'".

Jack gave a silent snort at this statement. "That ain't true. Trust a lawyer ta lie through his teeth. Just goes ta show, ya gotta get everything in writing. Ya can't trust nobody these days."

Caroline leaned forward and put a gentle hand on Jack's shoulder. "Shhh. Steven will take care of it."

Jack sighed but settled back to listen.

None of this exchange was heard on the floor, and Mr. Doleman continued. "Also, Mr. Hoyt emphasizes '. . . it was agreed by all those present that the details of the agreement would not be made public. Mr. Nash was confident that he and his business partner could avoid arrest and detainment just as they had always done. There was no agreement between Mr. Nash and the governor's office that the presiding governor would step in and reveal this agreement if either Mr. Nash or Mr. Kiefer were brought to trial.'"

Mr. Doleman returned his attention to the Justices. "This is not an uncommon arrangement, Your Honors. Enlisting known outlaws to switch sides in exchange for full or partial pardons has been beneficial to both parties. Unfortunately, often these deals become null and void when the outlaw reverts to type and continues to commit crimes during the time of expected clemency.

"This does not happen every time, but in the case of Mr. Nash, it did. He admitted in court to committing a crime in which a renowned businessman was scammed out of thousands of dollars.

"The pardon was intended to cover only the crimes Mr. Nash had committed before the agreement was made, but not for crimes committed during the period covered by the agreement. Mr. Hoyt wisely inserted a time period before giving Mr. Nash and Mr. Kiefer their pardons in order to assure that they could abide by the stipulations of the agreement. Mr. Nash could not.

"Mr. Nash also showed disrespect to the court by repeatedly speaking out of turn and even attempting to assault a witness while on the stand in an effort to prevent him from testifying."

Caroline saw the muscles in Jack's back tense. Again, her hand went out to his shoulder.

"Jack, you have to relax. I know it must be difficult for you to relive all this, but if you do anything to disrupt this court, Leon's appeal will be thrown out. Please, let Steven do his job."

"But it ain't right," Jack responded in a tight whisper. "We had our reasons for that con game, and they were good ones."

Beside Caroline, Josephine sat quietly with her eyes down and a guilty knot forming in her gut. She was still ashamed that her one mistake in judgment had cost her friend so dearly.

Mr. Doleman continued. "It was for these reasons that Mr. Nash lost his pardon and was sent to prison. Why Mr. Kiefer did not join him there is out of my realm of understanding."

Steven's jaw tightened at this damning comment, but he need not have worried.

"That is irrelevant to this case, Mr. Doleman," Chief Justice Maginnis reminded him. "It is Mr. Nash's trial and sentencing that are being questioned here, not Mr. Kiefer's."

"Of course. I apologize to Your Honors. In closing, Governor Warren feels that the sentence Mr. Nash received was just and warranted. Unlike Mr. Kiefer, Mr. Nash showed no remorse for his criminal activity. This, combined with Mr. Nash's disrespect to the court, convinced Judge Lacey that Mr. Nash would return to his former lifestyle and, indeed, had returned to it at the first opportunity.

"Though Mr. Kiefer and other un-disclosed individuals were involved with the crime, Mr. Nash was the instigator, as he had always been the instigator. He had given every indication that he would return to his criminal career with very little provocation.

"Mr. Nash is unrepentant and for the safety of our citizens, needs to remain in prison for the duration of his life."

"All right." Chief Justice Maginnis nodded. "Thank you."

"Thank you."

Doleman gathered his papers and returned to his seat.

Steven approached the bench again for his rebuttal.

"Mr. Doleman suggests that Mr. Nash's emotional outbursts were disrespect toward the court itself, but this was not the case. Mr. Nash was under duress due to previous revelations, and emotions were high. Mr. Nash's outburst was aimed at a man whom he once considered a friend when that man indicated his willingness to turn states evidence against their mutual benefactors who had taken them in as children and given them a home.

"Mr. Nash saw this as a betrayal of the highest—"

"Excuse me, Councilor," Justice Corn interrupted. "Does that not make Mr. Nash a hypocrite? Did he not agree to do the same thing in order to win his pardon?"

"No, Your Honor, it was not the same at all. Neither Mr. Nash nor Mr. Kiefer were expected to infiltrate their old gang or turn on men they had previously worked with. Most of their jobs through the Governor's Office were delivering important documents or tracking down missing persons. On occasion they were also expected to assist Detective Carlyle with security matters of a political or even personal nature.

"Indeed, one of the accusations of disrespect to the court was made when Mr. Nash refused to name his accomplices in the aforementioned criminal activity even though by doing so, he might have saved himself from the extreme sentence he received."

"Hmm. Thank you. Please continue."

"Thank you. To conclude the matter of disrespect to the court, on the contrary, Mr. Nash showed himself to be an honorable man despite his career choice, and he considers loyalty to his friends the highest bond there can be.

"Concerning the matter of Mr. Nash reverting to his criminal activities upon the slightest provocation, this accusation is not grounded in fact.

"Mr. Nash and Mr. Kiefer remained true to the terms of the arrangement for years past the original time agreed upon. In a deposition from Miss Josephine Janssen, she states, 'I threatened to expose the deal my friends made with the Governor of Wyoming in order to coerce them into helping me escape the clutches of a blackmailer. If word had gotten out to their criminal associates that Nash and Kiefer had switched sides and were working for the law, their lives, and their chance at a pardon, would have been placed in great jeopardy. I sincerely regret this action now and can only say in my defense that I was truly desperate.'"

Both Penny and Caroline turned accusing glares toward their friend. Josey shrunk as far down in her seat as she could and would not meet the eyes of either lady. Fortunately, Steven carried on with his narrative, and their attentions were diverted back to the room. For now.

"I suggest that loyalty," Steven continued, "and not an inherent inclination toward the criminal element, was Mr. Nash's downfall. Loyalty, and a desperate effort to save their chances for the pardons were his motivations for committing the crime. We concede that Mr. Nash did commit a criminal act during the period of their clemency, but we hold that this act was committed under duress and extenuating circumstances. Considering the agreement made between my client and the Governor's Office we suggest that Mr. Nash was wrongfully incarcerated and that time served is sufficient punishment for the crime commit.

"Thank you."

"Thank you, Councilor. The court will consider this information and you will receive our decision no later than June 30, 1888. This concludes the appeal of the sentence in The Territory of Wyoming vs. Napoleon Nash."

***

"That's nothin' like what I expected," Jack admitted to the group as they relaxed over lunch. "You really had to make your points fast. I figured we'd be in there all day."

"Oh no," Steven sipped his wine then set the glass down. "It's the two attorneys laying out their case as quickly and concisely as they can. Time is very limited."

"You did a good job," Caroline smiled at her man. "If that doesn't convince them that Napoleon has been misused, then I don't know what will."

Steven smiled at her. "I hope so."

"Yeah, but either way." Jack addressed the group. "I wanna thank all of ya for comin' forward like this and tryin' ta help. Not ta mention John Higgins. I barely noticed him even when he was in the room with us. Frank had to remind me who he was and then it all made sense. He did risk a lot comin' forward."

"Yes, he did. Governor Moonlight had nothing to do with arranging the deal, or in refusing to acknowledge that deal when you two were arrested. That being the case, I'm hopeful that Mr. Higgins won't lose his job. Perhaps Mr. Moonlight will see this as a sign of honesty and integrity."

"That settles it," Jack griped as he cut into his steak. "He's definitely going to get fired."

Frank snorted but Steven just rolled his eyes.

Jack chewed his steak then pointed his fork at the detective. "And Frank. I gotta admit, you surprised me. You started out hopin' me and Leon would mess things up. You ain't always been that supportive."

"Sure I have," Frank growled. "You just didn't appreciate my way of doin' things, that's all."

"Ha! By pullin' your gun on me and beatin' up on Leon. How is that supportive?"

"You made it out alive, didn't ya?"

"I did. The jury is still out on that one with Leon."

Frank sighed and leaned back in his chair. "Listen, Jack, I know you can't quite forgive me for what happened in Gillette—"

"Not ta mention before that," Jack sniped.

"Before that, I was just doin' my job. Nash accepts that and so would you, if you weren't so bull-headed. But what happened in Gillette was . . ." Frank simply shook his head, not finding the right words.

"Unforgiveable." Jack helped him out.

Frank was about to retaliate but Caroline beat him to it.

"What happened in Gillette?" she asked.

She and her sister shared a glance, then looked from one man to the other, expecting an answer.

Jack and Frank exchanged a quick glance, both realizing they had brought an old argument to the lunch table.

"Nothin'," Jack said. "It don't matter now." He then met Frank square on. "I guess you have supported us over the years. That does mean a lot."

"Well, finally!" Frank was adamant. "It took me comin' here today and putting my job with Wells Fargo on the line for you to finally give me credit."

"Yeah, okay," Jack said as the tension around the table eased. "But dammit, Frank. You ain't the easiest man ta like, ya know."

Frank stared at Jack for a beat then started laughing.

"I'll drink ta that!" he announced, then raised his glass in a salute.

Everyone at the table joined in, and with smiles and chuckles all around, the glasses clinked together in a toast.

"Do you really think you could lose your job over this?" Jack asked the detective.

Frank shrugged. "I doubt it. Just as with Mr. Higgins, I'm not in conflict with Governor Moonlight. If he does put pressure on Mr. Hume to fire me, well fine. I can always go back east and hook up with Mr. Hoag again. I might just do that anyway. We did make a good team."

Jack swallowed his resentment at this comment, as he didn't want to start the old argument up again. "Yeah, I suppose you could."

"Well, I certainly hope that something positive comes from all this," Josephine piped up, figuring it was about time they changed the subject "I'm ashamed enough about what I did, without having to admit it to a bunch of official looking men with white whiskers. Even if it was just in writing."

"Yes!" Caroline and Penelope rounded on their friend.

"How could you have done that?" Caroline demanded.

"I thought you were their friend!" Penny added.

Josephine rolled her eyes. She was never going to live that incident down.

Then Jack came to her rescue, "Ladies, ladies, don't be so hard on her. Josey's sorry for it and has done everything she can to make it up. We did tell her to stay away if we ever went to trial, and we did prevent her from testifyin' when she showed up ta do so. Cut her some slack, okay?"

The sisters looked repentant.

"All right."

"Sorry, Josephine."

***

Laramie, Wyoming
July 1888

Leon lay on his back, on his bunk, looking up at a ceiling that was closing in on top of him. He felt crushed, as though he were suffocating, even though he continued to draw oxygen into his lungs. That Supreme Court appeal had been his last chance, his last hope. What now? What next?

Oh, Steven had tried to be optimistic: *Moonlight can't stay in office forever. There's a presidential election coming up. A new president could mean a new governor, perhaps one who was more sympathetic to their plight. Just hang in there; we're not giving up!*

Throughout the whole meeting with Steven Granger, Napoleon and Jack had locked eyes and did not let go. It seemed to be all that held them together, that invisible but solid link of blue into brown. Steven's words didn't exist in their private world—only the partners existed. The partners, and their combined aura of disappointment.

"So," Leon had reiterated once Steven was finished. "They agreed to adjust my sentence to ten to twenty years, with possibility of parole at ten years, minus time served. So, I'm eligible for parole in about eight years."

"That's right." Steven looked from one man to the other. They continued to look at each other. "Although, if the governor and the warden are in agreement, you could be up for parole sooner."

Jack snorted.

Leon simply smiled. "Not much chance of that happening."

"I know." Steven shared their disappointment. "I had hoped for better, but it's an improvement, isn't it? Eight years is more manageable than twenty."

Leon turned his dark eyes to Steven. "That's it though, isn't it? This is the highest court in the land for this type of case, right?"

"Yes," Steven said, "This is not a federal case so the Wyoming Supreme Court is the highest court we can appeal to. Our best strategy now is to continue petitioning the governor's office. Sooner or later, they'll have to relent."

"No, they don't," Leon grumbled. "All the governor has to do is turn his back, and I'll be stuck in here until the day I die."

***

When Steven and Jack returned to Laramie, they continued through town and rode out to the orphanage to have a word with Mariam.

"Mariam!" Jack flagged her down as they entered the main foyer to the orphanage.

"Jack! What a pleasant surprise."

"Mariam, this is Steven Granger. He's Penny's brother-in-law, and also, Leon's lawyer. Steven, this is Dr. Mariam Soames."

"Good afternoon. I have heard much about you."

"All good, I hope?"

"Of course."

"So, what can I do for you, Jack," Mariam asked him. "How did the appeal go?"

"Not as well as we'd hoped," Jack admitted. "That's kinda what I wanted ta talk to ya about."

"Oh dear. Come, there's a sofa in the other room. Let's go sit."

The three of them made their way into the parlor and settled down to talk.

"What happened?" she asked.

"The Supreme Court agreed to make some changes to Mr. Nash's sentence, but it wasn't what we were hoping for."

"That's for sure," Jack grumbled.

Mariam put a consoling hand on Jack's arm. "Is it that bad?"

"The court would not grant him a pardon," Steven continued. "They did shorten his sentence to twenty years, with eligibility for parole after ten, including time served."

"Well, that's better than life, isn't it?"

"Yeah, I suppose," Jack grumbled. "It's just that Leon was disappointed. I'm afraid of what he might do."

Mariam nodded her understanding. "Yes, I see. You want me to keep an extra close eye on him over the next little while. Is that it?"

"If you don't mind," Jack concurred. "I know Kenny will be watching him, and Dr. Palin will keep him busy. But if I knew that you were keepin' an eye on him as well, then maybe I'll be able to sleep at night."

"Of course. You know that I will."

"Thank you."

***

Laramie, Wyoming

"You named your horse what?"

"Gov."

"Gov?"

"Yeah. Short for Governor."

"I know what it's short for. I just don't get why you named him that."

"I dunno." Jack shrugged. "I guess I was thinkin' that if I named him that, then it might bring us some luck where the governors are concerned. Maybe we'll get one in office that will actually be on our side."

"Hmm. Maybe." Leon was non-committal. "Don't count on it."

"What do ya mean, don't count on it? We gotta do somethin'. Leon, this ain't over yet."

"It isn't?"

"No, of course it ain't. What kinda talk is that?"

"Realistic kind?"

The partners sat and stared at each other.

"You're not givin' up on us, are ya?"

"Well, I know you're trying. I know all of you are, but where else can we go? The Supreme Court was our last real chance and, I guess it did help some, but . . . and I appreciate what all of you went through to get there. I know some of you put an awful lot on the line, and I really do appreciate that, but I don't see where else we can go."

"Yeah, I know. But like Steven says, there is an election comin' early in the new year. The way Steven and Cameron discuss things, it sounds like Wyoming could get statehood soon. That could change a whole lot a things. Them officials like ta celebrate major events like that by grantin' pardons and stuff. So who knows? There could be a lot a changes comin'. All ya gotta do is—"

"Hang on?"

Jack sighed. "What else is there?"

"Nothing."

"Leon, that ain't what I meant. Ya gotta hold on ta somethin', and for right now, that's it. It's somethin', right? The appeal did lighten your sentence, and there's gonna be an investigation into the accusations of abuse, so Mitchell will be held accountable. It ain't all bad."

"Hmm. Probably just make him mad." Leon sighed and decided to change the subject. "Besides, shouldn't you be getting on with your life, Jack? You've got a real special lady out there, just waiting to have your babies. Don't you think it's time you made her a happy woman?"

Jack felt exasperated and his expression showed it.

"I already told ya, if and when we do get married, it's gonna be with you there as my best man."

"Aww Jack, come on. Caroline said the same thing. She wanted to wait until I was released so I could be at their wedding. It's all very nice, and I do appreciate the sentiment, but it's not practical. Fortunately, she listened to me and went ahead with their wedding, and now they're both pleased as punch and staying true to the cause as well. No reason why you and Penny can't do the same.

"Get married, Jack. Don't wait for me. I won't be insulted. I want you to get married, start a family, get on with your life. I know you'll still be here for me; I know you're not gonna give up, even if I do. You're too damn stubborn!

"But in the meantime, I feel like I'm getting in your way; that I'm preventing you from moving forward. That's not right. That's not right at all."

Throughout this lecture, Jack's jawline tightened as the stubborn streak took hold.

"No. I already told ya, Penny and I discussed this, and we are waitin' until you get released, and that's the final word on that. Don't even bother bringin' it up again."

Leon sat back, feeling hurt.

"Jeez, you've gotten awfully masterful since you've had a chance to become your own man. Don't need a partner anymore, do you? Don't need your uncle hanging around, making the decisions."

Jack's temper let loose. "Goddammit, Leon. Jeez, you piss me off sometimes! What the hell kinda talk is that? You sound like you've just given up, like you're not even gonna try anymore."

Officer Pearson gave a quiet cough as a reminder to Jack to settle down.

Jack glanced at him, then sat back. He made a stressful, two-handed swipe through his curls, took a deep breath, and brought his temper under control. He glanced again at his uncle, and Leon sat slouched, his eyes fixed on his own shackled hands. He looked dejected, depressed—hopeless.

Jack was hit with remorse for yelling at him, and he took a step back.

"I know you've had a hard time lately, Leon, what with Elk Mountain, then Lobo gettin' killed, and . . . what happened after that."

"Yeah."

"I can't even imagine what that musta been like."

"No."

"Ya still goin' ta services?"

Non-committal shrug.

"Had much of a chance ta talk with Mariam?"

"Yeah, some."

"Well, ya haven't written David in quite a while. I know ya like 'im, and he's been askin' after ya. Why don't ya write to 'im?"

"Yeah, I suppose."

"C'mon Leon. Don't do this to me. How the hell am I supposed ta turn around and head for home knowin' that I'm leavin' ya in this mood? C'mon."

Leon took a deep breath, then smiled.

"Yeah, Jack. You're right. I'm sorry. How's Karma doing?"

Jack smiled back. "Good. She's really taken ta motherhood. That colt is gonna grow into a real beauty."

"Yeah. Well, that's worth hanging around for, isn't it?"

"Yeah, it is. And Daisy sure is growin'. She's a typical yearlin' now, all legs and attitude."

"Oww, Karma would not appreciate you calling her daughter 'typical'."

"Yeah, well. Sam's been workin' her in a halter, you know; teachin' her ground manners and all that stuff. She sure gives him a hard time about it. Then Penny comes along, and that filly follows her around like a dog—drives Sam nuts. Ohh—that reminds me . . ."

Leon perked up, his eyebrows asking the question.

"We got us a new hound dog at the ranch now." Jack laughed again as he remembered the antics of the new canine. "She's about four months old and full of big paws and craziness. It's all the two little dogs can do just ta stay out from under her. I can't count how many times she's tripped over 'em in her exuberance, and then comes crashin' down in a heap of puppy wiggles and indignant yappin'. Just wait 'til ya see her—what a hoot!"

Leon grinned, a sparkle coming back to his eye. "Yeah, sounds like a circus."

"Oh yeah. And Eli's gettin' big now too. He's talkin' real good, and even rides Midnight all by himself. He's gettin' to be quite the little man."

"Hmm. Midnight doesn't mind that?"

Jack shook his head. "Naw. I think he kinda likes the attention. And it's not like he's havin' ta work hard. It's mostly just around in the barnyard now. Maybe next summer, we'll take Eli up to the north pasture ta see the calves. He oughta enjoy that. And it shouldn't be too hard on Midnight, either."

"Sounds good."

"Okay fellas, sorry," Pearson broke in on their conversation. "Time to wrap it up. It's actually a bit over time, so . . ."

"Yeah, okay," Jack acknowledged, "thanks. Take it easy, Leon. All right? I'll see ya next month."

"Sure thing, Jack. Say 'hello' to everyone back home."

"Yeah, I will. And write to David; I know he'd like ta hear from ya'."

Leon grinned. "Yes, I will. Good idea."

The two friends parted company, and Pearson led Leon through the inner door and back into the life he could not escape.

***

As soon as the door to the processing room closed behind them, Pearson noticed a change in Leon's demeanor.

The smile left the inmate's face, and the sparkle died in his eyes. He stood placidly, completely subdued, and stared at a spot on the floor while Pearson removed the shackles. He moved when Pearson asked him to move, stood still when Pearson asked him to stand, and began walking forward when Pearson indicated that it was time for them to leave.

The guard could have left Leon as soon as they returned to the prison proper, but he didn't. He didn't like the look in Leon's eyes, not one little bit, and he wanted to be sure the inmate got to wherever he was going without incident.

Leon ignored him, and even though it was a pleasant spring day outside, the inmate simply returned to his cell, lay down on his cot and commenced to stare at the ceiling.

Pearson stood outside the cell door for a moment, watching the convict, yet still did not get any response or acknowledgement from the man lying on the cot. He sighed, and pushing himself away from the cell, turned and went in search of Mr. Reece.

***

Leon again lay on his cot, looking up into his own mind's eye. He really didn't know what he was going to do now. Even though he hadn't expected a miracle, the reality of what had come back to him was enough to send him into a spiral, even if it was just a temporary one. He'd give himself time to get over the disappointment, then reconsider his options.

He had eight years, after all. No need to be hasty.

Coming Soon

Volume Five: The Way Out

"HOLD HIM!" Boeman ordered his two cronies.

The two convicts responded instantly. They each grabbed an arm and held him in a grip that defied movement.

Boeman's eyes had turned cold and hard, and he came towards Nash, holding the scalpel so that Leon could see it.

Kenny tried to fight himself loose, but Harris tightened his grip and choked the guard back into submission.

Boeman paid them no heed; his complete focus was on his nemesis.

"Pull his head back," he ordered.

Leon began to fight, but he felt someone's arm wrap around his forehead and pull his head back, exposing his throat. Then he felt real fear—that primal, animalistic fear, when your most vulnerable area has been exposed to your enemy, and you're staring death in the face. Leon yelled and fought, trying to kick out as Boeman approached him.

Boeman just laughed at him, and Leon's head was pulled back further, until he felt as though his spine was going to snap.

"Oh, Nash, I have waited so long to do this," Boeman smirked at him. "You have no idea how much I'm gonna enjoy it."

"No . . ." Leon struggled in his desperation, but he couldn't break loose. He could hear, rather than see, Kenny struggling as well, because they both knew what was about to happen.

Boeman came and stood in front of Leon and smiled with manic pleasure.

Leon felt the tip of the scalpel pierce the epidermis, just below his right ear. His struggling increased, fear clutching at his heart and stealing the strength from his legs. He heard Kenny yelling, and then the yell being choked off. Slowly, Boeman slid the blade across

Leon's throat, applying just a touch more pressure to push the tip into the dermis, to cause blood to bead up, but not quite enough pressure yet, to actually cut into the jugular.

Boeman had waited too long for this; he was going to take his time.

List of Characters

- Barton, Harry: Leader of the Cripple Creek Gang
- Bill: Deputy, Cheyenne, Wyoming
- Blair, Jacob B.: Justice of the Wyoming Supreme Court. 1876 - 1888
- Boeman, Hank: Alpha inmate, Wyoming Territorial Prison
- Buchannan, Curly: Elk Mountain gang member, previously with the Red Sash Gang
- Carlyle, Frank: Wells Fargo detective
- Carmen, George: Outlaw. Survives train ambush, joins up with the Cripple Creek Gang.
- Carson, Floyd: Senior guard, Wyoming Territorial Prison
- Cartless, Roger: Teenage member of Elk Mountain gang. Best buddies with Les Howard
- Cobb, Malachi: Outlaw with the Elk Mountain Gang
- Corn, Samuel T.: Justice of the Wyoming Supreme Court. 1886 - 1900
- Dalton: Doctor. Mental Health Director on the Board of Penitentiary Commissioners
- Deke: Wrangler for the Rocking M Ranch
- Doleman, Hugo: Attorney for the Governor
- Douglas: Member of Cripple Creek Gang
- Ebner, Chuck: Elk Mountain gang member. Brother to Tom
- Ebner, Tom: Elk Mountain gang member
- Flannigan, Seth: Former Elk Mountain gang member who turns on gang to avoid prison sentence
- Gilmore, Ottus: Deputy in Medicine Bow
- Gov: Jack's new horse
- Hadden, Charlie: Elk Mountain gang member
- Hanson: Member of Cripple Creek Gang
- Harris, Carl: Inmate. Buddies up with Boeman
- Henderson, Matt: Elk Mountain gang member
- Higgins: Secretary to the Governor, Wyoming
- Howard, Les: Teenager killed at the train ambush
- Jackson, Black Henry: Elk Mountain gang member, previously with the Red Sash Gang
- Jansen, Josephine (Josey): Childhood friend of Jack and Leon

- Johnston: Inmate
- Jorgensen: Sharpshooter for Tom Morrison
- Kelly: Inmate
- Konachy, Harvey: Young inmate who committed suicide
- Kristiansen: Inmate
- Lancaster: Secretary for the Board of Penitentiary Commissioners
- Larson, Benny: Elk Mountain gang member
- Layton, Rick: Former deputy for Tom Morrison, rancher
- Lobinskie, Maurice: (Lobo) Elk Mountain gang member. Joins Nash in prison
- Ludlow: Chairman of the Wyoming Board of Penitentiary Commissioners
- Maginnis, William: Chief Justice of the Wyoming Supreme Court. 1886 - 1889
- Millie: Tricia's next-door neighbor
- Mitchell, Mason: Warden, Wyoming Territorial Prison
- Mukua: also known as Preacher. Shoshoni, member of Elk Mountain gang and Leon's maternal uncle (Ata'i)
- Murphy, Taggard: Sheriff of Medicine Bow. Former Elk Mountain gang member
- Murrey: Guard
- Palin, Walter (Doc): Doctor, Wyoming Territorial Prison
- Pearson: Guard
- Reece, Alexander: Youngest son of Kenny and Sarah
- Reece, Charlie: Middle son of Kenny and Sarah
- Reece, Connor: Eldest son of Kenny and Sarah
- Reece, Evelyn: Daughter and youngest child of Kenny and Sarah
- Reece, Kenny: Guard, Wyoming Territorial Prison
- Reece, Sarah: Kenny's wife
- Saufley, Micah C.: Justice of the Wyoming Supreme Court. 1888 - 1890
- Schulmeyer, Eric: Livery man. Arvada, Wyoming.
- Shaffer, Gus: Leader of the Elk Mountain Gang
- Schumacher, Mike: Deputy for Tom Morrison
- Simons: Doctor. Medical Director on the Board of Penitentiary Commissioners

- Soames, Mariam: Degrees in theology and philosophy. A friend to Jack and Leon, assistant to Dr. Palin, and runs the local orphanage at Laramie, Wyoming.
- Strode, Alex: Deputy of Tom Morrison. Rawlins, Wyoming
- Willoughby, Dan: Elk Mountain gang member

WYOMING GOVERNORS

In order of term

- Hoyt, John Wesley: 1878 – 1882
- Hale, William: 1882 – 1885
- Morgan, Elliot: 1885.
- Warren, Frances: 1885 – 1886
- Baxter, George: 1886
- Morgan, Elliot: 1886 – 1887
- Moonlight, Thomas: 1887 – 1889
- Warren, Frances: 1889 – 1890
- Barber, Amos: 1890 – 1893
- Osborn, John: 1893 – 1895
- Richards, William: 1895 - 1899
- Richards, DeForrest: 1899 – 1903

About the Author

I have always been a cowgirl at heart even though I have lived my whole life either on the West Coast of Canada and the USA., but our road trips always draw us east and south. Montana, Wyoming, Colorado; these are places where my imagination runs wild.

I've been an artist/writer all my life, painting and writing about my first passion; the West. I also found a nitch with painting pet portraits and animal studies. Now that I am retired, I can indulge in the things I love the most; my husband, my animals, my art and my writing. I'm busier now than I have ever been before, and I wouldn't have it any other way.

In 2021 we moved to Central Washington where the landscape and culture are more in keeping with my creativity. So far, it has been working out very well.

www.twoblazesartworks.com

Made in the USA
Columbia, SC
19 February 2023

12661558R00238